Before the Dawn

by Joseph A. Altsheler

CHAPTER I

A WOMAN IN BROWN

A tall, well-favoured youth, coming from the farther South, boarded the train for Richmond one raw, gusty morning. He carried his left arm stiffly, his face was thin and brown, and his dingy uniform had holes in it, some made by bullets; but his air and manner were happy, as if, escaped from danger and hardships, he rode on his way to pleasure and ease.

He sat for a time gazing out of the window at the gray, wintry landscape that fled past, and then, having a youthful zest for new things, looked at those who traveled with him in the car. The company seemed to him, on the whole, to lack novelty and interest, being composed of farmers going to the capital of the Confederacy to sell food; wounded soldiers like himself, bound for the same place in search of cure; and one woman who sat in a corner alone, neither speaking nor spoken to, her whole aspect repelling any rash advance.

Prescott always had a keen eye for woman and beauty, and owing to his long absence in armies, where both these desirable objects were scarce, his vision had become acute; but he judged that this lone type of her sex had no special charm. Tall she certainly was, and her figure might be good, but no one with a fair face and taste would dress as plainly as she, nor wrap herself so completely in a long, brown cloak that he could not even tell the colour of her eyes. Beautiful women, as he knew them, always had a touch of coquetry, and never hid their charms wholly.

Prescott's attention wandered again to the landscape rushing past, but finding little of splendour or beauty, it came back, by and by, to the lone woman. He wondered why she was going to Richmond and what was her name. She, too, was now staring out of the window, and the long cloak hiding her seemed so shapeless that he concluded her figure must be bad. His interest declined at once, but rose again with her silence and evident desire to be left alone.

As they were approaching Richmond a sudden jar of the train threw a small package from her lap to the floor. Prescott sprang forward, picked it up and handed it to her. She received it with a curt "Thanks," and the noise of the train was so great that Prescott could tell nothing about the quality of her voice. It might or might not be musical, but in any event she was not polite and showed no gratitude. If he had thought to use the incident as an opening for conversation, he dismissed the idea, as she turned her face back to the window at once and resumed her study of the gray fields.

"Probably old and plain," was Prescott's thought, and then he forgot her in the approach to Richmond, the town where much of his youth had been spent. The absence of his mother from the capital was the only regret in this happy homecoming, but he had received a letter from her assuring him of her arrival in the city in a day or two.

When they reached Richmond the woman in the brown cloak left the car before him, but he saw her entering the office of the Provost-Marshal, where all passes were examined with minute care, every one who came to the capital in those times of war being considered an enemy until proved a friend. Prescott saw then that she was not only tall, but very tall, and that she walked with a strong, graceful step. "After all, her figure may be good," he thought, revising his recent opinion.

Her pass was examined, found to be correct, and she left the office before his own time came. He would have asked the name on her pass, but aware that the officer would probably tell him to mind his own business, he refrained, and then forgot her in the great event of his return home after so long a time of terrible war. He took his way at once to Franklin Street, where he saw outspread before him life as it was lived in the capital of the Confederate States of America. It was to him a spectacle, striking in its variety and refreshing in its brilliancy, as he had come, though indirectly, from the Army of Northern Virginia, where it was the custom to serve half-rations of food and double rations of gunpowder. Therefore, being young, sound of heart and amply furnished with hope, he looked about him and rejoiced.

Richmond was a snug little town, a capital of no great size even in a region then lacking in city growth, but for the time more was said about it and more eyes were turned upon it than upon any other place in the world. Many thousands of men were dying in an attempt to reach this small Virginia city, and many other thousands were dying in an equally strenuous effort to keep them away.

Such thoughts, however, did not worry Prescott at this moment. His face was set resolutely toward the bright side of life, which is really half the battle, and neither the damp nor the cold was able to take from him the good spirits that were his greatest treasure. Coming from the bare life of a camp and the somber scenes of battlefields, he seemed to have plunged into a very whirlwind of gaiety, and his eyes sparkled with appreciation. He did not notice then that his captain's uniform was stained and threadbare enough to make him a most disreputable figure in a drawing-room, however gallant he might appear at the head of a forlorn hope.

The street was crowded, the pressure of the armies having driven much of the life of the country into the city, and Prescott saw men, women and children passing, some in rich and some in poor attire. He saw ladies, both young and old, bearing in their cheeks a faint, delicate bloom, the mark of the South, and he heard them as they spoke to each other in their soft, drawling voices, which reminded him of the waters of a little brook falling over a precipice six inches high.

It is said that soldiers, after spending a year or two in the serious business of slaying each other, look upon a woman as one would regard a divinity—a being to be approached with awe and respect; and such emotions sprang into the heart of Prescott when he glanced into feminine faces, especially youthful ones. Becoming suddenly conscious of his rusty apparel and appearance, he looked about him in alarm. Other soldiers were passing, some fresh and trim, some rusty as himself, but a great percentage of both had bandaged limbs or bodies, and he found no consolation in such company, wishing to appear well, irrespective of others.

He noticed many red flags along the street and heard men calling upon the people in loud, strident voices to come and buy. At other places the grateful glow of coal fires shone from half-opened doorways, and the faint but positive click of ivory chips told that games of chance were in progress.

"Half the population is either buying something or losing something," he said to himself.

A shout of laughter came from one of the open doorways beyond which men were staking their money, and a voice, somewhat the worse for a liquid not water, sang:

"Little McClellan sat eating a melon The Chickahominy by; He stuck in his spade, Then a long while delayed, And cried: 'What a brave general am I!'"

"I'll wager that you had nothing to do with driving back McClellan," thought Prescott, and then his mind turned to that worn army by the Rapidan, fighting with such endurance, while others lived in fat ease here in Richmond.

Half a dozen men, English in face and manner and rolling in their walk like sailors, passed him. He recognized them at once as blockade runners who had probably come up from Wilmington to sell their goods for a better price at the capital. While wondering what they had brought, his attention was distracted by one of the auctioneers, a large man with a red face and tireless voice.

"Come buy! Come buy!" he cried. "See this beautiful new uniform of the finest gray, a sample of a cargo made in England and brought over five days ago on a blockade runner to Wilmington."

Looking around in search of a possible purchaser, his eye caught Prescott.

"This will just suit you," he said. "A change of a strap or two and it will do for either captain or lieutenant. What a figure you will be in this uniform!" Then he leaned over and said persuasively: "Better buy it, my boy. Take the advice of a man of experience. Clothes are half the battle. They may not be so on the firing line, but they are here in Richmond."

Prescott looked longingly at the uniform which in colour and texture was all that the auctioneer claimed, and fingered a small package of gold in his pocket. At that moment some one bid fifty dollars, and Prescott surveyed him with interest.

The speaker was a man of his own age, but shorter and darker, with a hawk-like face softened by black eyes with a faintly humourous twinkle lurking in the corner of each. He seemed distinctly good-natured, but competition stirred Prescott and he offered sixty dollars. The other man hesitated, and the auctioneer, who seemed to know him, asked him to bid up.

"This uniform is worth a hundred dollars if it's worth a cent, Mr. Talbot," he said.

"I'll give you seventy-five dollars cash or five hundred on a credit," said Talbot; "now which will you take?"

"If I had to take either I'd take the seventy-five dollars cash, and I'd be mighty quick about making a choice," replied the auctioneer.

Talbot turned to Prescott and regarded him attentively for a moment or two. Then he said:

"You look like a good fellow, and we're about the same size. Now, I haven't a hundred dollars in gold, and I doubt whether you have. Suppose we buy this uniform together, and take turns in wearing it."

Prescott laughed, but he saw that the proposition was made in entire good faith, and he liked the face of the man whom the auctioneer had called Talbot.

"I won't do that," he replied, "because I have more money than you think. I'll buy this and I'll lend you enough to help you in buying another."

Friendships are quickly formed in war time, and the offer was accepted at once. The uniforms were purchased and the two young men strolled on together, each carrying a precious burden under his arm.

"My name is Talbot, Thomas Talbot," said the stranger. "I'm a lieutenant and I've had more than two years' service in the West. I was in that charge at Chickamauga when General Cheatham, leading us on, shouted: 'Boys, give 'em hell'; and General Polk, who had been a bishop and couldn't swear, looked at us and said: 'Boys, do as General Cheatham says!' Well, I got a bad wound in the shoulder there, and I've been invalided since in Richmond, but I'm soon going to join the Army of Northern Virginia."

Talbot talked on and Prescott found him entertaining, as he was a man who saw the humourous side of things, and his speech, being spontaneous, was interesting.

The day grew darker and colder. Heavy clouds shut out the sun and the rain began to fall. The people fled from the streets, and the two officers shivered in their uniforms. The wind rose and whipped the rain into their faces. Its touch was like ice.

"Come in here and wait till the storm passes," said Talbot, taking his new friend by the arm and pulling him through an open door. Prescott now heard more distinctly than ever the light click of ivory chips, mingled with the sound of many voices in a high or low key, and the soft movement of feet on thick carpets. Without taking much thought, he followed his new friend down a short and narrow hall, at the end of which they entered a large, luxurious room, well lighted and filled with people.

"Yes, it's a gambling room—The Nonpareil—and there are plenty more like it in Richmond, I can tell you," said Talbot. "Those who follow war must have various kinds of excitement. Besides, nothing is so bad that it does not have its redeeming point, and these places, without pay, have cared for hundreds and hundreds of our wounded."

Prescott had another errand upon which his conscience bade him hasten, but casting one glance through the window he saw the soaking streets and the increasing rain, swept in wild gusts by the fierce wind. Then the warmth and light of the place, the hum of talk and perhaps the spirit of youth infolded him and he stayed.

There were thirty or forty men in the room, some civilians and others soldiers, two bearing upon their shoulders the stripes of a general. Four carried their arms in slings and three had crutches beside their chairs. One of the generals was not over twenty-three years of age, but this war furnished younger generals than he, men who won their rank by sheer hard service on great battlefields.

The majority of the men were playing faro, roulette or keno, and the others sat in softly upholstered chairs and talked. Liquors were served from a bar in the corner, where dozens of brightly polished glasses of all shapes and sizes glittered on marble and reflected the light of the gas in vivid colours.

Prescott's mind traveled back to long, lonely watches in the dark forest under snow and rain, in front of the enemy's outposts, and he admitted that while the present might be very wicked it was also very pleasant.

He gave himself up for a little while to the indulgence of his physical senses, and then began to examine those in the room, his eyes soon resting upon the one who was most striking in appearance. It was a time of young men, and this stranger was young like most of the others, perhaps under twenty-five. He was of middle height, very thick and broad, and his frame gave the impression of great muscular strength and endurance. A powerful neck supported a great head surmounted by a crop of hair like a lion's mane. His complexion was as delicate as a woman's, but his pale blue eyes were bent close to the table as he wagered his money with an almost painful intentness, and Prescott saw that the gaming madness was upon him.

Talbot's eyes followed Prescott's and he smiled.

"I don't wonder that you are looking at Raymond," he said. "He is sure to attract attention anywhere. You are beholding one of the most remarkable men the South has produced."

Prescott recognized the name as that of the editor of the *Patriot*, a little newspaper published on a press traveling in a wagon with the Western army until a month since, when it had come over to the Army of Northern Virginia. The *Patriot* was "little" only in size. The wit, humour, terseness, spontaneous power of expression, and above all of phrase-making, which its youthful editor showed in its columns, already had made Raymond a power in the Confederacy, as they were destined in his maturity to win him fame in a reunited nation.

"He's a great gamester and thinks that he's a master of chance," said Talbot, "but as a matter of fact he always loses. See how fast his pile of money is diminishing. It will soon be gone, but he will find another resource. You watch him."

Prescott did not need the advice, as his attention was already concentrated on Raymond's broad, massive jaw and the aggressive curve of his strong face. His movements were quick and nervous; face and figure alike expressed the most absolute self-confidence. Prescott wondered if this self-confidence did not lie at the basis of all success, military, literary, mercantile or other, enabling one's triumphs to cover up his failures and make the people remember only the former.

Raymond continued to lose, and presently, all his money being gone, he began to feel in his pockets in an absent-minded way for more, but the hand came forth empty from each pocket. He did not hesitate.

A man only two or three years older was sitting next to Raymond, and he, too, was intent on the game. Beside him was a very respectable little heap of gold and notes, and Raymond, reaching over, took half of the money and without a word, putting it in front of himself, went on with his wagers. The second man looked up in surprise, but seeing who had robbed him, merely made a wry face and continued his game. Several who had noticed the action laughed.

"It's Raymond's way," said Talbot. "I knew that he would do it. That's why I told you to watch him. The other man is Winthrop. He's an editor, too—one of our Richmond papers. He isn't a genius like Raymond, but he's a slashing writer— loves to criticize anybody from the President down, and he often does it. He belongs to the F. F. V.'s himself, but he has no mercy on them—shows up all their faults. While you can say that gambling is Raymond's amusement, you may say with equal truth that dueling is Winthrop's."

"Dueling!" exclaimed Prescott in surprise. "Why, I never saw a milder face!"

"Oh, he doesn't fight duels from choice," replied Talbot. "It's because of his newspaper. He's always criticizing, and here when a man is criticized in print he challenges the editor. And the funny thing about it is, that although Winthrop can't shoot or fence at all, he's never been hurt. Providence protects him, I suppose."

"Has he ever hit anybody?" asked Prescott.

"Only once," replied Talbot, "and that was his eleventh duel since the war began. He shot his man in the shoulder and then jumped up and down in his pride. 'I hit him! I hit him!' he cried. 'Yes, Winthrop,' said his second, 'some one was bound to get in the way if you kept on shooting long enough.'"

The place, with its rich colours, its lights shining from glasses and mirrors, its mellow odours of liquids and its softened sounds began to have a soporific effect upon Prescott, used so long to the open air and untold hardships. His senses were pleasantly lulled, and the voice of his friend, whom he seemed now to have known for a long time, came from far away. He could have closed his eyes and gone to sleep, but Talbot talked on.

"Here you see the back door of the Confederacy," he said. "You men at the front know nothing. You are merely fighting to defend the main entrance. But while you are getting yourselves shot to pieces without knowing any special reason why, all sorts of people slip in at this back door. It is true not only of this government, but also of all others."

A middle-aged, heavy-faced man in a general's uniform entered and began to talk earnestly to one of the other generals.

"That is General Markham," said Talbot, "who is specially interesting not because of himself, but on account of his wife. She is years younger than he, and is said to be the most brilliant woman in Richmond. She has plans for the General, but is too smart to say what they are. I doubt whether the General himself knows."

Raymond and Winthrop presently stopped playing and Talbot promptly introduced his new friend.

"We should know each other since we belong to the same army," said Raymond. "You fight and I write, and I don't know which of us does the more damage; but the truth is, I've but recently joined the Army of Northern Virginia. I've been following the army in the West, but the news didn't suit me there and I've come East."

"I hope that you have many victories to chronicle," said Prescott.

"It's been a long time since there's been a big battle," resumed the editor, "and so I've come up to Richmond to see a little life."

He glanced about the room.

"And I see it here," he added. "I confess that the fleshpots of Richmond are pleasant."

Then he began to talk of the life in the capital, the condition of the army and the Confederate States, furnishing a continual surprise to Prescott, who now saw that beneath the man's occasional frivolity and epicurean tastes lay a mind of wonderful penetration, possessing that precious quality generally known as insight. He revealed a minute knowledge of the Confederacy and its chieftains, both civil and military, but he never risked an opinion as to its ultimate chances of success, although Prescott waited with interest to hear what he might say upon this question, one that often troubled himself. But however near Raymond might come to the point, he always turned gracefully away again.

They were sitting now in a cheerful corner as they talked, but at the table nearest them was a man of forty, with immense square shoulders, a heavy red face and an overbearing manner. He was playing faro and losing steadily, but every time he lost he marked the moment with an angry exclamation. The others, players and spectators alike, seemed to avoid him, and Winthrop, who noticed Prescott's inquiring glance, said:

"That's Redfield, a member of our Congress," and he named the Gulf State from which Redfield came. "He belonged to the Legislature of his State before the war, which he advocated with all the might of his lungs—no small power, I assure you—and he was leader in the shouting that one Southern gentleman could whip five Yankees. I don't know whether he means that he's the Southern gentleman, as he's never yet been on the firing line, but he's distinguishing himself just now by attacking General Lee for not driving all the Yankees back to Washington."

Redfield at length left the game, uttering with an oath his opinion that fair play was impossible in the Nonpareil, and turned to the group seated near him, regarding the Richmond editor with a lowering brow.

"I say, Winthrop," he cried, "I've got a bone to pick with you. You've been hitting me pretty hard in that rag of yours. Do you know what a public man down in the Gulf States does with an editor who attacks him! Why, he goes around to his office and cowhides the miserable little scamp until he can't lie down comfortably for a month."

A slight pink tint appeared in the cheeks of Winthrop.

"I am not well informed about the custom in the Gulf States, Mr. Redfield," he said, "but here I am always at home to my enemies, as you ought to know."

"Oh, nonsense!" exclaimed Raymond. "You two can't fight. We can't afford to lose Redfield. He's going to lead a brigade against the Yankees, and if he'll only make one of those fiery speeches of his it will scare all the blue-backs out of Virginia."

Redfield's red face flushed to a deeper hue, and he regarded the speaker with aversion, but said nothing in reply, fearing Raymond's sharp tongue. Instead, he turned upon Prescott, who looked like a mild youth fit to stand much hectoring.

"You don't introduce me to your new friend," he said to Talbot.

"Mr. Redfield, Captain Prescott," said Talbot. "Mr. Redfield is a Member of Congress and Captain Prescott comes from the Army of Northern Virginia, though by way of North Carolina, where he has been recently on some special duty."

"Ah, from the Army of Northern Virginia," said Redfield in a heavy growl. "Then can you tell me, Mr. Prescott, why General Lee does not drive the Yankees out of Virginia?"

A dark flush appeared on Prescott's face. Usually mild, he was not always so, and he worshiped General Lee.

"I think it is because he does not have the help of men like yourself," he replied.

A faint ray of a smile crossed the face of Raymond, but the older man was not pleased.

"Do you know, sir, that I belong to the Confederate Congress?" he exclaimed angrily; "and moreover, I am a member of the Military Committee. I have a right to ask these questions."

"Then," replied Prescott, "you should know that it is your duty to ask them of General Lee and not of me, a mere subaltern."

"Now, Mr. Redfield," intervened Raymond, "don't pick a quarrel with Captain Prescott. If there's to be a duel, Winthrop has first claim on you, and I insist for the honour of my profession that he have it. Moreover, since he is slender and you are far from it, I demand that he have two shots to your one, as he will have at least twice as much to kill."

Redfield growled out other angry words, which stopped under the cover of his heavy mustache, and then turned abruptly away, leaving Prescott in some doubt as to his personal courage but none at all as to his ill will.

"It is the misfortune of the South," said Raymond, "to have such men as that, who think to settle public questions by personal violence. They give us a bad name which is not wholly undeserved. In fact, personal violence is our great sin."

"And the man has a lot of power. That's the worst of it," added Talbot. "The boys at the front are hauled around so much by the politicians that they are losing confidence in everybody here in Richmond. Why, when President Davis himself came down and reviewed us with a great crowd of staff officers before Missionary Ridge, the boys all along the line set up the cry: 'Give us somethin' to eat, Mr. Jeff; give us somethin' to eat! We're hungry! We're hungry!' And that may be the reason why we were thrashed so badly by Grant not long after."

Prescott saw that the rain had almost ceased, and as he suggested that he must hurry on, the others rose to go with him from the house. He left them at the next corner, glad to have made such friends, and quickened his footsteps as he continued alone.

CHAPTER II

A MAN'S MOTHER

It was a modest house to which Prescott turned his steps, built two stories in height, of red brick, with green shutters over the windows, and in front a little brick-floored portico supported on white columns in the Greek style. His heart gave a great beat as he noticed the open shutters and the thin column of smoke rising from the chimney. The servants at least were there! He had been gone three years, and three years of war is a long time to one who is not yet twenty-five. There was no daily mail from the battlefield, and he had feared that the house would be closed.

He lifted the brass knocker and struck but once. That was sufficient, as before the echo died his mother herself, come before the time set, opened the door. Mrs. Prescott embraced her son, and she was even less demonstrative than himself, though he was generally known to his associates as a reserved man; but he knew the depth of her feelings. One Northern mother out of every ten had a son who never came back, but it was one Southern mother in every three who was left to mourn.

She only said: "My son, I feared that I should never see you again." Then she noticed the thinness of his clothing and its dampness. "Why, you are cold and wet," she added.

"I do not feel so now, mother," he replied.

She smiled, and her smile was that of a young girl. As she drew him toward the fire in a dusky room it seemed to him that some one else went out.

"I heard your footsteps on the portico," she said.

"And you knew that it was me, mother," he interrupted, as he reached down and patted her softly on the cheek.

He could not remember the time when he did not have a protecting feeling in the presence of his mother—he was so tall and large, and she so small. She scarcely reached to the top of his shoulder, and even now, at the age of forty-five, her cheeks had the delicate bloom and freshness of a young girl's.

"Sit by the fire here," she said, as she pushed him into an armchair that she pulled directly in front of the grate.

"No, you must not do that," she added, taking the poker from his hand. "Don't you know that it is a delight for me to wait upon you, my son come from the war!"

Then she prodded the coals until they glowed a deep red and the room was suffused with generous warmth.

"What is this bundle that you have?" she asked, taking it from him.

"A new uniform, mother, that I have just bought, and in which I hope to do you credit."

She flitted about the room attending to his wants, bringing him a hot drink, and she would listen to no account of himself until she was sure that he was comfortable. He followed her with his eyes, noting how little she had changed in the three years that had seemed so long.

She was a Northern woman, of a Quaker family in Philadelphia, whom his father had married very young and brought to live on a great place in Virginia. Prescott always believed she had never appreciated the fact that she was entering a new social world when she left Philadelphia; and there, on the estate of her husband, a just and generous man, she saw slavery under its most favourable conditions. It must have been on one of their visits to the Richmond house, perhaps at the slave market itself, that she beheld the other side; but this was a subject of which she would never speak to her son Robert. In fact, she was silent about it to all people, and he only knew that she was not wholly like the Southern women about him. When the war came she did not seek to persuade her son to either side, but when he made his choice he was always sure that he caused her pain, though she never said a word.

"Do you wear such thin clothing as this out there in those cold forests?" she asked, fingering his coat.

"Mother," he replied with a smile, "this is the style now; the shops recommend it, and you know we've all heard that a man had better be dead than out of the style."

"And you have become a great soldier?" she said, looking at him fondly.

He laughed, knowing that in any event he would seem great to her.

"Not great, mother," he replied; "but I know that I have the confidence of General Lee, on whose staff I serve."

"A good man and a great one," she said, clasping her hands thoughtfully. "It is a pity——"

She stopped, and her son asked:

"What is a pity, mother?"

She did not answer, but he knew. It was said by many that Lee hesitated long before he went with his State.

"Now," she said, "you must eat," and she brought him bread and meat and coffee, serving them from a little table that she herself placed by his side.

"How happens it, mother," he asked, "that this food is still warm? It must have been hours since you had breakfast."

A deep tint of red as of a blush suffused her cheeks, and she answered in a hesitating voice:

"Since there was a pause in the war, I knew that sooner or later you would come, and I remember how hungry you used to be as a growing boy."

"And through all these days you have kept something hot on the fire for me, ready at a moment's notice!"

She looked at him and there was a faint suspicion of tears in her eyes.

"Yes, yes, Robert," she replied. "Now don't scold me."

He had no intention of scolding her, but his thought was: "Has any other man a mother like mine?" Then he corrected himself; he knew that there must be myriads of others.

He said nothing in reply, merely smiling at her, and permitted her to do as she would. She went about the room with light, easy step, intent on her little services.

She opened the window shutters and the rich sunlight came streaming in, throwing a golden glow across the brown face of him who had left her a boy and come back a man. She sighed a little as she noticed how great was the change, but she hid the sigh from her son.

"Mother," he asked presently, "was there not some one else in this room when I came in? The light was faint, but I thought I saw a shadowy figure disappear."

"Yes," she answered; "that was Helen Harley. She was with me when you came. She may have known your footstep, too, and if not, she guessed it from my face, so she went out at once. She did not wish to be a mere curious onlooker when a mother was greeting her son, come home after three years in the war."

"She must be a woman now."

"She is a woman full grown in all respects. Women have grown old fast in the last three years. She is nearly a head taller than I."

"You have been comfortable here, mother?" he asked.

"As much so as one can be in such times," she replied. "I do not lack for money, and whatever deprivations I endure are those of the common lot—and this community of ill makes them amusing rather than serious."

She rose and walked to a door leading into the garden.

"Where are you going?" he asked.

"I shall return in a few moments."

When she came back she brought with her a tall young woman with eyes of dark blue and hair of brown shot with gold wherever the firelight fell upon it. This girl showed a sinuous grace when she walked and she seemed to Prescott singularly self-contained.

He sprang to his feet at once and took her hand in the usual Southern fashion, making a compliment upon her appearance, also in the usual Southern fashion. Then he realized that she had ceased to be a little girl in all other respects as well as in the physical.

"I have heard that gallantry in the face of the ladies as well as of the foe is part of a soldier's trade, Robert," she replied.

"And you do not know which requires the greater daring."

"But I know which your General ought to value the more."

After this she was serious. Neither of the younger people spoke much, but left the thread of the talk to Mrs. Prescott, who had a great deal to say. The elder woman, for all her gentleness and apparent timidity, had a bold spirit that stood in no awe of the high and mighty. She was full of curiosity about the war and plied her son with questions.

"We in Richmond know little that is definite of its progress," she said. "The Government announces victories and no defeats. But tell me, Robert, is it true, as I hear, that in the knapsacks of the slain Southern soldiers they find playing-cards, and in those of the North, Bibles?"

"If the Northern soldiers have Bibles, they do not use them," said Helen.

"And if the Southern soldiers have playing-cards, they do use them," said Mrs. Prescott.

Robert laughed.

"I daresay that both sides use their cards too much and their Bibles too little," he said.

"Do not be alarmed, Robert," said his mother; "such encounters between Helen and myself are of a daily occurrence."

"And have not yet resulted in bloodshed," added Miss Harley.

Prescott watched the girl while his mother talked, and he seemed to detect in her a certain aloofness as far as he was concerned, although he was not sure that the impression was not due to his absence so long from the society of women. It gave him a feeling of shyness which he found difficult to overcome, and which he contrasted in his own mind with her ease and indifference of manner.

When she asked him of her brother, Colonel Harley, the brilliant cavalry commander, whose exploits were recounted in Richmond like a romance, she showed enthusiasm, her eyes kindling with fire, and her whole face vivid. Her pride in her brother was large and she did not seek to conceal it.

"I hear that he is considered one of the best cavalry leaders of the age," she said, and she looked questioningly at Prescott.

"There is no doubt of it," he replied, but there was such a lack of enthusiasm in his own voice that his mother looked quickly at him. Helen did not notice. She was happy to hear the praises of her brother, and she eagerly asked more questions about him—his charge at this place, the famous ruse by which he had beaten the Yankees at that place, and the esteem in which he was held by General Lee; all of which Prescott answered readily and with pleasure. Mrs. Prescott looked smilingly at Miss Harley.

"It does not seem fair for a girl to show such interest in a brother," she said. "Now, if it were a lover it would be all right."

"I have no lover, Mrs. Prescott," replied Helen, a slight tint of pink appearing in her cheeks.

"It may be so," said the older woman, "but others are not like you." Then after a pause she sighed and said: "I fear that the girls of '61 will show an unusually large crop of old maids."

She spoke half humourously of what became in reality a silent but great tragedy, especially in the case of the South.

The war was prominent in the minds of the two women. Mrs. Prescott had truly said that knowledge of it in Richmond was vague. Gettysburg, it was told, was a great victory, the fruits of which the Army of Northern Virginia, being so far from its base, was unable to reap; moreover, the Army of the West beyond a doubt had won a great triumph at Chickamauga, a battle almost as bloody as Gettysburg, and now the Southern forces were merely taking a momentary rest, gaining fresh vigour for victories greater than any that had gone before.

Nevertheless, there was a feeling of depression over Richmond. Bread was higher, Confederate money was lower; the scarcity of all things needed was growing; the area of Southern territory had contracted, the Northern armies were coming nearer and nearer, and a false note sometimes rang in the gay life of the capital.

Prescott answered the women as he best could, and, though he strove to keep a bold temper, a tone of gloom like that which afflicted Richmond appeared now and then in his replies. He was sorry that they should question him so much upon these subjects. He was feeling so good, and it was such a comfort to be there in Richmond with his own people before a warm fire, that the army could be left to take care of itself for awhile. Nevertheless, he understood their anxiety and permitted no show of hesitation to appear in his voice. Miss Harley presently rose to go. The clouds had come again and a soft snow was falling.

"I shall see you home," said Prescott. "Mother, will you lend me an umbrella?"

Mrs. Prescott laughed softly.

"We don't have umbrellas in Richmond now!" she replied. "The Yankees make them, not we, and they are not selling to us this year."

"Mother," said Prescott, "if the Yankees ever crush us it will be because they make things and we don't. Their artillery, their rifles, their ammunition, their wagons, their clothes, everything that they have is better than ours."

"But their men are not," said Helen, proudly.

"Nevertheless, we should have learned to work with our hands," said Prescott.

They slipped into the little garden, now bleak with winter waste. Helen drew a red cloak about her shoulders, which Prescott thought singularly becoming. The snow was falling gently and the frosty air deepened the scarlet in her cheeks. The Harley house was only on the other side of the garden and there was a path between the two. The city was now silent. Nothing came to their ears save the ringing of a church bell.

"I suppose this does not seem much like war to you," said Helen.

"I don't know," replied Robert. "Just now I am engaged in escorting a very valuable convoy from Fort Prescott to Fort Harley, and there may be raiders."

"And here may come one now," she responded, indicating a horseman, who, as he passed, looked with admiring eyes over the fence that divided the garden from the sidewalk. He was a large man, his figure hidden in a great black cloak and his face in a great black beard growing bushy and unkempt up to his eyes. A sword, notable for its length, swung by his side.

Prescott raised his hand and gave a salute which was returned in a careless, easy way. But the rider's bold look of admiration still rested on Helen Harley's face, and even after he had gone on he looked back to see it.

"You know him?" asked Helen of Robert.

"Yes, I know him and so do you."

"If I know him I am not aware of it."

"That is General Wood."

Helen looked again at the big, slouching figure disappearing at the corner. The name of Wood was famous in the Confederacy. The greatest of all the cavalry commanders in a service that had so many, a born military genius, he was an illiterate mountaineer, belonging to that despised, and often justly despised, class known in the South as "poor white trash." But the name of Wood was now famous in every home of the revolting States. It was said that he could neither read nor write, but his genius flamed up at the coming of war as certainly as tow blazes at the touch of fire. Therefore, Helen looked after this singular man with the deepest interest and curiosity.

"And that slouching, awkward figure is the great Wood!" she said.

"He is not more slouching and awkward than Jackson was."

"I did not mean to attack him," she said quickly.

She had noticed Wood's admiring glance. In fact, it brought a tint of red to her cheeks, but she was not angry. They were now at her own door.

"I will not ask you to come in," she said, "because I know that your mother is waiting for you."

"But you will some other time?"

"Yes, some other time."

When he returned to his own house Mrs. Prescott looked at him inquiringly but said nothing.

CHAPTER III

THE MOSAIC CLUB

Prescott was a staff officer and a captain, bearing a report from the Commander of the Army of Northern Virginia to the President of the Confederacy; but having been told in advance that it was perfunctory in its nature, and that no haste was necessary in its delivery, he waited until the next morning before seeking the White House, as the residence of the President was familiarly called at Richmond, in imitation of Washington. This following of old fashions and old ways often struck Prescott as a peculiar fact in a country that was rebelling against them.

"If we succeed in establishing a new republic," he said to himself, "it will be exactly like the one that we quit."

He was told at the White House that the President was then in conference with the Secretary of War, but Mr. Sefton would see him. He had heard often of Mr. Sefton, whose place in the Government was not clearly defined, but of whose influence there was no doubt. He was usually known as the Secretary. "The Secretary of what?" "The Secretary of everything," was the reply.

Mr. Sefton received Prescott in a large dark room that looked like a workshop. Papers covered the tables and others were lying on the floor, indicating the office of a man who worked. The Secretary himself was standing in the darkest corner—a thin, dark, rather small man of about forty, one who seemed to be of a nervous temperament ruled by a strong will.

Prescott remembered afterward that throughout the interview the Secretary remained in the shadow and he was never once able to gain a clear view of his face. He found soon that Mr. Sefton, a remarkable man in all respects, habitually wore a mask, of which the mere shadow in a room was the least part.

Prescott gave his report, and the Secretary, after reading it attentively, said in a singularly soft voice:

"I have heard of you, Captain Prescott. I believe that you distinguished yourself in the great charge at Gettysburg?"

"Not more than five thousand others."

"At least you came out of the charge alive, and certainly five thousand did not do that."

Prescott looked at him suspiciously. Did he mean to cast some slur upon his conduct? He was sorry he could not see the Secretary's face more clearly, and he was anxious also to be gone. But the great man seemed to have another object in view.

"I hear that there is much discontent among the soldiers," said Mr. Sefton in a gentle, sympathetic voice. "They complain that we should send them supplies and reinforcements, do they not?"

"I believe I have heard such things said," reluctantly admitted Prescott.

"Then I have not been misinformed. This illustrates, Captain, the lack of serious reflection among the soldiers. A soldier feels hungry. He wants a beefsteak, soft bread and a pot of coffee. He does not see them and at once he is angry. He waves his hand and says: 'Why are they not here for me?' The Government does not own the secret of Arabian magic. We cannot create something where nothing is."

Prescott felt the Secretary gazing at him as if he alone were to blame for this state of affairs. Then the door opened suddenly and several men entered. One, tall, thin and severe of countenance, the typical Southern gentleman of the old school, Prescott recognized at once as the President of the Confederacy. The others he inferred were members of his Cabinet, and he rose respectfully, imitating the example of Mr. Sefton, but he did not fail to notice that the men seemed to be disturbed.

"A messenger from General Lee, Mr. President," said Mr. Sefton, in his smooth voice. "He repeats his request for reinforcements."

The worried look of the President increased. He ran his hand across his brow.

"I cannot furnish them," he said. "It is no use to send any more such requests to me. Even the conscription will not fill up our armies unless we take the little boys from their marbles and the grandfathers from their chimney-corners. I doubt whether it would do so then."

Mr. Sefton bowed respectfully, but added nothing to his statement.

"The price of gold has gone up another hundred points, Mr. Sefton," said the President. "Our credit in Europe has fallen in an equal ratio and our Secretary of State has found no way to convince foreign governments that they are undervaluing us."

Prescott looked curiously at the Secretary of State—it was the first time that he had ever seen him—a middle-aged man with broad features of an Oriental cast. He it was to whom many applied the words "the brains of the Confederacy." Now he was not disturbed by the President's evident annoyance.

"Why blame me, Mr. President?" he said. "How long has it been since we won a great victory? Our credit is not maintained here in Richmond nor by our agents in Europe, but on the battlefield."

Mr. Sefton looked at Prescott as if to say: "Just as I told you." Prescott thought it strange that they should speak so plainly before him, a mere subordinate, but policy might be in it, he concluded on second thought. They might desire their plain opinion to get back informally to General Lee. There was some further talk, all of which they seemed willing for him to hear, and then they returned to the inner room, taking Mr. Sefton, who bade Prescott wait.

The Secretary returned in a half-hour, and taking Prescott's arm with an appearance of great familiarity and friendliness, said:

"I shall walk part of the way with you, if you will let me, Captain Prescott. The President asks me to say to you that you are a gallant soldier and he appreciates your services. Therefore, he hopes that you will greatly enjoy your leave of absence in Richmond."

Prescott flushed with pleasure. He liked a compliment and did not deem it ignoble to show his pleasure. He was gratified, too, at the confidence that the Secretary, a man whose influence he knew was not exaggerated, seemed to put in him, and he thanked him sincerely.

So they walked arm in arm into the street, and those who met them raised their hats to the powerful Secretary, and incidentally to Prescott also, because he was with Mr. Sefton.

"If we win," said Mr. Sefton, "Richmond will become a great city—one of the world's capitals."

"Yes—if we win," replied Prescott involuntarily.

"Why, you don't think that we shall lose, do you?" asked the Secretary quickly.

Prescott was confused and hesitated. He regretted that he had spoken any part of his thoughts, and felt that the admission had been drawn from him, but now thought it better to be frank than evasive.

"Napoleon said that Providence was on the side of the heaviest battalions," he replied, "and therefore I hope ours will increase in weight soon."

The Secretary did not seem to be offended, leaning rather to the other side as he commended the frankness of the young Captain's speech. Then he began to talk to him at great length about the army, its condition, its prospects and the spirit of the soldiers. He revealed a knowledge of the camp that surprised Prescott and aroused in him admiration mingled with a lingering distrust.

Mr. Sefton seemed to him different, indeed, from the average Southerner. Very few Southern men at that time sought to conceal their feelings. Whatever their faults they were open, but Mr. Sefton wore his mask always. Prescott's mind went back unconsciously to the stories he had read of the agile Italian politicians of the Middle Ages, and for a moment paused at the doctrine of reincarnation. Then he was ashamed of himself. He was wronging Mr. Sefton, an able man devoted to the Southern cause—as everybody said.

They stopped just in front of Mrs. Prescott's house.

"You live here?" said the Secretary. "I know your mother. I cannot go in, but I thank you. And Miss Harley lives in the next house. I know her, too—a spirited and beautiful woman. Good-day, Captain Prescott; I shall see you again before you return to the army."

He left Prescott and walked back toward the White House. The young captain entered his own home, thinking of what he had seen and heard, and the impression remained that he had given the Secretary full information about the army.

Prescott received a call the next morning from his new friend Talbot.

"You are invited to a meeting of the Mosaic Club to-night at the house of Mrs. Markham," he said.

"And what is the Mosaic Club?" asked Prescott.

"The Mosaic is a club without organization, by-laws or members!" replied Talbot. "It's just the choice and congenial spirits of Richmond who have got into the habit of meeting at one another's houses. They're worth knowing, particularly Mrs. Markham, the hostess to-night. She heard of you and told me to invite you. Didn't write you a note—stationery's too high."

Prescott looked doubtfully at his mother.

"Why, of course you'll go," she said. "You did not come home to sit here all the time. I would not have you do that."

Talbot called for him shortly after dusk and the two strolled together toward the street where the Markham residence stood.

"Richmond is to be a great capital some day," said Talbot as they walked on, "but, if I may use the simile, it's a little ragged and out-at-elbows now."

This criticism was drawn from him by a misstep into the mud, but he quickly regained the ill-paved sidewalk and continued his course with unbroken cheerfulness. The night was dark, the few and widely scattered street lamps burned dimly, and the city loomed through the dusk, misshapen and obscure.

"Do you know," said Talbot, "I begin to believe that Richmond wouldn't amount to much of a town in the North?"

"It would not," replied Prescott; "but we of the South are agricultural people. Our pride is in the country rather than the towns."

A cheerful light shone from the windows of the Markham house as they approached it. When they knocked at the door it was opened by a coloured servant, and they passed into a large room, already full of people who were talking and laughing as if they had known one another all their lives. Prescott's first glimpse was of Helen Harley in a flowered silk dress, and he felt a thrill of gladness. Then he was presented to his hostess, Mrs. Markham, a small woman, very blonde, bright in attire and wearing fine jewels. She was handsome, with keen features and brilliant eyes.

"You are from General Lee's camp," she said, "and it is a Yankee bullet that has enabled you to come here. If it were not for those Yankee bullets we should never see our brave young officers; so it's an ill ball that brings nobody good."

She smiled into his eyes, and her expression was one of such great friendliness and candour that Prescott liked her at once. She held him and Talbot a few moments longer with light talk, and then he passed on.

It was a large room, of much width and greater length, containing heavy mahogany furniture, while the floor was carpeted in dark colours. The whole effect would have been somber without the presence of so many people, mostly young, and the cheerful fire in the grate glowing redly across the shades of the carpet.

There were a half-dozen men, some in uniform and some in civilian garb, around Helen Harley, and she showed all a young girl's keen and natural delight in admiration and in the easy flow of talk. Both Raymond and Winthrop were in the circle, and so was Redfield, wearing a black frock coat of unusual length and with rings on his fingers. Prescott wondered why such a man should be a member of this group, but at that moment some one dropped a hand upon his shoulder and, turning, he beheld the tall figure of Colonel Harley, Helen's brother.

"I, too, have leave of absence, Prescott," he said, "and what better could a man do than spend it in Richmond?"

Harley was a large, fair man, undeniably handsome, but with a slight expression of weakness about the mouth. He had earned his military reputation and he visibly enjoyed it.

"Where could one find a more brilliant scene than this?" continued the Colonel. "Ah, my boy, our Southern women stand supreme for beauty and wit!"

Prescott had been present before the war, both in his own country and in others, at occasions far larger and far more splendid; but none impressed him like the present, with the never-failing contrast of camp and battlefield from which he had come. There was in it, too, a singular pathos that appealed to his inmost heart. Some of the women wore dresses that had belonged to their mothers in their youth, the attire of the men was often strange and variegated, and nearly half the officers present had empty sleeves or bandaged shoulders. But no one seemed to notice these peculiarities by eye or speech, nor was their gaiety assumed; it was with some the gradual contempt of hardship brought about by use and with others the temporary rebound from long depression.

"Come," said Talbot to his friend, "you must meet the celebrities. Here's George Bagby, our choicest humourist; Trav. Daniel, artist, poet and musician; Jim Pegram, Innes Randolph, and a lot more."

Prescott was introduced in turn to Richmond's most noted men of wit and manners, the cream of the old South, and gradually all drew together in one great group. They talked of many things, of almost everything except the war, of the news from Europe, of the books that they had read—Scott and Dickens, Thackeray and Hugo—and of the music that they had heard, particularly the favourite arias of Italian opera.

Mrs. Markham and Miss Harley were twin stars in this group, and Prescott could not tell which had the greater popularity. Mrs. Markham was the more worldly and perhaps the more accomplished; but the girl was all youthful freshness, and there was about her an air of simplicity that the older woman lacked.

It gradually developed into a contest between them, heightened, so it seemed to Prescott, by the fact that Colonel Harley was always by the side of Mrs. Markham, and apparently made no effort to hide his admiration, while his sister was seeking without avail to draw him away. Prescott stood aside for a few moments to watch and then Raymond put his hand on his shoulder.

"You see in Mrs. Markham a very remarkable woman—the married belle," said the editor. "The married belle, I understand, is an established feature of life abroad, but she is as yet comparatively unknown in the South. Here we put a woman on the shelf at twenty—or at eighteen if she marries then, as she often does."

Coffee and waffles were served at ten o'clock. Two coloured women brought in the coffee and the cups on a tray, but the ladies themselves served it.

"I apologize for the coffee," said Mrs. Markham. "I have a suspicion that it is more or less bean, but the Yankee blockading fleet is very active and I dare any of you to complain."

"Served by your hand, the common or field bean becomes the finest mocha," said Mr. Pegram, with the ornate courtesy of the old South.

"And if any one dare to intimate that it is not mocha I shall challenge him immediately," said Winthrop.

"You will have to use a worse threat than that," said Mrs. Markham. "I understand that at your last duel you hit a negro plowing in a cornfield fifty yards from your antagonist."

"And scared the negro's mule half to death," added Raymond.

"But in your cause, Mrs. Markham, I couldn't miss," replied the gallant Winthrop, not at all daunted.

The waffles were brought in hot from the kitchen and eaten with the coffee. After the refreshments the company began to play "forfeit essay." Two hats were handed around, all drawing a question from one hat and a word from the other. It became the duty of every one to connect question and word by a poem, essay, song or tale in time to be recited at the next meeting. Then they heard the results of the last meeting.

"That's Innes Randolph standing up there in the corner and getting ready to recite," said Talbot to Prescott. "He's one of the cleverest men in the South and we ought to have something good. He's just drawn from one hat the words 'Daddy Longlegs' and from the other 'What sort of shoe was made on the last of the Mohicans?' He says he doesn't ask to wait until the next meeting, but he'll connect them extempore. Now we'll see what he has made out of them."

Randolph bowed to the company with mock humility, folded his hands across his breast and recited:

"Old Daddy Longlegs was a sinner hoary, And punished for his wickedness according to the story; Between him and the Indian shoes the likeness doth come in, One made a mock o' virtue and one a moccasin."

He was interrupted by the entrance of a quiet little man, modestly clad in a civilian's suit of dark cloth.

"Mr. Sefton," said some one, and immediately there was a halt in the talk, followed by a hush of expectation. Prescott noticed with interest that the company looked uncomfortable. The effect that Mr. Sefton produced upon all was precisely the same as that which he had experienced when with the Secretary.

Mr. Sefton was not abashed. He hurried up to the hostess and said:

"I hope I am not intrusive, Mrs. Markham, but I owed you a call, and I did not know that your little club was in session. I shall go in a few minutes."

Mrs. Markham pressed him to stay and become one of them for the evening, and her manner had every appearance of warmth.

"She believes he came to spy upon us," said Raymond, "and I am not sure myself that he didn't. He knew well enough the club was meeting here to-night."

But the Secretary quickly lulled the feelings of doubt that existed in the minds of the members of the Mosaic Club. He yielded readily to the invitation of Mrs. Markham and then exerted himself to please, showing a facile grace in manner and speech that soon made him a welcome guest. He quickly drifted to the side of Miss Harley, and talked so well from the rich store of his experience and knowledge that her ear was more for him than for any other.

"Is Mr. Sefton a bachelor?" asked Prescott of Winthrop.

Winthrop looked at the young Captain and laughed.

"Are you, too, hit?" Winthrop asked. "You need not flush, man; I have proposed to her myself three times and I've been rejected as often. I expect to repeat the unhappy experience, as I am growing somewhat used to it now and can stand it."

"But you have not answered my question: is the Secretary married?"

"Unfortunately, he is not."

There was an adjoining room to which the men were permitted to retire for a smoke if the spirit moved them, and when Prescott entered it for the first time he found it already filled, General Markham himself presiding. The General was a middle-aged man, heavy and slow of speech, who usually found the talk of the Mosaic Club too nimble for his wits and began his devotions to tobacco at an early hour.

"Have a cigar, Prescott," he said, holding up a box.

"That looks like a Havana label on the box," replied Prescott. "Are they genuine?"

"They ought to be genuine Havanas," replied the General. "They cost me five dollars apiece."

"Confederate money," added a colonel, Stormont; "and you'll be lucky if you get 'em next year for ten dollars apiece."

Colonel Stormont's eyes followed Prescott's round the room and he laughed.

"Yes, Captain Prescott," he said, "we are a somewhat peculiar company. There are now fourteen men in this room, but we can muster among us only twenty-one arms and twenty-four legs. It's a sort of general assembly, and I suppose we ought to send out a sergeant-at-arms for the missing members."

The Colonel touched his own empty left sleeve and added: "But, thank God, I've got my right arm yet, and it's still at the service of the Confederacy."

The Member of Congress, Redfield, came into the room at this moment and lighted a pipe, remarking:

"There will be no Confederacy, Colonel, unless Lee moves out and attacks the enemy."

He said this in a belligerent manner, his eyes half closed and his chin thrust forward as he puffed at his pipe.

An indignant flush swept over the veteran's face.

13

"Is this just a case of thumbs up and thumbs down?" he asked. "Is the Government to have a victory whenever it asks for it, merely because it does ask for it?"

Redfield still puffed slowly and deliberately at his pipe, and did not lower his chin a fraction from its aggravating height.

"General Lee overestimates the enemy," he said, "and has communicated the same tendency to all his men. It's a fatal mistake in war; it's a fatal mistake, I tell you, sir. The Yankees fight poorly."

The flush on the face of the Confederate colonel deepened. He tapped his empty sleeve and looked around at what he called the "missing members."

"You are in Congress, Mr. Redfield," he said, "and you have not seen the Yankees in battle. Only those who have not met them on the field say they cannot fight."

"I warn you that I am going to speak in Congress on the inaction of Lee and the general sloth of the military arm!" exclaimed Redfield.

"But, Mr. Redfield," said Prescott, seeking to soothe the Colonel and to still the troubled waters, "we are outnumbered by the enemy in our front at least two to one, we are half starved, and in addition our arms and equipment are much inferior to those of the Yankees."

Here Redfield burst into a passion. He thought it a monstrous shame, he said, that any subaltern should talk at will about the Southern Government, whether its military or civil arm.

Prescott flushed deeply, but he hesitated for an answer. His was not a hot Southern temper, nor did he wish to have a quarrel in a club at which he was only a guest. While he sought the right words, Winthrop spoke for him.

"I think, Mr. Redfield," said the editor, "that criticism of the Government is wholly right and proper. Moreover, not enough of it is done."

"You should be careful, Mr. Winthrop, how far you go," replied Redfield, "or you may find your printing presses destroyed and yourself in prison."

"Which would prove that instead of fighting for freedom we are fighting for despotism. But I am not afraid," rejoined the editor. "Moreover, Mr. Redfield, besides telling you my opinion of you here, I am also perfectly willing to print it in my paper. I shall answer for all that I say or write."

Raymond was sitting at a table listening, and when Winthrop finished these words, spoken with much fire and heat, he took out a note-book and regarded it gravely.

"Which would make, according to my entry here—if Mr. Redfield chooses to challenge—your ninth duel for the present season," he said.

There was an equivocal smile on the face of nearly every one present as they looked at the Member of Congress and awaited his reply. What that would have been they never knew, because just at that moment entered Mr. Sefton, breathing peace and good will. He had heard the last words, but he chose to view them in a humourous light. He pooh-poohed such folly as the rash impulses of young men. He was sure that his friend Redfield had not meant to cast any slur upon the army, and he was equally sure that Winthrop, whose action was right-minded were his point of view correct, was mistaken as to the marrow of Redfield's speech.

The Secretary had a peculiarly persuasive power which quickly exerted its influence upon Winthrop, Stormont and all the others. Winthrop was good-natured, avowing that he had no cause of quarrel with anybody if nobody had any with him, and Redfield showed clearly his relief. It seemed to Prescott that the Member of Congress had gone further than he intended.

No breath of these stormy airs was allowed to blow from the smoking-room upon the ladies, and when Prescott presently rejoined them he found vivacity and gaiety still prevalent. Prescott's gaze dwelt longest on Miss Harley, who was talking to the Secretary. He noted again the look of admiration in the eyes of Mr. Sefton, and that feeling of jealousy which he would not have recognized had it not been for Talbot's half-jesting words returned to him. He would not deny to himself now that Helen Harley attracted him with singular force. There was about her an elusive charm; perhaps it was the slight trace of foreign look and manner that added to her Southern beauty a new and piquant grace.

Mr. Sefton was talking in smooth, liquid tones, and the others had drawn back a little in deference to the all-powerful official, while the girl was pleased, too. She showed it in her slightly parted lips, her vivid eyes and the keen attention with which she listened to all that he said.

Mrs. Markham followed Prescott's look. An ironical smile trembled for a moment on her lips. Then she said:

"The Secretary, the astute Mr. Sefton, is in love."

She watched Prescott keenly to notice the effect upon him of what she said, but he commanded his countenance and replied with a pretense of indifference:

"I think so, too, and I give him the credit of showing extremely good taste."

Mrs. Markham said no more upon the subject, and presently Prescott asked of Miss Harley the privilege of taking her home when the club adjourned, after the universal custom among the young in Southern towns.

"My shoulder is a little lame yet, but I am sure that I shall guard you safely through the streets if you will only let me try," he added gallantly.

"I shall be pleased to have you go," she replied.

"I would lend you my carriage and horses," said Mrs. Markham, who stood by, "but two of my horses were killed in front of an artillery wagon at Antietam, another fell valourously and in like manner at Gettysburg, and the fourth is still in service at the front. I am afraid I have none left, but at any rate you are welcome to the carriage."

Prescott laughingly thanked her but declined. The Secretary approached at that moment and asked Miss Harley if he might see her home.

"I have just accepted Captain Prescott's escort, but I thank you for the honour, Mr. Sefton," she replied.

Mr. Sefton flashed Prescott a single look, a look that the young Captain did not like; but it was gone in a moment like a streak of summer lightning, and the Secretary was as bland and smiling as ever.

"Again do I see that we civilians cannot compete with the military," he said.

"It was not his shoulder straps; he was quicker than you," said Mrs. Markham with a soft laugh.

"Then I shall not be a laggard the next time," replied the Secretary in a meaning tone.

The meeting of the club came to an end a half-hour later, but first there was a little ceremony. The coffee was brought in for the third and last time and all the cups were filled.

"To the cause!" said General Markham, the host. "To the cause that is not lost!"

"To the cause that is right, the cause that is not lost," all repeated, and they drank solemnly.

Prescott's feelings as he drank the toast were of a curiously mingled nature. There was a mist in his eyes as he looked upon this gathering of women and one-armed men all turning so brave a face and so bold a heart to bad fortune. And he wished, too, that he could believe as firmly as they in the justice of the cause. The recurring doubts troubled him. But he drank the toast and then prepared for departure.

CHAPTER IV

THE SECRETARY MOVES

Nearly all the guests left the Markham house at the same time and stood for a few moments in the white Greek portico, bidding one another good-night. It seemed to Prescott that it was a sort of family parting.

The last good-by said, Robert and Helen started down the street, toward the Harley home six or seven blocks away. Her gloved hand rested lightly on his arm, but her face was hidden from him by a red hood. The cold wind was still blustering mightily about the little city and she walked close beside him.

"I cannot help thinking at this moment of your army. Which way does it lie, Robert?" she asked.

"Off there," he replied, and he pointed northward.

"And the Northern army is there, too. And Washington itself is only two hundred miles away It seems to me sometimes that the armies have always been there. This war is so long. I remember I was a child when it began, and now——"

She paused, but Prescott added:

"It began only three years ago."

"A long three years. Sometimes when I look toward the North, where Washington lies, I begin to wonder about Lincoln. I hear bad things spoken of him here, and then there are others who say he is not bad."

"The 'others' are right, I think."

"I am glad to hear you say so. I feel sorry for him, such a lonely man and so unhappy, they say. I wish I knew all the wrong and right of this cruel struggle."

"It would take the wisdom of the angels for that."

They walked on a little farther in silence, passing now near the Capitol and its surrounding group of structures.

"What are they doing these days up there on Shockoe?" asked Prescott.

"Congress is in session and meets again in the morning, but I imagine it can do little. Our fate rests with the armies and the President."

A deep mellow note sounded from the hill and swelled far over the city. In the dead silence of the night it penetrated like a cannon shot, and the echo seemed to Prescott to come back from the far forest and the hills beyond the James. It was quickly followed by another and then others until all Richmond was filled with the sound.

Prescott felt the hand upon his arm clasp him in nervous alarm.

"What does that noise mean?" he cried.

"It's the Bell Tower!" she cried, pointing to a dark spire-like structure on Shockoe Hill in the Capitol Square.

"The Bell Tower!"

"Yes; the alarm! The bell was to be rung there when the Yankees came! Don't you hear it? They have come! They have come!"

The tramp of swift feet increased and grew nearer, there was a hum, a murmur and then a tumult in the streets; shouts of men, the orders of officers and galloping hoof-beats mingled; metal clanked against metal; cannon rumbled and their heavy iron wheels dashed sparks of fire from the stones as they rushed onward. There was a noise of shutters thrown back and lights appeared at innumerable windows. High feminine voices shouted to each other unanswered questions. The tumult swelled to a roar, and over it all thundered the great bell, its echo coming back in regular vibrations from the hills and the farther shore of the river.

After the first alarm Helen was quiet and self-contained. She had lived three years amid war and its tumults, and what she saw now was no more than she had trained herself to expect.

Prescott drew her farther back upon the sidewalk, out of the way of the cannon and the galloping cavalry, and he, too, waited quietly to see what would happen.

The garrison, except those posted in the defenses, gathered about Capitol Square, and women and children, roused from their beds, began to throng into the streets. The whole city was now awake and alight, and the cries of "The Yankees! The Yankees!" increased, but Prescott, hardened to alarms and to using his eyes, saw no Yankees. The sound of scattered rifle shots came from a point far to the eastward, and he listened for the report of artillery, but there was none.

As they stood waiting and listening, Sefton and Redfield, who had been walking home together, joined them. The Secretary was keen, watchful and self-contained, but the Member of Congress was red, wrathful and excited.

"See what your General and your army have brought upon us," he cried, seizing Prescott by the arm. "While Lee and his men are asleep, the Yankees have passed around them and seized Richmond."

"Take your hand off my arm, if you please, Mr. Redfield," said Prescott with quiet firmness, and the other involuntarily obeyed.

"Now, sir," continued Robert, "I have not seen any Yankees, nor have you, nor do I believe there is a Yankee force of sufficient size to be alarming on this side of the Rapidan."

"Don't you hear the bell?"

"Yes, I hear the bell; but General Lee is not asleep nor are his men. If they had the habit of which you accuse them the Yankee army would have been in this city long ago."

Helen's hand was still lying on Prescott's arm and he felt a grateful pressure as he spoke. A thrill of delight shot through him. It was a pleasure to him to defend his beloved General anywhere, but above all before her.

The forces of cavalry, infantry and artillery increased and were formed about Capitol Square. The tumult decreased, the cries of the women and children sank. Order reigned, but everywhere there was expectation. Everybody, too, gazed toward the east whence the sound of the shots had come. But the noise there died and presently the great bell ceased to ring.

"I believe you are right, Captain Prescott," said the Secretary; "I do not see any Yankees and I do not believe any have come."

But the Member of Congress would not be convinced, and recovering his spirit, he criticized the army again. Prescott scorned to answer, nor did Helen or the Secretary speak. Soon a messenger galloped down the street and told the cause of the alarm. Some daring Yankee cavalrymen, a band of skirmishers or scouts, fifty or a hundred perhaps, coming by a devious way, had approached the outer defenses and fired a few shots at long range. The garrison replied, and then the reckless Yankees galloped away before they could be caught.

"Very inconsiderate of them," said the Secretary, "disturbing honest people on a peaceful night like this. Why, it must be at least half-past two in the morning."

"You will observe, Mr. Redfield," said Prescott, "that the Yankee army has not got past General Lee, and the city will not belong to the Yankees before daylight."

"Not a single Yankee soldier ought to be able to come so near to Richmond," said the Member of Congress.

"Why, this only gives us a little healthy excitement, Mr. Redfield," said the Secretary, smoothly; "stirs our blood, so to speak, and teaches us to be watchful. We really owe those cavalrymen a vote of thanks."

Then putting his hand on Redfield's arm, he drew him away, first bidding Prescott and Miss Harley a courteous good-night.

A few more steps and they were at Helen's home. Mr. Harley himself, a tall, white-haired man, with a self-indulgent face singularly like his son Vincent's, answered the knock, shielding from the wind with one hand the flame of a fluttering candle held in the other.

He peered into the darkness, and Prescott thought that he perceived a slight look of disappointment on his face when he saw who had escorted his daughter home.

"He wishes it had been the Secretary," thought Robert.

"I was apprehensive about you for awhile, Helen," he said, "when I heard the bell ringing the alarm. It was reported that the Yankees had come."

"They are not here yet," said Prescott, "and we believe it is still a long road to Richmond."

As he bade Helen good-night at the door, she urged him not to neglect her while he was in the capital, and her father repeated the invitation with less warmth. Then the two disappeared within, the door was shut and Robert turned back into the darkness and the cold.

His own house was within sight, but he had made his mother promise not to wait for him, and he hoped she was already asleep. Never had he been more wide awake, and knowing that he should seek sleep in vain, he strolled down the street, looking about at the dim and silent city.

He gazed up at the dark shaft of the tower whence the bell had rung its warning, at the dusky mass of the Capitol, at the spire of St. Paul's, and then down at a flickering figure passing rapidly on the other side of the street. Robert's eyes were keen, and a soldier's life had accustomed him to their use in the darkness. He caught only a glimpse of it, but was sure the figure was that of the Secretary.

Though wondering what an official high in the Government was about flitting through Richmond at such an hour, he remembered philosophically that it was none of his business. Soon another man appeared, tall and bony, his face almost hidden by a thick black beard faintly touched with silver in the light of the moon. But this person was not shifty nor evasive. He stalked boldly along, and his heavy footsteps gave back a hard metallic ring as the iron-plated heels of his boots came heavily in contact with the bricks of the sidewalk.

Prescott knew the second figure, too. It was Wood, the great cavalryman, the fierce, dark mountaineer, and, wishing for company, Robert followed the General, whom he knew well. Wood turned at the sound of his footsteps and welcomed him.

"I don't like this town nor its folks," he said in his mountain dialect, "and I ain't goin' to stay long. They ain't my kind of people, Bob."

"Give 'em a chance, General; they are doing their best."

"What the Gov'ment ought to do," said the mountaineer moodily, "is to get up ev'ry man there is in the country and then hit hard at the enemy and keep on hittin' until there ain't a breath left in him. But sometimes it seems to me that it's the business of gov'ments in war to keep their armies from winnin'!"

They were joined at the corner by Talbot, according to his wont brimming over with high spirits, and Prescott, on the General's account, was glad they had met him. He, if anybody, could communicate good spirits.

"General," said the sanguine Talbot, "you must make the most of the time. The Yankees may not give us another chance. Across yonder, where you see that dim light trying to shine through the dirty window, Winthrop is printing his paper, which comes out this morning. As he is a critic of the Government, I suggest that we go over and see the task well done."

The proposition suited Wood's mood, and Prescott's, too, so they took their way without further words toward Winthrop's office, on the second floor of a rusty two-story frame building. Talbot led them up a shabby staircase just broad enough for one, between walls from which the crude plastering had dropped in spots.

"Why are newspaper offices always so shabby," he asked. "I was in New York once, where there are rich papers, but they were just the same."

The flight of steps led directly into the editorial room, where Winthrop sat in his shirt sleeves at a little table, writing. Raymond, at another, was similarly clad and similarly engaged. A huge stove standing in the corner, and fed with billets of wood, threw out a grateful heat. Sitting around it in a semi-circle were four or five men, including the one-armed Colonel Stormont and another man in uniform. All were busy reading the newspaper exchanges.

Winthrop waved his hand to the new visitors.

"Be all through in fifteen minutes," he said. "Sit down by the stove. Maybe you'd like to read this; its Rhett's paper."

He tossed them a newspaper and went on with his writing. The three found seats on cane-bottomed chairs or boxes and joined the group around the stove.

Prescott glanced a moment at the newspaper which Winthrop had thrown to them. It was a copy of the Charleston *Mercury*, conducted by the famous secessionist Rhett, then a member of the Confederate Senate, and edited meanwhile by his son. It breathed much fire and brimstone, and called insistently for a quick defeat of the insolent North. He passed it on to his friends and then looked with more interest at the office and the men about him. Everything was shabby to the last degree. Old newspapers and scraps of manuscript littered the floor, cockroaches crawled over the desks, on the walls were double-page illustrations from *Harper's Weekly* and *Leslie's Weekly*, depicting battle scenes in which the frightened Southern soldiers were fleeing like sheep before the valiant sons of the North.

"It's all the same, Prescott," said Talbot. "We haven't any illustrated papers, but if we had they'd show the whole Yankee army running fit to break its neck from a single Southern regiment."

General Wood, too, looked about with keen eyes, as if uncertain what to do, but his hesitation did not last long. A piece of pine wood lay near him, and picking it up he drew from under his belt a great keen-bladed bowie-knife, with which he began to whittle long slender shavings that curled beautifully; then a seraphic smile of content spread over his face.

Those who were not reading drifted into a discussion on politics and the war. The rumble of a press just starting to work came from the next room. Winthrop and Raymond wrote on undisturbed. The General, still whittling his pine stick, began to stare curiously at them. At last he said:

"Wa'al, if this ain't a harder trade than fightin', I'll be darned!"

Several smiled, but none replied to the General's comment. Raymond presently finished his article, threw it to an ink-blackened galley-boy and came over to the stove.

"You probably wonder what I am doing here in the enemy's camp," he said. "The office of every newspaper but my own is the camp of an enemy, but Winthrop asked me to help him out to-night with some pretty severe criticism of the Government. As he's responsible and I'm not, I've pitched into the President, Cabinet and Congress of the Confederate States of America at a great rate. I don't know what will happen to him, because while we are fighting for freedom here we are not fighting for the freedom of the press. We Southerners like to put in some heavy licks for freedom and then get something else. Maybe we're kin to the old Puritans."

They heard a light step on the stair, and the two editors looked up expecting to see some one of the ordinary chance visitors to a newspaper office. Instead it was the Secretary, Mr. Sefton, a conciliatory smile on his face and a hand outstretched ready for the customary shake.

"You are surprised to see me, Mr. Winthrop," he said, "but I trust that I am none the less welcome. I am glad, too, to find so many good men whom I know and some of whom I have met before on this very evening. Good-evening to you all, gentlemen."

He bowed to every one. Winthrop looked doubtfully at him as if trying to guess his business.

"Anything private, Mr. Sefton?" he said "If so we can step into the next room."

"Not at all! Not at all!" replied the Secretary, spreading out his fingers in negative style. "There is nothing that your friends need not hear, not even our great cavalry leader, General Wood. I was passing after a late errand, and seeing your light it occurred to me that I might come up to you and speak of some strange gossip that I have been hearing in Richmond."

All now listened with the keenest interest. They saw that the wily Secretary had not come on any vague errand at that hour of the morning.

"And may I ask what is the gossip?" said Winthrop with a trace of defiance in his tone.

"It was only a trifle," replied the Secretary blandly; "but a friend may serve a friend even in the matter of a trifle."

He paused and looked smilingly around the expectant circle. Winthrop made an impatient movement. He was by nature one of the most humane and generous of men, but fiery and touchy to the last degree.

"It was merely this," continued the Secretary, "and I really apologize for speaking of it at all, as it is scarcely any business of mine, but they say that you are going to print a fierce attack on the Government."

"What then?" asked Winthrop, with increasing defiance.

"I would suggest to you, if you will pardon the liberty, that you refrain. The Government, of which I am but a humble official, is sensitive, and it is, too, a critical time. Just now the Government needs all the support and confidence that it can possibly get. If you impair the public faith in us how can we accomplish anything?"

"But the newspapers of the North have entire freedom of criticism," burst out Winthrop. "We say that the North is not a free country and the South is. Are we to belie those words?"

"I think you miss the point," replied the Secretary, still speaking suavely. "The Government does not wish to repress the freedom of the press nor of any individual, nor in fact have I had any such matter in mind in giving you this intimation. I think that if you do as I hear you purpose to do, some rather extreme men will be disposed to make you trouble. Now there's Redfield."

"The trouble with Redfield," broke in Raymond, "is that he wants all the twenty-four hours of every day for his own talking."

"True! true in a sense," said the Secretary, "but he is a member of the House Committee on Military Affairs and is an influential man."

"I thank you, Mr. Secretary," said Winthrop, "but the article is already written."

A shade crossed the face of Mr. Sefton.

"And as you heard," continued Winthrop, "it attacks the Government with as much vigour as I am capable of putting into it. Here is the paper now; you can read for yourself what I have written."

The galley-boy had come in with a half-dozen papers still wet from the press. Winthrop handed one to the Secretary, indicated the editorial and waited while Sefton read it.

The Secretary, after the perusal, put down the paper and spoke gently as if he were chiding a child: "I am sorry this is published, Mr. Winthrop," he said. "It can only stir up trouble. Will you permit me to say that I think it indiscreet?"

"Oh, certainly," replied Winthrop. "You are entitled to your opinion, and by the same token so am I."

"I don't think our Government will like this," said Mr. Sefton. He tapped the newspaper as he spoke.

"I should think it would not," replied Winthrop with an ironical laugh. "At least, it was not intended that way. But does our Government expect to make itself an oligarchy or despotism? If that is so, I should like to know what we are fighting for?"

Mr. Sefton left these questions unanswered, but continued to express sorrow over the incident. He did not mean to interfere, he said; he had come with the best purpose in the world. He thought that at this stage of the war all influences ought to combine for the public good, and also he did not wish his young friends to suffer any personal inconvenience. Then bowing, he went out, but he took with him a copy of the paper.

"That visit, Winthrop, was meant for a threat, and nothing else," said Raymond, when he was sure the Secretary was safely in the street.

"No doubt of it," said Winthrop, "but I don't take back a word."

They speculated on the result, until General Wood, putting up his knife and throwing down his pine stick, drew an old pack of cards from an inside pocket of his coat.

"Let's play poker a little while," he said. "It'll make us think of somethin' else and steady our nerves. Besides, it's mighty good trainin' for a soldier. Poker's just like war—half the cards you've got, an' half bluff. Lee and Jackson are such mighty good gen'rals 'cause they always make the other fellow think they've got twice as many soldiers as they really have."

Raymond, an inveterate gambler, at once acceded to the proposition; Winthrop and one of the soldiers did likewise, and they sat down to play. The others looked on.

"Shall we make the limit ten cents in coin or ten dollars Confederate money?" asked Winthrop.

"Better make it ten dollars Confederate; we don't want to risk too much," replied Raymond.

Soon they were deep in the mysteries and fascinations of the game. Wood proved himself a consummate player, a master of "raise" and "bluff," but for awhile the luck ran against him, and he made this brief comment:

"Things always run in streaks; don't matter whether it's politics, love, farmin' or war. They don't travel alone. At Antietam nearly half the Yankee soldiers we killed were red-headed. Fact, sure; but at Chancellorsville I never saw a single dead Yankee with a red head."

The luck turned by and by toward the General, but Prescott thought it was time for him to be seeking home and he bade good-night. Colonel Stormont accompanied him as he went down the rickety stairs.

"Colonel," asked Prescott, as they reached the street, "who, in reality, is Mr. Sefton?"

"That is more than any of us can tell," replied the Colonel; "nominally he is at the head of a department in the Treasury, but he has acquired a great influence in the Cabinet—he is so deft at the despatch of business—and he is at the White House as much as he is anywhere. He is not a man whom we can ignore."

Prescott was of that opinion, too, and when he got into his bed, not long before the break of day, he was still thinking of the bland Secretary.

CHAPTER V

AN ELUSIVE FACE

Walking abroad at noontime next day, Prescott saw Helen Harley coming toward Capitol Square, stepping lightly through the snow, a type of youthful freshness and vigour. The red hood was again over her head, and a long dark cloak, the hem of it almost touching the snow fallen the night before, enclosed her figure.

"Good-morning, Mr. Soldier," she said cheerily; "I hope that your dissipations at the Mosaic Club have not retarded the recovery of your injured shoulder."

Prescott smiled.

"I think not," he replied. "In fact, I've almost forgotten that I have a shoulder."

"Now, I can guess where you are going," she said.

"Try and see."

"You are on your way to the Capitol to hear Mr. Redfield reply to that attack of Mr. Winthrop's, and I'm going there, too."

So they walked together up the hill, pausing a moment by the great Washington monument and its surrounding groups of statuary where Mr. Davis had taken the oath of office two years before, and Mr. Sefton, who saw them from an upper window of that building, smiled sourly.

The doors of the Capitol were wide open, as they always stood during the sessions of Congress, and Robert and Helen passed into the rotunda, pausing a moment by the Houdon Washington, and then went up the steps to the second floor, where they entered the Senate Chamber, now used by the Confederate House of Representatives. The tones of a loud and tireless voice reached them; Mr. Redfield was already on his feet.

The honourable member from the Gulf Coast had risen on a question of personal privilege. Then he required the clerk of the House to read the offending editorial from Winthrop's newspaper, during which he stood haughtily erect, his feet rather wide apart, his arms folded indignantly across his breast, and a look of righteous wrath on his face. When the clerk finished, he spat plentifully in a spittoon at his feet, cleared his throat, and let loose the flood of rhetoric which was threatening already to burst over the dam.

The blow aimed by that villainous writer, the honourable gentleman said, was struck at him. He was a member of the Committee on Military Affairs, and he must reply ere the foul stain was permitted to tarnish his name. He came from a sunny land where all the women were beautiful and all the men brave, and he would rather die a thousand deaths than permit any obscure ink-slinger to impeach his fair fame. He carried the honour of his country in his heart; he would sooner die a thousand deaths than to permit—to permit—-

He paused, and waved his hand as he sought for a metaphor sufficiently strong-winged.

"Wait a minute, Mr. Redfield, and I'll help you down," dryly said a thin-faced member from the Valley of Virginia.

The sound of subdued laughter arose and the Speaker rapped for order. Mr. Redfield glared at the irreverent member from the Valley of Virginia, then resumed his interrupted flight. Unfortunately for him the spell was broken. Some of the members began to talk in low whispers and others to read documents. Besides the murmur of voices there was a sound of scraping feet. But the honourable member from the sunny shores of the Gulf helped himself down, though somewhat angrily, and choosing a tamer course began to come nearer to the point. He called for the suppression of the offending newspaper and the expulsion of its editor from the city. He spoke of Winthrop by name and denounced him. Robert saw Mr. Sefton appear upon the floor and once nod his head approvingly as Mr. Redfield spoke.

The House now paid more heed, but the dry member from the Valley of Virginia, in reply to Mr. Redfield, called the attention of the members to the fact that they could not suppress the newspapers. They might deny its representatives the privileges of the House, but they could go no further. He was opposed to spreading the thing to so great an extent, as it would be sure to reach the North and would be a standing advertisement to the Yankees that the South was divided against itself.

Then a motion was made to deny the privileges of the House to Winthrop, or any representative of his paper, but it was defeated by a narrow margin.

"That, I think," said Robert, "will be the end of this affair."

"I am glad of it," responded Helen, "because I like Mr. Winthrop."

"And, therefore, you believe everything he says is correct?"

"Yes; why not?"

"Women have more personal loyalty than men," said Robert, not replying directly. "Shall we go now?" he asked a moment later; "I think we have heard all of interest."

"No, I must stay a little," she replied with some embarrassment. "The fact is—I am—waiting to see Mr. Sefton."

"To see Mr. Sefton!" Prescott could not refrain from exclaiming in his surprise.

She looked at him with an air half defiance, half appeal.

"Yes," she said, "and my business is of considerable importance to me. You don't think that a mere woman can have any business of weight with so influential a personage as Mr. Sefton. You Southern men, with all your courtesy and chivalry, really undervalue us, and therefore you are not gallant at all."

Her defiant look and manner told Prescott that she did not wish him to know the nature of her business, so he made a light answer, asking her if she were about to undertake the affairs of the Government. He had no doubt some would be glad to get rid of them.

He excused himself presently and strolled into the rotunda, where he gazed absently at the Washington statue and the Lafayette bust, although he saw neither. Conscious of a feeling of jealousy, he began to wish ill to the clever Secretary. "What business can she have with a man like Sefton?" he said to himself.

Passing out of the rotunda, he walked slowly down the steps, and looking back saw Helen and Mr. Sefton in close and earnest conversation. Then he went on faster with increased ill temper.

"I have a piece of news for you," said Mrs. Prescott the next morning to her son at the breakfast table.

He looked at her with inquiring interest.

"Helen Harley has gone to work," she said.

"Gone to work! Mother, what do you mean?"

"The heiress of seven generations must work like a common Northern mill-hand to support that pompous old father of hers, the heir of six Virginia generations, who certainly would not work under any circumstances to support his daughter."

"Won't you explain yourself more clearly, mother?"

"It's this. The Harleys are ruined by the war. The Colonel is absorbed in his career and spends all his salary on himself. The old gentleman doesn't know anything about his financial affairs and doesn't want to; it's beneath his dignity. Helen, who does know about them, is now earning the bread for her father and herself. Think of a Southern girl of the oldest blood doing such a thing! It is very low and degrading, isn't it?"

She looked at him covertly. A sudden thought occurred to him.

"No, mother," he replied. "It is not low and degrading. You think just the contrary, and so do I. Where has Helen gone to work?"

"In the Treasury Department, under Mr. Sefton. She is copying documents there."

Robert felt a sudden relief and then alarm that she should owe so much to Sefton.

"I understand that Harley senior stormed and threatened for awhile," continued his mother. "He said no female member of his family had ever worked before, and he might have added, few male members either. He said his family would be disgraced forever by the introduction of such a low Yankee innovation; but Helen stood firm, and, moreover, she was urged by the hand of necessity. I understand that she has quite a good place and her salary is to be paid in gold. She will pass here every day at noon, coming home for her luncheon."

Prescott spent most of the morning at home, the remainder with his new friends, wandering about the city; but just before noon he was in front of the Custom House, waiting by the door through which Helen must come. She appeared promptly at the stroke of twelve and seemed surprised to see him there.

"I came merely to tell you how much I admire your resolution," he said. "I think you are doing a noble thing."

The colour in her cheeks deepened a little. He knew he had pleased her.

"It required no great amount of courage," she replied, "for the work is not hard and Mr. Sefton is very kind. And, aside from the money I am happier here. Did you never think how hard it was for women to sit with their hands folded, waiting for this war to end?"

"I have thought of it more than once," he replied.

"Now I feel that I am a part of the nation," she continued, "not a mere woman who does not count. I am working with the others for our success."

Her eyes sparkled like the eyes of one who has taken a tonic, and she looked about her defiantly as if she would be ready with a fitting reply to any who might dare to criticize her.

Prescott liked best in her this quality of independence and self-reliance, and perhaps her possession of it imparted to her that slight foreign air which he so often noticed. He thought the civilization of the South somewhat debilitating, so far as women were concerned. It wished to divide the population into just two classes—women of beautiful meekness and men of heroic courage.

Helen had broken down an old convention, having made an attempt that few women of her class and period would have dared, and at a time, too, when she might have been fearful of the results. She was joyous as if a burden had been lifted. Prescott rarely had seen her in such spirits. She, who was usually calm and grave, seemed to have forgotten the war. She laughed and jested and saw good humour in everything.

Prescott could not avoid catching the infection from the woman whom he most admired. The atmosphere—the very air—took on an unusual brilliancy. The brick walls and the shingled roofs glittered in the crisp, wintry sunshine; the schoolboys, caps over their ears and mittens on their fingers, played and shouted in the streets just as if peace reigned and the cannon were not rumbling onward over there beyond the trees.

"Isn't this world beautiful at times?" said Helen.

"It is," replied Robert, "and it seems all the more strange to me that we should profane it by war. But here comes Mrs. Markham. Let us see how she will greet you."

Mrs. Markham was in a sort of basket cart drawn by an Accomack pony, one of those ugly but stout little horses which do much service in Virginia and she was her own driver, her firm white wrists showing above her gloves as she held the reins. She checked her speed at sight of Robert and Helen and stopped abreast of them.

"I was not deceiving you the other night, Captain Prescott," she said, after a cheerful good-afternoon "when I told you that all my carriage horses had been confiscated. Ben Butler, here—I call him Ben Butler because he is low-born and has no manners—arrived only last night, bought for me by my husband with a whole wheelbarrowful of Confederate bills: is it not curious how we, who have such confidence in our Government, will not trust its money."

She flicked Ben Butler with her whip, and the pony reared and tried to bolt, but presently she reduced him to subjection.

"Did I not tell you that he had no manners," she said. "Oh, how I wish I had the real Ben Butler under my hand, too! I've heard what you've done, Helen. But, tell me, is it really true? Have you actually gone to work—as a clerk in an office, like a low-born Northern woman?"

The colour in Helen's cheeks deepened and Robert saw the faintest quiver of her lower lip.

"It is true," she replied. "I am a secretary in Mr. Sefton's office and I get fifteen dollars a week."

"Confederate money?"

"No, in gold."

"What do you do it for?"

"For the money. I need it."

Mrs. Markham flicked the pony's mane again and once more he reared, but, as before, the strong hand restrained him.

"What you are doing is right, Helen," she said. "Though a Southern woman, I find our Southern conventions weigh heavily upon me: but," she added quizzically, "of course, you understand that we can't know you socially now."

"I understand," said Helen, "and I don't ask it."

Her lips were pressed together with an air of defiance and there was a sparkle in her eyes.

Mrs. Markham laughed long and joyously.

"Why, you little goose," she said, "I believe you actually thought I was in earnest. Don't you know that we of the Mosaic Club and its circle represent the more advanced and liberal spirit of Richmond—if I do say it myself—and we shall stand by you to the utmost. I suspect that if you were barred, others would choose the same bars for themselves. Would they not, Captain Prescott?"

"I certainly should consider myself included in the list," replied the young man sturdily.

"And doubtless you would have much company," resumed she. "And now I must be going. Ben Butler is growing impatient. He is not accustomed to good society, and I must humour him or he will make a scene."

She spoke to the horse and they dashed down the street.

"A remarkable woman," said Prescott.

"Yes; and just now I feel very grateful to her," said Helen.

21

They met others, but not all were so frank and cordial as Mrs. Markham. There was a distinct chilliness in the manners of one, while a second had a patronizing air which was equally offensive. Helen's high spirits were dashed a little, but Robert strove to raise them again. He saw only the humourous features of such a course on the part of those whom they had encountered, and he exerted himself to ridicule it with such good effect that she laughed again, and her happy mood was fully restored when she reached her own gate.

The next was a festal day in Richmond, which, though always threatened by fire and steel, was not without its times of joyousness. The famous Kentucky raider, Gen. John H. Morgan, had come to town, and all that was best in the capital, both military and civil, would give him welcome and do him honour.

The hum and bustle of a crowd rose early in the streets, and Prescott, with all the spirits of youth, eager to see and hear everything of moment, was already with his friends, Talbot, Raymond and Winthrop.

"Richmond knows how to sing and dance even if the Yankee army is drawing near. Who's afraid!" said Winthrop.

"I have declined an honour," said Raymond. "I might have gone in one of the carriages in the procession, but I would rather be here on the sidewalk with you. A man can never see much of a show if he is part of it."

It was a winter's day, but Richmond was gay, nevertheless. The heavens opened in fold on fold of golden sunshine, and a bird of winter, rising above the city, poured out a flood of song. The boys had a holiday and they were shouting in the streets. Officers in their best uniforms rode by, and women, bringing treasured dresses of silk or satin from old chests, appeared now in gay and warm colours. The love of festivity, which war itself could not crush, came forth, and these people, all of whom knew one another, began to laugh and jest and to see the brighter side of life.

"Come toward the hotel," said Talbot to his friends; "Morgan and some of the great men of Kentucky who are with him have been there all night. That's where the procession starts."

Nothing loath, they followed him, and stayed about the hotel, talking with acquaintances and exchanging the news of the morning. Meanwhile the brilliant day deepened and at noon the time for the festivities to begin was at hand.

The redoubtable cavalry leader, whose fame was rivaling that of Stuart and Wood, came forth from the hotel, his friends about him, and the grand procession through the streets was formed. First went the Armory Band, playing its most gallant tunes, and after that the city Battalion in its brightest uniform. In the first carriage sat General Morgan and Mayor Joseph Mayo of Richmond, side by side, and behind them in carriages and on horseback rode a brilliant company; famous Confederate Generals like J. E. B. Stuart, Edward Johnson, A. P. Hill and others, Hawes, the so-called Confederate Governor of Kentucky, and many more.

Virginia was doing honour to Kentucky in the person of the latter's gallant son, John H. Morgan, and the crowd flamed into enthusiasm. Tumultuous applause arose. These were great men to the people. Their names were known in every household, and they resounded now, shouted by many voices in the crisp, wintry air. The carriages moved briskly along, the horses reared with their riders in brilliant uniforms, and their steel-shod hoofs struck sparks from the stones of the streets. Ahead of all, the band played dance music, and the brass of horn and trumpet flashed back the golden gleam of the sun. The great dark-haired and dark-eyed cavalryman, the centre and object of so much applause and enthusiasm, smiled with pleasure, and bowed to right and left like a Roman Caesar at his triumph.

The joy and enthusiasm of the crowd increased and the applause swelled into rumbling thunder. Richmond, so long depressed and gloomy, sprang up with a bound. Why cry when it was so much better to laugh! The flash of uniforms was in the eyes of all, and the note of triumphant music in every ear. What were the Yankees, anyway, but a leaderless horde? They could never triumph over such men as these, Morgan, Stuart, Wood, Harley, Hill, not to mention the peerless chief of them all, Lee, out there, always watching.

The low thunder of a cannon came faintly from the north, but there were few who heard it.

The enthusiasm of the crowd for Morgan spread to everybody, and mighty cheers were given in turn for all the Generals and the Mayor. The rebound was complete. The whole people, for the time being, looked forward to triumph, thorough and magnificent. The nearer the Yankees came to Richmond the greater would be their defeat and rout. High spirits were contagious and ran through the crowd like a fire in dry grass.

"Hurrah!" cried Talbot, clapping his hand heavily upon Prescott's shoulder. "This is the spirit that wins! We'll drive the Yankees into the Potomac now!"

"I've never heard that battles were won by shouting and the music of bands," replied Prescott dryly. "How many of these people who are making so much noise have anything whatever to do with the war?"

"That's your Puritan mind, old Gloomy Face," replied Talbot. "Nothing was ever won by being too solemn."

"And we mustn't hold too cheaply the enthusiasm of a crowd—even a crowd that is influenced merely by the emotion of the moment," said Raymond. "It is a force which, aimless in itself, may be controlled for good uses by others. Ha, look at Harley, there! Well done!"

Helen's brother was riding an unusually spirited horse that reared and curveted every time the band put forth an unusual effort. The Colonel himself was in gorgeous attire, wearing a brand new uniform with much gold lace, very large epaulets on his shoulders and a splendid silken sash around his waist. A great cavalry saber hung at his side. He was a resplendent figure and he drew much applause from the boys and the younger women. His eyes shone with pleasure, and he allowed his horse to curvet freely.

A little girl, perhaps pressed too much by the unconscious crowd or perhaps driven on by her own enthusiasm, fell directly in front of the rearing horse of Harley. It was too late for him to stop, and a cry of alarm arose from the crowd, who expected to see the iron-shod hoofs beat the child's body into the pavement, but Harley instantly struck his horse a mighty blow and the animal sprang far over the child, leaving her untouched.

The applause was thunderous, and Harley bowed and bowed, lifting his plumed hat again and again to the admiring multitude, while sitting his still-rearing horse with an ease and grace that was beyond criticism.

"The man's whole character was expressed in that act," said Raymond with conviction; "vain to the last degree, as fond of display and colours as a child, unconsciously selfish, but in the presence of physical danger quick, resourceful, and as brave as Alexander. What queer mixtures we are!"

Mr. Harley was in one of the carriages of the procession and his eyes glittered with pleasure and pride when he witnessed the act of his son. Moreover, in his parental capacity he appropriated part of the credit and also took off his hat and bowed.

The procession advanced along Main Street toward the south porch of the City Hall, where General Morgan was to be presented formally to the people, and the cheers never ceased for a moment. Talbot and the two editors talked continually about the scene before them, even the minds of the two professional critics becoming influenced by the unbounded enthusiasm; but Prescott paid only a vague attention, his mind having been drawn away by something else.

The young Captain saw in the throng a woman who seemed to him somewhat different from those around her. She was not cheering nor clapping her hands—merely floating with the stream. She was very tall and walked with a strong and graceful step, but was wrapped to her cheeks in a long brown cloak; only a pair of wonderfully keen eyes, which once met the glance of his, rose above its folds. Her look rested on him a moment and held him with a kind of secret power, then her eyes passed on; but it seemed to him that under a show of indifference she was examining everything with minute scrutiny.

It was the lady of the brown cloak, his silent companion of the train, and Prescott burned with curiosity at this unexpected meeting. He watched her for some time and he could make nothing of her. She spoke to no one, but kept her place among the people, unnoticed but noticing. He was recalled to himself presently by Talbot's demand to know why he stared so much at the crowd and not at the show itself.

Then he turned his attention away from the woman to the procession, but he resolved not to lose sight of her entirely.

At the south porch of the City Hall General Morgan was introduced with great ceremony to the inhabitants of the Confederate capital, who had long heard of his gallant deeds.

After the cheering subsided, the General, a handsome man of thirty-six or seven, made a speech. The Southern people dearly love a speech, and they gave him close attention, especially as he was sanguine, predicting great victories. Little he dreamed that his career was then close to its bloody end, and that the brilliant Stuart, standing so near, would be claimed even sooner; that Hill, over there, and others beside him, would never see the close of the war. There was no note of all this in the air now, and no note of it in Morgan's speech. Young blood and lively hope spoke in him, and the bubbling spirits of the crowd responded.

Prescott and his comrades stood beside the porch, listening to the address and the cheers, and Prescott's attention was claimed again by the strange woman in the throng. She was standing directly in front of the speaker, though all but her face was hidden by those around her. He saw the same keen eyes under long lashes studying the generals on the porch. "I'm going to speak to that woman," resolved Prescott. "Boys," he said to his comrades, "I've just caught the eye of an old friend whom I haven't seen in a long time. Excuse me for a minute."

He edged his way cautiously through the throng until he stood beside the strange woman. She did not notice his coming and presently he stumbled slightly against her. He recovered himself instantly and was ready with an apology.

"I beg your pardon," he said, "but we have met before. I seem to remember you, Miss, Miss——"

The woman looked startled, then set her lips firmly.

"You are rude, sir," she said. "Is it the custom of Southern gentlemen to accost ladies in this manner?"

She gave her shoulders a haughty shrug and turned her back upon him. Prescott flushed, but held his ground, and he would have spoken to her again had she given him the chance. But she began to move away and he was afraid to follow deliberately lest he make a scene. Instead, he went back to his friends.

The General's speech came to an end and was followed by a rolling thunder of cheers. Then all the people of consequence were presented to him, and forth from the Hustings court-room, where they had been biding their time, walked twenty of the most beautiful young ladies of Richmond, in holiday attire of pink, rose and lilac silk or satin, puffed and flounced, their hair adorned with pink and red roses from Richmond hothouses.

It was really a wonderful bit of feminine colouring amid the crowd, and the Southern people, ever proud of their women, cheered again. Helen was there—it was a holiday—in a wonderful old dress of rose-coloured satin, her cheeks glowing and her eyes shining, and as Prescott saw her he forgot the strange woman who had rebuffed him.

"The most beautiful girl of this score of beautiful girls is to present a wreath of roses to General Morgan. I wonder who it will be," said Raymond.

He looked quizzically at Prescott.

"I wonder," repeated Prescott, but he felt no doubt whatever upon the subject.

The cheering of the crowd ceased, and Helen, escorted by her brother, stepped from the unserried ranks of beauty to a table where the chaplet of roses lay. Then the General stood aside, and Helen, walking forward alone, made a little speech to General Morgan, in which she complimented him on his courage and brilliant achievements. She said that the sound of his voice would always strike terror in the North and kindle hope anew in the South. She was half afraid, half daring, but she spoke the words clearly. The big, black-bearded General stood before her, hat in hand and openly admiring. When she came to the end of her speech she reached up, rested the wreath for a moment on his bushy black crown of hair and then put it in his hands. Now the crowd gave its greatest burst of applause. The two figures standing there, the tall, brown soldier and the beautiful woman, appealed to all that was gallant in their nature.

"It does not look as if there would be any social ostracism of Miss Harley because she has turned working woman," said Winthrop.

"Cold and selfish emotions don't count at a time like this," said Raymond; "it's the silent pressure of time and circumstance that she'll have to reckon with."

Helen, her great deed performed, walked back, blushing somewhat, and hid herself among her companions. Then, the official ceremonies over, the occasion became informal, and soon generals and young women alike were surrounded by admirers, war and beauty having chances about equal in the competition. The good spirits of the crowd, moved by triumphant oratory, the beauty of the women and the blaze of uniforms, grew to such a pitch that no discordant note marred the cheerfulness of those gathered in the old Court House.

Prescott pressed into the crowd, but he found himself somewhat lost, or, rather, dimmed, amid the brilliant uniforms of the generals, who were as thick as corn in the field, and he despaired of securing more than a small part of Helen's attention. He had admired her beauty more than ever that day; her timid dignity when all critical eyes were upon her impressed him, and yet he felt no jealousy now when he saw her surrounded and so sincerely flattered by others. He was surprised at himself, and a little angry, too, that it should be so, but search his mind as he would he could not find the cause. At last he secured a word or two with her and passed on toward the porch; but looking back saw the great cavalry leader, Wood, the mountaineer, talking to her, his tall figure towering a head over hers, his black eyes sparkling with a new fire and lighting up his face like a blaze. His uniform was not too bright and he was an imposing figure—lionlike was the simile that occurred to Prescott.

But he felt no pang—again he was surprised at himself—and went on his way to the parlour, where the decorations were yet untouched, and gazed at the crowd, portions of which still lingered in the streets.

His eyes unconsciously sought one figure, a figure that was not there, and he came to himself with a start when he realized the cause that had drawn him to the place. Displeased with himself, he rejoined his friends in the court-room.

"Let's go into the hall and see the ladies and the great men," said Talbot, and his comrades willingly went with him. It was indeed an animated scene in the building, the same high spirits and confident hope for the future that had marked the crowd prevailing here.

Despite the winter without, it was warm in the rooms of the City Hall, and Prescott, after awhile, went back to the porch from which General Morgan had made his speech. Many of the enthusiastic throng of spectators still lingered and small boys were sending off amateur fireworks. Going outside, he became once more one of the throng, simply because he had caught another glimpse of a face that interested and mystified him.

It was the tall woman of the brown cloak, still watching everything with eyes that missed no detail. She annoyed Prescott; she had become an obsession like one of those little puzzles the solution of which is of no importance except when one cannot obtain it. So he lingered in her neighbourhood, taking care that she should not observe him, and he asked two or three persons concerning her identity. Nobody knew her.

As the crowd, by and by, began to diminish, the woman turned away. The outlines of her figure were not disclosed, but her step was swinging and free, as that of one who had an abundance of health and vigour. She spoke to nobody, but seemed sure of her way.

She went up Main Street, and Prescott, his curiosity increasing, followed at a distance. She did not look back, and he closed up gradually the gap between them, in order that he might not lose sight of her if she turned around a corner. This she did presently, but when he hastened and passed the corner, too, he found himself face to face with the woman in brown.

"Well, sir?" she said sharply.

"Ah, I—— Excuse me, I did not see you. I turned the corner with such suddenness," he said awkwardly, having an uneasy sense that he had been intrusive, yet anxious to solve the troublesome little mystery.

"You were following me—and for the second time to-day."

He was silent, but his flushed face confirmed the truth of her accusation. For the moment that he stood near he examined her features. He saw eyes so dark that he could not tell whether they were blue or black, eyelashes of unusual length, and a pale face remarkable for its strength. But it was youthful and finely cut, while a wisp of bronze hair at the edge of the hood showed a gleam of gold as the sunshine fell across it.

"I have heard that Southern gentlemen were always courteous, as I told you once before," she said.

"I thought I knew you, but made a mistake," Prescott replied, it being the first thing that came into his mind. "I fear that I have been rude and I ask your pardon."

He lifted his hat and bowed humbly.

"You can show contrition by ceasing to follow me," she said, and the sharp tone of her accusation was still in her voice.

Prescott bowed again and turned away. He fully meant to keep his implied promise, but curiosity was too strong for him, and watching once more from a distance, he saw her go up Shockoe Hill and into the Capitol through the wide-open doors. When he found it convenient presently to enter the Capitol in his turn, he saw no trace of her, and, disappointed and annoyed with himself, he went back to the City Hall. Here Talbot was the first whom he met.

"Where have you been?" asked his friend.

"Following a woman."

"Following a woman?"

Talbot looked at Prescott in surprise.

"I didn't know you were that kind of a man, Bob," he said; "but what luck?"

"None at all. I failed even to learn her name, where she lived or anything else about her. I'll tell you more this evening, because I want your advice."

The reception ended presently, and the ladies, escorted by the young men, went to their homes. Talbot, Winthrop and Raymond rejoined Prescott soon afterward near Shockoe Hill.

"Now tell us of the woman you were following," said Talbot.

"I don't think I shall," replied Prescott. "I've changed my intention about it—at least, for the present."

The affair had clung to his mind and the result of his second thought was a resolution to keep it to himself a while longer. He had formed a suspicion, but it might be wrong, and he would not willingly do injustice to any one, least of all to a woman. Her face, when he saw her close at hand, looked pure and good, and now that he recalled it he could remember distinctly that there had been in it a touch of reproach and the reproach was for him—she had seemed to ask why he annoyed her. No, he would wait before speaking of her to his friends.

Talbot regarded Prescott for a moment with an inquiring gaze, but said nothing more upon the subject.

Prescott left his friends at the Capitol and spent the remainder of the day with his mother, who on the plea of age had avoided the reception and the festivities, although she now had many questions to ask.

"I hear that great enthusiasm was shown and brilliant predictions were made," she said.

"It is quite true," he replied. "The music, the speeches and the high spirits, which you know are contagious in a crowd, have done good, I think, to the Southern cause."

"Did Morgan bring any new recruits for General Lee's army?"

"Now, mother," replied Prescott, laughing a little, "don't let your Northern blood carry you too far. I know, too, that wars are not won by music and shouting, and days like to-day bring nothing substantial—merely an increase of hope; but after all, that is what produces substantial results."

She smiled and did not answer, but went on quietly with her sewing. Prescott watched her for awhile and reflected what a beautiful woman his mother must have been, and was yet, for that matter.

"Mother," he said presently, "you do not speak it aloud, but you cannot disguise from me the fact that you think it would be better for the North to win."

She hesitated, but at last she said:

"I cannot rejoice whichever way this war ends. Are you not on the side of the South? All I can pray for is that it may end quickly."

"In your heart, mother, you have no doubt of the result."

She made no reply, and Prescott did not pursue the subject.

CHAPTER VI

THE PURSUIT OF A WOMAN

The silver lining which the reception to General Morgan put in the cloud always hanging over Richmond lasted until the next day, when the content of the capital was rudely shattered by news that important papers had been stolen from the office of the President in the granite building on Bank Street. The exact value of these papers the public did not know, but they contained plans, it was said, of the coming campaign and exact data concerning the military and financial condition of the Confederacy. They were, therefore, of value alike to the Government and its enemies, and great was the noise over their disappearance.

The theft, so supposition ran, was committed while nearly all the officials were present at the festivities of the preceding day, and when the guard about the public offices, never very strict, was relaxed more than usual. But the clue stopped there, and, so far as the city could hear, it bade fair to remain at that point, as the crush of great affairs about to decide the fate of a nation would not permit a long search for such a secret spring, though the leakage might prove expensive.

"Probably some faithless servant who hopes to sell them to the North for a large reward," said Raymond to Prescott.

"I think not," replied Prescott with emphasis.

"Ah, you don't? Then what do you think?" asked Raymond, looking at him sharply.

"A common spy," replied Prescott, not wishing to be surprised into further disclosure of his thought. "You know such must be here. In war no city or army is free from spies."

"But that's a vague generalization," said Raymond, "and leads to nothing."

"True," said Prescott, but he intended a further inquiry into the matter on his own account, and this he undertook as soon as he was free from others. He was perhaps better fitted than any one else in Richmond for the search, because he had sufficient basis upon which to build a plan that might or might not lead to a definite issue.

He went at once to the building in which the President had his office, where, despite the robbery of the day before, he roamed about among the rooms and halls almost as he pleased, inquiring and making suggestions which might draw from the attendants facts to them of slight importance. Yes, visitors had been there the day before, chiefly ladies, some from the farther South, drawn by veneration for their beloved President and a wish to see the severe and simple offices from which the destiny of eleven great States and the fate of the mightiest war the world had ever known was directed.

And who were the ladies? If their names were not known, could not a description of their appearance be given? But no one had any definite memory on these points; they were just like other sightseers. Was there a tall woman with a brown cloak among them? Prescott put this question to several people, but drew no affirmative reply until he found an old coloured man who swept the halls. The sweeper thought that he did remember seeing such a figure on the lower floor, but he was not sure, and with that Prescott was forced to be content.

He felt that his search had not been wholly in vain, leading as it did to what might be called the shadow of a clue, and he resolved to continue it. There had been leaks before in the Confederacy, some by chance and some by design, notably an instance of the former when Lee's message to his lieutenant was lost by the messenger and found by a Northern sympathizer, thus informing his opponents of his plan and compelling him to fight the costly battle of Antietam. If he pursued this matter and prevented its ultimate issue, he might save the Confederacy far more than he could otherwise.

Richmond was a small city, difficult of entrance without a pass, and for two or three days Prescott, abandoning the society of his friends, trod its streets industriously, not neglecting the smallest and meanest among them, seeking always a tall figure in a brown dress and brown cloak. It became an obsession with him, and, as he now recognized, there was even more in it than a mere hunt for a spy. This woman troubled him; he wished to know who and what she was and why she, a girl, had undertaken a task so unfitting. Yet war, he remembered, is a destroyer of conventions, and the mighty upheaval through which the country was going could account for anything.

He found on the third day his reward in another glimpse of the elusive and now tantalizing brown figure under the brow of Shockoe Hill, strolling along casually, as if the beauty of the day and the free air of the heavens alone attracted.

The brown dress had been changed, but the brown cloak remained the same, and Prescott felt a pang of remorse lest he had done an injustice to a woman who looked so innocent. Until this moment he had never seen her face distinctly, save one glimpse, but now the brown hood that she wore was thrown back a little and there shone beneath it clear eyes of darkest blue, illuminating a face as young, as pure, as delicate in outline as he could have wished for in a sister of his own. No harm could be there. A woman who looked like that could not be engaged upon an errand such as he suspected, and he would leave her undisturbed.

But, second thought came. He put together again all the circumstances, the occasions upon which he had seen her, especially that day of the Morgan reception, and his suspicions returned. So he followed her again, at a distance now, lest she should see him, and was led a long and winding chase about the capital.

He did not believe that she knew of his presence, and these vague meanderings through the streets of Richmond confirmed his belief. No one with a clear conscience would leave such crooked tracks, and what other purpose could she have now save to escape observation until the vigilance of the sentinels, on edge over the robbery, should relax a little and she could escape through the cordon of guards that belted in Richmond.

She passed at last into an obscure side street and there entered a little brown wooden cottage. Prescott, watching from the corner, saw her disappear within, and he resolved that he would see her, too, when she came out again. Therefore he remained at the corner or near it, sauntering about now and then to avoid notice, but always keeping within a narrow circle and never losing sight of the house.

He was aware that he might remain there a long time, but he had a stiff will and he was bent upon solving this problem which puzzled and irritated him.

It was about the middle of the afternoon when he traced her to the cottage, but the fragment of the day remaining seemed long to him. Golden shadows hung over the capital, but at last the sun went down in a sea of flame and the cold night of winter gathered all within its folds.

Prescott shivered as he trod his beat like a policeman, but he was of a tenacious fiber, and scorning alike the warnings of cold and hunger, he remained near the house, drawing closer and watching it more zealously than ever in the moonlight. His resolution strengthened, too; he would stay there, if necessary, until the sunset of the next day.

More hours passed at a limping gait. The murmur of the city died, and all was dark and still in the side street. Far into the night, nearly twelve, it must have been, when a figure stole from the cottage and glanced up the little ravine toward the main street, where Prescott stood invisible in the shadow of a high wooden fence.

She did not come by the front door, but stole out from the rear. He was convinced that he was right in his suspicions, and now every action of this unknown woman indicated guilt to his mind.

He crouched down in an angle of the fence, hidden completely by its shadow and the night, though he could see her well as she came up the little street, walking with light step and watching warily on every side. He noticed even then how strong and elastic her figure appeared and that every step was instinct with life and vitality. She must be a woman of more than common will and mould.

She came on, slightly increasing her speed, and did not see the dark figure of the man by the fence. A hood was drawn to her eyes and a fold of her cloak covered her chin. He could see now only a wisp of face like a sickle of a silver moon, and the feeling that disturbed him in the day did not return to him. He again imagined her cold and hard, a woman of middle age, battered by the world, an adventuress who did not fear to go forth in the night upon what he thought unholy errands.

She entered the main street, passed swiftly down it toward the barriers of the city, and Prescott, with noiseless footsteps, came behind; one shadow following the other.

None save themselves seemed to be abroad. The city was steeped in Sabbath calm and a quiet moon rode in a quiet heaven. Prescott did not stop now to analyze his feelings, though he knew that a touch of pique, and perhaps curiosity, too, entered into this pursuit, otherwise he should not have troubled himself so much with an unbidden task. But he was the hunter and she the hunted, and he was alive now with the spirit of the chase.

She turned toward the northwest, where the lines of earthwork were thinnest, where, in fact, a single person might slip between them in the darkness, and Prescott no longer had any doubt that his first surmise was correct. Moreover, she was wary to the last degree, looking cautiously on every side and stopping now and then to see that she was not followed. A fine moon sometimes shed its full rays upon her, and she seemed then to Prescott to be made of silver mist.

He, too, was most wary, knowing the need of it, and allowed the distance between them to lengthen, clinging meanwhile to the shadow of buildings and fences with such effect that when she looked back she never saw the man behind.

They passed into the suburbs, low and straggling, little groups of negro cabins stringing out now and then in the darkness, and the woman, save for her occasional pauses to see if she were pursued, kept a straight and rapid course as if she knew her mind and the way.

They came at last to a spot where there was a small break in the earthworks, and Prescott saw the sentinels walking their beats, gun on shoulder. Then the fugitive paused in the shadow of bushes and high grass and watched attentively.

The pursuit had become curiously unreal to Prescott. It seemed to him that he was in the presence of the mysterious and weird, but he was resolute to follow, and he wished only that she should resume her flight.

When the sentinels were some distance apart she slid between like a shadow, unseen and unheard, and Prescott, an adept at pursuit, quickly followed. They were now beyond the first line of earthworks, though yet within the ring of Richmond's outer defenses, but a single person with ordinary caution might pass the latter, too.

He followed her through bushes and clumps of trees which hung like patches of black on the shoulders of the hills, and he shortened the space between them, not caring now if she saw him, as he no longer had any doubt of her purpose. He looked back once and saw behind him an almost imperceptible glow which he knew was the city, and then on the left beheld another light, the mark of a Confederate fortress, set there as a guard upon the ways.

She turned to the right, leaving the fortress behind, passing into country still more desolate, and Prescott thought it was now time to end the pursuit. He pressed forward with increased speed, and she, hearing the sound of a footstep behind her, looked back. He heard in the dead stillness of the night the low cry of fright that broke from her. She stood for a moment as if the power of motion had departed, and then fled like a wounded deer, with Prescott, more than ever the hunter, swiftly following after.

He was surprised at her speed. Clearly she was long-limbed and strong, and for the time his energies were taxed to keep within sight of her fleeing figure. But he was a man, she a woman, and the pursuit was not long. At last she sank, panting, upon a fallen log, and Prescott approached her, a strange mingling of triumph and pity in his heart.

She looked up and there was appeal in her face. Again he saw how young she was, how pure the light of her eyes, how delicately moulded each feature, and surprise came, as a third emotion, to mingle with the triumph and pity, and not in a less degree.

"Ah, it is you," she said, and in her tone there was no surprise, only aversion.

"Yes, it is I," replied Prescott; "and you seemed to have expected me."

"Not in the way that you think," she replied haughtily.

A wonderful change came over her face, and her figure seemed to stiffen; every lineament, every curve expressed scorn and contempt. Prescott had never before seen such a remarkable transformation, and for the moment felt as if he were the guilty one and she the judge.

While he was wondering thus at her attractive personality, she rose and stood before him.

27

"Now, sir," she said, "you shall let me go, Mr.——Mr.——"

"I am Captain Robert Prescott of the Confederate Army," said Prescott. "I have nothing to conceal," and then he added significantly: "At present I am on voluntary duty."

"I have seen enough of you," she said in the same unbending tone. "You have given me a fright, but now I am recovered and I bid you leave me."

"You mistake, Madam or Miss," replied Prescott calmly, recovering his composure; "you and I have not seen enough of each other. I am a gentleman, I hope, at least I have passed for one, and I have no intent to insult you."

"What is your wish?" she asked, still standing before him, straight and tall, her tone as cold as ice.

"Truly," thought Prescott, "she can carry it off well, and if such business as this must be done by a woman, hers is a mind for the task." But aloud he said: "Madam—or—Miss—you see you are less frank than I; you do not supply the omission—certain documents important to the Government which I serve, and as important to our enemies if they can get them, were taken yesterday from the office of the President. Kindly give them to me, as I am a better custodian for them than you are."

Her face remained unchanged. Not by a single quiver of the lip or gleam of the eye did she show emotion, and in the same cold, even voice she replied:

"You are dreaming, Captain Prescott. Some freak of the fancy has mastered you. I know nothing of the documents. How could I, a woman, do such a thing?"

"It is not more strange than your flight from Richmond alone and at such an hour."

"What signifies that? These are times of war and strange times demand strange conduct. Besides, it concerns me alone."

"Not so," replied Prescott firmly; "give me the papers."

Her face now changed from its calm. Variable emotions shot over it. Prescott, as he stood there before her, was conscious of admiration. What vagary had sent a girl who looked like this upon such a task!

"The papers," he repeated.

"I have none," she replied.

"If you do not give them to me I shall be compelled to search you, and that, I fancy, you do not wish. But I assure you that I shall do it."

His tone was resolute. He saw a spark of fire in her eye, but he did not quail.

"I shall turn my back," he added, "and if the papers are not produced in one minute's time I shall begin my search."

"Would you dare?" she asked with flashing eyes.

"I certainly would," he replied. "I trust that I know my duty."

But in a moment the light in her eyes changed. The look there was an appeal, and it expressed confidence, too. Prescott felt a strange tremour. Her glance rested full upon him and it was strangely soft and pathetic.

"Captain Prescott," she said, "upon my honour—by the memory of my mother, I have no papers."

"Then what have you done with them?" said Prescott.

"I have never had any."

He looked at her doubtfully. He believed and yet he did not. But her eyes shone with the light of purity and truth.

"Then why are you out here at such an hour, seeking to escape from Richmond?" he asked at last.

"Lest I bring harm to another," she said proudly.

Prescott laughed slightly and at once he saw a deep flush dye her face, and then involuntarily he made an apology, feeling that he was in the presence of one who was his equal.

"But I must have those papers," he said.

"Then keep your threat," she said, and folding her arms proudly across her breast she regarded him with a look of fire.

Prescott felt the blood rising in his face. He could not fulfil his menace and now he knew it.

"Come," he said abruptly, "you must go back to Richmond with me. I can take you safely past the earthworks and back to the house from which you came; there my task shall end, but not my duty."

However, he comforted himself with the thought that she had not passed the last line of defenses and perhaps could not do so at another time.

The girl said nothing, but walked obediently beside him, tall, straight and strong. She seemed now to be subdued and ready to go wherever he directed.

Prescott recognized that his own position in following the course that he had chosen was doubtful. He might turn her over to the nearest military post and then his troubles concerning her would be at an end; but he could not choose that alternative save as a last resort. She had made an appeal to him and she was a woman, a woman of no ordinary type.

The night was far gone, but the moon was full, and now spread its veil of silver mist over all the hills and fields. The earth swam in an unreal light and again the woman beside Prescott became unreal, too. He felt that if he should reach out his hand and touch her he would touch nothing but air, and then he smiled to himself at such a trick of fancy.

"I have given you my name," he said. "Now what shall I call you?"

"Let it go for the time," she replied.

"I must, since I have no way to compel you," he said.

28

They approached the inner line of earthworks through which they had passed in the flight and pursuit, and now Prescott felt it his duty to find the way back, without pausing to reflect on the strangeness of the fact that he, a Confederate soldier, was seeking to escape the notice of the Confederate pickets for the sake of a spy belonging to the other side.

They saw again the sentinels walking back and forth, gun on shoulder, and waiting until they were farthest apart, Prescott touched the woman on the arm. "Now is our time," he said, and they slid with soundless footsteps between the sentinels and back into Richmond.

"That was well done!" said Prescott joyfully. "You can shut an army out of a town, but you can't close the way to one man or two."

"Captain Prescott," said the girl, "you have brought me back into Richmond. Why not let me go now?"

"I take you to the house from which you came," he replied.

"That is your Southern chivalry," she said, "the chivalry of which I have heard so much."

He was stung by the keen irony in her tone. She had seemed to him, for awhile, so humble and appealing that he had begun to feel, in a sense, her protector, and he did not expect a jeer at the expense of himself and his section. He had been merciful to her, too! He had sacrificed himself and perhaps injured his cause that he might spare her.

"Is a woman who plays the part of a spy, a part that most men would scorn, entitled to much consideration?" he asked bluntly.

She regarded him with a cold stare, and her figure stiffened as he had seen it stiffen once before.

"I am not a spy," she said, "and I may have reasons, powerful reasons, of which you know nothing, for this attempted flight from Richmond to-night," she replied; "but that does not mean that I will explain them to you."

Prescott stiffened in his turn and said with equal coldness:

"I request you, Madam or Miss, whichever you may be, to come with me at once, as we waste time here."

He led the way through the silent city, lying then under the moonlight, back to the little street in which stood the wooden cottage, neither speaking on the way. They passed nobody, not even a dog howled at them, and when they stood before the cottage it, too, was dark and silent. Then Prescott said:

"I do not know who lives there and I do not know who you are, but I shall consider my task ended, for the present at least, when its doors hide you from me."

He spoke in the cold, indifferent tone that he had assumed when he detected the irony in her voice. But now she changed again.

"Perhaps I owe you some thanks, Captain Prescott," she said.

"Perhaps, but you need not give them. I trust, madam, and I do not say it with any intent of impoliteness, that we shall never meet again."

"You speak wisely, Captain Prescott," she said.

But she raised the hood that hid her brow and gave him a glance from dark blue eyes that a second time brought to Prescott that strange tremour at once a cause of surprise and anger. Then she opened the door of the cottage and disappeared within.

He stood for a few moments in the street looking at the little house and then he hurried to his home.

CHAPTER VII

THE COTTAGE IN THE SIDE STREET

Prescott rose the next morning with an uneasy weight upon his mind—the thought of the prisoner whom he had taken the night before. He was unable to imagine how a woman of her manner and presence had ever ventured upon such an enterprise, and he contrasted her—with poor results for the unknown—with Helen Harley, who was to him the personification of all that was delicate and feminine.

After the influence of her eyes, her beauty and her voice was gone, his old belief that she was really the spy and had stolen the papers returned. She had made a fool of him by that pathetic appeal to his mercy and by a simulated appearance of truth. Now in the cold air of the morning he felt a deep chagrin. But the deed was past and could not be undone, and seeking to dismiss it from his mind he went to breakfast.

His mother, as he had expected, asked him nothing about his late absence the night before, but spoke of the reception to General Morgan and the golden haze that it cast over Richmond.

"Have you noticed, Robert," she asked, "that we see complete victory for the South again? I ask you once more how many men did General Morgan bring with him?"

"I don't know exactly, mother. Ten, perhaps."

"And they say that General Grant will have a hundred thousand new troops."

Prescott laughed.

"At that rate, mother," he replied, "the ten will have to whip the hundred thousand, which is a heavier proportion than the old one, of one Southern gentleman to five Yankees. But, seriously, a war is not won by mere mathematics. It is courage, enthusiasm and enterprise that count."

She did not answer, but poured him another cup of coffee. Prescott read her thoughts with ease. He knew that though hers had been a Southern husband and hers were a Southern son and a Southern home, her heart was loyal to the North, and to the cause that she considered the cause of the whole Union and of civilization.

"Mother," he said, the breakfast being finished, "I've found it pleasant here with you and in Richmond, but I'm afraid I can't stay much longer. My shoulder is almost cured now."

He swung his arm back and forth to show how well it was.

"But isn't there some pain yet?" she asked.

Prescott smiled a little. He saw the pathos in the question, but he shook his head.

"No, mother," he replied, "there is no pain. I don't mean to be sententious, but this is the death-grapple that is coming. They will need me and every one out there."

He waved his hand toward the north and his mother hid a little sigh.

Prescott remained at home all the morning, but in the afternoon he went to Winthrop's newspaper office, having a direct question in mind.

"Has anything more been heard of the stolen papers?" he asked of Winthrop.

"So far as I can learn, nothing," replied the editor; "but it's altogether likely that whoever took them has been unable to escape from the city. Besides, I understand that these plans were not final and the matter may not be so serious after all."

It seemed to Prescott in a moment of cold reason that the affair might well end now, but his desire would not have it so. He was seized with a wish to know more about that house and the woman in it. Who was she, why was she here, and what would be her fate?

The afternoon passed slowly, and when the night was advanced he set out upon his errand, resolved that he would not do it, and yet knowing that he would.

The little house was as silent and dark as ever, doors and shutters tightly closed. He watched it more than an hour and saw no sign of life. She must have gone from the city, he thought, and so concluding, he was about to turn away, when a hand was laid lightly upon his arm. It was the woman in brown, and the look upon her face was not all of surprise. It occurred suddenly to Prescott that she had expected him, and he wondered why. But his first question was rough.

"What are you doing here?" he asked.

"Nothing that I wish," she replied, the faintest trace of humour showing in her tone; "much that I do not wish. The reproof that your voice conveys is unwarranted. I have tried again to leave Richmond, but I cannot get past the outer lines of defenses. I am the involuntary guest of the rebel capital."

"Hardly that," replied Prescott, still somewhat roughly. He did not relish her jaunty tone, although he was much relieved to know that she could not escape. "You came uninvited, and you have no right to complain because you cannot leave when you wish."

"I see that I am in the presence of a sincere rebel patriot," she said with irony, "and I did not know before that the words 'rebel' and 'patriot' could go together so easily."

"I think that I should surrender you to the authorities," said Prescott.

"But you will not," she said with conviction. "Your conscience would reproach you too much."

Prescott was silent, uncertain what to say or to do. The woman annoyed him, and yet he did not conceal from himself that the slight protecting feeling, born of the fact that she was a woman and, it seemed, helpless, remained in his mind.

"Are you alone in that house?" he asked, still speaking curtly and pointing toward the wooden cottage.

"No," she replied.

Prescott looked at her inquiringly. He thought that he detected the faintest twinkle in her eyes. Could it be that a woman in such a position was laughing at the man who had helped her? He felt his face grow red.

"You wish to know who is there?" she said.

"I do not wish to know anything of the kind."

"You do, and I shall tell you. It is merely a woman, an old maid, perhaps as friendless as myself, Miss Charlotte Grayson. I need not add that she is a woman of right mind and sympathies."

"What do you mean by that?"

"She wishes to see the quick end of this hateful rebellion. Oh, I tell you there are many who think as she does, born and bred within the limits of this Confederacy. They are far more numerous than you rebels suspect."

She spoke with sudden fire and energy, and Prescott noticed again that abrupt stiffening of the figure. He saw, too, another curious effect—her eyes suddenly turned from dark-blue to black, an invariable change when she was moved by a passion.

"It is always safe for a woman to abuse a man," replied Prescott calmly.

"I am not attacking you, but the cause you serve—a hateful cause. How can honest men fight for it?" she said.

Prescott heard footsteps in the main street—it was not many yards from there to the point in the little side street where he stood—and he shrank back in the shadow of the fence.

"You do not wish to be seen with me," she said.

"Naturally," replied Prescott. "I might have to answer inquiries about you, and I do not wish to compromise myself."

"Nor me?" she said.

"Perhaps it is too late for that," replied Prescott.

Her face flushed scarlet, and again he saw that sudden change of the eyes from dark-blue to threatening black. It occurred to him then that she was handsome in a singular, challenging way.

"Why do you insult me?" she asked.

"I was not aware that I had done so," he replied coolly. "Your pursuits are of such a singular nature that I merely made some slight comment thereon."

She changed again and under drooping eyelids gave him that old imploring look, like the appeal of a child for protection.

"I am ungrateful," she said, "and I give your words a meaning that you do not intend. But I am here at this moment because I was just returning from another vain attempt to escape from the city—not for myself, I tell you again, and not with any papers belonging to your Government, but for the sake of another. Listen, there are soldiers passing."

It was the tread of a company going by and Prescott shrank still farther back into the shadow. He felt for the moment a chill in his bones, and he imagined what must be the dread of a traitor on the eve of detection. What would his comrades say of him if they caught him here? As the woman came close to him and put her hand upon his arm, he was conscious again of the singular thrill that shot through him whenever she touched him. She affected him as no other woman had ever done—nor did he know whether it was like or dislike. There was an uncanny fascination about her that attracted him, even though he endeavoured to shake it off.

The tread of the company grew louder, but the night was otherwise still. The moon silvered the soldiers as they passed, and Prescott distinctly saw their features as he hid there in the dark like a spy, fearing to be seen. Then he grew angry with himself and he shook the woman's hand from his arm; it had rested as lightly as dew.

"I think that you had better go back to Miss Charlotte Grayson, whoever she may be," he said.

"But one cannot stay there forever."

"That does not concern me. Why should it? Am I to care for the safety of those who are fighting me?"

"But do you stop to think what you are fighting for?" She put her hand on his arm, and her eyes were glowing as she asked the question. "Do you ever stop to think what you are fighting for, the wrong that you do by fighting and the greater wrong that you will do if you succeed, which a just God will not let happen?"

She spoke with such vehement energy that Prescott was startled. He was well enough accustomed to controversy about the right or wrong of the war, but not under such circumstances as these.

"Madam," he said, "we soldiers don't stop in the middle of a battle to argue this question, and you can hardly expect me to do so now."

She did not reply, but the fire still lingered in her eyes. The company passed, their tread echoed down the street, then died away.

"You are safe now," she said, with the old touch of irony in her voice; "they will not find you here with me, so why do you linger?"

"It may be because you are a woman," replied Prescott, "that I overlook the fact of your being a secret and disguised enemy of my people. I wish to see you safely back in the house there with your friends."

"Good-night," she said abruptly, and she slid away from him with soundless tread. He had noticed her noiseless walk before, and it heightened the effect of weird mystery.

She passed to the rear of the house, disappearing within, and Prescott went away. When he came back in a half-hour he noticed a light shining through one window of the little house, and it seemed more natural to him, as if its tenant, Miss Charlotte Grayson, had no reason to hide her own existence. Prescott was not fond of secrecy—his whole nature was open, and with a singular sense of relief he turned away for the second time, going to Winthrop's office, where he hoped to find more congenial friends.

Raymond, as he expected, was there with his brother editor, and so was Wood, the big cavalryman, who regarded Robert for a moment with an eye coldly critical. Raymond and Winthrop, who stood by, knew the cause, but Wood quickly relaxed and greeted with warmth the addition to the party. Others came in, and soon a dozen men who knew and liked each other well were gathered about the stove, talking in the old friendly Southern way and exchanging opinions with calm certainty on all recondite subjects.

After awhile Winthrop, who passed near the window on some errand, exclaimed:

"Gentlemen, behold Richmond in her bridal veil."

They looked out and saw the city, streets and roofs alike, sheeted in gleaming white. The snow which had come down so softly spoke only of peace and quietness.

"It's battle smoke, not a bridal veil, that Richmond must look for now," said Wood, "an' it's a pity."

There was a touch of sentiment in his voice, and Prescott looked at him with approval. As for himself, he was thinking at that moment of an unknown woman in a brown, wooden cottage. With the city snowed-in she might find the vigilance of the sentinels relaxed, but a flight through the frozen wilderness would be impossible for her. He was angry at himself again for feeling concern when he should be relieved that she could not escape; but, after, all she was a woman.

"Why so grave, Prescott?" asked Raymond. "A heavy snow like this is all in our favour, since we stand on the defensive; it makes it more difficult for the Yankee army to move."

"I was thinking of something else," replied Prescott truthfully. "I am going home now," he added. "Good-night."

As he passed out into the street the snow was still falling, soon covering his cap and military cloak, and clothing him, like the city, in a robe of white.

Raymond had said truthfully that a deep snow was to the advantage of the South, but as for himself, he resolved that on the next day he would investigate the identity of Miss Charlotte Grayson.

Prescott knew to whom it was best to turn for information in regard to the mysterious Charlotte Grayson, and in the doing so it was not necessary for him to leave his own home. His mother was likely to know everybody at all conspicuous in Richmond, as under her peaceful exterior she concealed a shrewd and inquiring mind.

"Mother," he said to her the next day as they sat before the fire, "did you ever hear of any lady named Miss Charlotte Grayson?"

She was knitting for the soldiers at the front, but she let the needles drop with a faint click into her lap.

"Grayson, Charlotte Grayson?" she said. "Is that the name of a new sweetheart of yours, Robert?"

"No, mother," replied he with a laugh; "it is the name of somebody whom I have never seen so far as I know, and of whom I never heard until a day or two ago."

"I recall the woman of whom you speak," she said, "an old maid without any relatives or any friends in particular. She was a seamstress here before the war. It was said that she went North at its outbreak, and as she was a Northern sympathizer it would seem likely; but she was a good seamstress; she made me a mantle once and I never saw a better in Richmond."

She waited for her son to offer an explanation of his interest in the whilom seamstress, but as he did not do so she asked no questions, though regarding him covertly.

He rose and, going to the window, looked out at the deep and all but untrodden snow.

"Richmond is in white, mother," he said, "and it will postpone the campaign which all Southern women dread."

"I know," she replied; "but the battle must come sooner or later, and a snow in Richmond means more coal and wood to buy. Do you ever think, Robert, what such questions as these, so simple in peace, mean now to Richmond?"

"I did not for the moment, mother," he replied, his face clouding, "but I should have thought of it. You mean that coal and wood are scarce and money still scarcer?"

She bowed her head, for it was a very solemn truth she had spoken. The coil of steel with which the North had belted in the South was beginning to press tighter and tighter during that memorable winter. At every Southern port the Northern fleets were on guard, and the blockade runners slipped past at longer and longer intervals. It was the same on land; everywhere the armies of the North closed in, and besides fire and sword, starvation now threatened the Confederacy.

There was not much news from the field to dispel the gloom in the South. The great battle of Chickamauga had been won not long before, but it was a barren victory. There were no more Fredericksburgs nor Chancellorsvilles to rejoice over. Gettysburg had come; the genius of Lee himself had failed; Jackson was dead and no one had arisen to take his place.

There were hardships now more to be feared than mere battles. The men might look forward to death in action, and not know what would become of the women and children. The price of bread was steadily rising, and the value of Confederate money was going down with equal steadiness.

The soldiers in the field often walked barefoot through the snow, and in summer they ate the green corn in the fields, glad to get even so little; but they were not sure that those left behind would have as much. They were conscious, too, that the North, the sluggish North, which had been so long in putting forth its full strength, was now preparing for an effort far greater than any that had gone before. The incompetent generals, the tricksters and the sluggards were gone, and battle-tried armies led by real generals were coming in numbers that would not be denied.

At such a time as this, when the cloud had no fragment of a silver lining, the spirit of the South glowed with its brightest fire—a spectacle sometimes to be seen even though a cause be wrong.

"Mother," said Prescott, and there was a touch of defiance in his tone, "do you not know that the threat of cold and hunger, the fear that those whom we love are about to suffer as much as ourselves, will only nerve us to greater efforts?"

"I know," she replied, but he did not hear her sigh.

He felt that his stay in Richmond was now shortening fast, but there was yet one affair on his mind to which he must attend, and he went forth for a beginning. His further inquiries, made with caution in the vicinity, disclosed the fact that Miss Charlotte Grayson, the occupant of the wooden cottage, and the Miss Charlotte Grayson whom his mother had in mind, were the same. But he could discover little else concerning her or her manner of life, save an almost positive assurance that she had not left Richmond either at the beginning of the war nor since. She had been seen in the streets, rarely speaking to any one, and at the markets making a few scanty purchases and preserving the same silence, ascribed, it was said, to the probable belief on her part that she would be persecuted because of her known Northern sympathies. Had any one been seen with her? No; she lived all alone in the little house.

Such were the limits of the knowledge achieved by Prescott, and for lack of another course he chose the direct way and knocked at the door of the little house, being compelled to repeat his summons twice before it was answered. Then the door was opened slightly; but with a soldier's boldness he pushed in and confronted a thin, elderly woman, who did not invite him to be seated.

Prescott took in the room and its occupant with a single glance, and the two seemed to him to be of a piece. The former—and he knew instinctively that it was Miss Grayson—was meager of visage and figure, with high cheek bones, thin curls flat down on her temples, and a black dress worn and old. The room exhibited the same age and scantiness, the same aspect of cold poverty, with its patched carpet and the slender fire smouldering on the hearth.

She stood before him, confronting him with a manner in which boldness and timidity seemed to be struggling with about equal success. There was a flush of anger on her cheeks, but her lips were trembling.

"I am speaking to Miss Grayson?" said Prescott.

"You are, sir," she replied, "but I do not know you, and I do not know why you have pushed yourself into my house."

"My name is Prescott, Robert Prescott, and I am a captain in the Confederate Army, as you may see by my uniform."

He noticed that the trembling of her lip increased and she looked fearfully at him; but the red flush of anger on her cheek deepened, too. The chief impression that she made on Prescott was pathetic, standing there in her poverty of dress and room, and he hastened to add:

"But I am here on my own private business; I have not come to annoy you. I merely want to inquire of a woman, a lodger of yours."

"I have no lodgers," she replied; "I am alone."

"I don't think I can be mistaken," said Prescott; "she told me that she was staying in this house."

"And may I ask the name of this lady who knows more about my own house than I do?" asked Miss Grayson with unconcealed sarcasm.

Prescott saw that her courage was now getting the better of her timidity. He hesitated and felt his cheeks redden.

"I do not know," he was forced to reply.

Miss Grayson's gaze became steady and triumphant.

"Does it not then occur to you, Captain Prescott, that you are proceeding upon a very slender basis when you doubt my word?"

"It is hardly that, Miss Grayson," he replied. "I thought—perhaps—that it might be an evasion, pardonable when it is made for a friend whom one thinks in danger."

His eye roamed around the room again and it caught sight of something disclosed to him for the first time by the sudden increase of the flickering blaze on the hearth. A flash of triumph appeared in his eye and his boldness and certainty returned to him.

"Miss Grayson," he said, "it is true that I do not know the name of the lady of whom I speak, but I have some proof of her presence here."

Miss Grayson started and her lips began to tremble again.

"I do not know what you mean," she said.

"I ask for the wearer of this," said Prescott, taking a long brown cloak from the chair on which it lay and holding it up before Miss Grayson's eyes.

"Then you ask for me," she replied bravely; "the cloak is mine."

"I have seen it several times before," said Prescott, "and it was always worn by some one else."

He looked significantly at her and he saw again the nervous trembling of the lip, but her eye did not quail. This woman, with her strange mingling of timidity and courage, would certainly protect the unknown if she could.

"The cloak is mine," she repeated. "It is a question of veracity between you and me, and are you prepared to say that you alone tell the truth?"

Prescott hesitated, not fancying this oblique method of attack, but a third person relieved them both from present embarrassment. A door to an inner apartment opened, and the woman in brown—but not in brown now—came into the room.

"You need not conceal my presence any longer, Charlotte," said the newcomer impressively. "I thank you, but I am sure that we need no protection from Captain Prescott."

"If you think so, Lucia," replied Miss Grayson, and Prescott distinctly heard her sigh of relief—a sigh that he could have echoed, as he had begun to feel as if he were acting not as a gentleman, but as a persecutor of a poor old maid. The girl—Lucia was her first name, he had learned that much—confronted him, and certainly there was no fear in her gaze. Prescott saw, too, at the first glance, that she was transformed. She was dressed in simple white, and a red rose, glowing by contrast against its whiteness, nestled in her throat. He remembered afterward a faint feeling of curiosity that in the dead of winter she should be wearing such a rose. Her eyes, black when she was angry, were now a deep, liquid blue, and the faint firelight drew gleams of red or gold, he knew not which, from her hair; the hair itself looked dark.

But it was her presence, her indefinable presence that pervaded the room. The thin little old maid was quite lost in it, and involuntarily Prescott found himself bowing as if to a great lady.

"I have meant no harm by coming here," he said; "the secrets of this house are safe as far as I am concerned. I merely came to inquire after your welfare. Miss—Miss——"

33

He stopped and looked inquiringly at her. A faint smile curved the corners of her mouth, and she replied:

"Catherwood; I am Miss Lucia Catherwood, but for the present I have nothing more to say."

"Catherwood, Lucia Catherwood," repeated Prescott. "It is a beautiful name, like——"

And then, breaking off abruptly, warned by a sudden lightning glance from her eyes, he walked to the window and pointed to the white world outside.

"I came to tell you, Miss Catherwood," he said, "that the snow lies deep on the ground—you know that already—but what I wish to make clear is the impossibility of your present escape from Richmond. Even if you passed the defenses you would almost certainly perish in the frozen wilderness."

"It is as I told you, Lucia," said Miss Grayson; "you must not think of leaving. My house is your house, and all that is here is yours."

"I know that, Charlotte," replied Miss Catherwood, "but I cannot take the bread from your mouth nor can I bring new dangers upon you."

She spoke the last words in a low tone, but Prescott heard her nevertheless. What a situation, he thought; and he, a Confederate soldier, was a party to it! Here in the dim little room were two women of another belief, almost another land, and around them lay the hostile city. He felt a thrill of pity; once more he believed her claim that she did not take the papers; and he tapped uneasily on the window pane with a long forefinger.

"Miss Catherwood," he said hesitatingly—that he should address her and not Miss Grayson seemed entirely proper—"I scarcely know why I am here, but I wish to repeat that I did not come with any bad intent. I am a Confederate soldier, but the Confederacy is not yet so far reduced that it needs to war on women."

Yet he knew as he spoke that he had believed her a spy and his full duty demanded that he deliver her to his Government; but perhaps there was a difference between one's duty and one's full duty.

"I merely wished to know that you were safe here," he continued, "and now I shall go."

"We thank you for your forbearance, Captain Prescott," said the elder woman, but the younger said nothing, and Prescott waited a moment, hoping that she would do so. Still she did not speak, and as she moved toward the door she did not offer her hand.

"She has no thanks for me, after all that I have done," thought Prescott, and there was a little flame of anger in his heart. Why should he trouble himself about her?

"Ladies," he said, with an embarrassed air, "you will pardon me if I open the door an inch or two and look out before I go. You understand why."

"Oh, certainly," replied Miss Catherwood, and again that faint smile lurked for a moment in the corners of her mouth. "We are Pariahs, and it would ill suit the fair fame of Captain Prescott to be seen coming from this house."

"You are of the North and I of the South and that is all," said Prescott, and, bowing, he left, forgetting in his annoyance to take that precautionary look before opening wide the door.

But the little street was empty and he walked thoughtfully back to his mother's house.

CHAPTER VIII

THE PALL OF WINTER

The deep snow was followed by the beginning of a thaw, interrupted by a sudden and very sharp cold spell, when the mercury went down to zero and the water from the melting snow turned to ice. Richmond was encased in a sheath of gleaming white. The cold wintry sun was reflected from roofs of ice, the streets were covered with it, icicles hung like rows of spears from the eaves, and the human breath smoked at the touch of the air.

And as the winter pressed down closer and heavier on Richmond, so did the omens of her fate. Higher and higher went the price of food, and lower and lower sank the hopes of her people. Their momentary joy under the influence of such events as the Morgan reception was like the result of a stimulant or narcotic, quickly over and leaving the body lethargic and dull. But this dullness had in it no thought of yielding.

On the second day of the great cold all the Harleys came over to take tea with Mrs. Prescott and her son, and then Helen disclosed the fact that the Government was still assiduous in its search for the spy and the lost documents.

"Mr. Sefton thinks that we have a clue," she said, identifying herself with the Government now by the use of the pronoun.

Prescott was startled a little, but he hid his surprise under a calm voice when he asked:

"What is this clue, or is it a secret?"

"No, not among us who are so loyal to the cause," she replied innocently; "and it may be that they want it known more widely because here in Richmond we are all, in a way, defenders of the faith—our faith. They say that it was a woman who stole the papers, a tall woman in a brown dress and brown cloak, who entered the building when nearly everybody was gone to the Morgan reception. Mr. Sefton has learned that much from one of the servants."

"Has he learned anything more?" asked Prescott, whose heart was beating in a way that he did not like.

"No, the traces stop at that point; but Mr. Sefton believes she will be found. He says she could not have escaped from the city."

"It takes a man like Sefton to follow the trail of a woman," interrupted Colonel Harley. "If it were not for the papers she has I'd say let her go."

Prescott had a sudden feeling of warmth for Vincent Harley, and he now believed a good heart to beat under the man's vain nature; but that was to be expected: he was Helen Harley's brother. However, it did not appeal to Helen that way.

"Shouldn't a woman who does such things suffer punishment like a man?" she asked.

"Maybe so," replied the Colonel, "but I couldn't inflict it."

The elder Harley advanced no opinion, but he was sure whatever Mr. Sefton did in the matter was right; and he believed, too, that the agile Secretary was more capable than any other man of dealing with the case. In fact, he was filled that day with a devout admiration of Mr. Sefton, and he did not hesitate to proclaim it, bending covert glances at his daughter as he pronounced these praises. Mr. Sefton, he said, might differ a little in certain characteristics from the majority of the Southern people, he might be a trifle shrewder in financial affairs, but, after all, the world must come to that view, and hard-headed men such as he would be of great value when the new Southern Republic began its permanent establishment and its dealings with foreign nations. As for himself, he recognized the fact that he was not too old to learn, and Mr. Sefton was teaching him.

Prescott listened with outward respect, but the words were so much mist to his brain, evaporating easily. Nor did Mr. Harley's obvious purpose trouble him as much as it had on previous occasions, the figure of the Secretary not looming so large in his path as it used to.

He was on his way, two hours later, to the little house in the side street, bending his face to a keen winter blast that cut like the edge of a knife. He heard the wooden buildings popping as they contracted under the cold, and near the outskirts of the town he saw the little fires burning where the sentinels stopped now and then on their posts to warm their chilled fingers. He was resolved now to protect Lucia Catherwood. The belief of others that the woman of the brown cloak was guilty aroused in him the sense of opposition. She must be innocent!

He knocked again at the door, and as before it did not yield until he had knocked several times. It was then Miss Charlotte Grayson who appeared, and to Prescott's heightened fancy she seemed thinner and more acidulous than ever. There was less of fear in her glance than when he came the first time, but reproach took its place, and was expressed so strongly that Prescott exclaimed at once:

"I do not come to annoy you, Miss Grayson, but merely to inquire after yourself and your friend, Miss Catherwood."

Then he went in, uninvited, and looked about the room. Nothing was changed except the fire, which was lower and feebler; it seemed to Prescott that the two or three lumps of coal on the hearth were hugging each other for scant comfort, and even as he looked at it the timbers of the house popped with the cold.

"Miss Catherwood is still with you, is she not?" asked Prescott. "My errand concerns her, and it is for her good that I have come."

"Why do you, a Confederate officer, trouble yourself about a woman who, you say, has acted as a spy for the North?" asked Miss Grayson, pointedly.

Prescott hesitated and flushed. Then he answered:

"I hope, Miss Grayson, that I shall never be able to overlook a woman in distress."

His eyes wandered involuntarily to the feeble fire, and then in its turn the thin face of Miss Grayson flushed. For a moment, in her embarrassment, she looked almost beautiful.

"Miss Catherwood is still here, is she not?" repeated Prescott. "I assure you that I came in her interest."

Miss Grayson gave him a look of such keenness that Prescott saw again the strength and penetration underlying her timid and doubtful manner. She seemed to be reassured and replied:

"Yes, she is here. I will call her."

She disappeared into the next room and presently Miss Catherwood came forth alone. She held her head as haughtily as ever, and regarded him with a look in which he saw much defiance, and he fancied, too, a little disdain.

"Captain Prescott," she said proudly, "I am not an object for military supervision."

"I am aware of that," he replied, "and I do not mean to be impolite, Miss Catherwood, when I say that I regret to find you still here."

She pointed through the window to the white and frozen world outside.

"I should be glad enough to escape," she said, "but that forbids."

"I know it, or at least I expected it," said Prescott, "and it is partly why I am here. I came to warn you."

"To warn me! Do I not know that I am in a hostile city?"

"But there is more. The search for those missing papers, and, above all, for the one who took them—a tall woman in a brown cloak, they say—has not ceased, nor will it; the matter is in the hands of a crafty, persistent man and he thinks he has a clue. He has learned, as I learned, that a woman dressed like you and looking like you was in the Government building on the day of the celebration. He believes that woman is still in the city, and he is sure that she is the one for whom he seeks."

35

Her face blanched; he saw for the first time a trace of feminine weakness, even fear. It was gone, however, like a mist before a wind, as her courage came back.

"But this man, whoever he may be, cannot find me," she said. "I am hidden unless some one chooses to betray me; not that I care for myself, but I cannot involve my generous cousin in such a trouble."

Prescott shook his head.

"Your trust I have not merited, Miss Catherwood," he said. "If I had chosen to give you up to the authorities I should have done so before this. And your confidence in your hiding place is misplaced, too. Richmond is small. It is not a great city like New York or Philadelphia, and those who would conceal a Northern spy—I speak plainly—are but few. It is easy to search and find."

Prescott saw her tremble a little, although her face did not whiten again, nor did a tear rise to her eye. She went again to the window, staring there at the frozen world of winter, and Prescott saw that a purpose was forming in her mind. It was a purpose bold and desperate, but he knew that it would fail and so he spoke. He pointed out to her the lines of defenses around Richmond, and the wilderness beyond all, buried under a cold that chained sentinels even to their fires; she would surely perish, even if she passed the watch.

"But if I were taken," she said, "I should be taken alone and they would know nothing of Miss Grayson."

"But I should never give up hope," he said. "After all, the hunted may hide, if warned, when the hunter is coming."

She gave him a glance, luminous, grateful, so like a shaft of light passing from one to another that it set Prescott's blood to leaping.

"Captain Prescott," she said, "I really owe you thanks."

Prescott felt as if he had been repaid, and afterward in the coolness of his own exclusive company he was angry with himself for the feeling—but she stirred his curiosity; he was continually conscious of a desire to know what manner of woman she was—to penetrate this icy mist, as it were, in which she seemed to envelop herself.

There was now no pretext for him to stay longer, but he glanced at the fire which had burned lower than ever, only two coals hugging each other in the feeble effort to give forth heat. Prescott was standing beside a little table and unconsciously he rested his right hand upon it. But he slipped the hand into his pocket, and when he took it out and rested it upon the table again there was something between the closed fingers.

Miss Grayson returned at this moment to the room and looked inquiringly at the two.

"Miss Catherwood will tell you all that I have said to her," said Prescott, "and I bid you both adieu."

When he lifted his hand from the table he left upon it what the fingers had held, but neither of the women noticed the action.

Prescott slipped into the street, looking carefully to see that he was not observed, and annoyed because he had to do so; as always his heart revolted at hidden work. But Richmond was cold and desolate, and he went back to the heart of the city, unobserved, meaning to find Winthrop, who always knew the gossip, and to learn if any further steps had been taken in the matter of the stolen documents.

He found the editor with plenty of time on his hands and an abundant inclination to talk. Yes, there was something. Mr. Sefton, so he heard, meant to make the matter one of vital importance, and the higher officers of the Government were content to leave it to him, confident of his ability and pertinacity and glad enough to be relieved of such a task.

Prescott, when he heard this, gazed thoughtfully at the cobwebbed ceiling. There was yet no call for him to go to the front, and he would stay to match his wits against those of the great Mr. Sefton; he had been drawn unconsciously into a conflict— a conflict of which he was perhaps unconscious—and every impulse in him told him to fight.

When he went to his supper that evening he found a very small package wrapped in brown paper lying unopened beside his plate. He knew it in an instant, and despite himself his face flooded with colour.

"It was left here for you an hour ago," said his mother, who in that moment achieved a triumph permitted to few mothers, burying a mighty curiosity under seeming indifference.

"Who left it, mother?" asked Prescott, involuntarily.

"I do not know," she replied. "There was a heavy knock upon the door while I was busy, and when I went there after a moment's delay I found this lying upon the sill, but the bringer was gone."

Prescott put the package in his pocket and ate his supper uneasily.

When he was alone in his room he drew the tiny parcel from his pocket and took off the paper, disclosing two twenty-dollar gold pieces, which he returned to his pocket with a sigh.

"At least I meant well," he said to himself.

A persistent nature feeds on opposition, and the failure of his first attempt merely prepared Prescott for a second. The affair, too, began to absorb his mind to such an extent that his friends noticed his lack of interest in the society and amusements of Richmond. He had been well received there, his own connections, his new friends, and above all his pleasing personality, exercising a powerful influence; and, coming from the rough fields of war, he had enjoyed his stay very keenly.

But he had a preoccupation now, and he was bent upon doing what he wished to do. Talbot and the two editors rallied him upon his absence of mind, and even Helen, despite her new interest in Wood, looked a little surprised and perhaps a little aggrieved at his inattention; but none of these things had any effect upon him. His mind was now thrown for the time being into one channel, and he could not turn it into another if he wished.

On the next morning after his failure he passed again near the little wooden house, the day being as cold as ever and the smoke of many chimneys lying in black lines against the perfect blue-and-white heavens. He looked at the chimney of the little wooden cottage, and there, too, was smoke coming forth; but it was a thin and feeble stream, scarcely making even a pale blur against the transparent skies. The house itself appeared to be as cold and chilly as the frozen snow outside.

Prescott glanced up and down the street. An old man, driving a small wagon drawn by a single horse, was about to pass him. Prescott looked into the body of the wagon and saw that it contained coal.

"For sale?" he asked.

The man nodded.

"How much for the lot?"

"Twenty dollars."

"Gold or Confederate money?"

The old man blew his breath on his red woolen comforter and thoughtfully watched it freeze there, then he looked Prescott squarely in the face and asked:

"Stranger, have you just escaped from a lunatic asylum?"

"Certainly not!"

"Then why do you ask me such a fool question?"

Prescott drew forth one of the two twenty-dollar gold pieces and handed it to the man.

"I take your coal," he said. "Now unload it into that little back yard there and answer no questions. Can you do both?"

"Of course—for twenty dollars in gold," replied the driver.

Prescott walked farther up the street, but he watched the man, and saw him fulfil his bargain, a task easily and quickly done. He tipped the coal into the little back yard of the wooden cottage, and drove away, obviously content with himself and his bargain. Then Prescott, too, went his way, feeling a pleasant glow.

He came back the next morning and the coal lay untouched. The board fence concealed it from the notice of casual passers, and so thieves had not been tempted. Those in the house must have seen it, yet not a lump was gone; and the feeble stream of smoke from the chimney had disappeared; nothing rose there to stain the sky. It occurred to Prescott that both the women might have fled from the city, but second thought told him escape was impossible. They must yet be inside the house; and surely it was very cold there!

He came back the same afternoon, but the coal was still untouched and the cold gripped everything in bands of iron. He returned a third time the next morning, slipping along in the shadow of the high board fence like a thief—he did have a somewhat guilty conscience—but when he peeped over the fence he uttered an exclamation.

Four of the largest lumps of coal were missing!

There was no doubt of it; he had marked them lying on the top of the heap, and distinguished by their unusual size.

"They are certainly gone," said Prescott to himself.

But it was not thieves. There in the snow he perceived the tracks of small feet leading from the coal-heap to the back door of the house.

Prescott felt a mighty sense of triumph, and gave utterance in a low voice to the unpoetic exclamation:

"They had to knuckle!"

But there was no smoke coming from the chimney, and he knew they had just taken the coal. "They!" It was "she," as there was only one trail in the snow, but he wondered which one. He was curiously inquisitive on this point, and he would have given much to know, but he did not dream of forcing an entrance into the house; yes "forcing" was now the word.

He was afraid to linger, as he did not wish to be seen by anybody either inside or outside the cottage, and went away; but he came back in an hour—that is, he came to the corner of the street, where he could see the feeble column of smoke rising once more from the chimney of the little wooden house.

Then, beholding this faint and unintentional signal, he smote himself upon the knee, giving utterance again to his feelings of triumph, and departed, considering himself a young man of perception and ability. His amiability lasted so long that his mother congratulated him upon it, and remarked that he must have had good news, but Prescott gallantly attributed his happiness to her presence alone. She said nothing in reply, but kept her thoughts to herself.

Inasmuch as the mind grows upon what it consumes, Prescott was soon stricken with a second thought, and the next day at twilight he bought as obscurely as he could a Virginia-cured ham and carried it away, wrapped in brown paper, under his arm.

Fortunately he met no one who took notice, and he reached the little street unobserved. Here he deliberated with himself awhile, but concluded at last to put it on the back door step.

"When they come for coal," he said to himself, "they will see it, or if they don't they will fall over it, if some sneak thief doesn't get it first."

He noticed, dark as it was, that the little trail in the snow had grown, and in an equal ratio the size of the coal pile had diminished.

Then he crept away, looking about him with great care lest he be seen, but some intuition sent him back, and when he stole along in the shadow of the fence he saw the rear door of the house open and a thin, angular figure appear upon the threshold. It was too dark for him to see the face, but he knew it to be Miss Grayson. That figure could not belong to the other.

She stumbled, too, and uttered a low cry, and Prescott, knowing the cause of both, was pleased. Then he saw her stoop and, raising his supply of manna in both her hands, unfold the wrappings of brown paper. She looked all about, and Prescott knew, in fancy, that her gaze was startled and inquisitive. The situation appealed to him, flattering alike his sense of pleasure and his sense of mystery, and again he laughed softly to himself.

A cloud which had hidden it sailed past and the moonlight fell in a silver glow on the old maid's thin but noble features; then Prescott saw a look of perplexity, mingled with another look which he did not wholly understand, but which did not seem hostile. She hesitated awhile, fingering the package, then she put it back upon the sill and beckoned to one within.

Prescott saw Miss Catherwood appear beside Miss Grayson. He could never mistake her—her height, that proud curve of the neck and the firm poise of the head. She wore, too, the famous brown cloak—thrown over her shoulders. He found a strange pleasure in seeing her there, but he was sorry, too, that Miss Grayson had called her, as he fancied now that he knew the result.

He saw them talking, the shrug of the younger woman's shoulders, the appealing gesture of the older, and then the placing of the package upon the sill, after which the two retreated into the house and shut the door.

Prescott experienced distinct irritation, even anger, and rising from his covert he walked away, feeling for the moment rather smaller than usual.

"Then some sneak thief shall have it," he said to himself, "for I will not take it again," and at that moment he wished what he said.

True to Redfield's prediction, the search for the hidden spy began the next morning, and, under the direction of Mr. Sefton, was carried on with great zeal and energy, attracting in its course, as was natural, much attention from the people of Richmond.

Some of the comments upon this piece of enterprise were not favourable, and conspicuous among them was that of Mrs. Prescott, who said to her son:

"If this spy has escaped from Richmond, then the search is useless; if still here, then no harm has been done and there is nothing to undo."

Prescott grew nervous, and presently he went forth to watch the hue and cry. The house of Miss Charlotte Grayson had not been searched yet, but it was soon to be, as Miss Grayson was well known for her Northern sympathies. He hovered in the vicinity, playing the rôle of the curious onlooker, in which he was not alone, and presently he saw a small party of soldiers, ten in number, headed by Talbot himself, arrive in front of the little brown cottage.

When he beheld his friend conducting this particular portion of the search, Prescott was tempted, if the opportunity offered, to confide the truth to Talbot and leave the rest to his generosity; but cool reflection told him that he had no right to put such a weight upon a friend, and while he sought another way, Talbot himself hailed him.

"Come along and hold up my hands for me, Bob," he said. "This is a nasty duty that they've put me to—it's that man Sefton—and I need help when I pry into the affairs of a poor old maid's house—Miss Charlotte Grayson."

Prescott accepted the invitation, because it was given in such a friendly way and because he was drawn on by curiosity—a desire to see the issue. It might be that Miss Catherwood, reasserting her claim of innocence, would not seek to conceal herself, but it seemed to him that the evidence against her was too strong. And he believed that she would do anything to avoid compromising Miss Grayson.

The house was closed, windows and doors, but a thin gray stream of smoke rose from the chimney. Prescott noticed, with wary eye, that the snow which lay deep on the ground was all white and untrodden in front of the house.

One of the soldiers, obedient to Talbot's order, used the knocker of the door, and after repeating the action twice and thrice and receiving no response, broke the lock with the butt of his rifle.

"I have to do it," said Talbot with an apologetic air to Prescott. "It's orders."

They entered the little drawing-room and found Miss Grayson, sitting in prim and dignified silence, in front of the feeble fire that burned on the hearth. It looked to Prescott like the same fire that was flickering there when first he came, but he believed now it was his coal.

Miss Grayson remained silent, but a high colour glowed in her face and much fire was in her eye. She shot one swift glance at Prescott and then ignored him. Talbot, Prescott and all the soldiers took off their caps and bowed, a courtesy which the haughty old maid ignored without rising.

"Miss Grayson," said Talbot humbly, "we have come to search your house."

"To search it for what?" she asked icily.

"A Northern spy."

"A fine duty for a Southern gentleman," she said.

Talbot flushed red.

"Miss Grayson," he said, "this is more painful to me than it is to you. You are a well-known Northern sympathizer and I am compelled to do it. It is no choice of mine."

Prescott noticed that Talbot refrained from asking her if she had any spy hidden in the house, not putting her word to the proof, and mentally he thanked him. "You are a real Southern gentleman," he thought.

Miss Grayson remained resolutely in her chair and stared steadily into the fire, ignoring the search, after her short and sharp talk with Talbot, who took his soldiers into the other rooms, glad to get out of her presence. Prescott lingered behind, anxious to catch the eye of Miss Grayson and to have a word with her, but she ignored him as pointedly as she had ignored Talbot, though he walked heavily about, making his boots clatter on the floor. Still that terrifying old maid stared into the fire, as if she were bent upon watching every flickering flame and counting every coal.

Her silence at last grew so ominous and weighed so heavily upon Prescott's spirits that he fled from the room and joined Talbot, who growled and asked him why he had not come sooner, saying: "A real friend would stay with me and share all that's disagreeable."

Prescott wondered what the two women would say of him when they found Miss Catherwood, but he was glad afterward to remember that his chief feeling was for Miss Catherwood and not for himself. He expected every moment that they would find her, and it was hard to keep his heart from jumping. He looked at every chair and table and sofa, dreading lest he should see the famous brown cloak lying there.

It was a small house with not many rooms, and the search took but a short time. They passed from one to another seeing nothing suspicious, and came to the last. "She is here," thought Prescott, "fleeing like a hunted hare to the final covert." But she was not there—and it was evident that she was not in the house at all. It was impossible for one in so small a space to have eluded the searchers. Talbot heaved a sigh of relief, and Prescott felt as if he could imitate him.

"A nasty job well done," said Talbot.

They went back to the sitting-room, where the lady of the house was still confiding her angry thoughts to the red coals.

"Our search is ended," said Talbot politely to Miss Grayson, "and I am glad to say that we have found nothing."

The lady's gaze was not deflected a particle, nor did she reply.

"I bid you good-day, Miss Grayson," continued Talbot, "and hope that you will not be annoyed again in this manner."

Still no reply nor any change in the confidences passing between the lady and the red coals.

Talbot gathered up his men with a look and hurried outside the house, followed in equal haste by Prescott.

"How warm it is out here!" exclaimed Talbot, as he stood in the snow.

"Warm?" said Prescott in surprise, looking around at the chill world.

"Yes, in comparison with the temperature in there," said Talbot, pointing to Miss Grayson's house.

Prescott laughed, and he felt a selfish joy that the task had been Talbot's and not his. But he was filled, too, with wonder. What had become of Miss Catherwood?

They had just turned into the main street, when they met Mr. Sefton, who seemed expectant.

"Did you find the spy, Mr. Talbot?" he asked.

"No," replied Talbot, with ill-concealed aversion; "there was nothing in the house."

"I thought it likely that some one would be found there," said the Secretary thoughtfully. "Miss Grayson has never hidden her Northern sympathies, and a woman is just fanatic enough to help in such a business."

Then he dismissed Talbot and his men—the Secretary had at times a curt and commanding manner—and took Prescott's arm in his with an appearance of great friendship and confidence.

"I want to talk with you a bit about this affair, Captain Prescott," he said. "You are going back to the front soon, and in the shock of the great battles that are surely coming such a little thing will disappear from your mind; but it has its importance, nevertheless. Now we do not know whom to trust. I may have seemed unduly zealous. Confess that you have thought so, Captain Prescott."

Prescott did not reply and the Secretary smiled.

"I knew it," he continued; "you have thought so, and so have many others in Richmond, but I must do my duty, nevertheless. This spy, I am sure, is yet in the city; but while she cannot get out herself, she may have ways of forwarding to the enemy what she steals from us. There is where the real danger lies, and I am of the opinion that the spy is aided by some one in Richmond, ostensibly a friend of the Southern cause. What do you think of it, Captain?"

The young Captain was much startled, but he kept his countenance and answered with composure:

"I really don't know anything about it, Mr. Sefton. I chanced to be passing, and as Mr. Talbot, who is one of my best friends, asked me to go in with him, I did so."

"And it does credit to your zeal," said the Secretary. "It is in fact a petty business, but that is where you soldiers in the field have the advantage of us administrators. You fight in great battles and you win glory, but you don't have anything to do with the little things."

"Our lives are occupied chiefly with little things; the great battles take but a few hours in our existence."

"But you have a free and open life," said the Secretary. "It is true that your chance of death is great, but all of us must come to that, sooner or later. As I said, you are in the open; you do not have any of the mean work to do."

The Secretary sighed and leaned a little on Prescott's arm. The young Captain regarded him out of the corner of his eye, but he could read nothing in his companion's face. Mr. Sefton's air was that of a man a-weary—one disgusted with the petty ways and intrigues of office.

They walked on together, though Prescott would have escaped could he have done so, and many people, noting the two thus arm in arm, said to each other that young Captain Prescott must be rising in favour, as everybody knew Mr. Sefton to be a powerful man.

Feeling sure that this danger was past for the present, Robert went home to his mother, who received him in the sitting-room with a slight air of agitation unusual in one of such a placid temper.

"Well, mother, what is the matter?" he asked. "One would think from your manner that you have been taking part in this search for the spy."

"And that I am suffering from disappointment because the spy has not been found?"

"How did you know that, mother?"

"The cook told me. Do you suppose that such an event as this would escape the notice of a servant? Why, I am prepared to gossip about it myself."

"Well, mother, there is little to be said. You told me this morning that you hoped the spy would not be found, and your wish has come true."

"I see no reason to change my wish," she said. "The Confederate Government has heavier work to do now than to hunt for a spy."

But Prescott noticed during the remainder of the afternoon and throughout supper that his mother's slight attacks of agitation were recurrent. There was another change in her. She was rarely a demonstrative woman, even to her son, and though her only child, she had never spoiled him; but now she was very solicitous for him. Had he suffered from the cold? Was he to be assigned to some particularly hard duty? She insisted, too, upon giving him the best of food, and Prescott, wishing to please her, quietly acquiesced, but watched her covertly though keenly.

He knew his mother was under the influence of some unusual emotion, and he judged that this house-to-house search for a spy had touched a soft heart.

"Mother," he said, after supper, "I think I shall go out for awhile this evening."

"Do go by all means," she said. "The young like the young, and I wish you to be with your friends while you are in Richmond."

Prescott looked at her in surprise. She had never objected to his spending the evening elsewhere, but this was the first time she had urged him to go. Yes, "urged" was the word, because her tone indicated it. However, she was so good about asking no questions that he asked none in return, and went forth without comment.

His steps, as often before, led him to Winthrop's office, where he and his friends had grown into the habit of meeting and discussing the news. To-night Wood came in, too, and sat silently in a chair, whittling a pine stick with a bowie-knife and evidently in deep thought. His continued stay in Richmond excited comment, because he was a man of such restless activity. He had never before been known to remain so long in one place, though now the frozen world, making military operations impossible or impracticable, offered fair excuse.

"That man Sefton came to see me to-day," he said after a long silence. "He wanted to know just how we are going to whip the enemy. What a fool question! I don't like Sefton. I wish he was on the other side!"

A slight smile appeared on the faces of most of those present. All men knew the reason why the mountain General did not like the Secretary, but no one ventured upon a teasing remark. The great black-haired cavalryman, sitting there, trimming off pine shavings with a razor-edged bowie-knife, seemed the last man in the world to be made the subject of a jest.

Prescott left at midnight, but he did not reach home until an hour later, having done an errand in the meanwhile. In the course of the day he had marked a circumstance of great interest and importance. Frame houses when old and as lightly built as that in the little side street are likely to sag somewhere. Now, at a certain spot the front door of this house failed to meet the floor by at least an eighth of an inch, and Prescott proposed to take advantage of the difference.

In the course of the day he had counted his remaining gold with great satisfaction. He had placed one broad, shining twenty-dollar piece in a small envelope, and now as he walked through the snow he fingered it in his pocket, feeling all the old satisfaction.

He was sure—it was an intuition as well as the logical result of reasoning—that Lucia Catherwood was still in the city and would return to Miss Grayson's cottage. Now he bent his own steps that way, looking up at the peaceful moon and down at the peaceful capital. Nothing was alight except the gambling houses; the dry snow crunched under his feet, but there was no other sound save the tread of an occasional sentinel, and the sharp crack of the timbers in a house contracting under the great cold.

A wind arose and moaned in the desolate streets of the dark city. Prescott bent to the blast, and shivering, drew the collar of his military cloak high about his ears. Then he laughed at himself for a fool because he was going to the help of two women who probably hated and scorned him; but he went on.

The little house was dark and silent. The sky above, though shadowed by night, was blue and clear, showing everything that rose against it; but there was no smoke from the cottage to leave a trail there.

"That's wisdom," thought Prescott. "Coal's too precious a thing now in Richmond to be wasted. It would be cheaper to burn Confederate money."

He stood for a moment, shivering by the gate, having little thought of detection, as use had now bred confidence in him, and then went inside. It was the work of but half a minute to slip a double eagle in its paper wrapping in the crack under the door, and then he walked away feeling again that pleasing glow which always came over him after a good deed.

He was two squares away when he encountered a figure walking softly, and the moonlight revealed the features of Mr. Sefton, the last man in the world whom he wished to see just then. He was startled, even more startled than he would admit to himself, at encountering this man who hung upon him and in a measure seemed to cut off his breath.

But he was convinced once more that it was only chance, as the Secretary's face bore no look of malice, no thought of suspicion, being, on the contrary, mild and smiling. As before, he took Prescott's unresisting arm and pointed up at the bright stars in their sea of blue.

"They are laughing at our passions, Mr. Prescott, perhaps smiling is the word," he said. "Such a peace as that appeals to me. I am not fond of war and I know that you are not. I feel it particularly to-night. There is poetry in the heavens so calm and so cold."

Prescott said nothing; the old sense of oppression, of one caught in a trap, was in full force, and he merely waited.

"I wish to speak frankly to-night," continued the Secretary. "There was at first a feeling of coldness, even hostility, between us, but in my case, and I think in yours too, it has passed. It is because we now recognize facts and understand that we are in a sense rivals—friendly rivals in a matter of which we know well."

The hand upon Prescott's arm did not tremble a particle as the Secretary thus spoke so clearly. But Prescott did not answer, and they went on in silence to the end of the square, where a man, a stranger to Prescott, was waiting.

Mr. Sefton beckoned to the stranger and, politely asking Prescott to excuse him a moment, talked with him a little while in low tones. Then he dismissed him and rejoined Prescott.

"A secret service agent," he said. "Unfortunately, I have to do with these people, though I am sure it could not be more repugnant to any one than it is to me; but we are forced to it. We must keep a watch even here in Richmond among our own people."

Prescott felt cold to the spine when the Secretary, with a courteous good-night, released him a few moments later. Then he hurried home and slept uneasily.

He was in dread at the breakfast table the next morning lest his mother should hand him a tiny package, left at the door, as she had done once before, but it did not happen, nor did it come the next day or the next.

The gold double eagle had been kept.

CHAPTER IX

ROBERT AND LUCIA

Two days passed, and neither any word nor his gold having come from the Grayson cottage, Prescott began to feel bold again and decided that he would call there openly and talk once more with Miss Grayson. He waited until the night was dusky, skies and stars alike obscured by clouds, and then knocked boldly at the door, which was opened by Miss Grayson herself. "Captain Prescott!" she exclaimed, and he heard a slight rustling in the room. When he entered Miss Catherwood was there. Certainly they had a strange confidence in him.

She did not speak, nor did he, and there was an awkward silence while Miss Grayson stood looking on. Prescott waited for the thanks, the hint of gratitude that he wished to hear, but it was not given; and while he waited he looked at Miss Catherwood with increasing interest, beholding her now in a new phase.

Hitherto she had always seemed to him bold and strong, a woman of more than feminine courage, one with whom it would require all the strength and resource of a man to deal even on the man's own ground. Now she was of the essence feminine. She sat in a low chair, her figure yielding a little and her face paler than he had ever seen it before. The lines were softened and her whole effect was that of an appeal. She made him think for a moment of Helen Harley.

"I am glad that our soldiers did not find you here when they searched this house," he said awkwardly.

"You were here with them, Captain Prescott—I have heard," she replied.

The colour rose to his face.

"It was pure chance," he said. "I did not come here to help them."

"I do not think that Captain Prescott was assisting in the search," interposed Miss Grayson. Prescott again looked for some word or sign of gratitude, but did not find it.

41

"I have wondered, Miss Catherwood, how you hid yourself," he said.

The shadow of a smile flickered over her pale face.

"Your wonder will have to continue, if it is interesting enough, Captain Prescott," she replied.

He was silent, and then a sudden flame appeared in her cheeks.

"Why do you come here?" she exclaimed. "Why do you interest yourself in two poor lone women? Why do you try to help them?"

To see her show emotion made him grow cooler.

"I do not know why I come," he replied candidly.

"Then do not do so any more," she said. "You are risking too much, and you, a Southern soldier, have no right to do it."

She spoke coldly now and her face resumed its pallor.

"I am with the North," she continued, "but I do not wish any one of the South to imperil himself through me."

Prescott felt hotly indignant that she should talk thus to him after all that he had done.

"My course is my own to choose," he replied proudly, "and as I told you once before, I do not make war on women."

Then he asked them what they proposed to do—what they expected Miss Catherwood's future to be.

"If she can't escape from Richmond, she'll stay here until General Grant comes to rescue her," exclaimed the fierce little old maid.

"The Northern army is not far from Richmond, but I fancy that it has a long journey before it, nevertheless," said Prescott darkly.

Then he was provoked with himself because he had made such a retort to a woman.

"It is not well to grow angry about the war now," said Miss Catherwood. "Many of us realize this; I do, I know."

He waited eagerly, hoping that she would tell of herself, who she was and why she was there, but she went no further.

He looked about the room and saw that it was changed; its furniture, always scanty, was now scantier than ever; it occurred to him with a sudden thrill that these missing pieces had gone to a pawnshop in Richmond; then his double eagle had not come too soon, and that was why it never returned to him. All his pity for these two women rose again.

He hesitated, not yet willing to go and not knowing what to say; but while he doubted there came a heavy knock at the door. Miss Grayson, who was still standing, started up and uttered a smothered cry, but Miss Catherwood said nothing, only her pallor deepened.

"What can it mean?" exclaimed Miss Grayson.

No one answered and she added hastily:

"You two must go into the next room!"

She made a gesture so commanding that they obeyed her without a word. Prescott did not realize what he was doing until he heard the door close behind him and saw that he was alone with Miss Catherwood in a little room in which the two women evidently slept. Then as the red blood dyed his brow he turned and would have gone back.

"Miss Catherwood, I do not hide from any one," he said, all his ingrained pride swelling up.

"It is best, Captain Prescott," she said quietly. "Not for your sake, but for that of two women whom you would not bring to harm."

A note of pathetic appeal appeared in her voice, and, hesitating, he was lost. He remained and watched her as she stood there in the centre of the room, her hand resting lightly upon the back of a chair and all her senses alert. The courage, the strength, the masculine power returned suddenly to her, and he had the feeling that he was in the presence of a woman who was the match for any man, even in his own special fields.

She was listening intently, and her figure, instinct with life and strength, seemed poised as if she were about to spring. The pallor in her cheeks was replaced by a glow and her eyes were alight. Here was a woman of fire and passion, a woman to whom danger mattered little, but to whom waiting was hard.

The sound of voices, one short and harsh and the other calm and even, came to them through the thin wall. The composed tones he knew were those of Miss Grayson, and the other, by the accent, the note of command, belonged to an officer. They talked on, but the words were not audible to either in the inner room.

His injured pride returned. It was not necessary for him to hide from any one, and he would go back and face the intruder, whoever he might be. He moved and his foot made a slight sound on the floor. Miss Catherwood turned upon him quickly, even with anger, and held up a warning finger. The gesture was of fierce command, and it said as plain as day, "Be still!" Instinctively he obeyed.

He had no fear for himself; he never thought then of any trouble into which discovery there might lead him, but the unspoken though eager question on his lips was to her: "What will *you* do if we are found?"

The voices went on, one harsh, commanding, the other calm, even argumentative; but the attitude of the woman beside Prescott never changed. She stood like a lithe panther, tense, waiting.

The harsh voice sank presently as if convinced, and they heard the sound of retreating footsteps, and then the bang of the front door as if slammed in disappointment.

"Now we can go back," said Miss Catherwood, and opening the door she led the way into the reception room, where Miss Grayson half lay in a chair, deadly pale and collapsed.

"What was it, Charlotte?" asked Miss Catherwood in a protecting voice, laying her hand with a soothing gesture upon Miss Grayson's head.

Miss Grayson looked up and smiled weakly.

"It lasted just a little too long for my nerves," she said. "It was, I suppose, what you might call a domiciliary visit. The man was an officer with soldiers, though he had the courtesy to leave the men at the door. He saw a light shining through a front window and thought he ought to search. I'm a suspect, a dangerous woman, you know—marked to be watched, and he hoped to make a capture. But I demanded his right, his orders—even in war there is a sort of law. I had been searched once, I said, and nothing was found; then it was by the proper authorities, but now he was about to exceed his orders. I insisted so much on my rights, at the same time declaring my innocence, that he became frightened and went away; but, oh, Lucia, I am more frightened now than he ever was!"

Miss Catherwood soothed her and talked to her protectingly and gently, as a mother to her frightened child, while Prescott admired the voice and the touch that could be at once so tender and so strong.

But the courageous half in Miss Grayson's dual nature soon recovered its rule over the timid half and she sat erect again, making apologies for her collapse.

"You see, now, Captain Prescott," said Miss Catherwood, still leaving a protecting hand upon Miss Grayson's shoulders, "that I was right when I wanted you to leave us. We cannot permit you to compromise yourself in our behalf and we do not wish it. You ran a great risk to-night. You might not fare so well the next time."

Her tone was cold, and, chilled by it, Prescott replied:

"Miss Catherwood, I may have come where I was not wanted, but I shall not do so again."

He walked toward the door, his head high. Miss Grayson looked at Miss Catherwood in surprise.

The girl raised her hand as if about to make a detaining gesture, but she let it drop again, and without another word Prescott passed out of the house.

One of the formal receptions, occurring twice a month, was held the next evening by the President of the Confederacy and his wife. Prescott and all whom he knew were there.

The parlours were crowded already with people—officers, civilians, curious transatlantic visitors—and more than one workman in his rough coat, for all the world was asked to come to the President's official receptions. They had obeyed the order, too, and came with their bravest faces and bravest apparel. In the White House of the Confederacy there were few somber touches that night.

The President and his wife, he elderly and severe of countenance, she young and mild, received in one of the parlours all who would shake the hand of Mr. Davis. It was singularly like a reception at that other White House on the Potomac, and the South, in declaring that she would act by herself, still followed the old patterns.

It was a varied gathering, varied in appearance, manners and temper. The official and civil society of the capital never coalesced well. The old families of Richmond, interwoven with nearly three centuries of life in Virginia, did not like all these new people coming merely with the stamp of the Government upon them, which was often, so they thought, no stamp at all; but with the ceaseless and increasing pressure from the North they met now on common ground at the President's official reception, mingling without constraint.

Prescott danced three times with Helen Harley and walked twice with her in the halls. She was at her best that night, beautiful in a gentle, delicate way, but she did not whip his blood like a wind from the hills, and he was surprised to find how little bitterness he felt when he saw her dancing with Mr. Sefton or walking with the great cavalry General like a rose in the shadow of an oak. But he loved her, he told himself again; she was the one perfect woman in the world, the one whom he must make his wife, if he could. These men were not to be blamed for loving her, too; they could not help it.

Then his eye roved to Colonel Harley, who, unlike General Wood, was as much at home here as in the field, his form expanding, his face in a glow, paying assiduous attention to Mrs. Markham, who used him as she would. He watched them a little, and, though he liked Mrs. Markham, he reflected that he would not be quite so complacent if he were in General Markham's place.

Presently Talbot tapped him on the shoulder, saying:

"Come outside."

"Why should I go out into the cold?" replied Prescott. "I'm not going to fight a duel with you."

"No, but you're going to smoke a cigar with me, a genuine Havana at that, a chance that you may not have again until this war ends. A friend just gave them to me. They came on a blockade runner last week by way of Charleston."

They walked back and forth to keep themselves warm. A number of people, drawn by the lights and the music, were lingering in the street before the house, despite the cold. They were orderly and quiet, not complaining because others were in the warmth and light while they were in the cold and dark. Richmond under the pressure of war was full of want and suffering, but she bred no mobs.

"Let's go back," said Talbot presently. "My cigar is about finished and I'm due for this dance with Mrs. Markham."

"Mine's not," replied Prescott, "and I'm not due for the dance with anybody, so I think I'll stay a little longer."

"All right; I must go."

Talbot went in, leaving his friend alone beside the house. Prescott continued to smoke the unfinished cigar, but that was not his reason for staying. He remained motionless at least five minutes, then he threw the cigar butt on the ground and moved farther along the side of the house, where he was wholly in shadow. His pretense of calm, of a lack of interest, was gone. His muscles were alert and his eye keen to see. He had on his military cap and he drew his cloak very closely about him until it shrouded his whole face and figure. He might pass unnoticed in a crowd.

Making a little circuit, he entered the street lower down, and then came back toward the house, sauntering as if he were a casual looker-on. No one noticed him, and he slid into a place in the little crowd, where he stood for a few moments, then made his way toward a tall figure near the fence.

When he was beside the house with Talbot he had seen that face under a black hood, looking over the fence, and the single glance was sufficient. Now he stood beside her and put his hand upon her arm as if he had come there with her, that no one might take notice.

She started, looked up into his face, checked a cry and was silent, though he could feel the arm quivering under the touch of his fingers.

"Why are you here?" he asked in a strained whisper. "Do you not know better than to leave Miss Grayson's house, and, above all, to come to this place? Are you a mad woman?"

Anger was mixed with his alarm. She seemed at that moment a child who had disobeyed him. She shrank a little at his words, but turned toward him luminous eyes, in which the appeal soon gave way to an indignant fire.

"Do you know what it is to stay in hiding—to be confined within the four walls of one room?" she said, and her voice was more intense even than his had been. "Do you know what it is to sit in the dark and the cold when you love the warmth and the light and the music? I saw you and the other man and the satisfaction on your faces. Do you think that you alone were made for enjoyment?"

Prescott looked at her in surprise, such was the fire and intensity of her tone and so unexpected was her reply. He had associated her with other fields of action, more strenuous phases of life than this of the ballroom, the dance and the liquid flow of music. All at once he remembered that she was a woman like another woman there in the ballroom in silken skirts and with a rose in her hair. Unconsciously he placed her by the side of Helen Harley.

"But the danger!" he said at last. "You are hunted, woman though you are, and Richmond is small. At such a time as this every strange form is noted."

"I am not afraid," she replied, and a peculiar kind of pride rang in her tone. "If I am sought as a criminal it does not follow that I am such."

"And you have left Miss Grayson alone?"

"Miss Grayson has often been alone. She may dislike loneliness, but she does not fear it. Listen, they are dancing again!"

The liquid melody of the music rose in a rippling flow, coming through the closed windows in soft minor chords. Standing there beside her, in the outer darkness and cold, Prescott began to understand the girl's feeling, the feeling of the hunted, who looks upon ease and joy. The house was gleaming with lights, even the measured tread of the dancers mingled with the flow of music; but here, outside, the wind began to whistle icily down the street, and the girl bent her head to its edge.

"You must go back at once to Miss Grayson's," urged Prescott, "and you must not come out again like this."

"You command merely for me to disobey," she said coolly. "By what right do you seek to direct my actions?"

"By the right of wisdom, or necessity, whichever you choose to call it," he replied. "Since you will not, of your own choice, care for yourself, I shall try to make you do so. Come!"

He put his hand upon her again. She sought to draw away, but he would not let go, and gradually she yielded.

"What a great thing is brute force! at least, you men think so," she said, as they walked slowly up the street.

"Yes, when properly exerted, as in the present instance."

They went on, the lights in the house became dimmer, and the sound of the music and the tread of the dance reached them no more.

She looked up into his face presently.

"Tell me one thing," she said.

"Certainly."

"Who is Helen?"

"Who is Helen?"

"Yes, I heard that man say how well she was looking to-night, and you agreed."

"We were both right. Helen is Miss Helen Harley, and they say she is the most beautiful woman in Richmond. She is the sister of Colonel Harley, one of our noted cavalry leaders."

She was silent for a little while, and then Prescott said:

"Now will you answer a question of mine?"

"I should like to hear the question first."

"Where were you hidden when we searched Miss Grayson's house?"

"That I will never tell you," she replied with sudden energy.

"Oh, well, don't do it then," he said in some disappointment.

They were now three or four squares away from the presidential mansion and were clothed in darkness, and silence save when the frozen snow crackled crisply under their feet.

"You cannot go any farther with me," she said. "I have warned you before that you must not risk yourself in my behalf."

"But if I choose to do so, nevertheless."

"Then I shall go back there to the house, where they are dancing."

She spoke in such a resolute tone that Prescott could not doubt her intent.

"If you promise to return at once to Miss Grayson's cottage I shall leave you here," he said.

"I make the promise, but for the present only," she replied. "You must remember that we are enemies; you are of the South, and I am treated as an enemy in Richmond. Good-night!"

She left him so quickly that he did not realize her departure until he saw her form flicker in the darkness and then disappear completely. A faint smile appeared on his face.

"No woman can ever successfully play the rôle of a man," he said to himself. Despite her former denial and her air of truth he was still thinking of her as a spy.

Then he walked thoughtfully back to the presidential mansion.

"You must have found that a most interesting cigar," said Talbot to him when he returned to the house.

"The most interesting one I ever smoked," replied Prescott.

Prescott found himself again with Mrs. Markham and walked with her into one of the smaller parlours, where Mr. Sefton, Winthrop, Raymond, Redfield and others were discussing a topic with an appearance of great earnestness.

"It is certainly a mystery, one of the most remarkable that I have ever encountered," said the Secretary with emphasis, as Prescott and Mrs. Markham joined them. "We are sure that it was a woman, a woman in a brown cloak and brown dress, and that she is yet in Richmond, but we are sure of nothing else. So far as our efforts are concerned, she might as well be in St. Petersburg as here in the capital city of the South. Perhaps the military can give us a suggestion. What do you think of it, Captain Prescott?"

He turned his keen, cold eye on Prescott, who never quivered.

"I, Mr. Sefton?" he replied. "I have no thoughts at all upon such a subject; for two reasons: first, my training as a soldier tells me to let alone affairs which are not my own; and second, you say this spy is a woman; know then that it is the prayer of every soldier that God will preserve him from any military duty which has to do with a woman, as it means sure defeat."

There was a laugh, and Mrs. Markham asked:

"Do you mean the second of your reasons as truth or as a mere compliment to my sex?"

"Madam," replied Prescott with a bow, "you are a living illustration of the fact that I could mean the truth only."

"But to return to the question of the spy," said Mr. Sefton, tenaciously, "have you really no opinion, Captain Prescott? I have heard that you assisted Mr. Talbot when he was detailed to search Miss Grayson's house—a most commendable piece of zeal on your part—and I thought it showed your great interest in the matter."

"Captain Prescott," said Mrs. Markham, "I am surprised at you. You really helped in the searching of Miss Grayson's house! The idea of a soldier doing such work when he doesn't have to!"

Prescott laughed lightly—a cloak for his real feelings—as Mrs. Markham's frank criticism stung him a little.

"It was pure chance, Mrs. Markham. I happened to be near there when Talbot passed with his detail, and as he and I are the best of friends, I went with him wholly out of curiosity, I assure you—not the best of motives, I am willing to admit."

"Then I am to imply, Mrs. Markham," said the Secretary in his smooth voice, "that you condemn me for instituting such a search. But the ladies, if you will pardon me for saying it, are the most zealous upholders of the war, and now I ask you how are we men to carry it on if we do not take warlike measures."

She shrugged her shoulders and the Secretary turned his attention again to Prescott.

"What do you think of our chances of capture, Captain?" he said. "Shall we take this woman?"

"I don't think so," replied Prescott, meeting the Secretary's eye squarely. "First, you have no clue beyond the appearance of a woman wearing a certain style of costume in the Government building on a certain day. You have made no progress whatever beyond that. Now, whoever this woman may be, she must be very clever, and I should think, too, that she has friends in the city who are helping her."

"Then," said the Secretary, "we must discover her friends and reach her through them."

"How do you propose going about it?" asked Prescott calmly.

"I have not made any arrangements yet, nor can I say that I have a settled plan in view," replied the Secretary; "but I feel sure of myself. A city of forty thousand inhabitants is not hard to watch, and whoever this spy's friends are I shall find them sooner or later."

His cold, keen eyes rested upon Prescott, but they were without expression. Nevertheless, a chill struck the young Captain to the marrow. Did the Secretary know, or were his words mere chance? He recognized with startling force that he was face to face with a man of craft and guile, one who regarded him as a rival in a matter that lay very close to the heart's desire, and therefore as a probable enemy.

But cold and keen as was the look of the Secretary, Prescott could read nothing in his face, and whether a challenge was intended or not he resolved to pick up the glove. There was something stubborn lying at the bottom of his nature, and confronted thus by formidable obstacles he resolved to protect Lucia Catherwood if it lay within his power.

General Wood, a look of discontent on his face, entered the room at this moment. An electrical current of antagonism seemed to pass between him and the Secretary, which Mrs. Markham, perhaps from an impulse of mischief and perhaps from a natural love of sport, fostered, permitting Prescott, to his relief, to retire into the background.

The Secretary's manner was smooth, silky and smiling; he never raised his voice above its natural pitch nor betrayed otherwise the slightest temper. He now led the talk upon the army, and gently insinuated that whatever misfortunes had befallen the Confederacy were due to its military arm; perhaps to a lack of concord among the generals, perhaps to hasty and imperfect judgment on the field, or perhaps to a failure to carry out the complete wishes of the Executive Department.

He did not say any of these things plainly, merely hinting them in the mildest manner. Prescott, though a representative of the army, did not take any of it to himself, knowing well that it was intended for the General, and he watched curiously to see how the latter would reply.

The General surprised him, developing a tact and self-command, a knowledge of finesse that he would not have believed possible in a rough and uneducated mountaineer. But the same quality, the wonderful perception, or rather intuition, that had made Wood a military genius, was serving him here, and though he perceived at once the drift of the Secretary's remarks and their intention, he preserved his coolness and contented himself for awhile with apparent ignorance. This, however, did not check the attack, and by and by Wood, too, began to deal in veiled allusions and to talk of a great general and devoted lieutenants hampered by men who sat in their chairs in a comfortable building before glowing fires and gossiped of faults committed by others amid the reek of desperate fields.

It was four o'clock in the morning when Prescott stood again in the street in the darkness and saw the Secretary taking Helen home in his carriage.

CHAPTER X

FEEDING THE HUNGRY

"It is now the gossip in Richmond," said Mrs. Prescott to her son as they sat together before the fire a day or two later, "that General Wood makes an unusually long stay here for a man who loves the saddle and war as he does."

"Who says so, mother?"

"Well, many people."

"Who, for instance?"

"Well, the Secretary, Mr. Sefton, as a most shining instance, and he is a man of such acute perceptions that he ought to know."

Prescott was silent.

"They say that Mr. Sefton wants something that somebody else wants," she continued. "A while back it was another person whom he regarded as the opponent to his wish, but now he seems to have transferred the rivalry to General Wood. I wonder if he is right."

She gazed over her knitting needles into the fire as if she would read the answer in the coals, but Prescott himself did not assist her, though he wondered at what his mother was aiming. Was she seeking to arouse him to greater vigour in his suit? Well, he loved Helen Harley, and he had loved her ever since they were little boy and little girl together, but that was no reason why he should shout his love to all Richmond. Sefton and Wood might shout theirs, but perhaps he should fare better if he were more quiet.

Lonely and abstracted, Prescott wandered about the city that evening, and when the hour seemed suitable, bending his head to the northern blast, he turned willing steps once more to the little house in the cross street, wondering meanwhile what its two inmates were doing and how they fared.

As he went along and heard the wind moaning among the houses he had the feeling that he was watched. He looked ahead and saw nothing; he looked back and saw nothing; then he told himself it was only the wind rattling among loose boards, but his fancy refused to credit his own words. This feeling that he was watched, spied upon, had been with him several days, but he did not realize it fully until the present moment, when he was again upon a delicate errand, one perhaps involving a bit of unfaithfulness to the cause for which he fought. He, the bold Captain, the veteran of thirty battles, shook slightly and then told himself courageously that it was not a nervous chill, but the cold. Yet he looked around fearfully and wished to hear other footsteps, to see other faces and to feel that he was not alone on such a cold and dark night—alone save for the unknown who watched him. At the thought he looked about again, but there was nothing, not even the faintest echo of a footfall.

The chill, the feeling of oppression passed for the time and he hastened to the side street and the little house. It was too dark for him to tell whether any wisp of smoke rose from the chimney, and no light shone from the window. He opened the little gate and passed into the little yard where the snow seemed to be yet unbroken. Then he slipped two of the beautiful gold double eagles under the door and almost ran away, the feeling that he was watched returning to him and hanging on his back like crime on the mind of the guilty.

Prescott's early ancestors had been great borderers, renowned Indian fighters and adepts in the ways of the forest, when the red men, silent and tenacious, followed upon their tracks for days and it was necessary to practise every art to throw off the pursuers, unseen but known to be there. Unconsciously a thin strain of heredity now came into play, and he began to wind about the city before going home, turning suddenly from one street into another, and gliding swiftly now and then in the darkest shadow, making it difficult for pursuer, if pursuer he had, to follow him.

He did not reach home until nearly two hours after he had left the cottage, and then his fingers and ears were blue and almost stiff with cold.

He wandered into the streets again the next morning, and ere long saw a slender figure ahead of him walking with decision and purpose. Despite the distance and the vagueness of her form he knew that it was Miss Grayson, and he followed more briskly, drawn by curiosity and a resolution to gratify it.

She went to one of the markets and began to barter for food, driving a sharp bargain and taking her time. Prescott loitered near and at last came very close. There were several others standing about, but if she noticed and recognized the Captain she gave no sign, going on imperturbably with her bargaining.

Prescott thought once or twice of speaking to her, but he concluded that it was better to wait, letting her make the advances if she would. He was glad of his decision a few minutes later, when he saw a new figure approaching.

The new arrival was Mr. Sefton, a fur-lined cloak drawn high around his neck and his face as usual bland and smiling. He nodded to Prescott and then looked at Miss Grayson, but for the moment said nothing, standing by as if he preferred to wait for whatever he had in mind.

Miss Grayson finished her purchases, and drawing her purse took forth the money for payment. A yellow gleam caught Prescott's eye and he recognized one of his double eagles. The knowledge sent a thrill through him, but he still stood in silence, glancing casually about him and waiting for one of the others to speak first.

Miss Grayson received her change and her packages and turned to go away, when she was interrupted by the Secretary, with no expression whatever showing through his blandness and his smiles.

"It is Miss Grayson, is it not?" he said smoothly.

She turned upon him a cold and inquiring look.

"I am Mr. Sefton of the Treasurer's office," he said in the same even tones—smooth with the smoothness of metal. "Perhaps it is too much to hope that you have heard of me."

"I have heard of you," she said with increasing coldness.

"And I of you," he continued. "Who in Richmond has not heard of Miss Charlotte Grayson, the gallant champion of the Northern Cause and of the Union of the States forever? I do not speak invidiously. On the contrary, I honour you; from my heart I do, Miss Grayson. Any woman who has the courage amid a hostile population to cling to what she believes is the right, even if it be the wrong, is entitled to our homage and respect."

He made a bow, not too low, then raised his hand in a detaining gesture when Miss Grayson turned to go.

"You are more fortunate than we—we who are in our own house—Miss Grayson," he said. "You pay in gold and with a large gold piece, too. Excuse me, but I could not help noticing."

Prescott saw a quiver on her lips and a sudden look of terror in her eyes; but both disappeared instantly and her features remained rigid and haughty.

"Mr. Sefton," she said icily, "I am a woman, alone in the world and, as you say, amid a hostile population; but my private affairs are my own."

There was no change in the Secretary's countenance; he was still bland, smiling, purring like a cat.

"Your private affairs, Miss Grayson," he said, "of course! None would think of questioning that statement. But how about affairs that are not private? There are certain public duties, owed by all of us in a time like this."

"You have searched my house," she said in the same cold tones; "you have exposed me to that indignity, and now I ask you to leave me alone."

"Miss Grayson," he said, "I would not trouble you, but the sight of gold, freshly coined gold like that and of so great a value, arouses my suspicions. It makes a question spring up in my mind, and that question is, how did you get it? Here is my friend, Captain Prescott; he, too, no doubt, is interested, or perhaps you know him already."

It was said so easily and carelessly that Prescott reproved himself when he feared a double meaning lurking under the Secretary's words. Nervousness or incaution on the part of Miss Grayson might betray much. But the look she turned upon Prescott was like that with which she had favoured the Secretary—chilly, uncompromising and hostile.

"I do not know your friend," she said.

"But he was with the officer who searched your house," said the Secretary.

"A good reason why I should not know him."

The Secretary smiled.

"Captain Prescott," he said, "you are unfortunate. You do not seem to be on the road to Miss Grayson's favour."

"The lady does not know me, Mr. Sefton," said Prescott, "and it cannot be any question of either favour or disfavour."

The Secretary was now gazing at Miss Grayson, and Prescott used the chance to study his face. This casual but constant treading of the Secretary upon dangerous ground annoyed and alarmed him. How much did he know, if anything? Robert would rather be in the power of any other man than the one before him.

When he had sought in vain to read that immovable face, to gather there some intimation of his purpose, the old feeling of fear, the feeling that had haunted him the night before when he went to the cottage, came over him again. The same chill struck him to the marrow, but his will and pride were too strong to let it prevail. It was still a calm face that he showed to the lady and the Secretary.

"If you have not known Captain Prescott before, you should know him now," the Secretary was saying. "A gallant officer, as he has proved on many battlefields, and a man of intelligence and feeling. Moreover, he is a fair enemy."

Prescott bowed slightly at the compliment, but Miss Grayson was immovable. Apparently the history and character of Captain Robert Prescott, C. S. A., were of no earthly interest to her, and Prescott, looking at her, was uncertain if the indifference were not real as well as apparent.

"Mr. Sefton," said Miss Grayson, "you asked an explanation and I said that I had none to give, nor have I. You can have me arrested if you wish, and I await your order."

"Not at all, Miss Grayson," replied the Secretary; "let the explanation be deferred."

"Then," she said with unchanging coldness, "I take pleasure in bidding you good-day."

"Good-day," rejoined the Secretary, and Prescott politely added his own.

Miss Grayson, without another word, gathered up her bundles and left.

"Slumbering fire," said the Secretary, looking after her.

"Is she to be blamed for it?" said Prescott.

"Did my tone imply criticism?" the Secretary asked, looking at Prescott.

CHAPTER XI

MR. SEFTON MAKES A CONFIDENCE

Prescott now resolved, whatever happened, to make another attempt at the escape of Lucia Catherwood. Threats of danger, unspoken, perhaps, but to his mind not the less formidable, were multiplying, and he did not intend that they should culminate in disaster. The figure of that woman, so helpless and apparently the sole target at this moment of a powerful Government, made an irresistible appeal to him.

But there were moments of doubt, when he asked himself if he were not tricked by the fancy, or rather by a clever and elusive woman—as cunning as she was elusive—who led him, and who looked to the end and not to the means. He saw something repellent in the act of being a spy, above all when it was a woman who took the part. His open nature rejected such a trade, even if it were confined to the deed of a moment done under impulse. She had assured him that she was innocent, and there was a look of truth in her face when she said it; but to say it and to look it was in the business of being a spy, and why should she differ from others?

But these moments were brief; they would come to his mind and yet his mind in turn would cast them out. He remembered her eyes, the swell of her figure, her noble curves. She was not of the material that would turn to so low a trade, he said to himself over and over again.

He was still thinking of a plan to save her and trying to find a way when a message arrived directing him to report at once to the Secretary of War. He surmised that he would receive instructions to rejoin General Lee as soon as possible, and he felt a keen regret that he should not have time to do the thing he wished most to do; but he lost no time in obeying the order.

The Secretary of War was in his office, sitting in a chair near the window, and farther away slightly in the shadow was another figure, more slender but stronger. Prescott recognized again, with that sudden and involuntary feeling of fear, the power of the man. It was Mr. Sefton, his face hidden in the shadows, and therefore wholly unread. But as usual the inflexibility of purpose, the hardening of resolve followed Prescott's emotion, and his figure stiffened as he stood at attention to receive the commands of the mighty—that is, the Secretary of War of the Confederate States of America.

But the Secretary of War was not harsh or fierce; instead, he politely invited the young Captain to a chair and spoke to him in complimentary terms, referring to his gallant services on many battlefields, and declaring them not unknown to those who held the strings of power. Mr. Sefton, from the security of the shadows, merely nodded to their guest, and Prescott returned the welcome in like fashion, every nerve attuned for what he expected to prove an ordeal.

48

"Many officers are brave," began the Secretary of War, "and it is not the highest compliment when we call you such, Captain Prescott. Indeed, we mean to speak much better of you when we say that you have bravery, allied with coolness and intelligence. When we find these in one person we have the ideal officer."

Prescott could not do less than bow to this flattery, but he wondered what such a curious prelude foreshadowed. "It means no good to me," he thought, "or he would not begin with such praise." But he said aloud:

"I am sure I have some zealous friend to thank for commendation so much beyond my desert."

"It is not beyond your desert, but you have a friend to thank nevertheless," replied the Secretary of War. "A friend, too, whom no man need despise. I allude to Mr. Sefton here, one of the ablest members of the Government, one who surpasses most of us in insight and pertinacity. It is he who, because of his friendship for you and faith in you, wishes to have you chosen for an important and delicate service which may lead to promotion."

Prescott stared at this man whose words rang so hollow in his ear, but he could see no sign of guile or satire on the face of the Secretary of War. On the contrary, it bore every appearance of earnestness, and he became convinced that the appearance was just. Then he cast one swift glance at the inscrutable Mr. Sefton, who still sat in the shadow and did not move.

"I thank you for your kind words," he said to the Secretary of War, "and I shall appreciate very much the honour, of which you give me an intimation."

The great man smiled. It is pleasant to us all to confer benefits and still pleasanter to know that they are appreciated.

"It is a bit of work in the nature of secret service, Captain Prescott," he continued, "and it demands a wary eye and a discerning mind."

Prescott shuddered with repulsion. Instinctively he foresaw what was coming, and there was no task which he would not have preferred in its place. And he was expected, too, at such a moment, to look grateful.

"You will recall the episode of the spy and the abstraction of the papers from the President's office," continued the Secretary of War in orotund and complaisant tones. "It may seem to the public that we have dropped this matter, which is just what we wish the public to think, as it may lull the suspicions of the suspected. But we are more resolved than ever to secure the guilty!"

Prescott glanced again at Mr. Sefton, but he still sat in the shadow, and Prescott believed that he had not yet moved either hand or foot in the whole interview.

"To be brief, Captain Prescott," resumed the Secretary of War, "we wish you to take charge of this service which, I repeat, we consider delicate and important."

"Now?" asked Prescott.

"No, not immediately—in two or three days, perhaps; we shall notify you. We are convinced the guilty are yet in Richmond and cannot escape. It is important that we capture them, as we may unearth a nest of conspirators. I trust that you see the necessity of our action."

Prescott bowed, though he was raging inwardly, and it was in his mind to decline abruptly such a service, but second thought told him a refusal might make a bad matter worse. He would have given much, too, to see the face of Mr. Sefton— his fancy painted there a smile of irony.

As the Secretary of War seemed to have said all that he intended, Prescott turned to go, but he added a word of thanks to Mr. Sefton, whose voice he wished to hear. Mr. Sefton merely nodded, and the young Captain, as he went out, hesitated on the doorstep as if he expected to hear sardonic laughter behind him. He heard nothing.

The fierce touch of the winter outside cooled his blood, and as he walked toward his home he tried to think of a way out of the difficulty. He kept repeating to himself the words of the Secretary of War: "In two or three days we shall send for you," and from this constant repetition an idea was born in his head. "Much may be done in two or three days," he said to himself, "and if a man can do it I will!" and he said it with a sense of defiance.

His brain grew hot with the thought, and he walked about the city, not wishing yet to return to his home. He had been walking, he knew not how long, when a hand fell lightly upon his arm and, turning, he beheld the bland face of Mr. Sefton.

"May I walk a little with you, Captain Prescott?" he said. "Two heads are sometimes better than one."

Prescott was hot alike with his idea and with wrath over his recent ordeal; moreover, he hated secret and underhand parts, and spoke impulsively:

"Mr. Secretary, I have you to thank for this task, and I do not thank you at all!"

"Why not? Most young officers wish a chance for promotion."

"But you set me spying to catch a spy! There are few things in the world that I would rather not do."

"You say 'you set me spying'! My dear sir, it was the Secretary of War, not I."

"Mr. Sefton," exclaimed Prescott angrily, "why should we fence with words any longer? It is you and you alone who are at the bottom of this!"

"Since that is your theory, my dear Captain, what motive would you assign?"

Prescott was slow to wrath, but when moved at last he had little fear of consequences, and it was so with him now. He faced the Secretary and gazed at him steadily, even inquiringly. But, as usual, he read nothing in the bland, unspeaking countenance before him.

"There is a motive, an ulterior motive," he replied. "For days now you have been persecuting me and I am convinced that it is for a purpose."

"And if so ready to read an unspoken purpose in my mind, then why not read the cause of it?"

Prescott hesitated. This calm, expressionless man with the impression of power troubled him. The Secretary again put his hand lightly upon his arm.

"We are near the outskirts of the city, Captain," said Mr. Sefton, "and I suggest that we walk on toward the fortifications in order that none may overhear what we have to say. It may be that you and I shall arrive at such an understanding that we can remain friends."

There was suggestion in the Secretary's words for the first time, likewise a command, and Prescott willingly adopted his plan. Together the two strolled on through the fields.

"I have a tale to tell," began the Secretary, "and there are preliminaries and exordiums, but first of all there is a question. Frankly, Captain Prescott, what kind of a man do you think I am?"

Prescott hesitated.

"I see you do not wish to speak," continued the Secretary, "because the portrait you would paint is unflattering, but I will paint it for you—at least, the one that you have in your mind's eye. You think me sly and intriguing, eaten up by ambition, and caring for nobody in the world but myself. A true portrait, perhaps, so far as the external phases go, and the light in which I often wish to appear to the world, but not true in reality."

Prescott waited in silence to hear what the other might have to say, and whatever it was he was sure that it would be of interest.

"That I am ambitious is true," continued the Secretary; "there are few men not old who are not so, and I think it better to have ambition than to be without it. But if I have ambition I also have other qualities. I like my friends—I like you and would continue to like you, Captain Prescott, if you would let me. It is said here that I am not a true Southerner, whatever may be my birth, as my coldness, craft and foresight are not Southern characteristics. That may be true, but at least I am Southern in another character—I have strong, even violent emotions, and I love a woman. I am willing to sacrifice much for her."

The Secretary's hand was still resting lightly on Prescott's arm, and the young Captain, feeling it tremble, knew that his companion told the truth.

"Yes," resumed Mr. Sefton, "I love a woman, and with all the greater fire because I am naturally undemonstrative and self-centred. The stream comes with an increased rush when it has to break through the ice. I love a woman, I say, and I am determined to have her. You know well who it is!"

"Helen Harley," said Prescott.

"I love Helen Harley," continued the Secretary, "and there are two men of whom I am jealous, but I shall speak first of one—the one whom I have feared the longer and the more. He is a soldier, a young man commended often by his superiors for gallantry and skill—deservedly so, too—I do not seek to deny it. He is here in Richmond now, and he has known Helen Harley all his life. They were boy and girl together. But he has become mixed in an intrigue here. There is another woman——"

"Mr. Sefton! You proposed that we understand each other, and that is just what I wish, too. You have been watching me all this time."

"Watching you! Yes, I have, and to purpose!" exclaimed the Secretary. "You have done few things in Richmond that have not come to my knowledge. Again I ask you what kind of a man do you think I am? When I saw you standing in my path I resolved that no act of yours should escape me. You know of this spy, Lucia Catherwood, and you know where she is. You see, I have even her name. Once I intended to arrest her and expose you to disgrace, but she had gone. I am glad now that we did not find her. I have a better use for her uncaught, though it annoys me that I cannot yet discover where she was when we searched that house."

The cold chill which he had felt before in the presence of this man assailed Prescott again. He was wholly within his power, and metaphorically, he could be broken on the wheel if the adroit and ruthless Secretary wished it. He bit his dry lip, but said nothing, still waiting for the other.

"I repeat that I have a better use for Miss Catherwood," continued Mr. Sefton. "Do you think I should have gone to all this trouble and touched upon so many springs merely to capture one misguided girl? What harm can she do us? Do you think the result of a great war and the fate of a continent are to be decided by a pair of dark eyes?"

They were walking now along a half-made street that led into the fields. Behind them lay the city, and before them the hills and the forest, all in a robe of white. Thin columns of smoke rose from the earthworks, where the defenders hovered over the fires, but no one was near enough to hear what the two men said.

"Then why have you held your hand?" asked Prescott.

"Why?" and the Secretary actually laughed, a smooth, noiseless laugh, but a laugh nevertheless, though so full of a snaky cunning that Prescott started as if he had been bitten. "Why, because I wished you, Robert Prescott, whom I feared, to become so entangled that you would be helpless in my hands, and that you have done. If I wish I can have you dismissed from the army in disgrace—shot, perhaps, as a traitor. In any event, your future lies in the hollow of my hand. You are wholly at my mercy. I speak a word and you are ruined."

"Why not speak it?" Prescott asked calmly. His first impulse had passed, and though his tongue was dry in his mouth the old hardening resolve to fight to the last came again.

"Why not speak it? Because I do not wish to do so—at least, not yet. Why should I ruin you? I do not dislike you; on the contrary, I like you, as I have told you. So, I shall wait."

"What then?"

"Then I shall demand a price. I am not in this world merely to pass through it mechanically, like a clock wound up for a certain time. No; I want things and I intend to have them. I plan for them and I make sacrifices to get them. My one desire most of all is Helen Harley, but you are in the way. Stand out of it—withdraw—and no word of mine shall ever tell what I know. So far as I am concerned there shall be no Lucia Catherwood. I will do more: I will smooth her way from Richmond for her. Now, like a wise man, pay this price, Captain Prescott. It should not be hard for you."

He spoke the last words in a tone half insinuating, half ironical. Prescott flushed a deep red. He did love Helen Harley; he had always loved her. He had not been away from her so much recently because of any decrease in that love; it was his misfortune—the pressure of ugly affairs that compelled him. Was the love he bore her to be thrown aside for a price? A price like that was too high to pay for anything.

"Mr. Secretary," he replied icily, "they say that you are not of the South in some of your characteristics, and I think you are not. Do you suppose that I would accept such a proposition? I could not dream of it. I should despise myself forever if I were to do such a thing."

He stopped and faced the Secretary angrily, but he saw no reflection of his own wrath in the other's face; on the contrary, he had never before seen him look so despondent. There was plenty of expression now on his countenance as he moodily kicked a lump of snow out of his way. Then Mr. Sefton said:

"Do you know in my heart I expected you to make that answer. You would never have put such an alternative to a rival, but I—I am different. Am I responsible? No; you and I are the product of different soils and we look at things in a different way. You do not know my history. Few do here in Richmond—perhaps none; but you shall know, and then you will understand."

Prescott saw that this man, who a moment ago was threatening him, was deeply moved, and he waited in wonder.

"You have never known what it is," resumed the Secretary, speaking in short, choppy tones so unlike his usual manner that the voice might have belonged to another man, "to belong to the lowest class of our people—a class so low that even the negro slaves sneered at and despised it; to be born to a dirt floor, and a rotten board roof and four log walls! A goodly heritage, is it not? Was not Providence kind to me? And is it not a just and kind Providence?"

He laughed with concentrated bitterness, and a feeling of pity for this man whom he had been dreading so much stole over Prescott.

"We talk of freedom and equality here in the South," continued the Secretary, "and we say we are fighting for it; but not in England itself is class feeling stronger, and that is what we are fighting to perpetuate. I say that you have no such childhood as mine to look back to—the squalour, the ignorance, the sin, the misery, and above all the knowledge that you have a brain in your head and the equal knowledge that you are forbidden to use it—that places and honours are not for you!"

Again he fiercely kicked a clump of snow from his path and gazed absently across the fields toward the wintry horizon, his face full of passionate protestation. Prescott was still silent, his own position forgotten now in the interest aroused by this sudden outburst.

"If you are born a clod it is best to be a clod," continued the Secretary, "but that I was not. As I said, I have a brain in my head, and eyes to see. From the first I despised the squalour and the misery around me, and resolved to rise above it despite all the barriers of a slave-holding aristocracy, the most exclusive aristocracy in the world. I thought of nothing else. You do not know my struggles; you cannot guess them—the years and the years and all the bitter nights. They say that any oppressed and despised race learns and practises craft and cunning. So does a man; he must—he has no other choice.

"I learned craft and cunning and practised them, too, because I had to do so. I did things that you have never done because you were not driven to them, and at last I saw the seed that I had planted begin to grow. Then I felt a joy that you can never feel because you have never worked for an object, and never will work for it, as I have done. I have triumphed. The best in the South obey me because they must. It is not the title or the name, for there are those higher than mine, but it is the power, the feeling that I have the reins in my hand and can guide."

"If you have won your heart's desire why do you rail at fate?" asked Prescott.

"Because I have not won my wish—not all of it. They say there is a weak spot in every man's armour; there is always an Achilles' heel. I am no exception. Well, the gods ordained that I, James Sefton, a man who thought himself made wholly of steel, should fall in love with a piece of pink-and-white girlhood. What a ridiculous bit of nonsense! I suppose it was done to teach me I am a fool just like other men. I had begun to believe that I was exceptional, but I know better now."

"Then you call this a weakness and regret it?"

"Yes, because it interferes with all my plans. The time that I should be devoting to ambition I must sacrifice for a weakness of the heart."

The low throb of a distant drum came from a rampart, and the Secretary raised his head, as if the sound gave a new turn to his thoughts.

"Even the plans of ambition may crumble," he said. "Since I am speaking frankly of one thing, Captain Prescott, I may speak likewise of another. Have you ever thought how unstable may prove this Southern Confederacy for which we are spending so much blood?"

"I have," replied Prescott with involuntary emphasis.

"So have I; again I speak to you with perfect frankness, because it will not be to your profit to repeat what I say. Do you realize that we are fighting against the tide, or, to put it differently, against the weight of all the ages? When one is championing a cause opposed to the tendency of human affairs his victories are worse than his defeats because they merely postpone the certain catastrophe. It is impossible for a slave-holding aristocracy under any circumstances to exist much longer in the world. When the apple is ripe it drops off the tree, and we cannot stay human progress. The French Revolution was bound to triumph because the institutions that it destroyed were worn out; the American Colonies were bound to win in their struggle with Britain because nature had decreed the time for parting; and even if we should succeed in this contest we should free the slaves ourselves inside of twenty years, because slavery is now opposed to common sense as well as to morality."

"Then why do you espouse such a cause?" asked Prescott.

"Why do you?" replied the Secretary very quickly.

It was a question that Prescott never yet had been able to answer to his own complete satisfaction, and now he preferred silence. But no reply seemed to be expected, as the Secretary continued to talk of the Southern Confederacy, the plan upon which it was formed, and its abnormal position in the world, expressing himself, as he had said he would, with the most perfect frankness, displaying all the qualities of a keen analytical and searching mind. He showed how the South was one-sided, how it had cultivated only one or two forms of intellectual endeavour, and therefore, so he said, was not fitted in its present mood to form a calm judgment of great affairs.

"The South is not sufficiently arithmetical," he said; "statistics are dry, but they are very useful on the eve of a great war. The South, however, has always scorned mathematics; she doesn't know even now the vast resources of the North, her tremendous industrial machinery which also supports the machinery of war, and above all she does not know that the North is only now beginning to be aroused. Even to this day the South is narrow, and, on the whole, ignorant of the world."

Prescott, who knew these things already, did not like, nevertheless, to hear them said by another, and he was in arms at once to defend his native section.

"It may be as you say, Mr. Secretary," he replied, "and I have no doubt it is true that the North is just gathering her full strength for the war, but you will see no shirking of the struggle on the part of the Southern people. They are rooted deep in the soil, and will make a better fight because of the faults to which you point."

The Secretary did not reply. They were now close to the fortifications and could see the sentinels, as they walked the earthworks, blowing on their fingers to keep them warm. On one side they caught a slight glimpse of the river, a sheet of ice in its bed, and on the other the hills, with the trees glittering in icy sheaths like coats of mail.

"It is time to turn back," said Mr. Sefton, "and I wish to say again that I like you, but I also warn you once more that I shall not spare you because of it; my weakness does not go so far. I wish you out of my way, and I have offered you an alternative which you decline. Many men in my position would have crushed you at once; so I take credit to myself. You adhere to your refusal?"

"Certainly I do," replied Prescott with emphasis.

"And you take the risk?"

"I take the risk."

"Very well, there is no need to say more. I warn you to look out for yourself."

"I shall do so," replied Prescott, and he laughed lightly and with a little irony.

They walked slowly back to the city, saying no more on the subject which lay nearest to their hearts, but talking of the war and its chances. A company of soldiers shivering in their scanty gray uniforms passed them.

"From Mississippi," said the Secretary; "they arrived only yesterday, and this, though the south to us, is a cruel north to them. But there will not be many like these to come."

They parted in the city, and the Secretary did not repeat his threats; but Prescott knew none the less that he meant them.

CHAPTER XII

A FLIGHT BY TWO

It was about ten by the watch, and a very cold, dark and quiet night, when Prescott reached the Grayson cottage and paused a moment at the gate, the dry snow crumbling under his heels. There was no light in the window, nor could he see any smoke rising from the chimney. The coal must be approaching the last lump, he thought, and the gold would be gone soon, too. But there was another and greater necessity than either of those driving him on, and, opening the gate, he quickly knocked upon the door. It was low but heavy, a repeated and insistent knock, like the muffled tattoo of a drum, and at last Miss Grayson answered, opening the door a scant four inches and staring out with bright eyes.

"Mr. Prescott!" she exclaimed, "it is you! You again! Ah, I have warned you and for your own good, too! You cannot enter here!"

"But I must come in," he replied; "and it is for my own good, too, as well as yours and Miss Catherwood's."

She looked at him with searching inquiry.

"Don't you see that I am freezing on your doorstep?" he said humourously.

He saw her frown plainly by the faint flicker of the firelight, and knew she did not relish a jest at such a time.

"Let me in and I will tell you everything," he added quickly. "It is an errand more urgent than any on which I have come before."

She opened the door slowly, belief and unbelief competing in her mind, and when it was closed again Prescott insisted upon knowing at once if Miss Catherwood were still in the house.

"Yes, she is here," Miss Grayson replied at last and reluctantly.

"Then I must see her and see her now," said Prescott, as he quietly took a seat in the chair before her.

"You cannot see her again," said Miss Grayson.

"I do not move from this chair until she comes," said Prescott resolutely, as he spread his fingers out to the tiny blaze.

Miss Grayson gave him one angry glance; her lips moved as if she would say something, but changing her mind, she took a chair on the other side of the fire and her face also bore the cast of resolution.

"It is no use, Miss Grayson," said Prescott. "I am here for the best of purposes, I assure you, and I will not stir. Please call Miss Catherwood."

Miss Grayson held out for a minute or two longer, and then, a red spot in either cheek, she walked into the next room and returned with Lucia.

Prescott knew her step, light as it was, before she came, and his heart beat a little more heavily. He rose, too, and bowed with deep respect when she appeared, feeling a strange thrill of pleasure at seeing her again.

He had wondered in what aspect she would appear, she whose nature seemed to him so varied and contradictory, and whose face was the index to these changing phases. She came in quietly, a young girl, pale, inquiring, yet saying no word; but there was a sparkle in her gaze that made the blood leap for a moment to Prescott's face.

"Miss Catherwood," he said, "you forbade me to return here, but I have come nevertheless."

She was still silent, her inquiring look upon him.

"You must leave Richmond to-night!" he said. "There must be no delay."

She made a gesture as if she would call his attention to the frozen world outside and said:

"I am willing enough to leave Richmond if I knew a way."

"I will find the way—I go with you!"

"That I cannot permit; you shall not risk your future by making such an attempt with me."

"It will certainly be risked greatly if I do not make the attempt with you," he replied.

They looked at him in wonder. Prescott saw now, by a sudden intuition, the course of action that would appeal to them most, and he said:

"It is as much for my sake as it is for yours. That you are here is known to a man powerful in this Government, and he knows also that I am aware of your presence. There is to be another search for you and I shall be forced to lead it. It means my ruin unless you escape before that search begins."

Then he explained to them as much as he thought necessary, although he did not give Mr. Sefton's name, and dwelt artfully upon his own peril rather than upon hers.

Lucia Catherwood neither moved nor spoke as Prescott told the story. Once there was a strange light in her eyes as she regarded him, but it was momentary, gone like a flash, and her face remained expressionless.

"But is there a way?" asked Miss Grayson in doubt and alarm.

"I shall find a way," replied Prescott confidently. "Lift the curtain from the window and look. The night is dark and cold; all who can will be under roofs, and even the sentinels will hug walls and earthworks. Now is our time."

"You must go, Lucia," said Miss Grayson decisively.

Miss Catherwood bowed assent and went at once to the next room to prepare for the journey.

"Will you care for her as if she were your own, your sister?" asked Miss Grayson, turning appealingly to Prescott.

"As God is my witness," he replied, and the ring in his tone was so deep and true that she could not doubt it.

"I believe you," said this bravest of old maids, looking him steadfastly in the eye for a few moments and then following the girl into the next room.

Prescott sat alone by the fire, staring at three or four coals that glowed redly on the hearth, and wondering how he should escape with this girl from Richmond. He had said confidently that he should find a way and he believed he would, but he knew of none.

They came back presently, the girl wrapped to the eyes in a heavy black cloak.

"It is Miss Grayson's," she said with a touch of humour. "She has consented to take my brown one in its place."

"Overshoes?" said Prescott, interrogatively.

Her feet peeped from beneath her dress.

"Two pairs," she replied. "I have on both Charlotte's and my own."

"Gloves?"

She held out her hands enclosed in the thickest mittens.

"You will do," said Prescott; "and now is the time for us to go."

He turned his back while these two women, tried by so many dangers, wished each other farewell. There were no tears, no vehement protestations; just a silent, clinging embrace, a few words spoken low, and then the parting. Prescott's own eyes were moist. There must be unusual qualities in these two women to inspire so deep an attachment, so much capacity for sacrifice.

He opened the door an inch or so and, looking out, beheld a city silent and dark, like a city of the dead.

"Come," he said, and the two went out into the silence and cold desolation. He glanced back and saw the door yet open a few inches. Then it closed and the brave old maid was left alone.

The girl shivered at the first touch of the night and Prescott asked anxiously if she found the cold too great.

"Only for a moment," she replied. "Which way shall we go?"

He started at the question, not yet having chosen a course, and replied in haste:

"We must reach the Baltimore road; it is not so far to the Northern pickets, and when we approach them I can leave you."

"And you?" she said, "What is to become of you?"

All save her eyes was hidden by the dark cloak, but she looked up and he saw there a light like that which had shone when she came forth to meet him in the house.

"I?" he replied lightly. "Don't worry about me. I shall return to Richmond and then help my army to fight and beat your army. Really General Lee couldn't spare me, you know. Come!"

They stole forward, two shadows in the deeper shadow, the dry snow rustling like paper under their feet. From some far point came the faint cry of a sentinel, announcing to a sleepy world that all was well, and after that the silence hung heavily as ever over the city. The cold was not unpleasant to either of them, muffled as they were in heavy clothing, for it imparted briskness and vigour to their strong young bodies, and they went on at a swift pace through the densest part of the city, into the thinning suburbs and then toward the fields and open spaces which lay on the nearer side of the earthworks. Not a human being did they see not a dog barked at them as they passed, scarcely a light showed in a window; all around them the city lay in a lethargy beneath its icy covering.

Involuntarily the girl, oppressed by the loneliness which had taken on a certain weird quality, walked closer to Prescott, and he could faintly hear her breathing as she fled with him, step for step.

"The Baltimore road lies there," he said, "and yonder are earthworks. See! Where the faint light is twinkling! that low line is what we have to pass."

They heard the creaking of wagons and the sound of voices as of men speaking to horses, and stopped to listen. Then they beheld lights nearer by on the left.

"Stay here a moment and I'll see what it is," said Prescott.

"Oh, don't leave me!" she cried with a sudden tremour.

"It is only for a moment," he replied, glad to hear that sudden tremour in her voice.

Turning aside he found close at hand an obscure tavern, and beside it at least a dozen wagons, the horses hitched as if ready for a journey. He guessed immediately that these were the wagons of farmers who had been selling provisions in the city. The owners were inside taking something to warm them up for the home journey and the horses outside were stamping their feet with the same purpose.

"Not likely to bother us," was Prescott's unspoken comment as he returned to the girl who stood motionless in the snow awaiting him. "It is nothing," he said. "We must go forward now, watch our chance and slip through the earthworks."

She did not speak, but went on with him, showing an infinite trust that appealed to every fiber of his being. The chill of the wintry night had been driven away by vigourous exercise, but its tonic effect remained with both, and now their courage began to rise as they approached the first barrier. It seemed to them that they could not fail on such a night.

"There is an interval yonder between two of the earthworks," said Prescott. "I'm sure we can pass them."

Silently they approached the opening. The moon glimmered but faintly across the white snow, and no sign of life came from the earthworks. But as they drew near a sentinel, gun on shoulder, appeared walking back and forth, and beyond where his post ended was another soldier, likewise walking back and forth, gun on shoulder.

"It is evident that our way doesn't lie there," said Prescott, turning back quickly lest the sentinel should see them and demand an explanation.

"What shall we do?" she asked, seeming now to trust to him implicitly.

"Why, try another place," he replied lightly. "If at first you don't succeed, try, try again."

They tried again and failed as before. The sentinels of the Confederacy everywhere were watchful, despite the wintry night and the little apparent need of precaution. Yet the two were drawn closer and closer together by the community of hope and despair, and when at last they drifted back toward the tavern and the wagons Prescott felt as if he, too, were seeking to escape from Richmond to join the Army of the North. He even found it in his heart to condemn the vigilance of his own.

"Captain Prescott," said the girl, as they stood watching the light in the tavern window, "I insist that you leave me here. I wish to make an attempt alone. Why should you risk yourself?"

"Even if you passed the fortifications," he replied, "you would perish in the frozen hills beyond. Do you think I have come so far to turn back now?"

Staring at the wagons and the stamping horses, he noticed one of the farmers come out of the tavern. His appearance gave Prescott a happy inspiration.

"Stay here a moment or two, Miss Catherwood," he said. "I want to talk to that man."

She obeyed without a word of protest, and he approached the farmer, who lurched toward one of the wagons. Prescott had marked this suggestive lurch, and it gave him an idea.

The farmer, heated by many warm drinks, was fumbling with the gear of his horses when Prescott approached, and to his muddled eyes the stranger seemed at least a general, looming very stiff and very tall with his great military cloak drawn threateningly about him.

"What is your name?" asked Prescott sternly.

The severe tone made a deep and proper impression on the intoxicated gentleman's agricultural mind, so he replied promptly, though with a stutter:

"Elias Gardner."

"Where are you from, Elias, and what are you doing here?"

The military discipline about Richmond was very strict, and the farmer, anxious to show his good standing, replied with equal promptness:

"From Wellsville. I've been selling a load of farm truck in Richmond. Oh, I've got my pass right enough, Colonel."

He took his pass from his pocket and handed it to the man who from the dignity and severity of his manner might be a general officer. Prescott looking at it felt a thrill of joy, but there was no change in the sternness of his tone when he addressed the farmer again.

"Why, this pass," he said, "is made out to Elias Gardner *and wife*. You said nothing about your wife."

The farmer was somewhat confused, and explained hastily that his wife was going to stay awhile in Richmond with relatives, while he went home alone. In three or four days he would be back with another load of provisions and then he could get her. The face of the stern officer gradually relaxed and he accused the good Mr. Gardner of taking advantage of his wife's absence to enjoy himself. Prescott nodded his head slightly toward the tavern, and the farmer, taking courage from the jocular contraction of the Colonel's left eye, did not resent the insinuation. On the contrary, he enjoyed it, feeling that he was a devil of a fellow, and significantly tapped the left pocket of his coat, which gave forth a ring as of glass.

"The quality of yours is bad," said Prescott. "Here, try mine; it's like velvet to the throat, a tonic to the stomach, and it means sweet sleep to-morrow."

Drawing from his pocket his own well-filled flask, with which from prudential motives he had provided himself before undertaking his journey, he handed it to Mr. Gardner of Wellsville and made him drink deep and long.

When the farmer finished he sighed deeply, and words of appreciation and gratitude flowed from his tongue.

"Bah, man!" said Prescott, "you cannot drink at all. You do not get the real taste of it with one little sip like that on such a cold night as this. Here, drink it down a real drink, this time. Are you a girl to refuse such liquor?"

The last taunt struck home, and Mr. Gardner of Wellsville, making a mighty suspiration, drank so long and deep that the world wavered when he handed the flask back to Prescott, and a most generous fire leaped up and sparkled in his veins. But when he undertook to step forward the treacherous earth slid from under his feet, and it was only the arm of the friendly officer that kept him from falling. He tried to reach his wagon, but it unkindly moved off into space.

Prescott helped him to the wagon and then into it. "How my head goes round!" murmured the poor farmer.

"Another taste of this will put you all right," said Prescott, and he forced the neck of his flask into Elias Gardner's mouth. Elias drank deeply, either because he wanted to or because he could not help himself, and closing his eyes dropped off to slumber as peacefully as a tired child.

Prescott laid Mr. Gardner down in the bed of his own wagon, and then this chivalrous Confederate officer picked a man's pocket—deliberately and with malice aforethought. But he did not take much—only a piece of paper with a little writing on it, which he put in the pocket of his waistcoat. Moreover, as a sort of compensation he pulled off the man's overcoat—which was a poor one—and putting it on his own shoulders, wrapped his heavy military cloak around the prostrate farmer. Then he stretched him out in a comfortable place in the wagon bed and heaped empty sacks above him until Elias was as cozy as if he had been in his own bed at home.

Having placed empty chicken crates on either side of Elias and others across the top, to form a sort of roof beneath which the man still slept sweetly, though invisibly, Prescott contemplated his work for a moment with deep satisfaction. Then he summoned the girl, and the two, mounting the seat, drove the impatient horses along the well-defined road through the snow towards the interval between the earthworks.

"It is necessary for me to inform you, Miss Catherwood, that you're not Miss Catherwood at all," said Prescott.

A faint gleam of humour flickered in her eye.

"And who am I, pray?" she asked.

"You are a much more respectable young woman than that noted Yankee spy," replied Prescott in a light tone. "You are Mrs. Elias Gardner, the wife of a most staid and worthy farmer, of strong Southern proclivities, living twenty miles out on the Baltimore road."

"And who are you?" she asked, the flicker of humour reappearing in her eye.

"I am Mr. Elias Gardner, your husband, and, as I have just said, a most honest and worthy man, but, unfortunately, somewhat addicted to the use of strong liquors, especially on a night as cold as this."

If Prescott's attention had not been demanded then by the horses he would have seen a rosy glow appear on her face. But it passed in a moment, and she remained silent.

Then he told her of the whole lucky chance, his use of it, and how the way now lay clear before them.

"We shall take Mr. Gardner back home," he said, "and save him the trouble of driving. It will be one of the easiest and most comfortable journeys that he ever took, and not a particle of harm will come to him from it."

"But you? How will you get back into Richmond?"

She looked at him anxiously as she spoke.

"How do you know that I want to return?"

"I am speaking seriously."

"I am sure it will not be a difficult matter," he said. "A man alone can pass the fortifications of any city without much trouble. It is not a matter that I worry about at all. But please remember that you are Mrs. Elias Gardner, my wife, as questions may be asked of you before this night's journey ends."

The flush stole over her cheeks again, but she said nothing.

Prescott picked up the long whip, called a "black snake," which was lying on the seat and cracked it over the horses, a fine, sturdy pair, as he had noticed already. They stepped briskly along, as if anxious to warm themselves after their long wait in the cold, and Prescott, who was a good driver, felt the glorious sensation of triumph over difficulties glowing within him.

"Ho, for a fine ride, Mrs. Gardner!" he said gaily to the girl.

His high spirits were infectious and she smiled back at him.

"With such an accomplished driver holding the lines, and so fine a chariot as this, it ought to be," she replied.

The horses blew the steam from their nostrils, the dry snow crunched under their heels, and the real Elias Gardner slumbered peacefully under his own chicken crates as they approached the earthworks.

As before, when they had walked instead of coming in their own private carriage, they soon saw the sentinel, half frozen but vigilant, and he promptly halted them. Prescott produced at once the pass that he had picked from the pocket of the unconscious Elias, and the sentinel called the officer of the guard, who appeared holding a dim lantern and yawning mightily.

Now this officer of the guard was none other than Thomas Talbot, Esquire, himself, as large as life but uncommonly sleepy, and anxious to have done with his task. Prescott was startled by his friend's appearance there at such a critical moment, but he remembered that the night was dark and he was heavily muffled.

Talbot looked at the pass, expressed his satisfaction and handed it back to Prescott, who replaced it in his waistcoat pocket with ostentatious care.

"Cold night for a long drive," said Talbot, wishing to be friendly.

Prescott nodded but did not speak.

"Especially for a lady," added Talbot gallantly.

Miss Catherwood nodded also, and with muttered thanks Prescott, gathering up the lines, drove on.

"That was a particular friend of mine," he said, when they were beyond the hearing of the outpost, "but I do not recall a time when the sight of him was more unwelcome."

"Well, at any rate, he was less troublesome than friends often are."

"Now, don't forget that you are still Mrs. Elias Gardner of Wellsville," he continued, "as there are more earthworks and outposts to pass."

"I don't think that fugitives often flee from a city in their own coach and four," she said with that recurring flicker of humour.

"At least not in such a magnificent chariot as ours," he said, looking around at the lumbering farm wagon. The feeling of exultation was growing upon him. When he had resolved to find a way he did not see one, but behold, he had found it and it was better than any for which he had hoped. They were not merely walking out of Richmond—they were driving and in comfort. The road seemed to have been made smooth and pleasant for them.

There was another line of earthworks and an outpost beyond, but the pass for honest Elias Gardner and wife was sufficient. The officer, always a young man and disposed to be friendly, would glance at it, wave them on their way and retreat to shelter as quickly as possible.

The last barrier was soon crossed and they were alone in the white desolation of the snow-covered hills and forests. Meanwhile, the real Elias Gardner slumbered peacefully in his own wagon, the "world forgetting and by the world forgot."

"You must go back, Captain Prescott, as I am now well beyond the Confederate lines encircling Richmond and can readily care for myself," said Miss Catherwood.

But he refused to do so, asserting with indignation that it was not his habit to leave his tasks half finished, and he could not abandon her in such a frozen waste as that lying around them. She protested no further, and Prescott, cracking his whip over the horses, increased their speed, but before long they settled into an easy walk. The city behind sank down in the darkness, and before them curved the white world of hills and forests, white even under its covering of a somber night.

CHAPTER XIII

LUCIA'S FAREWELL

Prescott has never forgotten that night, the long ride, the relief from danger, the silent woman by his side; and there was in all a keen enjoyment, of a kind deeper and more holy than he had ever known before. He had saved a woman, a woman whom he could admire, from a great danger; it was hers rather than his own that appealed to him, and he was thankful. In her heart, too, was a devout gratitude and something more.

The worthy Elias Gardner, slumbering so peacefully under his crates, was completely forgotten, and they two were alone with the universe. The clouds by and by passed away and the heavens shone blue and cold; a good moon came out, and the white hills and forests, touched by it, flashed now and then with the gleam of silver. All the world was at peace; there was no sign of war in the night nor in those snowy solitudes. Before them stretched the road, indicated by a long line of wheel tracks in the snow, and behind them was nothing. Prescott, by and by, let the lines drop on the edge of the wagon-bed, and the horses chose their own way, following with mere instinct the better path.

He began now to see himself as he was, to understand the impulse that had driven him on. Here by his side, her warm breath almost on his face, was the girl he had saved, but he took no advantage of time and place, infringing in no degree upon the respect due to every woman. He had come even this night believing her a spy, but now he held her as something holy.

She spoke by and by of the gratitude she owed him, not in many words, but strong ones, showing how deeply she felt all she said, and he did not seek to silence her, knowing the relief it would give her to speak.

Presently she told him of herself. She came from that borderland between North and South which is of both though not wholly of either, but her sympathies from the first had turned to the North, not so much through personal feeling, but because of a belief that it would be better for the North to triumph. The armies had come, her uncle with whom she had lived had fallen in battle, and their home was destroyed, by which army she did not know. Then she turned involuntarily to her nearest relative, Miss Grayson, in whose home she knew she would receive protection, and who, she knew, too, would share her sympathies. So she had come to Richmond.

She said nothing of the accusation, the affair of the papers, and Prescott longed to ask her again if she were guilty, and to hear her say that she was not. He was not willing to believe her a spy, that she could ever stoop to such an act; and here in the darkness with her by his side, with only purity and truth in her eyes, he could not believe her one. But when she was away he knew that his doubts would return. Then he would ask himself if he had not been tricked and used by a woman as beautiful and clever as she was ruthless. Now he saw only her beauty and what seemed to him the truth of her eyes, and he swore again silently and for the twentieth time that he would not leave her until he saw her safe within the Northern lines. So little thought he then of his own risks, and so willing a traitor was he, for a moment, and for the sake of one woman's eyes, to the cause that he served. But a traitor only in seeming, and not in reality, he would have said of himself with truth.

"What do you intend to do now?" asked Prescott at last.

"There is much in the trail of our army that I can do," she said. "There will be many wounded soon."

"Yes, when the snow goes," said Prescott. "Doesn't it seem strange that the dead cold of winter alone should mean peace nowadays?"

Both spoke solemnly. For the time the thought of war inspired Prescott with the most poignant repulsion, since he was taking this girl to the army which he expected to fight.

"There is one question which I should like to ask you," he said after awhile.

"What is it?"

"Where were you hidden that day my friend Talbot searched for you and I looked on?"

She glanced quickly up into his face, and her lips curved in the slightest smile. There was, too, a faint twinkle in her eye.

"You have asked me for the second time the one question that I cannot answer," she replied. "I am sorry to disappoint you, Captain Prescott, but ask me anything else and I think I can promise a reply. This one is a secret not mine to tell."

57

Silence fell once more over them and the world about them. There was no noise save the soft crush of the horses' feet in the snow and the crunch of the wagon wheels. The silvery glow of the moon still fell across the hills, and the trees stood motionless like white but kindly sentinels.

Prescott by and by took his flask from his pocket.

"Drink some of this," he said; "you must. The cold is insidious and you should fend it off."

So urged she drank a little, and then Prescott, stopping the horses, climbed back in the wagon-bed.

"It would be strange," he said, "if our good farmer prepared for a twenty-mile drive without taking along something to eat."

"And please see that he is comfortable," she said. "I know these are war times, but we are treating him hardly."

Prescott laughed.

"You shouldn't feel any remorse," he said. "Our worthy Elias was never more snug in his life. He's still sleeping as sweetly as a baby, and is as warm as a rabbit in its nest. Ah, here we are! Cold ham, light bread, and cold boiled eggs. I'll requisition them, but I'll pay him for them. It's a pity we can't feed the horses, too."

He took a coin from his pocket and thrust it into that of the sleeping farmer. Then he spread the food upon the seat of the wagon, and the two ate with hearty appetites due to the cold, their exertions and the freedom from apprehension.

Prescott had often eaten of more luxurious fare, but none that he enjoyed more than that frugal repast, in a lonely wagon on a cold and dark winter morning. Thrilled with a strange exhilaration, he jested and found entertainment in everything, and the girl beside him began to share his high spirits, though she said little, but laughed often at his speeches. Prescott never before had seen in her so much of feminine gentleness, and it appealed to him, knowing how strong and masculine her character could be at times. Now she left the initiative wholly to him, as if she had put herself in his hands and trusted him fully, obeying him, too, with a sweet humility that stirred the deeps of his nature.

At last they finished the crumbs of the farmer's food and Prescott regretfully drove on.

"The horses have had a good rest, too," he said, "and I've no doubt they needed it."

The character of the night did not change, still the same splendid white silence, and just they two alone in the world.

"We must be at least twenty miles from Richmond," said the girl.

"I haven't measured the time," Prescott replied, "but it's an easy progress. I am quite sure that if we keep on going long enough we'll arrive somewhere at last."

"I think it likely," she said, smiling. "I wonder that we don't see any houses."

"Virginia isn't the most densely peopled country in the world, and we are coming to a pretty sterile region that won't support much life in the best of times."

"Are we on doubtful ground?"

"That or very near it."

They passed at least one or two houses by the roadside, but they were lone and dark. No lean Virginia dogs howled at them and the solitary and desolate character of the country did not abate.

"Are you cold?" asked Prescott.

"Not at all," she replied. "I have never in my life taken an easier journey. It seems that fortune has been with us."

"Fortune favours the good or ought to do so."

"How long do you think it is until daylight?"

"I don't know; an hour, I suppose; why bother about it?"

Certainly Prescott was not troubling his head by trying to determine the exact distance to daylight, but he began to think for the first time of his journey's end. He must leave Miss Catherwood somewhere in comparative safety, and he must get back to Richmond, his absence unnoted. These were problems which might well become vexing, and the exaltation of the moment could not prevent their recurrence. He stopped the wagon and took a look at the worthy Elias, who was slumbering as peacefully as ever. "A sound conscience makes a sound sleeper," he quoted, and then he inspected the country.

It was a little wilderness of hills and scrub forest, all lying under the deep snow, and without sign of either human or animal life.

"There is nothing to do but drive on," he said. "If I only dared to wake our friend, the farmer, we might find out from him which way the nearest Northern pickets lie."

"You should let me go now, Captain Prescott, I beg you again."

"Abandon you in this snowy waste! I claim to be an American gentleman, Miss Catherwood. But if we don't strike a promising lead soon I shall waken our friend Elias, and he will have to point a way, whether he will or no."

But that threat was saved as a last resort, and he drove quietly around the curve of a hill. When they reached the other side, there was the rapid crunch of hoofs in the snow, an abrupt command to halt, and they found themselves surrounded by a dozen troopers. Prescott recognized the faded blue uniform and knew at once that he was in the midst of Yankee horsemen. The girl beside him gave one start at the sudden apparition and then became calm and impassive.

"Who are you?" asked the leader of the horsemen, a lieutenant.

"Elias Gardner of Wellsville," replied Prescott in a drawling, rural voice.

"That tells nothing," said the Lieutenant.

"It's my name, anyhow," replied Prescott coolly, "and if you don't believe it, here's a pass they gave me when I went into Richmond with a load of produce."

The Lieutenant read the paper by the moonlight and then handed it back to its temporary owner.

"It's all right," he said; "but I want to know, Mr. Elias Gardner and Mrs. Elias Gardner, what you mean by feeding the enemy."

"I'd sell to you at the same price," replied Prescott.

Some of the troopers were looking at the barrels and crates in the wagons to see if they were really empty, and Prescott was in dread lest they come upon the sleeping farmer; but they desisted soon, satisfied that there was nothing left to eat.

The Lieutenant cocked a shrewd eye on Prescott.

"So you've been in Richmond, Mr. Farmer; how long were you there?" he asked.

"Only a day."

"Don't you think it funny, Mr. Farmer, that you should go so easily into a town that armies of a hundred thousand men have been trying for more than two years to enter and have failed?"

"Maybe I showed better judgment," Prescott replied, unable to restrain a gibe.

The Lieutenant laughed.

"Perhaps you are right," he said; "but we'll have Grant soon. Now, Mr. Gardner, you've been in Richmond, and I've no doubt you used your eyes while you were there, for you look to me like a keen, observant man. I suspect that you could tell some interesting things about their earthworks, forts and so forth."

Prescott held up his hands in mock consternation.

"I ain't no soldier," he replied in his drawling tone. "I wouldn't know a fort if I saw one, and I never get near such things if I know it."

"Then perhaps Mrs. Gardner took notice," continued the Lieutenant in a wheedling tone. "Women are always observant."

Miss Catherwood shook her head.

"See here, you two," said the Lieutenant, "if you'll only tell me about those fortifications I'll pay you more than you got for that load of produce."

"We don't know anything," said Prescott; "ain't sure there are any fortifications at all."

"Confound it!" exclaimed the Lieutenant in a vexed tone, "a Northern man can never get anything out of these Virginia farmers!"

Prescott stared at him and grinned a little.

"Go on!" said the Lieutenant, waving his hand in anger. "There's a camp of ours a mile farther ahead. They'll stop you, and I only hope they'll get as much out of you as I have."

Prescott gladly obeyed the command and the Northern horsemen galloped off, their hoof-beats making little noise in the snow. But as he drove on he turned his head slightly and watched them until they were out of sight. When he was sure they were far away he stopped his own horses.

"Will you wait here a moment in the wagon, Miss Catherwood, until I go to the top of the hill?" he asked.

She nodded, and springing out, Prescott ran to the crest. There looking over into the valley, he saw the camp of which the Lieutenant had spoken, a cluster of tents and a ring of smoking fires with horses tethered beyond, the brief stopping place of perhaps five hundred men, as Prescott, with a practised eye, could quickly tell.

He saw now the end of the difficulty, but he did not rejoice as he had hoped.

"Beyond this hill in the valley, and within plain view from the crest, is the camp of your friends, Miss Catherwood," he said. "Our journey is over. We need not take the wagon any farther, as it belongs to our sleeping friend, the farmer, but you can go on now to this Northern detachment—a raiding party, I presume, but sure to treat you well. I thank God that the time is not yet when a woman is not safe in the camp of either North or South. Come!"

She dismounted from the wagon and slowly they walked together to the top of the hill. Prescott pointed to the valley, where the fires glowed redly across the snow.

"Here I leave you," he said.

She looked up at him and the glow of the fires below was reflected in her eyes.

"Shall we ever see each other again?" she asked.

"That I cannot tell," he replied.

She did not go on just yet, lingering there a little.

"Captain Prescott," she asked, "why have you done so much for me?"

"Upon my soul I do not know," he replied.

She looked up in his face again, and he saw the red blood rising in her cheeks. Borne away by a mighty impulse, he bent over and kissed her, but she, uttering a little cry, ran down the hill toward the Northern camp.

He watched her until he saw her draw near the fires and men come forward to meet her. Then he went back to the wagon and drove it into a side path among some trees, where he exchanged outer clothing again with the farmer, awakening the amazed man directly afterward from his slumbers. Prescott offered no explanations, but soothed the honest man's natural anger with a gold eagle, and, leaving him there, not three miles from his home, went back on foot.

He slipped easily into Richmond the next night, and before morning was sleeping soundly in his own bed.

CHAPTER XIV

PRESCOTT'S ORDEAL

Prescott was awakened from his sleep by his mother, who came to him in suppressed anxiety, telling him that a soldier was in the outer room with a message demanding his instant presence at headquarters. At once there flitted through his mind a dream of that long night, now passed, the flight together, the ride, the warm and luminous presence beside him and the last sight of her as she passed over the hill to the fires that burned in the Northern camp. A dream it was, vague and misty as the darkness through which they had passed, but it left a delight, vague and misty like itself, that refused to be dispelled by the belief that this message was from Mr. Sefton, who intended to strike where his armour was weakest.

With the power of repression inherited from his Puritan mother he hid from her pleasure and apprehension alike, saying:

"Some garrison duty, mother. You know in such a time of war I can't expect to live here forever in ease and luxury."

The letter handed to him by the messenger, an impassive Confederate soldier in butternut gray, was from the commandant of the forces in Richmond, ordering him to report to Mr. Sefton for instructions. Here were all his apprehensions justified. The search had been made, the soldiers had gone to the cottage of Miss Grayson, the girl was not there, and the Secretary now turned to him, Robert Prescott, as if he were her custodian, demanding her, or determined to know what he had done with her. Well, his own position was uncertain, but she at least was safe—far beyond the lines of Richmond, now with her own people, and neither the hand of Sefton nor of any other could touch her. That thought shed a pleasant glow, all the more grateful because it was he who had helped her. But toward the Secretary he felt only defiance.

As he went forth to obey the summons the city was bright, all white and silver and gold in its sheet of ice, with a wintry but golden sun above; but something was missing from Richmond, nevertheless. It suddenly occurred to him that Miss Grayson must be very lonely in her bleak little cottage.

He went undisturbed by guards to the Secretary's room—the Confederate Government was never immediately surrounded with bayonets—and knocked upon the door. A complete absence of state and formality prevailed.

The Secretary was not alone, and Prescott was not surprised. The President of the Confederacy himself sat near the window, and just beyond him was Wood, in a great armchair, looking bored. There were present, too, General Winder, the commander of the forces in the city, another General or two and members of the Cabinet.

"An inquisition," thought Prescott. "This disappointed Secretary would ruin me."

The saving thought occurred to him that if he had known of Miss Catherwood's presence in Richmond Mr. Sefton also had known of it. The wily Secretary must have in view some other purpose than to betray him, when by so doing he would also betray himself. Prescott gathered courage, and saluting, stood respectfully, though in the attitude of one who sought no favour.

All the men in the room looked at him, some with admiration of the strong young figure and the open, manly face, others with inquiry. He wondered that Wood, a man who belonged essentially to the field of battle, should be there; but the cavalry leader, for his great achievements, was high in the esteem of the Confederate Government.

It was the Secretary, Mr. Sefton, who spoke, for the others seemed involuntarily to leave to him subjects requiring craft and guile—a tribute or not as one chooses to take it.

"The subject upon which we have called you is not new to us nor to you," said the Secretary in expressionless tones. "We revert to the question of a spy—a woman. It is now known that it was a woman who stole the important papers from the office of the President. The secret service of General Winder has learned that she has been in this city all the while—that is, until the last night or two."

He paused here a few moments as if he would mark the effect of his words, and his eyes and those of Prescott met. Prescott tried to read what he saw there—to pierce the subconscious depths, and he felt as if he perceived the soul of this man—a mighty ambition under a silky exterior, and a character in which a dual nature struggled. Then his eyes wandered a moment to Wood. Both he and Sefton were mountaineers in the beginning, and what a contrast now! But he stood waiting for the Secretary to proceed.

"It has become known to us," continued the Secretary, "that this dangerous spy—dangerous because of the example she has set, and because of the connections that she may have here—has just escaped from the city. She was concealed in the house of Miss Charlotte Grayson, a well-known Northern sympathizer—a house which you are now known, Captain Prescott, to have visited more than once."

Prescott looked again into the Secretary's eyes and a flash of intelligence passed between them. He read once more in their depths the desire of this man to torture him—to drag him to the edge of the abyss, but not to push him over.

"There is a suspicion—or perhaps I ought to say a fear—that you have given aid and comfort to the enemy, this spy, Captain Prescott," said the Secretary.

Prescott's eyes flashed with indignant fire.

"I have been wounded five times in the service of the Confederacy," he replied, "and I have here an arm not fully recovered from the impact of a Northern bullet." He turned his left arm as he spoke. "If that was giving aid and comfort to the enemy, then I am guilty."

A murmur of approval arose. He had made an impression.

"It was by my side at Chancellorsville that he received one of his wounds," said Wood in his peculiar slow, drawling tones.

Prescott shot him a swift and grateful glance.

But the Secretary persisted. He was not to be turned aside, not even by the great men of the Confederacy who sat in the room about him.

"No one doubts the courage of Captain Prescott," he said, "because that has been proved too often—you see, Captain, we are familiar with your record—but even the best of men may become exposed to influences that cause an unconscious change of motive. I repeat that none of us is superior to it."

Prescott saw at once the hidden meaning in the words, and despite himself a flush rose to his face. Perhaps it was true.

The Secretary looked away toward the window, his glance seeming to rest on the white world of winter outside, across which the yellow streaks of sunlight fell like a golden tracery. He interlaced his fingers thoughtfully upon his knees while he waited for an answer. But Prescott had recovered his self-possession.

"I do not know what you mean," he said. "I am not accustomed, perhaps, to close and delicate analysis of my own motives, but this I will say, that I have never knowingly done anything that I thought would cause the Confederacy harm; while, on the contrary, I have done all I could—so far as my knowledge went—that would do it good."

As he spoke he glanced away from the Secretary toward the others, and he thought he saw the shadow of a smile on the face of the President. What did it mean? He was conscious again of the blood flushing to his face. It was the President himself who next spoke.

"Do you know where this woman is, Captain Prescott?" he asked.

"No, I do not know where she is," he replied, thankful that the question had come in such a form.

Wood, the mountaineer, moved impatiently. He was of an impetuous disposition, untrammeled by rule, and he stood in awe of nobody.

"Gentlemen," he said, "I can't exactly see the drift of all this talk. I'd as soon believe that any of us would be a traitor as Captain Prescott, an' I don't think we've got much time to waste on matters like this. Grant's a-comin'. I tell you, gentlemen, we've got to think of meetin' him and not of huntin' for a woman spy."

He spoke with emphasis, and again Prescott shot him another swift and grateful glance.

"There is no question of treason, General Wood," said Mr. Sefton placidly. "None of us would wrong Captain Prescott by imputing to him such a crime. I merely suggested an unconscious motive that might have made him deflect for a moment, and for a moment only, from the straight and narrow path of duty."

Prescott saw a cruel light in the Secretary's eyes and behind it a suggestion of enjoyment in the power to make men laugh or quiver as he wished; but he did not flinch, merely repeating:

"I have done my duty to the Confederacy as best I could, and I am ready to do it again. Even the children among us know that a great battle is coming, and I ask that I be permitted again to show my loyalty at the front."

"Good words from a good man," exclaimed Wood.

"General," said the President quietly, "comments either for or against are not conducive to the progress of an examination."

Wood took the rebuke in good part, lifted a ruler from the table and with an imaginary pocket-knife began to trim long shavings from it.

Prescott, despite his feeling that he had done no moral wrong—though technically and in a military sense he had sinned—could not escape the sensation of being on trial as a criminal, and his heart rose up in indignant wrath. Those five wounds were ample reply to such a charge. He felt these questions to be an insult, and cold anger against the Secretary who was seeking to entrap or torture him rose in his heart. There came with it a resolve not to betray his part in the escape of the girl; but they never asked him whether or not he had helped her in her flight. When he noticed this his feeling of apprehension departed, and he faced the Secretary, convinced that the duel was with him alone and that these others were but seconds to whom Mr. Sefton had confided only a part of what he knew.

The Secretary asked more questions, but again they were of a general nature and did not come to the point, as he made no mention of Miss Grayson or her cottage.

Wood said nothing, but he was growing more impatient than ever, and the imaginary shavings whittled by his imaginary knife were increasing in length.

"Gentlemen," he exclaimed, "it still 'pears to me that we are wastin' time. I know Prescott an' he's all right. I don't care two cents whether or not he helped a woman to escape. S'pose she was young and pretty."

All smiled saved Sefton and Prescott.

"General, would you let gallantry override patriotism?" asked the President.

"There ain't no woman in the world that can batter down the Confederacy," replied the other stoutly. "If that is ever done, it'll take armies to do it, and I move that we adjourn."

The President looked at his watch.

"Yes," he said, "we must go. Mr. Sefton, you may continue the examination as you will and report to me. Captain Prescott, I bid you good-day, and express my wish that you may come clear from this ordeal."

Prescott bowed his thanks, but to Wood, whose active intervention in his behalf had carried much weight, he felt deeper gratitude, though he said nothing, and still stood in silence as the others went out, leaving him alone with the Secretary.

Mr. Sefton, too, was silent for a time, still interlacing his fingers thoughtfully and glancing now and then through the window. Then he looked at Prescott and his face changed. The cruelty which had lurked in his eyes disappeared and in its place came a trace of admiration, even liking.

"Captain Prescott," he said, "you have borne yourself very well for a man who knew he was wholly in the power of another, made by circumstances his enemy for the time being."

"I am not wholly in the power of anybody," replied Prescott proudly. "I repeat that I have done nothing at any time of which I am ashamed or for which my conscience reproaches me."

"That is irrelevant. It is not any question of shame or conscience, which are abstract things. It is merely one of fact—that is, whether you did or did not help Miss Catherwood, the spy, to escape. I am convinced that you helped her—not that I condemn you for it or that I am sorry you did so. Perhaps it is for my interest that you have acted thus. You were absent from your usual haunts yesterday and the night before, and it was within that time that the spy disappeared from Miss Grayson's. I have no doubt that you were with her. You see, I did not press the question when the others were here. I halted at the critical point. I had that much consideration for you."

He stopped again and the glances of these two strong men met once more; Prescott's open and defiant, Sefton's cunning and indirect.

"I hear that she is young and very beautiful," said the Secretary thoughtfully.

Prescott flushed.

"Yes, young and very beautiful," continued the Secretary. "One might even think that she was more beautiful than Helen Harley."

Prescott said nothing, but the deep flush remained on his face.

"Therefore," continued the Secretary, "I should imagine that your stay with her was not unpleasant."

"Mr. Sefton," exclaimed Prescott, taking an angry step forward, "your intimation is an insult and one that I do not propose to endure."

"You mistake my meaning," said the Secretary calmly. "I intended no such intimation as you thought, but I wonder what Helen Harley would think of the long period that you have spent with one as young and beautiful as herself."

He smiled a little, showing his white teeth, and Prescott, thrown off his guard, replied:

"She would think it a just deed."

"Then you admit that it is true?"

"I admit nothing," replied Prescott firmly. "I merely stated what I thought would be the opinion of Helen Harley concerning an act of mercy."

The Secretary smiled.

"Captain Prescott," he said, "I am not sorry that this has happened, but be assured that I am not disposed to make war upon you now. Shall we let it be an armed peace for the present?"

He showed a sudden warmth of manner and an easy agreeableness that Prescott found hard to resist. Rising from the chair, he placed his hand lightly upon Robert's arm, saying:

"I shall go with you to the street, Captain, if you will let me."

Together they left the room, the Secretary indicating the way, which was not that by which Prescott had come. They passed through a large office and here Prescott saw many clerks at work at little desks, four women among them. Helen Harley was one of the four. She was copying papers, her head bent down, her brown hair low on her forehead, unconscious of her observers.

In her simple gray dress she looked not less beautiful than on that day when, in lilac and rose, drawing every eye, she received General Morgan. She did not see them as they entered, for her head remained low and the wintry sunshine from the window gleamed across her brown hair.

The Secretary glanced at her casually, as it were, but Prescott saw a passing look on his face that he could translate into nothing but triumphant proprietorship. Mr. Sefton was feeling more confident since the examination in the room above.

"She works well," he said laconically.

"I expected as much," said Prescott.

"It is not true that people of families used to an easy life cannot become efficient when hardship arrives," continued the Secretary. "Often they bring great zeal to their new duties."

Evidently he was a man who demanded rigid service, as the clerks who saw him bent lower to their task, but Helen did not notice the two until they were about to pass through a far door. Her cheeks reddened as they went out, for it hurt her pride that Prescott should see her there—a mere clerk, honest and ennobling though she knew work to be.

The press of Richmond was not without enterprise even in those days of war and want, and it was seldom lacking in interest. If not news, then the pungent comment and criticism of Raymond and Winthrop were sure to find attentive readers, and on the day following Prescott's interview with the Secretary they furnished to their readers an uncommonly attractive story.

It had been discovered that the spy who stole the papers was a beautiful woman—a young Amazon of wonderful charms. She had been concealed in Richmond all the while—perhaps she might be in the city yet—and it was reported that a young Confederate officer, yielding to her fascinations, had hidden and helped her at the risk of his own ruin.

Here, indeed, was a story full of mystery and attraction; the city throbbed with it, and all voices were by no means condemnatory. It is a singular fact that in war people develop an extremely sentimental side, as if to atone for the harsher impulses that carry them into battle. Throughout the Civil War the Southerners wrote much so-called poetry and their newspapers were filled with it. This story of the man and the maid appealed to them. If the man had fallen—well, he had fallen in a good cause. He was not the first who had been led astray by the tender, and therefore pardonable, emotion. What did it matter if she was a Northern girl and a spy? These were merely added elements to variety and charm. If he had made a sacrifice of himself, either voluntarily or involuntarily, it was for a woman, and women understood and forgave.

They wondered what this young officer's name might be—made deft surmises, and by piecing circumstance to circumstance proved beyond a doubt that sixteen men were certainly he. It was somewhat tantalizing that at least half of these men, when accused of the crime, openly avowed their guilt and said they would do it again. Prescott, who was left out of all these calculations, owing to the gravity and soberness of his nature, read the accounts with mingled amusement and vexation. There was nothing in any of them by which he could be identified, and he decided not to inquire how the story reached the newspapers, being satisfied in his own mind that he knew already. The first to speak to him of the matter was his friend Talbot.

"Bob," he said, "I wonder if this is true. I tried to get Raymond to tell me where he got the story, but he wouldn't, and as all the newspapers have it in the same way, I suppose they got it from the same source. But if there is such a girl, and if she has been here, I hope she has escaped and that she'll stay escaped."

It was pleasant for Prescott to hear Talbot talk thus, and this opinion was shared by many others as he soon learned, and his conscience remained at ease, although he was troubled about Miss Grayson. But he met her casually on the street about a week afterward and she said:

"I have had a message from some one. She is safe and well and she is grateful." She would add no more, and Prescott did not dare visit her house, watched now with a vigilance that he knew he could not escape; but he wondered often if Lucia Catherwood and he in the heave and drift of the mighty war should ever meet again.

The gossip of Richmond was not allowed to dwell long on the story of the spy, with all its alluring mystery of the man and the maid. Greater events were at hand. A soft wind blew from the South one day. The ice broke up, the snow melted, the wind continued to blow, the earth dried—winter was gone and spring in its green robe was coming. The time of play was over. The armies rose from their sleep in the snows and began to brush the rust from the cannon. Horses stretched themselves and generals studied their maps anew. Three years of tremendous war was gone, but they were prepared for a struggle yet more gigantic.

To those in Richmond able to bear arms was sent an order—"Come at once to the front"—and among them was Prescott, nothing loath. His mother kissed him a tearless good-by, hiding her grief and fear under her Puritan face.

"I feel that this is the end, one way or the other," she said.

"I hope so, mother."

"But it may be long delayed," she added.

To Helen he said a farewell like that of a boy to the girl who has been his playmate. Although she flushed a little, causing him to flush, too, deep tenderness was absent from their parting, and there was a slight constraint that neither could fail to notice.

Talbot was going with him, Wood and Colonel Harley were gone already, and Winthrop and Raymond said they should be at the front to see. Then Prescott bade farewell to Richmond, where in the interval of war he had spent what he now knew to be a golden month or two.

CHAPTER XV

THE GREAT RIVALS

A large man sat in the shadow of a little rain-washed tent one golden May morning and gazed with unseeing eyes at the rich spectacle spread before him by Nature. The sky was a dome of blue velvet, mottled with white clouds, and against the line of the horizon a belt of intense green told where the forest was springing into new life under the vivid touch of spring. The wind bore a faint, thrilling odour of violets.

The leader was casting up accounts and trying in vain to put the balance on his own side of the ledger. He dealt much with figures, but they were never large enough for his purpose, and with the brave man's faith he could trust only in some new and strange source of supply. Gettysburg, that drawn field of glorious defeat, lay behind him, and his foe, as he knew, was gathering all his forces and choosing his ablest leader that he might hurl his utmost strength upon these thin battalions. But the soul of the lonely man rose to the crisis.

Everything about him was cast in a large mould, and the dignity and slow gravity of his manner added to his size. Thus he was not only a leader, but he had the look of one—which is far from being always so. Yet his habitual expression was of calm benevolence, his gestures whenever he moved were gentle, and his gray eyes shed a mild light. His fine white hair and beard contributed to his fatherly appearance. One might have pointed him out as the president of a famous college or the leader of a reform movement—so little does Nature indicate a man's trade by his face.

Those around the gray-haired chief, whose camp spread for miles through the green forest, were singularly unlike him in manner and bearing, and perhaps it was this sharp contrast that gave to him as he sat among his battalions the air of a patriarch. He was old; they were young. He was white of head, but one might search in vain through these ragged regiments for a gray hair. They were but boys, though they had passed through some of the greatest battles the world has ever known, and to-day, when there was a pause in the war and the wind blew from the south, they refused to be sad or to fear for the future. If the truth be told, the future was the smallest item in their reckoning. Men of their trade, especially with their youth, found the present so large that room was left for nothing else. They would take their ease now and rejoice.

Now and then they looked toward the other and larger army that lay facing them not far away, but it did not trouble them greatly. There was by mutual though tacit consent an interval of peace, and these foes, who had learned in fire and smoke to honour each other, would not break it through any act of bad faith. So some slept on the grass or the fresh-cut boughs of trees; others sang or listened to the music of old violins or accordions, while more talked on any subject that came into their minds, though their voices sank when it was of far homes not seen since long ago. Of the hostile camp facing theirs a like tale might have been told.

It seemed to Prescott, who sat near the General's tent, as if two huge picnic parties had camped near each other with the probability that they would join and become one in a short time—an illusion arising from the fact that he had gone into the war without any deep feeling over its real or alleged causes.

"Why do you study the Yankees so hard?" asked Talbot, who lay in the shade of a tree. "They are not troubling us, and I learned when I cut my eye teeth not to bother with a man who isn't bothering me—a rule that works well."

"To tell you the truth, Talbot," replied Prescott, "I was wondering how all this would end."

"The more fool you," rejoined Talbot. "Leave all that to Marse Bob. Didn't you see how hard he was thinking back there?"

Prescott scarcely heard his words, as his eyes were caught by an unusual movement in the hostile camp. He carried a pair of strong glasses, being a staff officer, and putting them to his eyes he saw at once that an event of uncommon interest was occurring within the lines of the Northern army. There was a great gathering of officers near a large tent, and beyond them the soldiers were pressing near. A puff of smoke appeared suddenly, followed by a spurt of flame, and the sound of a cannon shot thundered in their ears.

Talbot uttered an angry cry.

"What do they mean by firing on us when we're not bothering them?" he cried.

But neither shot nor shell struck near the lines of the Southern army. Peace still reigned unbroken. There was another flash of fire, another cannon shot, and then a third. More followed at regular intervals. They sounded like a signal or a salute.

"I wonder what it can mean?" said Prescott.

"If you want to find out, ask," said Talbot, and taking his comrade by the arm, he walked toward a line of Northern sentinels posted in a wood on their right.

"I've established easy communication," said Talbot; "there's a right good fellow from Vermont over here at the creek bank. He talks through his nose, but that don't hurt him. I traded him some whisky for a pouch of tobacco last night, and he'll tell us what the row is about."

Prescott accepted his suggestion without hesitation. It was common enough for the pickets on either side to grow friendly both before and after those terrific but indecisive battles so characteristic of the Civil War, a habit in which the subordinate officers sometimes shared while those of a higher rank closed their eyes. It did no military injury, and contributed somewhat to the smoothness and grace of life. The thunder of the guns, each coming after its stated interval, echoed again in their ears. A great cloud of yellowish-brown smoke rose above the trees. Prescott used his glasses once more, but he was yet unable to discover the cause of the commotion. Talbot, putting his fingers to his lips, blew a soft, low but penetrating whistle, like the distant note of a mocking-bird. A tall, thin man in faded blue, with a straggling beard on his face and a rifle in his hand, came forward among the trees.

"What do you want, Johnny Reb?" he asked in high and thin but friendly tones.

"Nothing that will cost you anything, Old Vermont," replied Talbot.

"Wall, spit it out," said the Vermonter. "If I'd been born in your State I'd commit suicide if anybody found it out. Ain't your State the place where all they need is more water and better society, just the same as hell?"

"I remember a friend of mine," said Talbot, "who took a trip once with four other men. He said they were a gentleman from South Carolina, a man from Maryland, a fellow from New York, and a damned scoundrel from Vermont. I think he hit it off just about right."

The Vermonter grinned, his mouth forming a wide chasm across the thin face. He regarded the Southerner with extreme good nature.

"Say, old Johnny Reb," he asked, "what do you fellows want anyway?"

"We'd like to know when your army is going to retreat, and we have come over here to ask you," replied Talbot.

The cannon boomed again, its thunder rolling and echoing in the morning air. The note was deep and solemn and seemed to Prescott to hold a threat. Its effect upon the Vermonter was remarkable. He straightened his thin, lean figure until he stood as stiff as a ramrod. Then dropping his rifle, he raised his hand and gave the cannon an invisible salute.

"This army never retreats again," he said. "You hear me, Johnny Reb, the Army of the Potomac never goes back again. I know that you have whipped us more than once, and that you have whipped us bad. I don't forget Manassas and Fredericksburg and Chancellorsville, but all that's done past and gone. We didn't have good generals then, and you won't do it again—never again, I say. We're comin', Johnny Reb, with the biggest and best army we've had, and we'll just naturally sweep you off the face of the earth."

The emphasis with which he spoke and his sudden change of manner at the cannon shot impressed Prescott, coming, too, upon his own feeling that there was a solemn and ominous note in the sound of the gun.

"What do those shots mean?" he asked. "Are they not a salute for somebody?"

"Yes," replied the Vermonter, a glow of joy appearing in his eye. "Grant has come!"

"Ah!"

"He's to command us now," the Vermonter continued, "and you know what that means. You have got to stand up and take your medicine. You hear me telling you!"

A sudden thrill of apprehension ran through Prescott's veins. He had been hearing for a long time of this man Grant and his great deeds in the West, where no general of the South seemed able to stand before him. Now he was here in the East among that group of officers yonder, and there was nothing left for either side but to fight. Grant would permit no other choice; he was not like the other Northern generals—he would not find excuses, and in his fancy double and triple the force before him, but he would drive straight for the heart of his foe.

It was a curious chance, but as the echo of the last gun rolled away among the trees the skies were darkened by leaden clouds rolling up from the southwest and the air became somber and heavy. Prescott saw as if in a vision the mighty battles that were to come and the miles of fallen scattered through all the wilderness that lay around them.

But Talbot, gifted with a joyous soul that looked not far into the future, never flinched. He saw the cloud on the face of Prescott and the glow in the eyes of the Vermonter, but he was stirred by no tumult.

"Never mind," he said calmly. "You've got your Grant and you are welcome to him, but Marse Bob is back there waiting for him." And he nodded over his shoulder toward the tent where the lone man had been sitting. His face as he spoke was lighted by the smile of supreme confidence.

They thanked the man for his news and walked slowly back to their camp, Prescott thoughtful all the way. He knew now that the crisis had come.

The two great protagonists stood face to face at last.

When Robert announced the arrival of Grant to his Commander-in-Chief a single flash appeared in the eye of Lee and then the mask settled back over his face, as blank and expressionless as before.

Then Prescott left the General's tent and walked toward a little house that stood in the rear of the army, well beyond the range of a hostile cannon shot. The arrival of Grant, now conceded by North and South alike to be the ablest general on the Northern side, was spreading with great swiftness among the soldiers, but these boys, veterans of many fields, showed little concern; they lived in the present and thought little of "next week."

Prescott noted, as he had noted so many times before, the motley appearance of the army, but with involuntary motion he began to straighten and smooth his own shabby uniform. He was about to enter the presence of a woman and he was young and so was she.

The house was a cheap and plain structure, such as a farmer in that sterile region would build for himself; but farmer and family were gone long since, swept away by the tide of war, and their home was used for other purposes.

Prescott knocked lightly at the door and Helen Harley opened it.

"Can the Colonel see me?" he asked.

"He will see any one if we let him," she replied.

"Then I am just 'any one'!"

"I did not say that," she replied with a smile.

She stood aside and Prescott entered the room, a bare place, the rude log walls covered with neither lath nor plaster, yet not wholly lacking in proof that woman was present. The scanty articles of furniture were arranged with taste, and against the walls were tacked a few sheets from last year's New York and London illustrated weeklies. Vincent Harley lay on a pallet of blankets in the corner, a petulant look on his face.

"I'm glad to see you, Prescott," he said, "and then I'm not, because you fill my soul with envy. Here I am, tied to these blankets, while you can walk about and breathe God's air as you will. I wouldn't mind it so much if I had got that bullet in a big battle, say like Gettysburg, but to be knocked off one's horse as nice as you please in a beggarly little skirmish. It's too much, I say."

"You ought to be thankful that the bullet, instead of putting you on the ground, didn't put you under it," replied Prescott.

"Now, don't you try the pious and thankful dodge on me!" cried Harley. "Helen does it now and then, but I stop her, even if I have to be impolite to a lady. I wouldn't mind *your* feelings at all."

His sister sat down on a camp stool. It was easy to see that she understood her brother's temper and knew how to receive his outbursts.

"There you are again, Helen," he cried, seeing her look. "A smile like that indicates a belief in your own superiority. I wish you wouldn't do it. You hurt my vanity, and you are too good a sister for that."

Prescott laughed.

"I think you are getting well fast, Harley," he said. "You show too much energy for an invalid."

"I wish the surgeon thought the same," replied Harley, "but that doctor is feeble-minded; I know he is! Isn't he, Helen?"

"Perhaps he's keeping you here because he doesn't want us to beat the Yankees too soon," she replied.

"Isn't it true, Prescott, that a man is always appreciated least by his own family?" he asked.

He spoke as if in jest, but there was a trace of vanity, and Prescott hesitated for a reply, not wishing to appear in a false light to either brother or sister.

"Slow praise is worth the most," he replied ambiguously. Harley showed disappointment. He craved a compliment and he expected it.

While they talked Prescott was watching Helen Harley out of the corner of his eye. Outside were the wild soldiers and war; here, between these narrow log walls, he beheld woman and peace. He was seized with a sudden sick distaste of the war, its endless battles, its terrible slaughter, and the doubt of what was to come after.

Harley claimed his attention, for he could not bear to be ignored. Moreover, he was wounded, and with all due deference to his sister, the visit was to him.

"Does either army mean to move?" he asked.

"I think so; I came to tell you about it," replied Prescott.

Harley at once was full of eagerness. This touched him on his strongest side. He was a warrior by instinct, and his interest in the affairs of the army could never be languid.

"Why, what news have you?" he asked quickly.

"Grant has come!"

He uttered an exclamation, but for a little while made no further comment. Like all the others, he seemed to accept the arrival of the new Northern leader as the signal for immediate action, and he wished to think over it.

"Grant," he said presently, "will attack us, and you don't know what it costs me to be lying here. I must be up and I will. Don't you see what is coming? Don't you see it, I say?"

"What is it that you see?" asked Prescott.

"Why, General Lee is going to win the greatest victory of the age. He will beat their biggest army, led by their best General. Why, I see it now! It will be the tactics of Chancellorsville over again. What a pity Jackson is gone! But there's Wood. He'll make a circuit with ten thousand men and hit 'em on the right flank, and at the same time I'll go around with my cavalry and dig into 'em on the left. The Yankees won't be dreaming of it, for Bobby Lee will be pounding 'em in front and they'll have eyes only for him. Won't it be grand, magnificent!"

There was a flash in his eye now and he was no longer irritable or impatient.

"Isn't war a glorious game?" he said. "Of course it is best not to have war, but if we must have it, it draws out of a man the best that is in him, if he's any good at all."

There was a light knock at the door, and Prescott, who was contrasting brother and sister, noticed their countenances change oddly and in a manner as different as their characters. Evidently they knew the knock. She closed her lips tightly and a faint pink tint in her cheeks deepened. He looked up quickly and the light in his eyes spoke welcome. "Come in!" he called in a loud voice, but his sister said nothing.

The lady who entered was Mrs. Markham, as crisp as the breath of the morning. Her dress was fresh and bright in colour, a brilliant note in a somber camp.

"Oh, Colonel!" she cried, going forward and taking both of Harley's hands in the warmth of her welcome. "I have been so anxious to see you again, and I am glad to know that you are getting well."

A pleased smile came over Harley's face and remained there. Here was one, and above all a woman, who could appreciate him at his true value, and whom no small drop of jealousy or envy kept from saying so.

"You give me too much credit, Mrs. Markham," he said.

"Not at all, my dear Colonel," she replied vivaciously. "It is not enough. One who wins laurels on such a terrible field as war has a right to wear them. Do not all of us remember that great charge of yours just at the critical moment, and the splendid way in which you covered the retreat from Gettysburg. You always do your duty, Colonel."

"My brother is not the only man in the army who does his duty," said Miss Harley, "and there are so many who are always true that he does not like to be singled out for special praise."

Colonel Harley frowned and Mrs. Markham shot a warning side glance at Miss Harley. Prescott, keenly watching them both, saw a flash as of perfect understanding and defiance pass between two pairs of eyes and then he saw nothing more. Miss Harley was intent upon her work, and Mrs. Markham, blonde, smiling and innocent, was talking to the Colonel, saying to him the words that he liked to hear and soothing his wounded spirit.

Mrs. Markham had just come from Richmond to visit the General, and she told gaily of events in the Southern capital.

"We are cheerful there, Colonel," she said, "confident that such men as you will win for us yet. Oh, we hear what is going on. They print news on wall-paper, but we get it somehow. We have our diversions, too. It takes a thousand dollars, Confederate money, to buy a decent calico dress, but sometimes we have the thousand dollars. Besides, we have taken out all the old spinning-wheels and looms and we've begun to make our own cloth. We don't think it best that the women should spend all their time mourning while the men are at the front fighting so bravely."

Mrs. Markham chattered on; whatever might be the misfortunes of the Confederacy they did not seem to impress her. She was so lively and cheerful, and so deftly mingled compliments with her gaiety, that Prescott did not wonder at Harley's obvious attraction, but he was not sorry to see the frown deepen on the face of the Colonel's sister. The sound of some soldiers singing a gay chorus reached their ears and he asked Helen if she would come to the door of the house and see them. She looked once doubtfully at the other woman, but rose and went with him, the two who were left behind making no attempt to detain her.

"Too much watching is not good, Helen," said Prescott, reproachfully. "You are looking quite pale. See how cheerful the camp is! Did you ever before hear of such soldiers?"

She looked over the tattered army as far as she could see and her eyes grew wet.

"War is a terrible thing," she replied, "and I think that no cause is wholly right; but truly it makes one's heart tighten to see such devotion by ragged and half-starved soldiers, hardly a man of whom is free from wound or scar of one."

The rolling thunder of a cannon shot came from a point far to the left.

"What is that?" she asked.

"It means probably that the tacit truce is broken, but it is likely that it is more in the nature of a range-finding shot than anything else. We are strongly intrenched, and as wise a man as Grant will try to flank us out of here, before making a general attack. I am sure there will be no great battle for at least a week."

"And my brother may be well in that time," she said. "I am so anxious to see him once more in the saddle, where he craves to be and where he belongs."

There are women who prefer to see the men whom they love kept back by a wound in order that they might escape a further danger, but not of such was Helen. Prescott remembered, too, the single glance, like a solitary signal shot, that had passed between her and Mrs. Markham.

"We are all anxious to see Colonel Harley back in the saddle," he replied, "and for a good reason. His is one of our best sabers."

Then she asked him to tell her of the army, the nature of the position it now occupied, the movements they expected, and he replied to her in detail when he saw how unaffected was her interest. It pleased him that she should be concerned about these things and should understand them as he explained their nature; and she, seeing his pleasure, was willing to play upon it. So talking, they walked farther and farther from the house and were joined presently by the cheerful Talbot.

"It's good of you to let us see you, Miss Harley," he said. "We are grateful to your brother for getting wounded so that you had to come and nurse him; but we are ungrateful because he stays hurt so long that you can't leave him oftener."

Talbot dispensed a spontaneous gaiety. It was his boast that he could fall in love with every pretty girl whom he saw without committing himself to any. "That is, boys," he said, "I can hover on the brink without ever falling over, and it is the most delightful sensation to know that you are always in danger and that you will always escape it. You are a hero without the risk."

He led them away from more sober thoughts, talking much of Richmond and the life there.

They went back presently to the house and met Mrs. Markham at the door just as she was leaving.

"The Colonel is so much better," she said sweetly to Miss Harley. "I think that he enjoys the visits of friends."

"I do not doubt it," replied the girl coldly, and she went into the room.

CHAPTER XVI

THE GREAT REVIVAL

Two men sat early the next morning in a tent with a pot of coffee and a breakfast of strips of bacon between them. One was elderly, calm and grave, and his face was known well to the army; the other was youngish, slight, dark and also calm, and the soldiers were not familiar with his face. They were General Lee and Mr. Sefton.

The Secretary had arrived from Richmond just before the dawn with messages of importance, and none could tell them with more easy grace than he. He was quite unembarrassed now as he sat in the presence of the great General, announcing the wishes of the Government—wishes which lost no weight in the telling, and whether he was speaking or not he watched the man before him with a stealthy gaze that nothing escaped.

"The wishes of the Cabinet are clear, General Lee," he said, "and I have been chosen to deliver them to you orally, lest written orders by any chance should fall into the hands of the enemy."

"And those wishes are?"

"That the war be carried back into the enemy's own country. It is better that he should feel its ills more heavily than we. You will recall, General, how terror spread through the North when you invaded Pennsylvania. Ah, if it had not been for Gettysburg!"

He paused and looked from under lowered eyelashes at the General. There had been criticism of Lee because of Gettysburg, but he never defended himself, taking upon his shoulders all the blame that might or might not be his. Now when Mr. Sefton mentioned the name of Gettysburg in such a connection his face showed no change. The watchful Secretary could not see an eyelid quiver.

"Yes, Gettysburg was a great misfortune for us," said the General, in his usual calm, even voice. "Our troops did wonders there, but they did not win."

"I scarcely need to add, General," said the Secretary, "that the confidence of the Government in you is still unlimited."

Then making deferential excuses, Mr. Sefton left the tent and Lee followed his retreating figure with a look of antipathy.

The Secretary wandered through the camp, watching everything. He had that most valuable of all qualities, the ability to read the minds of men, and now he set himself to the discovery of what these simple soldiers, the cannon food, were thinking. He did it, too, without attracting any attention to himself, by a deft question here, a suggestion there, and then more questions, always indirect, but leading in some fashion to the point. Curiously, but truly, his suggestions were not optimistic, and after he talked with a group of soldiers and passed on the effect that he left was depressing. He, too, looked across toward the Northern lines, and, civilian though he was, he knew that their tremendous infolding curve was more than twice as great as that forming the lines of the South. A singular light appeared in the Secretary's eyes as he noticed this, but he made no verbal comment, not even to himself.

The Secretary's steps led straight toward the house in which the wounded Colonel Harley lay, and when the voice bidding him to enter in response to his knock was feminine, he smiled slightly, entered with light step, and bowed with all the old school's courteous grace over the hand of Helen Harley.

"There are some women, Miss Harley," he said, "who do not fear war and war's alarms."

"Some, Mr. Sefton!" she replied. "There are many—in the South, I know—and there must be as many in the North."

"It is your generous heart that speaks," he said, and then he turned to Colonel Harley, who was claiming the attention of an old acquaintance.

The two men shook hands with great warmth. Here was one who received the Secretary without reserve. Miss Harley, watching, saw how her brother hung upon the words of this accomplished man of the world; how he listened with a pleased air to his praise and how he saw in the Secretary a great man and a friend.

He asked Helen presently if she would not walk with him a little in the camp and her brother seconded the idea. He was not intentionally selfish, and he loved his sister.

"She sits here all the time nursing me," he said, "when I'm almost well, and she needs the fresh air. Take her out, Mr. Sefton, and I'll thank you if she doesn't."

But she was willing to go. She was young; red blood flowed in her veins; she wished to be happy; and the world, despite this black cloud of war which hung over her part of it, was curious and interesting. She was not fond of close rooms and sick beds, so with a certain relief she walked forth by the side of the Secretary.

It was another of those beautiful days in May which clothe the Virginia earth in a gauze of spun silver. Nature was blooming afresh, and peace, disturbed by the vain battle of the night before, had returned to the armies.

"It seems to me a most extraordinary thing to behold these two armies face to face and yet doing nothing," said Helen.

"Wars consist of much more than battles," replied the Secretary.

"I am learning that," she said.

She looked about her with eager interest, custom not dimming to her the strange sights of an army in camp and on the eve of a great conflict. Nothing was like what she imagined it would be. The soldiers seemed to have no fear of death; in fact, nothing, if they could be judged by their actions, was further from their thoughts; they were gay rather than sad, and apparently were enjoying life with an indifference to circumstances that was amazing.

They were joined presently by Prescott, who thought it no part of his cue to avoid the Secretary. Mr. Sefton received him with easy courtesy, and the three strolled on together.

The Secretary asked the news of the camp, and Prescott replied that the Reverend Doctor Warren, a favourite minister, was about to preach to the soldiers.

"He is worth hearing," said Prescott. "Doctor Warren is no ordinary man, and this is Sunday, you know."

This army, like other armies, included many wild and lawless men who cherished in their hearts neither the fear of God nor the fear of man; but the South was religious, and if the battle or march did not forbid, Sunday was observed with the rites of the church. The great Jackson, so eager for the combat on other days, would not fight on Sunday if it could be helped.

The crowd was gathering already to hear the minister, who would address them from a rude little platform built in the centre of a glade.

The day was so calm, so full of the May bloom that Helen felt its peace steal over her, and for the moment there was no war; this was not an army, but just a great camp-meeting in the woods, such as the South often had and still has.

The soldiers were gathered already to the number of many thousands, some sitting on stumps and logs and others lying on the ground. All were quiet, inspired with respect for the man and his cloth.

"Let us sit here and listen," said Prescott, and the three, sitting on a convenient log, waited.

Doctor Warren, for he was an M.A. and a Ph.D. of a great American university and had taken degrees at another in Germany, ascended his rude forest pulpit. He was then about forty years of age; tall, thin, with straight black hair, slightly long, and with angular but intellectual features.

"A good man," thought Helen, and she was deeply impressed by his air of authority and the respect that he so evidently inspired.

He spoke to them as to soldiers of the cross, and he made his appeal directly to their hearts and minds, never to their passions. He did not inquire into the causes of the conflict in which they were engaged, he had no criticism for the men on the other side; he seemed rather to include them in his address. He said it was a great war, marked by many terrible battles as it would be marked by many more, and he besought them so to bear themselves that whatever the issue none could say that he had not done his duty as he saw it. And whether they fell in battle or not, that would be the great comfort to those who were at home awaiting their return.

Prescott noticed many general officers in the crowd listening as attentively as the soldiers. All sounds in the camp had died and the speaker's clear voice rose now and penetrated far through the forest. The open air, the woods, the cannon at rest clothed the scene with a solemnity that no cathedral could have imparted. The same peace enfolded the Northern army, and it required but little fancy to think that the soldiers there were listening, too. It seemed at the moment an easy and natural thing for them both to lay down their arms and go home.

The minister talked, too, of home, a place that few of those who heard him had seen in two years or more, but he spoke of it not to enfeeble them, rather to call another influence to their aid in this struggle of valour and endurance. Prescott saw tears rise more than once in the eyes of hardened soldiers, and he became conscious again of the power of oratory over the Southern people. The North loved to read and the South to hear speeches; that seemed to him to typify the difference in the sections.

The minister grew more fiery and more impassioned. His penetrating voice reached far through the woods and around him was a ring of many thousands. Few have ever spoken to audiences so large and so singular; of women there were not twenty, just men, and men mostly young, mere boys the majority, but with faces brown and scarred and clothing tattered and worn, men hardened to wounds and reckless of death, men who had seen life in its wildest and most savage phases. But all the brown and scarred faces were upturned to the preacher, and the eyes of the soldiers as they listened gleamed with emotional fire. The wind moaned now and then, but none heard it. Around them the smoky camp-fires flared and cast a distorting light over those who heard.

Prescott's mind, as he listened to the impassioned voice of the preacher and looked at the brown, wild faces of those who listened, inevitably went back to the Crusades. There was now no question of right or wrong, but he beheld in it the spirit of men stirred by their emotions and gathering a sort of superhuman fire for the last and greatest conflict, for Armageddon. Here was the great drama played against the background of earth and sky, and all the multitude were actors.

The spirit of the preacher, too, was that of the crusading priest. The battlefields before them were but part of the battle of life; it was their duty to meet the foe there as bravely as they met the temptation of evil, and then he preached of the reward afterward, the Heaven to come. His listeners began to see a way into a better life through such a death, and many shook with emotion.

The spell was complete. The wind still moaned afar, and the fires still flared, casting their pallid light, but all followed the preacher. They saw only his deepset, burning eyes, the long pale face, and the long black hair that fell around it. They followed only his promises of death and life. He besought them to cast their sins at the feet of the Master—to confess and prepare for the great day to come.

Prescott was a sober man, one who controlled his emotions, but he could not help being shaken by the scene, the like of which the world has not witnessed since the Crusades—the vast forest, the solemn sky overhead, the smoky fires below, and the fifty thousand in the shadow of immediate death who hung on the words of one man.

The preacher talked of olden days, of the men who, girding themselves for the fight, fell in the glory of the Lord. Theirs was a beautiful death, he said, and forgiveness was for all who should do as they and cast away their sins. Groans began to arise from the more emotional of the soldiers; some wept, many now came forward and, confessing their sins, asked that prayers be said for their souls. Others followed and then they went forward by thousands. Over them still thundered the voice of the preacher, denouncing the sin of this world and announcing the glory of the world to come. Clouds swept up the heavens and the fires burned lower, but no one noticed. Before them flashed the livid face and burning eyes of the preacher, and he moved them with his words as the helmsman moves the ship.

Denser and denser grew the throng that knelt at his feet and begged for his prayers, and there was the sound of weeping. Then he ceased suddenly and, closing his eyes and bending his head, began to pray. Involuntarily the fifty thousand, too, closed their eyes and bent their heads.

He called them brands snatched from the burning; he devoted their souls to God. There on their knees they had confessed their sins and he promised them the life everlasting. New emotions began to stir the souls of those who mourned. Death? What was that? Nothing. A mere dividing place between mortality and immortality, a mark, soon passed, and nothing more. They began to feel a divine fire. They welcomed wounds and death, the immortal passage, and they longed for the battlefield and the privilege of dying for their country. They thought of those among their comrades who had been so fortunate as to go on before, and expected joyfully soon to see them again.

Prescott looked up once, and the scene was more powerful and weird than any he had ever seen before. The great throng of people stood there with heads bowed listening to the single voice pouring out its invocation and holding them all within its sweep and spell.

The preacher asked the blessing of God on every one and finished his prayer. Then he began to sing:

"I've found a friend in Jesus, He is everything to me, He's the fairest of ten thousand to my soul; The Lily of the Valley in Him alone I see— All I need to cleanse and make me fully whole.

"He's my comfort in trouble, In sorrow He's my stay; He tells me every care on Him to roll. He's the Lily of the Valley, the Bright and Morning Star He's the fairest of ten thousand to my soul."

He sang one verse alone, and then the soldiers began to join, at first by tens, then by hundreds and then by thousands, until the grand chorus, rolling and majestic, of fifty thousand voices swelled through all the forest:

"He's the Lily of the Valley, the Bright and Morning Star, He's the fairest of ten thousand to my soul."

The faces of the soldiers were no longer sad. They were transfigured now. Joy had come after sorrow and then forgiveness. They heard the promise.

"The best of all ways to prepare soldiers for battle," said a cynical voice at Prescott's elbow.

It was Mr. Sefton.

"But it is not so intended," rejoined Prescott.

"Perhaps not, but it will suffice."

"His is what I call constructive oratory," presently continued the Secretary in a low voice. "You will notice that what he says is always calculated to strengthen the mind, although the soldiers themselves do not observe it."

"But no man could be more sincere," said Helen.

"I do not doubt it," replied the Secretary.

"It is impossible for me to think that the men singing here may fall in battle in a few days," said Helen.

The singing ended and in a few minutes the soldiers were engaged in many avocations, going about the business of the day. Prescott and Mr. Sefton took Helen back to the house and then each turned to his own task.

Several officers were gathered before a camp-fire on the following morning mending their clothes. They were in good humour because Talbot was with them and gloom rarely endured long in his presence.

"After all, why should the spirit of mortal be proud?" said Talbot. "Will it profit me more to be killed in a decent uniform than in a ragged one?"

"Don't you want to make a respectable casualty?" asked Prescott.

"Yes; but I don't like to work so much for it," replied Talbot. "It's harder to dress well now than it is to win a battle. You can get mighty little money and it's worth mighty little after you get it. The 'I promise to pay' of the Confederate States of America has sunk terribly low, boys."

He held up a Confederate bill and regarded it with disgust.

"It would take a wheelbarrow full of those to buy a decent suit of clothes," he said. "Do you know the luck I had yesterday when I tried to improve my toilet?"

All showed interest.

"More than six months' pay was due me," said Talbot, "and thinking I'd buy something to wear, I went around to old Seymour, the paymaster, for an installment. 'See here, Seymour,' I said, 'can't you let me have a month's pay. It's been so long since I have had any money that I've forgotten how it looks. I want to refresh my memory.'

"You ought to have seen the look old Seymour put on. You'd have thought I'd asked him for the moon. 'Talbot' he said, 'you're the cheekiest youngster I've met in a long time.'

"'But the army owes me six months' pay,' I said. 'What's that got to do with it?' he asked. 'I'd like to know what use a soldier has for money?' Then he looked me up and down as if it wouldn't work a footrule hard to measure me. But I begged like a good fellow—said I wanted to buy some new clothes, and I'd be satisfied if he'd let me have only a month's pay. At last he gave me the month's pay—five hundred dollars—in nice new Confederate bills, and I went to a sutler to buy the best he had in the way of raiment.

"I particularly wanted a nice new shirt and found one just to suit me. 'The price?' I said to the sutler. 'Eight hundred dollars,' he answered, as if he didn't care whether I took it or not. That settled me so far as the shirt question was concerned—I'd have to wait for that until I was richer; but I looked through his stock and at last I bought a handkerchief for two hundred dollars, two paper collars for one hundred dollars each, and I've got this hundred dollars left. Oh, I'm a bargainer!"

And he waved the Confederate bill aloft in triumph.

"I'd give this hundred dollars for a good cigar," he added, "but there isn't one in the army."

One of the men sang:

"I am busted, mother, busted. Gone the last unhappy check; And the infernal sutler's prices Make every pocket-book a wreck."

Prescott sat reading a newspaper. It was the issue of the *Richmond Whig* of April 30, 1864, and his eyes were on these paragraphs:

"That the great struggle is about to take place for the possession of Richmond is conceded on all sides. The enemy is marshaling his cohorts on the Rapahannock and the Peninsula, and that a last desperate effort will be made to overrun Virginia and occupy her ancient capital is admitted by the enemy himself. What, then, becomes the duty of the people of Richmond in view of the mighty conflict at hand? It is evidently the same as that of the commander of a man-of-war who sails out of port to engage the foes of his flag in mortal combat. The decks are cleared for action; non-combatants are ordered below or ashore; the supply of ammunition and food is looked to, and a short prayer uttered that Heaven will favour the right and protect the land and the loved ones for whom the battle is waged.

"We sincerely hope and pray that the red waves of battle may not, as in 1862, roll and break and hiss against the walls of the capital, and the ears of our suffering but resolute people may never again be saluted by the reports of hostile guns. But our hopes may be disappointed; the enemy may come again as he has come before, and, for aught we know, the battle may be fought on these hills and in these streets. It is with a view of this possible contingency that we would urge upon our people to make all needful preparation for whatever fate betides them, and especially to give our brave and unconquerable defenders a clear deck and open field. And above all, let the living oracles of our holy religion, and pious men and women of every persuasion, remember that God alone giveth the victory, and that His ear is ever open to the prayer of the righteous."

Prescott's thoughts the next morning were of Lucia Catherwood, who had floated away from him in a sort of haze. It seemed a long time since they parted that night in the snow, and he found himself trying to reproduce her face and the sounds of her voice. Where was she now? With that army which hung like a thunder cloud on their front? He had no doubt of it. Her work would be there. He felt that they were going to meet again, and it would not be long.

That day the Southern breeze blew stronger and sweeter than ever. It came up from the Gulf, laden with a million odours, and the little wild flowers in delicate tints of pink and purple and blue peeped up amid the shades of the forest.

That night Grant, with one hundred and thirty thousand men and four hundred guns, crossed the Rapidan and advanced on the Army of Northern Virginia.

The fiercest and bloodiest campaign recorded since history rose from the past was about to begin.

CHAPTER XVII

THE WILDERNESS

There is in Virginia a grim and sterile region the name of which no American ever hears without a shudder. When you speak to him of the Wilderness, the phantom armies rise before him and he hears the thunder of the guns as the vast struggle sweeps through its shades. He sees, too, the legions of the dead strewn in the forest, a mighty host, and he sighs to think so many of his countrymen should have fallen in mutual strife.

It is a land that deserves its name. Nature there is cold and stern. The rock crops up and the thin red soil bears only scrub forest and weary bushes. All is dark, somber and lonely, as if the ghosts of the fallen had claimed it for their playground.

The woodchopper seeks his hut early at night, and builds high the fire for the comfort of the blaze. He does not like to wander in the dark over the ground where vanished armies fought and bled so long. He sees and hears too much. He knows that his time—the present—has passed with the day, and that when the night comes it belongs again to the armies; then they fight once more, though the battle is soundless now, amid the shades and over the hills and valleys.

Now and then he turns from the fire and its comradeship and looks through the window into the darkness. He, too, shudders as he thinks of the past and remembers the long roll, Chancellorsville, the Wilderness, Spottsylvania and the others. Even the poor woodchopper knows that this melancholy tract of ground has borne more dead men's bones than any other of which history tells, and now and then he asks why, but no one can give him the answer he wishes. They say only that the battles were fought, that here the armies met for the death struggle which both knew was coming and which came as they knew.

The Wilderness has changed but little in the generation since Grant and Lee met there. The sullen soil is sullen and unyielding still. As of old it crops up here in stone and there turns a thin red tint to the sun. The sassafras bushes and the scrub oaks moan sadly in the wind, and few human beings wander over the desolate hills and valleys.

At Gettysburg there is a city, and the battlefield is covered with monuments in scores and scores, and all the world goes to see them. The white marble and granite shafts and pillars and columns, the green hills and fields around, the sunshine and the sound of many voices are cheerful and tell of life; you are not with the dead—you are simply with the glories of the past.

But it is different when you come to the Wilderness. Here you really walk with ghosts. There are no monuments, no sunshine, no green grass, no voices; all is silent, somber and lonely, telling of desolation and decay. To many it is a more real monument than the clustering shafts of Gettysburg. All this silence, all this abandonment tell in solemn and majestic tones that here not one great battle was fought, but many; that here in one year shone the most brilliant triumph of the South; and here, in another year, she fought her death struggle.

When you walk among the bushes and the scrub oaks and listen to the desolate wind you need no inscription to tell you that you are in the Wilderness.

CHAPTER XVIII

DAY IN THE WILDERNESS

Helen Harley saw the sun rise in a shower of red and gold on a May morning, and then begin a slow and quiet sail up a sky of silky blue. It even touched the gloomy shades of the Wilderness with golden gleams, and shy little flowers of purple, nestling in the scant grass, held up their heads to the glow. From the window in the log house in which she had nursed her brother she looked out at the sunrise and saw only peace, and the leaves of the new spring foliage moving gently in the wind.

The girl's mind was not at rest. In the night she had heard the rumbling of wheels, the tread of feet, and many strange, muffled sounds. Now the morning was here and the usual court about her was missing. Gone were the epaulets, the plumes and the swords in sheath. The generals, Raymond and Winthrop, who had come only the day before. Talbot, Prescott and Wood, were all missing.

The old house seemed desolate, abandoned, and she was lonely. She looked through the window and saw nothing that lived among the bushes and the scrub oaks only the scant grass and the new spring foliage waving in the gentle wind. Here smouldered the remains of a fire and there another, and yonder was where the tent of the Commander had stood; but it was gone now, and not a sound came to her ears save those of the forest. She was oppressed by the silence and the portent.

Her brother lay upon the bed asleep in full uniform, his coat covering his bandages, and Mrs. Markham was in the next room, having refused to return to Richmond. She would remain near her husband, she said, but Helen felt absolutely alone, deserted by all the world.

No, not alone! There, coming out of the forest, was a single horseman, the grandest figure that she had ever seen—a man above six feet in height, as strong and agile as a panther, his head crowned with magnificent bushy black hair, and his face covered with a black beard, through which gleamed eyes as black as night. He rode, a very king, she thought.

The man came straight toward the window of the log house, the feet of his horse making no sound upon the turf. Here was one who had come to bid her good-by.

She put her hand through the open window, and General Wood, the mountaineer, bending low over his horse's neck, kissed it with all the grace and gallantry of an ancient knight.

"I hope that you will come back," she said softly.

"I will, I must, if you are here," he said.

He kissed her hand again.

"Your brother?" he added.

"He is still asleep."

"What a pity his wounds are so bad! We'll need him to-day."

"Is it coming? Is it really coming to-day, under these skies so peaceful and beautiful?" she asked in sudden terror, though long she had been prepared for the worst.

"Grant is in the Wilderness."

She knew what that meant and asked no more.

Wood's next words were those of caution.

"There is a cellar under this house," he said. "If the battle comes near you, seek shelter in it. You promise?"

"Yes, I promise."

"And now good-by."

"Good-by," she said.

He kissed her hand again and, without another word, turned and rode through the forest and away. She watched him until he was quite out of sight, and then her eyes wandered off toward the east, where the new sun was still piling up glowing bands of alternate red and gold.

Her brother stirred on the bed and awoke. He was fretful that morning.

"Why is the place so silent?" he asked, with the feeling of a vain man who does not wish to be left alone.

"I do not know," she replied, though well she knew.

There was a knock at the door and Mrs. Markham entered, dressed as if for the street—fresh, blonde and smiling.

"You two are up early, Helen," she said. "What do you see there at the window?"

"Nothing," replied Helen. She did not tell any one of the parting with Wood. That belonged to her alone.

A coloured woman came with the breakfast, which was served on a little table beside Harley's bed. He propped himself up with a pillow and sat at the table with evident enjoyment. The golden glory of the new sun shone there through the window and fell upon them.

"How quiet the camp is!" said Mrs. Markham after awhile. "Surely the army sleeps late. I don't hear any voices or anything moving."

"No," said Helen.

"No, not a thing!" exclaimed Mrs. Markham.

"Eh?" cried Harley.

His military instinct leaped up. Silence where noise has been is ominous.

"Helen," he said, "go to the window, will you?"

"No. I'll go," said Mrs. Markham, and she ran to the window, where she uttered a cry of surprise.

"Why, there is nothing here!" she exclaimed. "There are no tents, no guns, no soldiers! Everything is gone! What does it mean?"

The answer was ready.

From afar in the forest, low down under the horizon's rim, came the sullen note of a great gun—a dull, sinister sound that seemed to roll across the Wilderness and hang over the log house and those within it.

Harley threw himself on the bed with a groan of grief and rage.

"Oh, God," he cried, "that I should be tied here on such a day!"

Helen ran to the window but saw nothing—only the waving grass, the somber forest and the blue skies and golden sunshine above. The echo of the cannon shot died and again there was silence, but only for a moment. The sinister note swelled up again from the point under the horizon's rim far off there to the left, and it was followed by another, and more and more, until they blended into one deep and sullen roar.

Unconsciously Constance Markham, the cynical, the worldly and the self-possessed, seized Helen Harley's hand in hers.

"The battle!" she cried. "It is the battle!"

"Yes," said Helen; "I knew that it was coming."

"Ah, our poor soldiers!"

"I pity those of both sides."

"And so do I. I did not mean it that way."

The servant was cowering in a corner of the room. Harley sprang to his feet and stood, staggering.

"I must be at the window!" he said.

Helen darted to his support.

"But your wounds," she said. "You must think of them!"

"I tell you I shall stay at the window!" he exclaimed with energy. "If I cannot fight, I must see!"

She knew the tone that would endure no denial, and they helped him to the window, where they propped him in a chair with his eyes to the eastern forest. The glow of battle came upon his face and rested there.

"Listen!" he cried. "Don't you hear that music? It's the big guns, not less than twenty. You cannot hear the rifles from here. Ah if I were only there!"

The three looked continually toward the east, where a somber black line was beginning to form against the red-and-gold glow of the sunrise. Louder and louder sounded the cannon. More guns were coming into action, and the deep, blended and violent note seemed to roll up against the house until every log, solid as it was, trembled with the concussion. Afar over the forest the veil of smoke began to grow wider and thicker and to blot out the red-and-gold glory of the sunrise.

Harley bent his head. He was listening—not for the thunder of the great guns, but for the other sounds that he knew went with it—the crash of the rifles, the buzz and hiss of the bullets flying in clouds through the air, the gallop of charging horsemen, the crash of falling trees cut through by cannon shot, and the shouts and cries. But he heard only the thunder of the great guns now, so steady, so persistent and so penetrating that he felt the floor tremble beneath him.

He searched the forest with eyes trained for the work, but saw no human being—only the waving grass, the somber woods, and a scared lizard rattling the bark of a tree as he fled up it.

In the east the dull, heavy cloud of smoke was growing, spreading along the rim of the horizon, climbing the concave arch and blotting out all the glory of the sunrise. The heavy roar was like the sullen, steady grumbling of distant thunder, and the fertile fancy of Harley, though his eyes saw not, painted all the scene that was going on within the solemn shades of the Wilderness—the charge, the defense, the shivered regiments and brigades; the tread of horses, cannon shattered by cannon, the long stream of wounded to the rear, and the dead, forgotten amid the rocks and bushes. He had beheld many such scenes and he had been a part of them. But who was winning now? If he could only lift that veil of the forest!

Every emotion showed on the face of Harley. Vain, egotistic, and often selfish, he was a true soldier; his was the military inspiration, and he longed to be there in the field, riding at the head of his horsemen as he had ridden so often, and to victory. He thought of Wood, a cavalry leader greater than himself, doing a double part, and for a moment his heart was filled with envy. Then he flushed with rage because of the wounds that tied him there like a baby. What a position for him, Vincent Harley, the brilliant horseman and leader! He even looked with wrath upon his sister and Mrs. Markham, two women whom he admired so much. Their place was not here, nor was his place here with them. He was eaten with doubt and anxiety. Who was losing, who was winning out there beyond the veil of the forest where the pall of smoke rose? He struck the window-sill angrily with his fist.

"I hate this silence and desolation here around us," he exclaimed, "with all that noise and battle off there where we cannot see! It chills me!"

But the two women said nothing, still sitting with their hands in each other's and unconscious of it; forgetting now in this meeting of the two hundred thousand the petty personal feelings that had divided them.

Louder swelled the tumult. It seemed to Helen, oblivious to all else, that she heard amid the thunder of the cannon other and varying notes. There was a faint but shrill incessant sound like the hum of millions of bees flying swiftly, and another, a regular but heavier noise, was surely the tread of charging horsemen. The battle was rolling a step nearer to them, and she began to see, low down under the pall of smoke, flashes of fire like swift strokes of lightning. Then it rolled another step nearer and its tumult beat heavily and cruelly on the drums of her ears. Yet the deathly stillness in the scrub oaks around the house continued. They waved as peacefully as ever in the gentle wind from the west. It was still a battle heard but not seen.

She would have left the window to cower in the corner with the coloured woman who served them, but this struggle, of which she could see only the covering veil, held her appalled. It was misty, intangible, unlike anything of which she had read or heard, and yet she knew it to be real. They were in conflict, the North and the South, there in the forest, and she sat as one in a seat in a theatre who looked toward a curtained stage.

When she put her free hand once on the window-sill she felt beneath her fingers the faint, steady trembling of the wood as the vast, insistent volume of sound beat upon it. The cloud of smoke now spread in a huge, somber curve across all the east, and the swift flashes of fire were piercing through it faster and faster. The volume of sound grew more and more varied, embracing many notes.

"It comes our way," murmured Harley, to himself rather than to the women.

Helen felt a quiver run through the hand of Mrs. Markham and she looked at her face. The elder woman was pale, but she was not afraid. She, too, would not leave the window, held by the same spell.

"Surely it is a good omen!" murmured Harley; "the field of Chancellorsville, where we struck Hooker down, is in this same Wilderness."

"But we lost there our right arm—Jackson," said Mrs. Markham.

"True, alas!" said Harley.

The aspect of the day that had begun so bright and clear was changing. The great pall of smoke in the east gave its character to all the sky. From the west clouds were rolling up to meet it. The air was growing close, sultry and hot. The wind ceased to blow. The grass and the new leaves hung motionless. All around them the forest was still heavy and somber. The coloured woman in the corner began to cry softly, but from her chest. They could hear her low note under the roar of the guns, but no one rebuked her.

"It comes nearer and nearer," murmured Harley.

There was relief, even pleasure in his tone. He had forgotten his sister and the woman to whom his eyes so often turned. That which concerned him most in life was passing behind the veil of trees and bushes, and its sound filled his ears. He had no thought of anything else. It was widening its sweep, coming nearer to the house where he was tied so wretchedly by wounds; and he would see it—see who was winning—his own South he fiercely hoped.

The thoughts of brother and sister at that moment were alike. All the spirit and fire of the old South flushed in every vein of both. They were of an old aristocracy, with but two ambitions, the military and the political, and while they prayed for complete success in the end, they wanted another great triumph on the field of battle. Gettysburg, that insuperable bar, was behind them, casting its gloomy memory over the year between; but this might take its place, atoning for it, wiping it out. But there was doubt and fear in the heart of each; this was a new general that the North had, of a different kind from the old—one who did not turn back at a defeat, but came on again and hammered and hammered. They repeated to themselves softly the name "Grant." It had to them a short, harsh, abrupt sound, and it did not grow pleasant with repetition.

An odour, the mingled reek of smoke, burnt gunpowder, trampled dust and sweating men, reached them and was offensive to their nostrils. Helen coughed and then wiped her face with her handkerchief. She was surprised to find her cheeks damp and cold. Her lips felt harsh and dry as they touched each other.

The trembling of the house increased, and the dishes from the breakfast which they had left on the table kept up an incessant soft, jarring sound. The battle was still spreading; at first a bent bow, then a semi-circle, the horns of the crescent were now extending as if they meant to meet about the house, and yet they saw not a man, not a horse, not a gun; only afar off the swelling canopy of smoke, and the flashes of light through it, and nearer by the grass and the leaves, now hanging dull and lifeless.

Harley groaned again and smote the unoffending window-sill with his hand.

"Why am I here—why am I here," he repeated, "when the greatest battle of all the world is being fought?"

The clouds of smoke from the cannon and the clouds from the heated and heavy air continued to gather in both heavens and were now meeting at the zenith. The skies were dark, obscure and somber. Most trying of all was the continuous, heavy jarring sound made by the thunder of the guns. It got upon the nerves, it smote the brain cruelly, and once Helen clasped her hands over her ears to shut it out, but she could not; the sullen mutter was still there, no less ominous because its note was lower.

A sudden tongue of flame shot up in the east above the forest, but unlike the others did not go out again; it hung there a red spire, blood-red against the sky, and grew taller and broader.

"The forest burns!" murmured Harley.

"In May?" said Helen.

"What a cannonade it must be to set green trees on fire!" continued Harley.

The varying and shriller notes heard through the steady roar of the great guns now grew more numerous and louder; and most persistent among them was a nasty buzz, inconceivably wicked in its cry.

"The rifles! A hundred thousand of them at least!" murmured Harley, to whose ear all these sounds were familiar.

New tongues of fire leaped above the trees and remained there, blood-red against the sky; sparks at first fugitive and detached, then in showers and millions, began to fly. Columns of vapour and smoke breaking off from the main cloud floated toward the house and assailed those at the window until eyes and nostrils tingled. The strange, nauseous odour, the mingled reek of blood and dust, powder and human sweat grew heavier and more sickening.

Helen shuddered again and again, but she could not turn away. The whole look of the forest had now changed to her. She saw it through a red mist: all the green, the late green of the new spring, was gone. All things, the trees, the leaves, the grass and the bushes, seemed burnt, dull and dead.

"Listen!" cried Harley. "Don't you hear that—the beat of horses' feet! A thousand, five thousand of them! The cavalry are charging! But whose cavalry?"

His soul was with them. He felt the rush of air past him, the strain of his leaping horse under him, and then the impact, the wild swirl of blood and fire and death when foe met foe. Once more he groaned and struck the window-sill with an angry hand.

Nearer and nearer rolled the battle and louder and shriller grew its note. The crackle of the rifles became a crash as steady as the thunder of the great guns, and Helen began to hear, above all the sound of human voices, cries and shouts of command. Dark figures, perfectly black like tracery, began to appear against a background of pallid smoke, or ruddy flame, distorted, shapeless even, and without any method in their motions. They seemed to Helen to fly back and forth and to leap about as if shot from springs like jumping-jacks and with as little of life in them—mere marionettes. The great pit of fire and smoke in which they fought enclosed them, and to Helen it was only a pit of the damned. For the moment she had no feeling for either side; they were not fellow beings to her—they who struggled there amid the flame and the smoke and the falling trees and the wild screams of the wounded horses.

The coloured woman cowering in the corner continued to cry softly, but with deep sobs drawn from her chest, and Helen wished that she would stop, but she could not leave the window to rebuke her even had she the heart to do so.

The smoke, of a close, heavy, lifeless quality, entered the window and gathered in the rooms, penetrating everything. The floor and the walls and the furniture grew sticky and damp, but the three at the window did not notice it. They had neither eyes nor heart now save for the tremendous scene passing before them. No thought of personal danger entered the mind of either woman. No, this was a somber but magnificent panorama set for them, and they, the spectators, were in their proper seats. They were detached, apart from the drama which was of another age and another land, and had no concern with them save as a picture.

Helen could not banish from her mind this panoramic quality of the battle. She was ashamed of herself; she ought to draw from her heart sympathy for those who were falling out there, but they were yet to her beings of another order, and she remained cold—a spectator held by the appalling character of the drama and not realizing that those who played the part were human like herself.

"The battle is doubtful," said Harley.

"How do you know?"

"See how it veers to and fro—back and forth and back and forth it goes again. If either side were winning it would all go one way. Do you know how long we have been here watching?"

"I have no idea whatever."

He looked at his watch and then pointed upward at the heavens where in the zenith a film of light appeared through the blur of cloud and smoke.

"There's the sun," he said; "it's noon. We've been sitting here for hours. The time seems long and again it seems short. Ah, if I only knew which way fortune inclined! Look how that fire in the forest is growing!"

Over in the east the red spires and pillars and columns united into one great sheet of flame that moved and leaped from tree to tree and shot forth millions of sparks.

"That fire will not reach us," said Harley. "It will pass a half-mile to the right."

But they felt its breath, far though hot, and again Helen drew her handkerchief across her burning face. The deadly, sickening odour increased. A light wind arose, and a fine dust of ashes, borne on its breath, began to enter the window and sweep in at every possible crevice and cranny of the old house. It powdered the three at the window and hung a thin, gray and pallid veil over the floor and the scanty furniture. The faint jarring of the wood, so monotonous and so persistent, never ceased. And distinctly through the sounds they heard the voice of the coloured woman, crying softly from her chest, always the same, weird, unreal and chilling.

The struggle seemed to the three silent watchers to swing away a little, the sounds of human voices died, the cries, the commands were heard no more; but the volume of the battle grew, nevertheless. Harley knew that new regiments, new brigades, new batteries were coming into action; that the area of conflict was spreading, covering new fields and holding the old. He knew by the rising din, ever swelling and beating upon the ear, by the vast increase in the clouds of smoke, the leaping flashes of flame and the dust of ashes, now thick and drifting, that two hundred thousand men were eye to eye in battle amid the gloomy thickets and shades of the Wilderness, but God alone knew which would win.

Some of the awe that oppressed the two women began to creep over Harley and to chill the blood in his veins. He had gone through many battles; he had been with Pickett in that fiery rush up Cemetery Hill in the face of sixty thousand men and batteries heaped against each other; but there he was a part of things and all was before him to see and to hear: here he only sat in the dusk of the smoke and the ashes and the clouds, while the invisible battle swung to and fro afar. He heard only the beat of its footsteps as it reeled back and forth, and saw only the mingled black and fiery mists and vapours of its own making that enclosed it.

The dun clouds were still rolling up from both heavens toward the zenith, shot now and then with yellow streaks and scarlet gleams. Sometimes they threw back in a red glare the reflection of the burning forest, and then again the drifting clouds of smoke and ashes and dust turned the whole to a solid and dirty brown. It was now more than a battle to Harley. Within that cloud of smoke and flashing flame the fate of a nation hung—the South was a nation to him—and before the sun set the decree might be given. He was filled with woe to be sitting there looking on at so vast an event. Vain, selfish and superficial, depths in his nature were touched at last. This was no longer a scene set as at a theatre, upon which one might fight for the sake of ambition or a personal glory. Suddenly he sank into insignificance. The fortunes or the feelings of one man were lost in mightier issues.

"It's coming back!" exclaimed Mrs. Markham.

The battle again approached the old house, the clouds swept up denser and darker, the tumult of the rifles and the great guns grew louder; the voices, the cries and the commands were heard again, and the human figures, distorted and unreal, reappeared against the black or fiery background. To Helen's mind returned the simile of a huge flaming pit in which multitudes of little imps struggled and fought. She was yet unable to invest them with human attributes like her own, and the mystic and unreal quality in this battle which oppressed her from the first did not depart.

"It is all around us," said Mrs. Markham.

Helen looked up and saw that her words were true. The battle now made a complete circuit of the house, though yet distant, and from every point came the thunder of the cannon and the rifles, the low and almost rhythmic tread of great armies in mortal struggle, and the rising clouds of dust, ashes and smoke shot with the rapid flame of the guns, like incessant sheet-lightning.

The clouds had become so dense that the battle, though nearer, grew dimmer in many of its aspects; but the distorted and unreal human figures moved like shadows on a screen and were yet visible, springing about and crossing and recrossing in an infinite black tracery that the eye could not follow. But to neither of the three did the thought of fear yet come. They were still watchers of the arena, from high seats, and the battle was not to take them in its coils.

The flame, the red light from the guns, grew more vivid, and was so rapid and incessant that it became a steady glare, illuminating the vast scene on which the battle was outspread; the black stems of the oaks and pines, the guns—some wheelless and broken now, the charging lines, fallen horses scattered in the scrub, all the medley and strain of a titanic battle.

The sparks flew in vast showers. Bits of charred wood from the burning forest, caught up by the wind, began to fall on the thin roof of the old house, and kept up a steady, droning patter. The veil of gray ashes upon the floor and on the scanty furniture grew thicker. The coloured woman never ceased for a moment to cry drearily.

"It is still doubtful!" murmured Harley.

His keen, discerning eye began to see a method, an order in all this huge tumult—signs of a design, and of another design to defeat it—the human mind seeking to achieve an end. One side was the North and another the South—but which was his own he could not tell. For the present he knew not where to place his sympathies, and the fortunes of the battle were all unknown to him.

He looked again at his watch. Mid-afternoon. Hours and hours had passed and still the doubtful battle hung on the turning of a hair; but his study of it, his effort to trace its fortune through all the intricate maze of smoke and flame, did not cease. He sought to read the purposes of the two master minds which marshaled their forces against each other, to evolve order from chaos and to read what was written already.

Suddenly he uttered a low cry. He could detect now the colour of the uniforms. There on the right was the gray, his own side, and Harley's soul dropped like lead in water. The gray were yielding slowly, almost imperceptibly, but nevertheless were yielding. The blue masses were pouring upon them continually, heavier and heavier, always coming to the attack.

Harley glanced at the women. They, too, saw as he saw. He read it in the deathly pallor of their faces, their lips parted and trembling, the fallen look of their eyes. It was not a mere spectacle now—something to gaze at appalled, not because of the actors in it, but because of the spectacle itself. It was beginning now to have a human interest, vital and terrible—the interest of themselves, their friends and the South to which they belonged.

Helen suddenly remembered a splendid figure that had ridden away from her window that morning—the figure of the man who alone had come to bid her good-by, he who had seemed to her a very god of war himself; and she knew he must be there in that flaming pit with the other marionettes who reeled back and forth as the master minds hurled fresh legions anew to the attack. If not there, one thing alone had happened, and she refused to think of that, though she shuddered; but she would not picture him thus. No; he rode triumphant at the head of his famous brigade, sword in hand, bare and shining, and there was none who could stand before its edge. It was with pride that she thought of him, and a faint blush crept over her face, then passed quickly like a mist before sunshine.

The battle shifted again and the faces of the three who watched at the window reflected the change in a complete and absolute manner. The North was thrust back, the South gained—a few feet perhaps, but a gain nevertheless, and joy shone on the faces where pallor and fear had been before. To the two women this change would be permanent. They could see no other result. The North would be thrown back farther and farther, overwhelmed in rout and ruin. They looked forward to it eagerly and in fancy saw it already. The splendid legions of the South could not be beaten.

But no such thoughts came to Harley. He felt all the joy of a momentary triumph, but he knew that the fortune of the battle still hung in doubt. Strain eye and ear as he would, he could see no decrease in the tumult nor any decline in the energy of the figures that fought there, an intricate tracery against the background of red and black. The afternoon was waning, and his ears had grown so used to the sounds without that he could hear everything within the house. The low, monotonous crying of the coloured woman was as distinct as if there were no battle a half-mile away.

The dense fine ashes crept into their throats and all three coughed repeatedly, but did not notice it, having no thought for anything save for what was passing before them. They were powdered with it, face, hair and shoulders, until it lay over them like a veil, but they did not know nor care.

The battle suddenly changed again and the South was pressed back anew. Once more their faces fell, and the hearts of the women, raised to such heights, sank to the depths. It was coming nearer, too. There was a fierce hiss, a shrill scream and something went by.

"A shell passed near us then," said Harley, "and there's another. The battle is swinging close."

Still the element of fear did not enter into the minds of any of the three, not even into those of the women, although another shell passed by and then others, all with a sharp, screaming note, full of malignant ferocity. Then they ceased to come and the battle again hovered in the distance, growing redder and redder than ever against a black background as the day darkened and the twilight approached. Its sound now was a roar and a hum—many varying notes blending into a steady clamour, which was not without a certain rhythm and music—like the simultaneous beating of a million mighty bass drums.

"They still press us back," murmured Harley; "the battle is wavering."

With the coming of the twilight the light in the forest of scrub oaks and pines, the light from so many cannon and rifles, assumed vivid and unearthly hues, tinged at the edges with a yellow glare and shot through now and then with blue and purple streaks. Over it hung the dark and sullen sky.

"It comes our way again," said Harley.

It seemed now to converge upon them from all sides, to contract its coils like a python, but still the house was untouched, save by the drifting smoke and ashes. Darker and darker the night came down, a black cap over all this red struggle, but with its contrast deepening the vivid colours of the combat that went on below.

Nearer it came, and suddenly some horsemen shot from the flame-cloud and stood for a moment in a huddled group, as if they knew not which way to turn. They were outlined vividly against the red battle and their uniforms were gray. Even Helen could see why they hesitated and doubted. Riderless horses galloped out of the smoke and, with the curious attraction that horses have for the battlefield, hovered near, their empty saddles on their backs.

A groan burst from Harley.

"My God," he cried, "those cavalrymen are going to retreat!"

Then he saw something that struck him with a deeper pang, though he was silent for the moment. He knew those men. Even at the distance many of the figures were familiar.

"My own troop!" he gasped. "Who could have thought it?"

Then he added, in sad apology: "They need a leader."

The horsemen were still in doubt, although they seemed to drift backward and away from the field of battle. A fierce passion lay hold of Harley and inflamed his brain. He saw his own men retreating when the fate of the South hung before them. He thought neither of his wounds nor of the two women beside him, one his sister. Springing to his feet while they tried in vain to hold him back, he cried out that he had lingered there long enough. He threw off their clinging hands, ran to the door, blood from his own wounds streaking his clothes, and they saw him rush across the open space toward the edge of the forest where the horsemen yet lingered. They saw him, borne on by excitement, seize one of the riderless horses, leap into the saddle and turn his face toward the battle. They almost fancied that they could hear his shout to his troops: "Come on, men; the way is here, not there!"

The horse he had seized was that of a slain bugler, and the bugle, tied by a string to the horn of the saddle, still hung there. Harley lifted it to his lips, blew a note that rose, mellow and inspiring, above all the roar of the cannon and the rifles, and then, at the head of his men, rode into the heart of the battle.

CHAPTER XIX

NIGHT IN THE WILDERNESS

The two women clasped hands again and looked at each other as Harley disappeared amid the smoke.

"He has left us," said Mrs. Markham.

"Yes, but he has gone to his country's need," said his sister proudly.

Then they were silent again. Night, smoky, cloudy and dark, thick with vapours and mists, and ashes and odours that repelled, was coming down upon the Wilderness. Afar in the east the fire in the forest still burned, sending up tongues of scarlet and crimson over which sparks flew in myriads. Nearer by, the combat went on, its fury undimmed by the darkness, its thunder as steady, as persistent and terrible as before.

Helen was struck with horror. The battle, weird enough in the day, was yet more so in the darkness, and she could not understand why it did not close with the light. It partook of an inhuman quality, and that scene out there was more than ever to her an inferno because the flaming pit was now enclosed by outer blackness, completely cut off from all else—a world to itself in which all the passions strove, and none could tell to which would fall the mastery.

She felt for the moment horror of both sides, North and South alike, and she wished only that the unnatural combat would cease; she did not care then—a brief emotion, though—which should prove the victor.

It was a dark and solemn night that came down over the Wilderness and the two hundred thousand who had fought all day and still fought amid its thickets. Never before had that thin, red soil—redder now—borne such a crop, and many were glad that the darkness hid the sight from their enemies. The two Generals, the master minds who had propelled their mighty human machines against each other, were trying to reckon their losses—with the battle still in progress—and say to themselves whether they had won or lost. But this battlefield was no smooth and easy chessboard where the pawns might be moved as one wills and be counted as they fell, but a wilderness of thickets and forests and hills and swamps and valleys where the vast lines bent or twisted or interlaced and were lost in the shades and the darkness. Count and reckon as they would, the two Generals, equal in battle, face to face for the first time—could not give the total of the day. It was still an unadded sum, and the guns, despite the night, were steadily contributing new figures. This was the flaw in their arithmetic; nothing was complete, and they saw that they would have to begin again to-morrow. So, with this day's work yet unfinished, they began to prepare, sending for new regiments and brigades, massing more cannon, and planning afresh.

But all these things were unknown to Helen as she sat there at the window with Mrs. Markham. Her thoughts wandered again to Wood, that splendid figure on horseback, and she sought to identify him there among the black marionettes that gyrated against the red background. But with the advance of night the stage was becoming more indistinct, the light shed over it more pallid and shifting, and nothing certain could be traced there. All the black figures were mixed in a confused whirl, and where stood the South and where the North neither Helen nor Mrs. Markham could tell.

The night was thick and hot, rank with vapours and mists and odours that oppressed throat and nostrils. The wind seemed to have died, but the fine dust of ashes still fell and the banks of nauseous smoke floated about aimlessly.

New fear assailed the two women for the first time—not so much fear of the shells and the bullets, but of the night and its mysteries and the weird combat that was still going on there where the light was so pallid and uncertain. Once again those who fought had become for them unreal—not human beings, but imps in an inferno of their own creation. They wished now that Harley was still with them. Whatever else he might be, he was brave and he would defend them. They looked around fearfully at the shadows that were encroaching upon the house. The rain of ashes and dust began to annoy them, and they moved a little closer to each other.

Helen glanced back once. The inside of the house was now in total darkness, and out of it came the monotonous wailing of the black woman. It occurred suddenly to Helen that the servant had crouched there crying the whole day long. But she said nothing to her and turned her back to the window.

"It is dying now," said Mrs. Markham.

The dull red light suddenly contracted and then broke into intermittent flashes. The sound of the cannon and the rifles sank into the low muttering of distant thunder. The two women felt the house under them cease to tremble. Then the intermittent flashes, too, disappeared, the low rumbling died away like the echo of a distant wind, and a sudden and complete silence, mystic and oppressive in its solemnity, fell over the Wilderness. Only afar the burning forest glowed like a torch.

The silence was for awhile more terrifying than the battle to which they had grown used. It hung over the forest and them like something visible that enfolded them. They breathed a hot, damp air heavy with ashes and smoke and dust, and their pulses throbbed painfully in their temples. Around them all the time was that horrible deathlike pall of silence.

They spoke, and their voices, attuned before to the roar of the battle, sounded loud, shrill and threatening. Both started, then laughed weakly.

"Is it really over?" exclaimed Mrs. Markham, hysterically.

"Until to-morrow," replied Helen, with solemn prevision.

She turned to the inner blackness of the house and lighted a candle, which she placed on the table, where it burned with an unsteady yellow light, illuminating the centre of the room with a fitful glow, but leaving the corners still in darkness. Everything lay under its veil of ashes—the table, the floor, and the bed on which Harley had slept.

Helen felt a strange sort of strength, the strength of excitement and resolve. She shook the black woman by the arm and bade her bring food.

"We must eat, for we shall have work to do," she said to Mrs. Markham, and nodded her head toward the outside.

It was the task of but a few minutes, and then the two women prepared to go forth. They knew they would be needed on this night, and they listened to hear the ominous sounds that would be a call to them. But they heard nothing. There was the same dead, oppressive stillness. Not a leaf, not a blade of grass seemed to stir. Helen looked once more from the window. Afar in the east the forest still burned, but the light there was pallid, grayish, more of the quality of moonlight than of fire, and looked dim. Directly before her in the forest where the battle had been all was black, silent and impenetrable. It was true there were faint lights here and there as of torches that had burned badly, but they were pin-points, serving only to deepen the surrounding blackness. Once or twice she thought she saw figures moving slowly, but she was not sure. She heard nothing.

Helen was in an unreal world. An atmosphere new, fiery and surcharged surrounded her, and in its heat little things melted away. Only the greater remained. That life in Richmond, bright and gay in many of its aspects, lived but a few days since, was ages and ages ago; it belonged to another world. Now she was in the forest with the battle and the dead, and other things did not count.

The door stood wide open, and as Helen prepared to go another woman entered there, a woman young like herself, tall, wrapped in a long brown cloak, but bareheaded. Two or three stray locks, dark but edged with red gold, strayed down. Her face, clear and feminine though it was, seemed to Helen stronger than any other woman's face that she had ever seen.

Helen knew instinctively that this was a woman of the North, or at least one with the North, and her first feeling was of hostility. So, as the two stood looking at each other, her gaze at first was marked by aversion and defiance. Who was she who had come with the other army, and why should she be there?

But Lucia Catherwood knew both the women in the old house. She remembered a day in Richmond when this girl, in lilac and rose, so fair a representative of her South, welcomed a gallant general; and she remembered another, a girl of the same years, lonely, an outcast in the farthest fringe of the crowd—herself. Her first emotion, too, was hostility, mingled with another feeling closely akin to it. She had seen her with Prescott, and unwillingly had confessed them well matched. She, too, asked what this woman was doing here in the forest beside the battle; but these feelings had only a short life with her. There were certain masculine qualities in Lucia Catherwood that tended to openness and frankness. She advanced and offered her hand like a man to Helen.

"We come under different flags," she said, "but we cannot be enemies here; we must be friends at least to-night, and I could wish that it should always be so."

Her smile was so frank, so open, so engaging that Helen, whose nature was the same, could resist her no longer. Despite herself she liked this girl, so tall, so strong, with that clear, pure face showing a self-reliance such as she had never before seen on the face of a woman. Mrs. Markham yet hung back a little, cool, critical and suspicious, but presently she cast this manner from her and spoke as if Lucia Catherwood was her friend, one of long and approved standing.

"I think that our work is to be the same," said Helen simply, and the other bowed in silent assent. Then the three went forth.

The field of battle, or rather the portion of it which came nearest to them—it wound for miles through the thickets—lay a half-mile from the house under the solid black veil of a cloudy night, the forest, and the smoke that yet drifted about aimlessly. Outside the house the strange, repellent odours grew stronger, as if it were the reek of some infernal pit.

They advanced over open ground, and the field of conflict was still black and soundless, though there was a little increase in the lights that moved dimly there. The smoke assailed them again, and fine ashes from the distant fire in the east now and then fell upon them. But they noticed none of these things, still advancing with steady step and unshrinking faces toward the forest.

The twinkling lights increased and sounds came at last. Helen would not say to herself what they were. She hoped that her fancy deceived her; but the three women did not stop. Helen looked at the tall, straight young figure beside her, so strong, so self-reliant, and she drew strength from her companion—now she was such. They walked side by side, and Mrs. Markham came behind. Helen began to feel the influence of a personality, a will stronger than her own, and she yielded to it without further question and without reluctance, having the feeling that she had known this girl a long time.

The trembling lights of the forest increased, moving about like so many fireflies in the night; the nauseous odours grew heavier, more persistent, and for a moment Helen felt ill; her head began to spin around at the thought of what she was going to see, but quickly she recovered herself and went on by the side of the girl who never faltered. Helen wondered at such courage, and wondering, she admired.

The ground grew rougher, set with tiny hillocks and stones and patch after patch of scrub bushes. Once Helen stumbled against something that felt cold even through the leather of her shoe, and she shuddered. But it was only a spent cannon ball lying peacefully among the bushes, its mission ended.

They reached burnt ground—spots where the scanty grass or the bushes had been set on fire by the cannon or the rifles. Many places still burned slowly and sent up languid sparks and dull smoke. In other places the ground was torn as if many ploughs had been run roughly over it, and Helen knew that the shells and the cannon balls had passed in showers. There were other objects, too, lying very quiet, but she would not look at them, though they increased fast as they went on, lying like seed sown above ground.

They were at the edge of the forest now, and here the air was thicker and darker. The mists and vapours floated among the trees and lay like warm, wet blankets upon their faces. They saw now many moving figures, some bending down as if they would lift something from the earth, and others who held lights. Occasionally they passed women like themselves, but not often. Some of the men were in gray uniform and some in blue, but they passed and repassed each other without question, doing the work they had come there to do.

Here in the forest the area of burnt ground was larger, and many coils of smoke rose languidly to join the banks of it that towered overhead. The still objects, too, were lying as far as one could see, in groups here, somewhat scattered there, but the continuity never broken, many with their faces upturned to the sky as if they awaited placidly the last call. Helen was struck by this peace, this seeming confidence in what was to come. The passage, then, had not been so hard! Here, when she stood in the centre of it all, the old feelings of awe returned, and the real world, the world that she had known before this day, swung farther and farther away.

There was still but little noise, for those who yet lived were silent, waiting patiently, and the vast peace was more powerful in its impression upon the mind than any tumult could have been. Helen looked up once at the skies. They were black and overcast. But few stars twinkled there. It was a fit canopy for the Wilderness, the gloomy forest that bore such a burden. From a far point in the southwest came the low rumble of thunder, and lightning, like the heat-lightning of a summer night, glimmered fitfully. Then there was a faint, sullen sound, the report of a distant cannon shot. Helen started, more in anger than terror. Would they fight again at such a time? She felt blame for both, but the shot was not repeated then. A signal gun, she thought, and went on, unconsciously going where the strong young figure of Lucia Catherwood led the way. She heard presently another distant cannon shot, its solemn echoes rolling all around the horizon, but she paid no heed to it. Her mind was now for other things.

An inky sky overhung the battlefield and all it held. Those nights in the Wilderness were among the blackest in both ways this country has ever known. Brigades and batteries moving in the dense scrub, seeking better places for the fresh battle on the morrow, wandered sometimes through each other's lines. Soldiers, not knowing whether they were among friends or enemies, and not caring, drank in the darkness from the same streams, and, overpowered by fatigue, North and South alike often slept a soundless sleep under trees not fifty yards from one another; but the two Generals, who were the supreme expression of the genius of either side, never slept. They had met for the first time; each nearly always a victor before, neither had now won. The result yet to come lay hidden in the black Wilderness, and by smoking camp-fires they planned for the next day, knowing well that they would meet again in a combat fiercer, longer and deadlier than ever, the one always seeking to drive on, the other always seeking to hold him back.

The Wilderness enclosed many secrets that night, hiding dead and living alike. Many of the fallen lay unseen amid the ravines and hollows, and the burning forest was their funeral pyre. Never did the Wilderness more deserve its name; gloomy at any time, it had new attributes of solemn majesty. Everything seemed to be in unison with those who lay there—the pitchy blackness, the low muttering of distant thunder, the fitful glimmer of the lightning, the stems of trees twisted and contorted by the gleam of the uncertain flashes, the white faces of the slain upturned to the sky seen dimly by the same light, the banks of smoke and vapour yet floating through the forest, the strange, repellent odours, and the heavy, melancholy silence.

Those who had come upon the field after the night began worked without talk, the men from either side passing and repassing each other, but showing no hostility. The three women, too, began to help them, doing the errand upon which they had come, and their service was received without question and without comment. No one asked another why he was there; his duty lay plain before him.

It was Lucia Catherwood who took the lead, neither Helen nor Mrs. Markham disputing her fitness for the place, too apparent to all to be denied; it was she who never flinched, who, if she spoke at all, spoke words of cheer, whose strength and courage seemed never to fail.

Thus the hours passed, and the character of the night in the Wilderness did not change. There was yet compared with the tumult of the day a heavy, oppressive silence; the smoke and the vapours did not go away, the heavy atmosphere did not thin, and at intervals the distant thunder rumbled and the fitful lightning glared over a distorted forest.

The three worked in silence, like those around them, faithful, undaunted. Mrs. Markham, the cynical and worldly, was strangely changed, perhaps the most changed of the three; all her affectations were gone, and she was now only an earnest woman. And while the three worked they always watched for one man. And this man was not the same with any one of the three.

It was past midnight and Helen did not know how long she had been upon the battlefield, working as she did in a kind of a dream, or rather mist, in which everything was fanciful and unreal, with her head full of strange sights and unheard sounds, when she saw two men ride side by side and silently out of the black forest—two figures, one upright, powerful, the other drooping, with head that swayed slightly from side to side.

She knew them at once despite the shadows of the trees and the faint moonlight—and it was what her thoughts had told her would come true. It had never occurred to her that the one who sat in the saddle so erect and so powerful could fall; nor had he.

She and Mrs. Markham advanced to meet them. Harley's head swayed slightly from side to side, and his clothing showed red in the dim moonlight. Wood held him in the saddle with one hand and guided the two horses with the other. Both women were white to the lips, but it was Helen who spoke first.

"I expected you," she said to Wood.

Wood replied that Harley was not hurt save by exhaustion from his previous wounds. He had come, too, at a critical moment, and his coming had been worth much to the South. But now he was half unconscious; he must rest or die. The General spoke in simple words, language that one would have called dialect, but Helen did not think of those things; his figure was grander than ever before to her, because, despite the battle, he had remembered to bring back her brother.

Mrs. Markham was quiet, saying no word, but she went with them to the house, where Harley was placed on the very bed on which he had slept the night before. Lucia Catherwood did not turn back, and was left alone on the field, but she was neither afraid nor lonely. She, too, was looking for some one—one whom she was in dread lest she find and whom she wished to find nevertheless. But she had a feeling—how or whence it came she did not know—that she would find him there. Always while she helped the others, hour after hour, she looked for him, glancing into every ravine and hollow, and neglecting no thicket or clump of bushes that she passed. She believed that she would know him if she saw but the edge of his coat or his hand.

At last she reached the fringe of the battlefield. The fallen forms were fewer and the ground less torn by the tramplings of men and horses and the wheels of guns, though the storm had passed, leaving its track of ruin. Here, too, were burned spots, the grass still smouldering and sending up tiny sparks, a tree or two twisted out of shape and half-consumed by flames; a broken cannon, emblem of destruction, lying wheelless on the ground. Lucia looked back toward the more populous field of the fallen and saw there the dim lights still moving, but decreasing now as the night waned. Low, blurred sounds came to her ears. As for herself, she stood in the darkness, silvered dimly by a faint moonlight, a tall, lithe young figure, self-reliant, unafraid.

She began now to search every hollow, to look among the bushes and the ravines. She had heard from men of his own company that he was missing, and she would not turn back while he was unfound. It was for this that she had come, and he would need her.

She was on the farthest rim of the battlefield, where the lights when she looked back were almost lost, and it seemed to be enclosed wholly by the darkness and the vapours. No voice came from it, but in the forest before her were new sounds—a curious tread as of many men together stepping lightly, the clanging of metal, and now and then a neigh coming faintly. This, she knew, were the brigades and the batteries seeking position in the darkness for a new battle; but she was not afraid.

81

Lucia Catherwood was not thinking then of the Wilderness nor of the vast tragedy that it held, but of a flight one snowy night from a hostile capital, a flight that was not unhappy because of true companionship. Formed amid hard circumstances, hers was not a character that yielded quickly to sentiment, but when the barriers were broken down she gave much.

She heard a tread in the brushwood. Some horses, saddles on and bridles hanging—their riders lost, she well knew how—galloped near her, looked at her a moment or two with wide eyes, and then passed on. Far to the right she heard a faint cannon shot. If they were going to fight again, why not wait until the next day? It could not be done in all this darkness. A blacker night she had never seen.

She came to a tiny valley, a mere cup in the bleak, red ridges, well set with rich green grass as if more fertile soil had gathered there, but all torn and trampled, showing that one of the fiercest eddies of the battle had centred in this spot. At the very edge lay two horses with their outstretched necks crossed united in death. In the trampled grass lay other dark figures which she could not pass without a shudder.

She paused here a moment because it seemed to be growing darker. The low rumble of thunder from the far western horizon came again, all the more threatening because of its faintness and distance. The lightning gleamed a moment and by its quick flash she saw the one she was seeking.

He lay at the far edge of the little valley where the grass had grown richest and tallest, and he was almost hidden by the long stems. It was his face that she saw first, white and still in the lightning's glare, but she did not believe that he was dead. Ah! that could not happen.

Raising his head in her arms, she rested it upon her knee, moistening his lips with water that she carried in a flask. She was a strong woman, both physically and mentally, far beyond the average of her sex, and now she would not yield to any emotion. No; she would do what it was necessary to do, and not until then would she even put her finger upon his wrist to find if the pulse were still beating.

The wound was on the side of the head, under the hair, and she remembered afterward how glad she was that the scar would always be hidden by the hair. Strong enough to examine the nature of the injury, she judged that it had been done by a fragment of shell, and she believed that the concussion and loss of blood, rather than any fatal wound, had caused Prescott's fall.

As she drew away the hair, washed the wound and bound it up with a strip from her own dress, she was filled with a divine gladness. Not only was she doing that which she wished most to do, but she was making repayment. He would have died there had she not found him, and no one else would have found him in that lone spot.

Not yet did she seek to move him or to bring help. She would have him to herself for awhile—would watch over him like a mother, and she could do as much as any surgeon. She was glad Helen and the other woman had turned aside, for she alone had found him. No one else could claim a share in saving him. He was for the time hers and hers alone, and in this she rejoiced.

As his pulse was growing stronger she knew that he would live. No doubt of it now occurred to her mind, and she was still happy. The battle of the day that was gone and of the day that was to come, and all the thousands, the living and the fallen, were alike forgotten. She remembered only him.

Again came the tramp of riderless horses, and for a moment she was in dread—not for herself, but for him—but again they turned and passed her by. When the low, threatening note of the cannon shot came once more she trembled lest the battle be renewed in the darkness and surge over this spot; but silence only followed the report. Misty forms filed past in the thicket. They were in blue, a regiment of her own people passing in the darkness. She crouched low in the grass, holding his head upon her knees, hiding again, not for herself, but for him. She would not have him a prisoner, but preferred to become one herself, and cared nothing for it. This was repayment. His pulse was growing stronger and stronger and he uttered half-spoken words while his head moved slightly upon her knees.

She did not know how long she had been there, and she looked back again toward the field. It was now wholly in darkness, then lighted dimly by a fitful flash of lightning. She must carry him to shelter, and without taking thought, she tried to lift him in her arms. He was heavy, lying like lead, and she put him down again, but very softly. She must go for help. Then she heard once more the tread of those riderless horses and feared for him. She could not leave him there alone. She made a mighty effort, lifted him in her arms, and staggered toward the battlefield.

CHAPTER XX

THE SECRETARY LOOKS ON

The old house in the woods which still lay within the Confederate lines became a hospital before morning, and when General Wood turned away from it he beheld a woman staggering through the darkness, carrying a strange burden. It was Lucia Catherwood, and when she came nearer he knew that the burden was a man. He saw then that the girl's expression was one that he had never before seen on the face of woman. As he ran forward she gasped:

"Take him; it is Captain Prescott!"

Full of wonder, but with too much delicacy under his rough exterior to ask questions, the mountaineer lifted Prescott in his arms and carried him into the house, where he was placed on the bed beside Harley, who was unconscious, too. Lucia Catherwood followed alone. She had been borne up by the impulse of excessive emotion, but she was exhausted now by her mighty effort. She thought she was going to faint—she who had never fainted in her life—and leaned against the outside wall of the house, dizzy and trembling. Black shadows, not those of the night, floated before her eyes, and the house moved away; but she recovered herself in a few moments and went in.

Improvised beds and cots were in every room, and many of the wounded lay on the floor, too. Mixed with them were some in blue just as on the other side of the battlefield were some in gray mixed with the blue. There was a powerful odour of drugs, of antiseptics, and Helen and Mrs. Markham were tearing cloth into strips.

Prescott lay a long time awaiting his turn at the surgeon's hand—so long that it seemed to Lucia Catherwood it would never come; but she stayed by his side and did what she could, though conscious that both Mrs. Markham and Helen were watching her at times with the keenest curiosity, and perhaps a little hostility. She did not wonder at it; her appearance had been so strange, and was still so lacking in explanation, that they could not fail, after the influence of the battlefield itself had somewhat passed, to be curious concerning her. But she added nothing to what she had said, doing her work in silence.

The surgeon came at last and looked at Prescott's head and its bandages. He was a thin man of middle age, and after his examination he nodded in a satisfied way.

"You did this, I suppose," he said to Lucia—it was not the first woman whom he had seen beside a wounded man. When she replied in the affirmative, he added:

"I could not have done better myself. He's suffering chiefly from concussion, and with good nursing he'll be fit for duty again in a few weeks. You can stay with him, I suppose? You look strong, and women are good for such work."

"Yes; I will stay with him," she replied, though she felt a sudden doubt how she should arrange to do so.

The surgeon gave a few instructions and passed on—it was a busy night for him and all his brethren, and they could not linger over one man. Lucia still sat by the side of Prescott, applying cooling bandages, according to the surgeon's instructions, and no one sought to interfere with her.

The house, which contained so many wounded, was singularly quiet. Hardly one of them groaned. There was merely the sound of feet moving softly. Two or three lights burned very low. Outside was the same silence and darkness. Men came in or went away and the others took no notice.

A man entered presently, a slender man, of no particular presence, with veiled eyes, it seemed to Lucia, and she observed that his coming created a faint rustle of interest, something that had not happened with any other. He was not in uniform, and his first glance was for Helen Harley. Then he came toward Lucia and, bending down, looked keenly at the face of her patient.

"It is Captain Prescott," he said. "I am sorry. Is he badly hurt?"

"No," she replied; "he is suffering chiefly from concussion, the surgeon says, and will be well again in two or three weeks."

"With good nursing?"

"Yes, with good nursing." She glaced up in a little surprise.

Revelation, comprehension, resolve, shot over James Sefton's face. He was genuinely pleased, and as he glanced at Lucia Catherwood again her answering gaze was full of understanding.

"Your name is Lucia Catherwood," he said.

"Yes," she replied, without surprise.

"It does not matter how I knew it," he continued; "it is sufficient that I do know it. I know also that you are the best nurse Robert Prescott could have."

Her look met his, and, despite herself, the deep red dyed her face, even her neck. There was a swift look of admiration on the Secretary's face. Then he smiled amiably. He had every reason to feel amiable. He realized now that he had nothing to fear from Prescott's rivalry with Helen Harley so long as Lucia Catherwood was near. Then why not keep her near?

"You are to be his nurse," he continued, "and you must have the right to go through our lines, even to Richmond if necessary. Here is a pass for you."

He took pencil and paper from his pocket and wrote an order which he handed to her.

The Secretary's next concern was for Harley, and he spoke in low tones of him to Mrs. Markham and his sister. He had heard of his heroic charge at a critical moment—of a man rising from his bed of wounds to lead back his wavering regiment; the army was ringing with it. In the new republic such a hero should have a great reward. Helen flushed with pleasure, but Mrs. Markham, shrewder and keener, said nothing. Her own husband, unhurt, came an hour later, and he was proud of his wife at work there among the wounded. The Secretary stayed a long while, and Lucia felt at times that he was watching her with an eye that read her throughout; but when she saw him looking at Helen Harley she thought she knew the reason of his complacency. She, too, was acute.

The Secretary brought news of the battle, and as he prophesied that the next day would be bloodier than the one just closed, he glanced through the window at the black Wilderness with real awe upon his face.

Lucia followed his look, and despite herself she felt a certain pride. This general, who struck so hard and never ceased striking, was her general. She had known that it would be so, but these people about her had not known it until now. She felt in her heart that the end was coming, but she knew it would be over the roughest road ever traveled by a victorious army.

She formed plans, too, as she sat there, and was thankful for the pass that she concealed in her dress. No matter how it had come, she had it and it was all-powerful. She did not fear this Secretary whom others seemed to fear. If necessary she would go to Richmond again, and she would there join her cousin, Miss Grayson, her nearest living relative, who could now give her protection that no one could question.

About three o'clock in the morning a young man whose face and manner she liked came in and looked at Prescott. He showed deep concern, and then relief, when assured that the wound was not serious. His name was Talbot—Thomas Talbot, he said—and he was a particular friend of Prescott's. He gave Lucia one or two glances, but in a few moments he went away to take his part in the next day's battle.

Lucia dozed a little by and by, her sleep being filled with strange dreams. She was awakened by a low, distant sound, one that the preceding day had made familiar—the report of a cannon shot. She looked out of the window, and it was still so dark that the forest, but a short distance away, was invisible.

"They have begun early," she murmured.

She saw Prescott stir as if he had heard a call, and his eyes half opened. Then he made an effort to move, but she put her hand gently upon his forehead and he sank back to rest. She saw in his half-open eyes a fleeting look of comprehension, gratitude and joy, then the eyes closed again, and he floated off once more into the land of peace where he abode for the present. Lucia felt singularly happy and she knew why, for so engrossed was she in Prescott that she scarcely heard the second cannon shot, replying to the first. There came others, all faint and far, but each with its omen. The second day's battle had begun.

The supreme commanders of either side were now ready. Human minds had never been more busy than theirs had been. Grant was still preparing to attack; no thought of failure entered his resolute soul. If he did not succeed to-day, then he would succeed on the next day or next week or next month; he would attack and never cease attacking. Lee stood resolutely in his path, resolved to beat him back, not only on this line, but on every other line, always bringing up his thinning brigade for a new defense.

The Wilderness still held secrets for both, but they intended to solve them that day, to see which way the riddle ran, and the Wilderness itself was as dark, as calm and as somber as ever. It had been torn by cannon balls, pierced by rifle bullets and scorched by fire; but the two armies were yet buried in it and it gave no sign to the world outside.

In the house, despite the wounded, there was deep attention and a concern that nothing could suppress. The scattered cannon shots blended into a steady thunder already, but it was distant and to the watchers told nothing. The darkness, too, was still so great that they could see no flashes.

The Secretary, mounted on an Accomack pony, rode out of the woods and looked a little while at the house, then turned away and continued in the direction of the new battle. He was in a good humour that morning, smiling occasionally when no one could see. The combat already begun did not trouble Mr. Sefton, although it was his business there to see how it was going and supplement, or, rather, precede, the General's reports with such news as he could obtain, and so deft a mind as his could obtain much. Yet he was not worried over either its progress or its result. He had based his judgment on calculations made long ago by a mind free from passion or other emotion and as thoroughly arithmetical as a human mind can be, and he had seen nothing since to change the estimates then formed.

When he thought how they missed Jackson it was with no intention of depreciating Wood. Both were needed, and he knew that the mountain General would be wherever the combat was fiercest that day. And then, he might not come back! The Secretary pondered over this phase of the matter. He had been growing suspicious of late, and Wood was a good general, but he was not sure that he liked him. But pshaw! There was nothing to dread in such a crude, rough mountaineer.

He glanced to the left and saw there the heads of horses and horsemen rising and falling like waves as they swept over the uneven ground. He believed them to be Wood's troopers, and, taking his field-glass, he studied the figure that rode at their head. It was Wood, and the Secretary saw that they were about to strike the Northern flank. He was not a soldier, but he had an acute mind and a keen eye for effect. He recognized at once the value of the movement, the instinct that had prompted it and the unflinching way in which it was being carried out. "Perhaps Wood will fall there! He rides in the very van," he thought, but immediately repented, because his nature was large enough to admit of admiration for a very brave man.

The sun shone through the clouds a little and directly upon the point in the Northern lines where Wood was aiming to strike, and the Secretary watched intently. He saw the ranks of horsemen rising and falling quickly and then pausing for a second or two before hurling themselves directly upon the Northern flank. He saw the flash of sabers, the jets of white smoke from rifle or pistol, and then the Northern line was cut through. But new regiments came up, threw themselves upon the cavalry, and all were mingled in a wild pell-mell among the thickets and through the forests. Clouds of smoke, thick and black, settled down, and horse and foot, saber and gun were hidden from the Secretary.

"Stubborn! As stubborn as death!" he murmured; "but the end is as certain as the setting of the sun."

Turning his horse, he rode to a new hill, from which he made another long and careful examination. Then he rode a mile or two to the rear and stopped at a small improvised telegraph station, whence he sent three brief telegrams. The first was to President Jefferson Davis of the Southern Confederacy in Richmond; the others, somewhat different in nature, were for two great banking houses—one in London, the other in Paris—and these two despatches were to be forwarded from a seaport by the quickest steamer.

This business despatched, Mr. Sefton, rubbing his hands with pleasure, rode back toward the battle.

A figure, black-bearded, gallant and large, came within the range of his glasses. It was Wood, and the Secretary breathed a little sigh of sorrow. The General had come safely out of the charge and was still a troublesome entity, but Mr. Sefton checked himself. General Wood was a brave man, and he could respect such splendid courage and ability.

Thinking deeply on the way and laying many plans, he turned his pony and rode back toward the house which was still outside the area of battle, and the Secretary judged that it would not come within it on that day at least. More than one in that log structure waited to hear what news he would bring.

Prescott, shortly after daylight, had opened his ears to a dull, steady, distant sound, not unpleasant, and his eyes to a wonderful, luminous face—a face that he knew and which he once had feared he might never see again.

"Lucia Catherwood!" he said.

"Yes, it is I," she replied softly, so softly that no one else could hear.

"I think that you must have found me and brought me here," he said. An intuition had told him this.

She answered evasively: "You are not hurt badly. It was a piece of shell, and the concussion did the harm."

Prescott looked a question. "You will stay by me?" his eyes said to her as plain as day.

"Yes, I will stay by you," was her positive reply in the same language.

Then he lay quite still, for his head was dull and heavy; but it was scarcely an ache, and he did not suffer pain. Instead, a soothing content pervaded his entire system and he felt no anxiety about anything. He tried to remember his moments of unconsciousness, but his mind went back only to the charge, the blow upon the head, and the fall. There everything had stopped, but he was still sure that Lucia Catherwood had found him and somehow had brought him here. He would have died without her, of that he had no doubt, and by and by he should learn about it all.

Men came into the house and went away, but he felt no curiosity. That part of him seemed to be atrophied for the present, but after awhile something aroused his interest. It was not any of the men or women who passed and repassed, but that curious, dull, steady, distant sound which had beat softly upon his ears the moment he awoke. He remembered now that it had never ceased, and it began to trouble him, reminding him of the buzzing of flies on a summer afternoon when he was a boy and wanted to sleep. He wondered what it was, but his brain was still dulled and gave no information. He tried to forget but could not, and looked up at Lucia Catherwood for explanation, but she had none to offer.

He wished to go to sleep, but the noise—that soft but steady drumming on the ear—would not let him. His desire to know grew and became painful. He closed his eyes in thought and it came to him with sudden truth it was the sound of guns, cannon and rifles. The battle, taken up where it was left off the night before, was going on.

North and South were again locked in mortal strife, and the Wilderness still held its secret, refusing to name the victor. Prescott felt a sudden pang of disappointment. He knew the straits of the South; he knew that she needed every man, and he was lying there helpless on a bed while the persistent Grant was hammering away and would continue to hammer away as no general before him had done. He tried to move, but Lucia put her cool hand upon his forehead. That quieted him, but he still listened intently to the sound of battle, distinguishing with a trained ear the deep note of the cannon and the sharper crash of the rifle. All waited anxiously for the return of the Secretary, confident that he would come and confident that he would bring true news of the battle's fortunes. It required but a short acquaintance with Mr. Sefton to produce upon every one the impression that he was a man who saw.

The morning had not been without pleasure to Prescott. His nurse seemed to know everything and to fear nothing. Lucia understood her peculiar position. She had a full sense that she was an outsider, but she did not intend to go away, being strongly fortified by the feeling that she was making repayment. Once as she sat by Prescott, Helen came, too, and leaned over him. Lucia drew away a little as if she would yield to another who had a better claim, but Helen would not have it so.

"Do not go," she said. "He is yours, not mine."

Lucia did not reply, but a tacit understanding arose between the two women, and they were drawn toward each other as friends, since there was nothing to divide them.

The Secretary at that moment was riding slowly toward the house, turning now and then to look at the battle which yet hung in doubt, in its vast canopy of smoke. He studied it with keen eyes and a keener mind, but he could yet make nothing of it, and could give no news upon his arrival at the house.

The long day waned at last, but did not bring with its shadows any decrease in the violence of the battle. Its sound was never absent for a moment from the ears of those in the house, and the women at the windows saw the great pyramid of flame from the forest fire, but their anxiety was as deep as ever. No word came to indicate the result. Night fell, close, heavy and black, save where the forest burned, and suddenly the battle ceased.

News came at length that the South had held her lines. Grant had failed to break through the iron front of Lee. A battle as bloody as Gettysburg had been fought and nothing was won; forty thousand men had been struck down in the Wilderness, and Grant was as far as ever from Richmond.

The watchers in the house said little, but they rejoiced—all save Lucia Catherwood, who sat in silence. However the day might have ended, she did not believe the campaign had ended with it, and her hope continued.

A messenger arrived in haste the next day. The house must be abandoned by all who could go. Grant had turned on his left flank and was advancing by a new road. The Southern army must also turn aside to meet him.

It was as Lucia Catherwood expected. Meade, a victor at Gettysburg, had not attacked again. Grant, failing in the Wilderness, moved forward to fight within three days another battle as great.

The story of either army was the same. The general in his tent touched the spring that set all things in motion. The soldiers rose from the hot ground on which they lay in a stupor rather than sleep. Two streams of wounded poured to the rear, one to the North and one to the South. The horses, like their masters, worn and scarred like them, too, were harnessed to cannon and wagon; the men ate as they worked; there was no time for delay. This was to be a race, grand and terrible in its nature, with great battles as incidents. The stakes were high, and the players played with deadly earnestness.

Both Generals sent orders to hurry and themselves saw that it was done. The battle of yesterday and the day before was as a thing long past; no time to think of it now. The dead were left for the moment in the Wilderness as they had fallen. The air was filled with commands to the men, shouts to the horses, the sough of wheels in the mud, the breaking of boughs under weight, and the clank of metal. The Wilderness, torn now by shells and bullets and scorched by the fires, waved over two armies gloomier and more somber than ever, deserving to the full its name.

They were still in the Wilderness, and it had lost none of its ominous aspects. Far to left and right yet burned the forest fires set by the shells, flaring luridly in the intense blackness that characterized those nights. The soldiers as they hurried on saw the ribbons and coils of flame leaping from tree-top to tree-top, and sometimes the languid winds blew the ashes in their faces. Now and then they crossed parts of the forest where it had passed, and the earth was hot to their feet. Around them lay smouldering logs and boughs, and from these fallen embers tongues of flame arose. Overhead, the moon and stars were shut out by the clouds and smoke and vapour.

Even with a passion for a new conflict rising in them, the soldiers as they hurried on felt the weirdness, the satanic character of the battleground. The fitful flashes of lightning often showed faces stamped with awe; wet boughs of low-growing trees held them back with a moist and sticky touch; the low rumble of thunder came from the far horizon and its tremendous echo passed slowly through the Wilderness; and mingled again with this sound was an occasional cannon shot as the fringes of the two armies hastening on passed the time of night.

The tread of either army was heavy, dull and irregular, and the few torches they carried added little light to the glare of the lightning and the glow of the burning forest. The two marched on in the dark, saying little, making little noise for numbers so great, but steadily converging on Spottsylvania, where they were destined to meet in a conflict rivaling in somber grandeur that of the past two days.

CHAPTER XXI

A DELICATE SITUATION

The wounded and those who watched them in the old house learned a little of the race through the darkness. The change of the field of combat, the struggle for Spottsylvania and the wheel-about of the Southern army would leave them in the path of the North, and they must retreat toward Richmond.

The start next morning was through a torn and rent Wilderness, amid smoke and vapours, with wounded in the wagons, making a solemn train that wound its way through the forest, escorted on either flank by troopers, commanded by Talbot, slightly wounded in the shoulder. The Secretary had gone again to look on at the battle.

It was thus that Lucia Catherwood found herself on the way, of her own free will, to that Richmond from which she had recently escaped with so much trouble. There was no reason, real or conventional, why she should not go, as the precious pass from the Secretary removed all danger; and there in Richmond was Miss Grayson, the nearest of her blood. Helen removed the last misgiving.

"You will go with us? We need you," she said.

"Yes," replied Lucia simply; "I shall go to Richmond. I have a relative there with whom I can stay until the end of the war."

Helen was contented with this. It was not a time to ask questions. Then they rode together. Mrs. Markham was with them, quiet and keen-eyed. Much of the battle's spell had gone from her, and she observed everything, most of all Lucia Catherwood. She had noticed how the girl's eyes dwelled upon Prescott, the singular compound of strength and tenderness in her face, a character at once womanly and bold, and the astute Mrs. Markham began to wonder where these two had met before; but she said nothing to any one.

Prescott was in a wagon with Harley. Fate seemed to have linked for awhile these two who did not particularly care for each other. Both were conscious, and Prescott was sitting up, refreshed by the air upon his face, a heavy and noxious atmosphere though it was. So much of his strength had returned that he felt bitter regret at being unable to take part in the great movement which, he had gathered, was going on, and it was this feeling which united him and Harley for the time in a common bond of sympathy; but the latter presently spoke of something else:

"That was a beautiful girl who replaced your bandage this morning, Prescott. Upon my honour, she is one of the finest women I ever saw, and she is going with us, I hear. Do you know anything about her?"

Prescott did not altogether like Harley's tone, but he knew it was foolish to resent it and he replied:

"She is Miss Lucia Catherwood, a relative of Miss Charlotte Grayson, who lives in Richmond, and whom I presume she is going there to join. I have seen Miss Catherwood once or twice in Richmond."

Then he relapsed into silence, and Harley was unable to draw from him any more information; but Prescott, watching Lucia, saw how strong and helpful she was, doing all she could for those who were not her own. A woman with all a woman's emotions and sympathies, controlled by a mind and body stronger than those of most women, she was yet of the earth, real and substantial, ready to take what it contained of joy or sorrow. This was one of her qualities that most strongly attracted Prescott, who did not like the shadowy or unreal. Whilst he was on the earth he wished to be of it, and he preferred the sure and strong mind to the misty and dreamy.

He wished that she would come again to the wagon in which he rode, but now she seemed to avoid him—to be impelled, as it were, by a sense of shyness or a fear that she might be thought unfeminine. Thus he found scant opportunity during the day to talk to her or even to see her, as she remained nearly all the time in the rear of the column with Helen Harley.

Harley's vagrant fancy was caught. He was impressed by Lucia's tall beauty, her silence, her self-possession, and the mystery of her presence. He wished to discover more about her, who she was, whence she came, and believing Prescott to be his proper source of information, he asked him many questions, not noticing the impatient or taciturn demeanour of his comrade until Robert at last exclaimed with a touch of anger:

"Harley, if you wish to know so much about Miss Catherwood, you had better ask her these questions, and if she wishes she will answer them."

"I knew that before," replied Harley coolly; "and I tell you again, Prescott, she's a fine girl—none finer in Richmond."

Prescott turned his back in so far as a wounded man in that narrow space could turn, and Harley presently relapsed into silence.

They were yet in the Wilderness, moving among scrub pines, oaks and cedars, over ground moist with rain and dark with the shadow of the forest. It was Talbot's wish to keep in the rear of the Southern army until the way was clear and then turn toward Richmond. But this was not done with ease, as the Southern army was a shifting quantity, adapting its movements to those of the North; and Talbot often was compelled to send scouts abroad, lest he march with his convoy of wounded directly into the Northern ranks. Once as he rode by the side of Prescott's wagon he remarked:

"Confound such a place as this Wilderness; I don't think any region ever better deserved its name. I'll thank the Lord when I get out of it and see daylight again."

They were then in a dense forest, where the undergrowth was so thick that they broke a way through it with difficulty. The trees hung down mournful boughs dripping with recent rain; the wheels of the wagons and the feet of the horses made a drumming sound in the soft earth; the forest fire still showed, distant and dim, and a thin mist of ashes came on the wind at intervals; now and then they heard the low roll of a cannon, so far away that it seemed but an echo.

Thomas Talbot was usually a cheerful man who shut one eye to grief and opened the other to joy; but he was full of vigilance to-day and thought only of duty. Riding at the head of his column, alert for danger, he was troubled by the uncertainties of the way. It seemed to him that the two armies were revolving like spokes around a hub, and he never knew which he was going to encounter, for chance might bring him into the arc of either. He looked long at the gloomy forest, gazed at the dim fire which marked the latest battlefield, and became convinced that it was his only policy to push on and take the risk, though he listened intently for distant cannon shots and bore away from them.

They stopped about the middle of the afternoon to rest the horses and serve men and women with scanty food. Prescott felt so strong that he climbed out of the wagon and stood for a moment beside it. His head was dizzy at first, but presently it became steady, and he walked to Lucia Catherwood, who was standing alone by a great oak tree, gazing at the forest.

She did not notice him until she heard his step in the soft earth close behind her, when she started in surprise and alarm, exclaiming upon the risk he took and cautioning against exertion.

"My head is hard," he said, "and it will stand more blows than the one I received in the battle. Really I feel well enough to walk out here and I want to speak to you."

She was silent, awaiting his words. A shaft of sunshine pierced an opening in the foliage and fell directly upon her. Golden gleams appeared here and there in her hair and the colour in her cheeks deepened. Often Prescott had thought how strong she was; now he thought how very womanly she was.

"You are going with the wounded to Richmond?" he said.

"Yes," she replied. "I am going back to Miss Grayson's, to the house and the city from which you helped me with so much trouble and danger to escape."

"I am easier in my conscience because I did so," he said. "But Miss Catherwood, do you not fear for yourself? Are you not venturing into danger again?"

She smiled once more and replied in a slightly humourous tone:

"No; there is no danger. I went as one unwelcome before; I go as a guest now. You see, I am rising in the Confederacy. One of your powerful men, Mr. Sefton, has been very kind to me."

"What has he done for you?" asked Prescott, with a sudden jealous twinge.

"He has given me this pass, which will take me in or out of Richmond as I wish."

She showed the pass, and as Prescott looked at it he felt the colour rise in his face. Could the heart of the Secretary have followed the course of his own?

"I am here now, I may say, almost by chance," she continued. "After I left you I reached the main body of the Northern army in safety, and I intended to go at once to Washington, where I have relatives, though none so near and dear as Miss Grayson—you see I am really of the South, in part at least—but there was a long delay about a pass, the way of going and other such things, and while I was waiting General Grant began his great forward movement. There was nothing left for me to do then but to cling to the army—and—and I thought I might be of some use there. Women may not be needed on a battlefield, but they are afterward."

"I, most of all men, ought to know that," said Prescott, earnestly. "Don't I know that you, unaided, brought me to that house? Were it not for you I should probably have died alone in the Wilderness."

"I owed you something, Captain Prescott, and I have tried to repay a little," she said.

"You owe me nothing; the debt is all mine."

"Captain Prescott, I hope you do not think I have been unwomanly," she said.

"Unwomanly? Why should I think it?"

"Because I went to Richmond alone, though I did so really because I had nowhere else to go. You believe me a spy, and you think for that reason I was trying to escape from Richmond!"

She stopped and looked at Prescott, and when she met his answering gaze the flush in her cheeks deepened.

"Ah, I was right; you do think me a spy!" she exclaimed with passionate earnestness, "and God knows I might have been one! Some such thought was in my mind when I went to Miss Grayson's in Richmond. That day in the President's office, when the people were at the reception I was sorely tempted, but I turned away. I went into that room with the full intention of being a spy. I admit it. Morally, I suppose that I was one until that moment, but when the opportunity came I could not do it. The temptation would come again, I knew, and it was one reason why I wished to leave Richmond, though my first attempt was made because I feared you—I did not know you then. I do not like the name of spy and I do not want to be one. But there were others, and far stronger reasons. A powerful man knew of my presence in that office on that day; he could have proved me guilty even though innocent, and he could have involved with my punishment the destruction of others. There was Miss Grayson—how could I bring ruin upon her head! And—and——"

She stopped and the brilliant colour suffused her face.

"You used the word 'others,'" said Prescott. "You mean that so long as you were in Richmond my ruin was possible because I helped you?"

She did not reply, but the vivid colour remained in her face.

"It is nothing to me," said Prescott, "whether you were or were not a spy, or whether you were tempted to be one. My conscience does not reproach me because I helped you, but I think that it would give me grievous hurt had I not done so. I am not fitted to be the judge of anybody, Miss Catherwood, least of all of you. It would never occur to me to think you unwomanly."

"You see that I value your good opinion, Captain Prescott," she said, smiling slightly.

"It is the only thing that makes my opinion of any worth."

Talbot approached at that moment. Prescott introduced him with the courtesy of the time, not qualified at all by their present circumstances, and he regarded Talbot's look of wonder and admiration with a secret pleasure. What would Talbot say, he thought, if he were to tell him that this was the girl for whom he had searched Miss Grayson's house?

"Prescott," said Talbot, "a bruised head has put you here and a scratched arm keeps me in the same fix, but this is almost our old crowd and Richmond again—Miss Harley and her brother, Mrs. Markham, you and myself. We ought to meet Winthrop, Raymond and General Wood."

"We may," added Prescott, "as they are all somewhere with the army; Raymond is probably printing an issue of his paper in the rear of it—he certainly has news—and as General Wood is usually everywhere we are not likely to miss him."

"I think it just as probable that we shall meet a troop of Yankee cavalry," said Talbot. "I don't know what they would want with a convoy of wounded Confederates, but I'm detailed to take you to safety and I'd like to do it."

He paused and looked at Lucia. Something in her manner gave him a passing idea that she was not of his people.

"Still there is not much danger of that," he continued. "The Yankees are poor horsemen—not to be compared with ours, are they, Miss Catherwood?"

She met his gaze directly and smiled.

"I think the Yankee cavalry is very good," she said. "You may call me a Yankee, too, Captain Talbot. I am not traveling in disguise."

Talbot stroked his mustache, of which he was proud, and laughed.

"I thought so," he said; "and I can't say I'm sorry. I suppose I ought to hate all the Yankees, but really it will add to the spice of life to have with us a Yankee lady who is not afraid to speak her mind. Besides, if things go badly with us we can relieve our minds by attacking you."

Talbot was philosophical as well as amiable, and Prescott saw at once that he and Lucia would be good friends, which was a comfort, as it was in the power of the commander of the convoy to have made her life unpleasant.

Talbot stayed only a minute or two, then rode on to the head of the column, and when he was gone Lucia said:

"Captain Prescott, you must go back to your wagon; it is not wise for you to stay on your feet so long—at least, not yet."

He obeyed her reluctantly, and in a few moments the convoy moved on through the deep woods to the note of an occasional and distant cannon shot and a faint hum as of great armies moving. An hour later they heard a swift gallop and the figure of Wood at the head of a hundred horsemen appeared.

The mountaineer seemed to embrace the whole column in one comprehensive look that was a smile of pleasure when it passed over the face of Helen Harley, a glance of curiosity when it lingered on Lucia Catherwood, and inquiry when it reached Talbot, who quickly explained his mission. All surrounded Wood, eager for news.

"We're going to meet down here somewhere near a place they call Spottsylvania," said the General succinctly. "It won't be many days—two or three, I guess—and it will be as rough a meeting as that behind us was. If I were you, Talbot, I'd keep straight on to the south."

Then the General turned with his troopers to go. It was not a time when he could afford to tarry; but before starting he took Helen Harley's hand in his with a grace worthy of better training:

"I'll bring you news of the coming battle, Miss Harley."

She thanked him with her eyes, and in a moment he was gone, he and his troopers swallowed up by the black forest. The convoy resumed its way through the Wilderness, passing on at a pace that was of necessity slow owing to the wounded in the wagons and the rough and tangled nature of the country, which lost nothing of its wild and somber character. The dwarf cedars and oaks and pines still stretched away to the horizon. Night began to come down in the east and there the Wilderness heaved up in a black mass against the sullen sky. The low note of a cannon shot came now and then like the faint rumble of dying thunder.

Lucia walked alone near the rear of the column. She had grown weary of the wagons and her strong young frame craved exercise. She was seldom afraid or awed, but now the sun sinking over the terrible Wilderness and the smoke of battle around chilled her. The long column of the hurt, winding its way so lonely and silent through the illimitable forest, seemed like a wreck cast up from the battles, and her soul was full of sympathy. In a nature of unusual strength her emotions were of like quality, and though once she had been animated by a deep and passionate anger against that South with which she now marched, at this moment she found it all gone—slipped away while she was not noticing. She loved her own cause none the less, but no longer hated the enemy. She had received the sympathy and the friendship of a woman toward whom she had once felt a sensation akin to dislike. She did not forget how she had stood in the fringe of the crowd that day in Richmond and had envied Helen Harley when, in her glowing beauty, she received the tribute of the multitude. Now the two women were drawn together. Something that had been between them was gone, and in her heart Lucia knew what it was; but she rejoiced in a companionship and a friendship of her own sex when she was among those who were not of her cause.

It was impossible to resist sharing the feelings of the column: when it was in dread lest some wandering echo might be the tread of Northern horsemen, she, too, was in dread. She wanted this particular column to escape, but when she looked toward another part of the Wilderness, saw the dim light and heard the far rumble of another cannon shot, she felt a secret glow of pride. Grant was still coming, always coming, and he would come to the end. The result was no longer in doubt; it was now merely a matter of time and patience.

The sun sank behind the Wilderness; the night came down, heavy, black and impenetrable; slow thunder told of rain, and Talbot halted the convoy in the densest part of the forest, where the shelter would be best—for he was not sure of his way and farther marching in the dark might take him into the enemy's camp. All day they had not passed a single house nor met a single dweller in the Wilderness; if they had been near any woodcutter's hut it was hidden in a ravine and they did not see it. If a woodcutter himself saw them he remained in his covert in the thicket and they passed on, unspoken.

Talbot thought it best to camp where they were for the night, and he drew up the wagons in a circle, in the centre of which were built fires that burned with a smoky flame. All hovered around the blaze, as they felt lonely in this vast Wilderness and were glad when the beds of coal began to form and glow red in the darkness. Even the wounded in the wagons turned their eyes that way and drew cheer from the ruddy glow.

A rumour arose presently, and grew. It said that a Yankee woman was among them, traveling with them. Some one added that she bore a pass from the powerful Mr. Sefton and was going to Richmond, but why he did not know. Then they looked about among the women and decided that it could be none save Lucia; but if there was any feeling of hostility toward her it soon disappeared. Other women were with the column, but none so strong, none so helpful as she. Always she knew what to do and when to do it. She never grew tired nor lost her good humour; her touch had healing in it, and the wounded grew better at the sight of her face.

"If all the Yankees are like her, I wish I had a few more with this column," murmured Talbot under his breath.

Lucia began to feel the change in the atmosphere about her. The coldness vanished. She looked upon the faces that welcomed her, and being a woman she felt warmth at her heart, but said nothing.

Prescott crawled again from his wagon and said to her as she passed:

"Why do you avoid me, Miss Catherwood?"

A gleam of humour appeared in her eye.

"You are getting well too fast. I do not think you will need any more attention," she replied.

He regarded her with an unmoved countenance.

"Miss Catherwood," he said, "I feel myself growing very much worse. It is a sudden attack and a bad one."

But she passed on, disbelieving, and left him rueful.

The night went by without event, and then another day and another night, and still they hovered in the rear of their army, uncertain which way to go, tangled up in the Wilderness and fearing at any moment a raid of the Northern cavalry. They yet saw the dim fire in the forest, and no hour was without its distant cannon shot.

On the second day the two editors, Raymond and Winthrop, joined them.

"I've been trying to print a paper," said Raymond ruefully, "but they wouldn't stay in one place long enough for me to get my press going. This morning a Yankee cannon shot smashed the press and I suppose I might as well go back to Richmond. But I can't, with so much coming on. They'll be in battle before another day."

Raymond spoke in solemn tones (even he was awed and oppressed by what he had seen) and Winthrop nodded assent.

"They are converging upon the same point," said Winthrop, "and they are sure to meet inside of twenty-four hours."

When Lucia awoke the next morning the distant guns were sounding in her ears and a light flame burned under the horizon in the north. Day had just come, hot and close, and the sun showed the colour of copper through the veil of clouds hanging at the tops of the trees.

"It's begun," she heard Talbot say briefly, but she did not need his words to tell her that the armies were joined again in deadly strife in the Wilderness.

They ate breakfast in silence, all watching the glowing light in the north and listening to the thunder of the guns. Prescott, strong after his night's rest and sleep, came from the wagon and announced that he would not ride as an invalid any more; he intended to do his share of the work, and Talbot did not contradict him; it was a time when a man who could serve should be permitted to do it.

Talbot said they would remain in the camp for the present and await the fortunes of the battle; it was not worth while to continue a retreat when none knew in which direction the right path lay. But the men as they listened were seized with a fever of impatience. The flame of the cannon and the thunder of the battle had a singular attraction for them. They wished to be there and they cursed their fate because they were here. The wounded lamented their wounds and the well were sad because they were detailed for such duty; the new battle was going on without them, and the result would be decided while they waited there in the Wilderness with their hands folded. How they missed the Secretary with his news!

The morning went slowly on. The sun rose high, but it still shone with a coppery hue through the floating clouds, and a thick blanket of damp heat enclosed the convoy. The air seemed to tremble with the sound from the distant battle; it came in waves, and save for it the forest was silent; no birds sang in the trees, nothing moved in the grass. There was only the rumble of guns, coming wave upon wave. Thus hour after hour passed, and the fever of impatience still held the souls of those in this column. But the black Wilderness would tell no tale; it gave back the sound of conflict and nothing more. They watched the growing smoke and flame, the forest bursting into fresh fires, and knew only that the battle was fierce and desperate, as before.

Prescott's strength was returning rapidly, and he expected in another day or two to return to the army. The spirit was strong within him to make the trial now, but Talbot would not hear of it, saying that his wound was not healed sufficiently. On the morning of that second day he stood beside Lucia, somewhat withdrawn from the others, and for awhile they watched the distant battle. It was the first time in twenty-four hours that he had been able to speak to her. She had not seemed exactly to avoid him, but she was never in his path. Now he wished to hold her there with talk.

"I fear that you will be lonely in Richmond," he said at random.

"I shall have Miss Grayson," she replied, "and the panorama of the war will pass before me; I shall not have time for loneliness."

"Poor Richmond! It is desolate now."

"Its condition may become worse," she said meaningly.

He understood the look in her eyes and replied:

"You mean that Grant will come?"

"Yes!" she exclaimed, pointing toward the flame of the battle. "Can't you see? Don't you know, Captain Prescott, that Grant will never turn back? It is but three days since he fought a battle as great as Gettysburg, and now he is fighting another. The man has come, and the time for the South is at hand."

"But what a price—what a price!" said Prescott.

"Yes," she replied quickly; "but it is the South, not the North, that demands payment."

Then she stopped, and brilliant colour flushed into her face.

"Forgive me for saying such things at such a time," she said. "I do not hate anybody in the South, and I am now with Southern people. Credit it to my bad taste."

But Prescott would not have it so. It was he who had spoken, he said, and she had the right to reply. Then he asked her indirectly of herself, and she answered willingly. Hers had been a lonely life, and she had been forced to develop self-reliance, though perhaps it had taken her further than she intended. She seemed still to fear that he would think her too masculine, a bit unwomanly; but her loneliness, the lack of love in her life, made a new appeal to Prescott. He admired her as she stood there in her splendid young beauty and strength—a woman with a mind to match her beauty—and wondered how his fleeting fancy could ever have been drawn to any other. She was going to that hostile Richmond, where she had been in such danger, and she would be alone there save for one weak woman, watched and suspected like herself. He felt a sudden overwhelming desire to protect her, to defend her, to be a wall between her and all danger.

Far off on the northern horizon the battle flamed and rumbled, and a faint reflection of its lurid glow fell on the forest where they stood. It may be that its reflection fell on Prescott's ardent mind and hastened him on.

"Lucia," he exclaimed, "you are going back to Richmond, where you will be suspected, perhaps insulted! Give me the right to protect you from everybody!"

"Give you the right!" she exclaimed, in surprise; but as she looked at him the brilliant colour dyed her face and neck.

"Yes, Lucia," he said, "the greatest and holiest of all rights! Do you not see that I love you? Be my wife! Give me the right as your husband to stand between you and all danger!"

Still she looked at him, and as she gazed the colour left her face, leaving it very pale, while her eyes showed a dazzling hue. The forgotten battle flamed and thundered on the horizon.

"No," she replied, "I cannot give you such a promise."

"Lucia! You do not mean that! I know you do not. You must care for me a little. One reason why you fled from Richmond was to save me!"

"Yes, I do care for you—a little. But do you care for me enough—ah! do not interrupt me! Think of the time, the circumstances! One may say things now which he might not mean in a cooler moment. You wish to protect me—does a man marry a woman merely to protect her? I have always been able to protect myself."

There was a flash of pride in her tone and her tall figure grew taller. Prescott flushed a little and dropped his eyes for a moment.

"I have been unfortunate in my words, but, believe me, Lucia, I do not mean it in that way. It is love, not protection, that I offer. I believe that I loved you from the first—from the time I was pursuing you as a spy; and I pursue you now, though for myself."

She shook her head sadly, though she smiled upon him. She was his enemy, she said—she was of the North and he of the South—what would he say to his friends in Richmond, and how could he compromise himself by such a marriage? Moreover, it was a time of war, and one must not think of love. He grew more passionate in his declaration as he saw that which he wished slipping from him, and she, though still refusing him, let him talk, because he said the things that she loved best to hear. All the while the forgotten battle flamed and thundered on the northern horizon. Its result and progress alike were of no concern to them; both North and South had floated off in the distance.

Talbot came that way as they talked, and seeing the look on their faces, started and turned back. They never saw him. Lucia remained fixed in her resolve and only shook her head at Prescott's pleading.

"But at least," said Prescott, "that 'no' is not to apply forever. I shall refuse to despair."

She smiled somewhat sadly without reply, and there was no opportunity to say more, as others drew near, among them Mrs. Markham, wary and keen-eyed as ever. She marked well the countenances of these two, but reserved her observations for future use.

The battle reclaimed attention, silhouetted as it was in a great flaming cloud against a twilight sky, and its low rumble was an unbroken note.

When night fell a messenger came with terrible news. Grant had broken through at last! The thin lines of the Confederates could not stand this steady, heavy hammering day after day. They must retreat through the Wilderness and draw fresh breath to fight again. Sadly the convoy took its way to the south, and in three hours it was enveloped by the remnants of a broken brigade, retreating in the fear of hot pursuit by both cavalry and infantry. The commander of the brigade, by virtue of his rank, became commander of the whole, and Talbot, longing for action, fell back to the rear, resolved to watch for the enemy.

Talbot hated to exercise authority, preferring to act alone; and now he became a picket, keen-eyed, alert, while his friends went into camp ahead on the bank of a narrow but deep river. Presently he heard shots and knew that the skirmishers of the enemy were advancing, though he wondered why they should show such pernicious activity on so black a night. They were in battle with some other retreating Southern force—probably a regiment, he thought—and if they wanted to fight he could not help it.

CHAPTER XXII

THE LONE SENTINEL

The desultory firing troubled the ears of Talbot as he trod to and fro on his self-imposed task, as he could not see the use of it. The day for fighting and the night for sleep and rest was the perfect division of a soldier's life.

The tail of the battle writhed on without regard for his feelings or theories, though its efforts became gradually feebler, and he hoped that by and by the decent part of both armies would settle into lethargy, leaving the night to the skirmishers, who never sleep and are without conscience.

He went back a little to an open spot where a detail of about twenty men were posted. But he did not remain with them long. Securing a rifle, he returned toward the enemy, resolved to watch on his own account—a voluntary picket.

Talbot was not troubled for his friends alone. The brigade had been beaten and driven back upon the river, and with the press of numbers against it he feared that the next day would bring its destruction. The coming of the night, covering friend and foe alike and making activity hazardous, was opportune, since it would give his comrades time to rest and gather their strength for the stand in the morning. He could hear behind him even now the heavy tread of the beaten companies as they sought their places in the darkness, the clank of gun wheels, and now and then the neigh of a tired horse.

The crash of a volley and another volley which answered came from his right, and then there was a spatter of musketry, stray shots following each other and quickly dying away. Talbot saw the flash of the guns, and the smell of burnt gunpowder came to his nostrils. He made a movement of impatience, for the powder poisoned the pure air. He heard the shouts of men, but they ceased in a few moments, and then farther away a cannon boomed. More volleys of rifle shots and the noise of the cheering or its echo came from his left; but unable to draw meaning from the tumult, he concluded at last it was only the smouldering embers of the battle and continued to walk his voluntary beat with steady step.

The night advanced and the rumbling in the encampment behind him did not cease at all, the sounds remaining the same as they were earlier in the evening—that is, the drum of many feet upon the earth, the rattle of metal and the hum of many voices. Talbot concluded that the men would never go to sleep, but presently a light shot up in the darkness behind him, rising eight or ten feet above the earth and tapering at the top to a blue-and-pink point. Presently another arose beside it, and then others and still others, until there were thirty, forty, fifty or more.

Talbot knew these were the campfires and he wondered why they had not been lighted before. At last the men would go to sleep beside the cheerful blaze. The fires comforted him, too, and he looked upon the rosy flame of each, shining there in the darkness, as he would have looked upon a personal friend. They took away much of his lonely feeling, and as they bent a little before the wind seemed to nod to him a kind of encouragement in the dangerous work upon which he had set himself. He could see only the tops of these rosy cones; all below was hidden by the bushes that grew between. He could not see even the dim figure of a soldier, but he knew that they were there, stretched out in long rows before the fires, asleep in their blankets, while others stood by on their arms, ready for defense should the pickets be driven in.

The troublesome skirmishers seemed to be resting just then, for no one fired at him and he could not hear them moving in the woods. The scattering shots down the creek ceased and the noises in the camp began to die. It seemed as if night were about to claim her own at last and put everybody to rest. The fires rose high and burned with a steady flame.

A stick broke under his feet with a crackling noise as he walked to and fro, and a bullet sang through the darkness past his ear. He fired at the flash of the rifle, and as he ran back and forth fired five or six times more, slipping in the bullets as quickly as he could, for he wished to create an illusion that the patrol consisted of at least a dozen men. The opposing skirmishers returned his fire with spirit, and Talbot heard their bullets clipping the twigs and pattering among the leaves, but he felt no great alarm, since the night covered him and only a chance ball could strike him.

His opponents were wary, and only two or three times did he see the shadows which he knew to be their moving figures. He fired at these but no answering cry came, and Talbot could not tell whether any of his bullets struck, though it did not matter. His lead served well enough as a warning, and the skirmishers must know that the nearer they came the better aim they would have to face. Presently their fire ceased and he was disappointed, as his blood had risen to fever heat and he was in fighting humour.

The night went on its slow way, and Talbot, stopping a moment to rest and listen for the skirmishers, calculated that it was not more than two hours until day. The long period through which he had watched began to press upon him. Weights dragged at his feet, and he noticed that his rifle when he shifted it from one shoulder to the other appeared many pounds heavier than before. His knees grew stiff and he felt like an old man; but he allowed himself no rest, continuing his walk back and forth at a slower pace, for he believed he could feel his joints grate as he stepped. He looked at the fires with longing and was tempted to go; but no, he must atone for the neglect of that chief of brigade.

Just when the night seemed to be darkest the skirmishers made another attack, rushing forward in a body, firing with great vigour and shouting, though hitherto they had fought chiefly in silence. Talbot considered it an attempt to demoralize him and was ready for it. He retreated a little, sheltered himself behind a tree and opened fire, skipping between shots from one tree to another in order that he might protect the whole of his battle line and keep his apparent numbers at their height.

His assailants were so near now that he could see some of them springing about, and one of his shots was followed by a cry of pain and the disappearance of the figure. After that the fire of his antagonists diminished and soon ceased. They had shown much courage, but seemed to think that the defenders were in superior numbers and a further advance would mean their own destruction.

Again silence came, save for the hum of the camp. The fires burnt brightly behind him, and far off in front he saw the flickering fires of the enemy. As the wind increased the lights wavered and the cones split into many streams of flame before it. The leaves and boughs whistled in the rush of air and the waters of the creek sang a minor chord on the shallows. Talbot had heard these sounds a hundred times when a boy in the wilderness of the deep woods, and it was easy enough for him to carry himself back there, with no army or soldier near. But he quickly dismissed such thoughts as would lull him only into neglect of his watch. After having kept it so long and so well it would be the height of weakness to fail now, when day could not be much more than two hours distant.

The silence remained unbroken. An hour passed and then another, and in the east he saw a faint shade of dark gray showing through the black as if through a veil.

The gray tint brightened and the black veil became thinner. Soon it parted and a bar of light shot across the eastern horizon, broadening rapidly till the world of hills, fields and forests rose up from the darkness. A trumpet sounded in the hostile camp.

Skirmishers filled the woods in front of Talbot and pressed toward him in a swarm.

"Surrender!" cried out one of them, an officer. "It is useless for you to resist! We are a hundred and you are one! Don't you see?"

Talbot turned and looked back at the fires burning in the empty camp of his comrades. The light of the morning showed everything, even to the last boat-load of the beaten brigade landing on the farther shore; he understood all.

"Yes, I will surrender," he said, as his eyes gleamed with sudden comprehension of his great triumph, "but I've held you back till the last company of our division has passed the river and is safe."

CHAPTER XXIII

OUT OF THE FOREST

The retreating brigade, the river behind it and the pursuit seemingly lost on the farther shore, passed on in the golden sunshine of the morning through, a country of gentle hills, green fields and scattered forest.

It was joined three hours after sunrise by no less a person than Mr. Sefton himself, fresh, immaculate and with no trace of discomposure on his face. He was on horseback, and told them he had just come across the fields from another division of the army not more than three miles away. He gave the news in a quiet tone, without any special emphasis upon the more important passages. The South had been compelled to give ground; Grant had lost more than fifty thousand men, but he was coming through the Wilderness and would not be denied. He was still fighting as if he had just begun, and reinforcements were constantly pouring forward to take the places of the fallen in his ranks.

Prompted by a motive which even his own analytical mind could not define, the Secretary sought Lucia Catherwood. He admired her height, her strength and resolved beauty—knew that she was of a type as admirable as it was rare, and wondered once or twice why he did not love her instead of Helen Harley. Here was a woman with a mind akin to his own—bold, keen and penetrating. And that face and figure! He wished he could see her in a drawing-room, dressed as she should be, and with the lights burning softly overhead. Then she would be indeed a princess, if there were any such beings, in the true meaning of the word, on this earth. She would be a fit wife for a great man—the greater half of himself.

But he did not love her; he loved Helen Harley—the Secretary confessed it to himself with a smothered half-sigh. At times he was pleased with this sole and recently discovered weak spot in his nature, because it brought to him some fresh and pleasing emotions, not at all akin to any that he had ever felt before; but again it troubled him, as a flaw in his armour. His love for Helen Harley might interfere with his progress—in fact, was doing so already, but he said to himself he could not help it. Now he was moved to talk to Lucia Catherwood. Dismounting from his horse, he took a place by her side.

She was walking near the rear of the column and there were others not many feet away, but she was alone in the truest sense, having a feeling of personal detachment and aloofness. These people were kind to her, and yet there was a slight difference in their manner toward her and toward one another—a difference almost imperceptible and perhaps not intended, but sufficient to show her that she was not of them. Just now it gave her such a sense of loneliness and exclusion that she almost welcomed the smile of the Secretary when he spoke to her. As ready to recognize the power in him as he was to note her own strong and keen mind, she waited guardedly to hear what he had to say.

93

"Miss Catherwood," he said, "I was glad to assist you in your plan of returning to Richmond, but I have wondered why you should wish to return. If I may use a simile, Richmond is the heart of the storm, and having escaped from such a place, it seems strange that you should go back to it."

"There are many other women in Richmond," she replied, "and as they will not be in any greater danger than I, should I be less brave than they?"

"But they have no other choice."

"Perhaps I have none either. Moreover, a time is coming when it is not physical courage alone that will be needed. Look back, Mr. Sefton."

She pointed to the Wilderness behind them, where they saw the crimson glow of flames against the blue sky, and long, trailing clouds of black smoke. The low mutter of guns, a continuous sound since sunrise, still came to their ears.

"The flames and the smoke," she said, "are nearer to Richmond than they were yesterday, just as they were nearer yesterday than they were the day before."

"It is yet a long road to Richmond."

"But it is being shortened. I shall be there at the end. The nearest and dearest of all my relatives is in Richmond and I wish to be with her. There are other reasons, too, but the end of which I spoke is surely coming and you know it as well as I. Perhaps you have long known it. As for myself, I have never doubted, despite great defeats."

"It is not given to men to have the faith of women."

"Perhaps not; but in this case it does not require faith: reason alone is sufficient. What chance did the South ever have? The North, after all these years, is just beginning to be aroused. Until the present you have been fighting only her vanguard. Sometimes it seems to me that men argue only from passion and sentiment, not from reason. If reason alone had been applied this war would never have been begun."

"Nor any other. It is a true saying that neither men nor women are ever guided wholly for any long period by reason. That is where philosophers,—idealogists, Napoleon called them—make their mistake, and it is why the science of government is so uncertain—in fact, it is not a question of science at all, but of tact."

The Secretary was silent for awhile, but he still walked beside Miss Catherwood, leading his horse by the bridle. Prescott presently glancing back, beheld the two together and set his teeth. He did not like to see Lucia with that man and he wondered what had put them side by side. He knew that she had a pass from Mr. Sefton, and this fresh fact added to his uneasiness. Was it possible those two had a secret in common?

The Secretary saw the frown on Prescott's face and was pleased, though he spoke of him and his great services. "He has more than courage—he has sense allied with it. Sometimes I think that courage is one of the commonest of qualities, but it is not often that it is supported by coolness, discrimination and the ability to endure. A fine young man, Robert Prescott, and one destined to high honours. If he survive the war, I should say that he will become the Governor of his State or rise high in Congress."

He watched the girl closely out of the corner of his eye as he spoke, for he was forming various plans and, as Lucia Catherwood was included in his comprehensive schemes, he wished to see the effect upon her of what he said, but she betrayed nothing. So far as her expression was concerned Prescott might have been no more to her than any other chance acquaintance. She walked on, the free, easy stride of her long limbs carrying her over the ground swiftly. Every movement showed physical and mental strength. Under the tight sleeve of her dress the muscle rippled slightly, but the arm was none the less rounded and feminine. Her chin, though the skin upon it was white and smooth like silk, was set firmly and marked an indomitable will.

Curious thoughts again flowed through the frank mind of the Secretary. Much of his success in life was due to his ability to recognize facts when he saw them. If he made failures he never sought to persuade himself that they were successes or even partial successes; thus he always went upon the battlefield with exact knowledge of his resources. He wondered again why he did not fall in love with Lucia Catherwood. Here was the exact complement of himself, a woman with a mind a fit mate to his own. He had come far already, but with her to aid him there were no heights to which he—no, they—might not climb. And she was beautiful—beautiful, with a grace, a stateliness and dignity beyond compare.

Mr. Sefton glanced down the column and saw there a head upon which the brown hair curled slightly. The eyes were turned away, but the Secretary knew they were blue and that there was something in the face which appealed to strong men for protection. He shook his head slowly. The tricky little god was making sport of him, James Sefton, the invincible, and he did not like it.

A sense of irritation against Lucia Catherwood rose in Mr. Sefton's mind. As he could not stir her in any obvious manner by speaking of Prescott, he felt a desire to move her in some way, to show his power over her, to compel from her an appeal for mercy. It would be a triumph to bring a woman at once so strong and so proud to her knees. He would not proceed to extreme measures, and would halt at the delicate moment, but she must be made to feel that he was master of the situation.

So he spoke again of her return to Richmond, suggesting plans for her pleasant stay while there, mentioning acquaintances of his whom he would like her to know, and making suggestions to which he thought she would be compelled to return answers that would betray more or less her position in Richmond.

She listened at first with a flush on her face, giving way soon to paleness as her jaw hardened and her lips closed firmly. The perception of Lucia Catherwood was not inferior to that of the Secretary, and she took her resolve.

"Mr. Sefton," she said at length, "I am firmly convinced of one thing."

"And what is that?"

"That you know I am the alleged spy for whom you were so long looking in Richmond."

The Secretary hesitated for an answer. Her sudden frankness surprised him. It was so different from his own methods in dealing with others that he had not taken it into account.

"Yes, you know it," she continued, "and it may be used against me, not to inflict on me a punishment—that I do not dread—but to injure the character and reputation that a woman loves—things that are to her the breath of life. But I say that if you choose to use your power you can do so."

The Secretary glanced at her in admiration, the old wonder concerning himself returning to him.

"Miss Catherwood," he said, "I cannot speak in too high praise of your courage. I have never before seen a woman show so much. Your surmise is correct. You were the spy or alleged spy, as you prefer to say, for whom I was looking. As for the morality of your act, I do not consider that; it never entered into my calculations; but in going back to Richmond you realize that you will be wholly in the power of the Confederate Government. Whenever it wants you you will have to come, and in very truth you will have to walk in the straight and narrow path."

"I am not afraid," she said, with a proud lifting of her head. "I will take the risks, and if you, Mr. Sefton, for some reason unknown to me, force me to match my wits with yours, I shall do the best I can."

The haughty uplift of her neck and the flash of her eye showed that she thought her "best" would be no mean effort, but this attitude appealed to the Secretary more than a humble submission ever would have done. Here was one with whom it would be a pleasure to make a test of skill and force. Certainly steel would be striking sparks from steel.

"I am not making any threats, Miss Catherwood," he said. "That would be unworthy, I merely wish you to understand the situation. I am a frank man, I trust, and, like most other men, I seek my own advancement; it would further no interest of mine for me to denounce you at present, and I trust that you will not at any time make it otherwise."

"That is, I am to serve you if you call upon me."

"Let us not put it so bluntly."

"I shall not do anything that I do not wish to do," she said, with the old proud uplift of her head. "And listen! there is something which may soon shatter all your plans, Mr. Sefton."

She pointed backward, where the purplish clouds hung over the Wilderness, whence came the low, sullen mutter, almost as faint as the distant beat of waves on a coast.

The Secretary smiled deprecatingly.

"After all, you are like other women, Miss Catherwood. You suppose, of course, that I stake my whole fortune upon a single issue, but it is not so. I wish to live on after the war, whatever its result may be, and the tide of fortune in that forest may shift and change, but mine may not shift and change with it."

"You are at least frank."

"The South may lose, but if she loses the world will not end on that account. I shall still wish to play my part. Ah, here comes Captain Prescott."

Prescott liked little this long talk between Lucia and the Secretary and the deep interest each seemed to show in what the other said. He bore it with patience for a time, but it seemed to him, though the thought was not so framed in his mind, that he had a certain proprietary interest in her because he had saved her at great risk.

The Secretary received him with a pleasant smile, made some slight remark about duty elsewhere and dropped easily away. Prescott waited until he was out of hearing before he said:

"Do you like that man, Miss Catherwood?"

"I do not know. Why?"

"You were in such close and long conversation that you seemed to be old friends."

"There were reasons for what we said."

She looked at him so frankly that he was ashamed, but she, recognizing his tone and the sharpness of it, was not displeased. On the contrary, she felt a warm glow, and the woman in her urged her to go further. She spoke well of the Secretary, his penetrating foresight and his knowledge of the world and its people—men, women and children. Prescott listened in a somewhat sulky mood, and she, regarding him with covert glances, was roused to a singular lightness that she had not known for many days. Then she changed, showing him her softer side, for she could be as feminine as any other woman, not less so than Helen Harley, and she would prove it to him. Becoming all sunshine with just enough shadow to deepen the colours, she spoke of a time when the war should have passed—when the glory of this world with the green of spring and the pink of summer should return. Her moods were so many and so variable, but all so gay, that Prescott began to share her spirits, and although they were retreating from a lost field and the cannon still muttered behind them, he forgot the war and remembered only this girl beside him, who walked with such easy grace and saw so bright an outlook.

95

Thus the retreat continued. The able-bodied soldiers of the brigade were drafted away, but the women and wounded men went on. Grant never ceased his hammer strokes, and it was necessary for the Southern leaders to get rid of all superfluous baggage. Prescott, singularly enough, found himself in command of this little column that marched southward, taking the place of his friend Talbot, lost in a mysterious way to the regret of all.

Mr. Sefton left them the day after his talk with Lucia, and Prescott was not sorry to see him go, for some of his uneasiness departed with him. Harley, vain, fretful and complaining, gave much trouble, yielding only to the influence of Mrs. Markham, with whom Prescott did not like to see him, but was helpless in the matter. Helen and Lucia were the most obedient of soldiers and gave no trouble at all. Helen, a warm partisan, seemed to think little of the great campaign that was going on behind her, and to concern herself more about something else. Yet she was not unhappy—even Prescott could see it—and the bond between her and Lucia was growing strong daily. Usually they were together, and once when Mrs. Markham spoke slightingly of the "Northern woman," as she called Lucia, Helen replied with a sharpness very remarkable for her—a sharpness that contributed to the growing coldness between them, which had begun with the power Mrs. Markham exercised over Helen's brother.

Prescott noticed these things more or less and sometimes they pained him; but clearly they were outside his province, and in order to give them no room in his mind he applied himself more diligently than ever to his duties, his wound now permitting him to do almost a man's work.

They marched slowly and it gave promise of being a long journey. The days grew very hot; the sun burned the grass, and over them hung clouds of steamy vapour. For the sake of the badly wounded who had fever they traveled often by night and rested by day in the shade. But that cloud of war never left them.

The days passed and distant battles still hung on their skirts. The mutter of the guns was seldom absent, and they yet saw, now and then, on the horizon, flashes like heat-lightning. One morning there was a rapid beat of hoofs, a glitter of sabers issuing from a wood, and in a moment the little convoy was surrounded by a troop of cavalry in blue.

"Only wounded men and women," said their leader, a young colonel with a fine, open face. "Bah, we have no time to waste with them!"

He bowed contritely, touching his hat to the ladies and saying that he did not mean to be ungallant. Then in a moment he and his men were gone at gallop in a cloud of dust, disappearing in a whirlwind across the plain, leaving the little convoy to proceed at its leisure.

Prescott gazed after them, shading his eyes with his hands. "There must be some great movement at hand," he said, "or they would have asked us questions, at least."

The day grew close and sultry. Columns of steamy vapour moved back and forth and enclosed them, and the sun set in a red mist. At night it rained, but early the next morning the mutter of the cannon grew to a rumble and then a storm. The hot day came and all the east was filled with flashes of fire. The crash of the cannon was incessant, and in fancy every one in that little convoy heard the tramping of brigades and the clatter of hoofs as the horsemen rushed on the guns.

"They have met again!" said Lucia.

"Yes," replied Prescott. "It's Grant and Lee. How many great battles is this since they met first in the Wilderness?"

Nobody could tell; they had lost count.

The tumult lasted about an hour and then died away, to be succeeded by a stillness intense and painful. The sun shone with a white glare. No wind stirred. The leaves and the grass drooped. The fields were deserted; there was not a sign of life in them, either human or animal. The road lay before them, a dusty streak.

None came to tell of the battle, and, oppressed by anxiety, Prescott moved on. Some horsemen appeared on the hills the next morning, and as they approached, Prescott, with indescribable joy, recognized in the lead the figure of Talbot, whose unknown fate they had mourned. Talbot delightedly shook hands with them all, not neglecting Lucia Catherwood. His honest face glowed with emotion.

"I am on a scout around our army now," he said, "and I thought I should find you near here somewhere. I wanted to tell you what had become of me. I was captured that night we were crossing the river—some of my blundering—but I escaped the next night. It was easy enough to do. There was so much fighting and so much of everything going on that I just rose up and walked out of the Yankee camp. Nobody had time to pay any attention to me. I got back to Lee—somehow I knew I must do it, as he could never win the war without me—and here I am."

"There was a battle yesterday morning; we heard it," said Prescott.

Talbot's face clouded and the corners of his mouth drooped.

"We have won a great victory," he said, "but it doesn't pay us. The Yankees lost twelve or fifteen thousand men, but we haven't gained anything. That firing you heard was at Cold Harbour. It was a great battle, an awful one. I hope to God I shall never see its like again. I saw fifteen thousand men stretched out on the bloody ground in rows. I don't believe that so many men ever before fell in so short a time. I have heard of a whirlwind of death, but I never saw one till then.

"We had gone into intrenchments and Grant moved against us with his whole army. They came on; you could hear 'em, the tramp of regiments and brigades, scores of thousands, and the sun rising up and turning to gold over their heads. Our cannon began. What a crash! It was like twenty thunderbolts all at once. We swept that field with tons and tons of metal. Then our rifles opened and the whistling of the bullets was like the screaming of a wind on a plain. You could see the men of that army shoot up into the air before such a sheet of metal, and you heard the cracking of bones like the breaking up of ice. After awhile those that lived had to turn back; human beings could not stand more, and we were glad when it was all over."

Talbot stayed a little while with them. Then he and his men, like the Northern cavalry, whirled off in a cloud of dust, and the little convoy resumed its solemn march southward, reaching Richmond in safety.

CHAPTER XXIV

THE DESPATCH BEARER

Leaves of yellow and red and brown were falling, and the wind that came up the valley played on the boughs like a bow on the strings of a violin. The mountain ridges piled against each other cut the blue sky like a saber's edge, and the forests on the slopes rising terrace above terrace burned in vivid colours painted by the brush of autumn. The despatch bearer's eye, sweeping peaks and slopes and valleys, saw nothing living save himself and his good horse. The silver streams in the valleys, the vivid forests on the slopes and the blue peaks above told of peace, which was also in the musical note of the wind, in the shy eyes of a deer that looked at him a moment then fled away to the forest, and in the bubbles of pink and blue that floated on the silver surface of the stream at his feet.

Prescott had been into the far South on a special mission from the Confederate Government in Richmond after his return from the Wilderness and complete recovery from his wound, and now he was going back through a sea of mountains, the great range that fills up so much of North Carolina and its fifty thousand square miles, and he was not sorry to find the way long. He enjoyed the crisp air, the winds, the burning colours of the forest, the deep blue of the sky and the infinite peace. But the nights lay cold on the ridges, and Prescott, when he could find no cabin for shelter, built a fire of pine branches and, wrapping himself in his blanket, slept with his feet to the coals. The cold increased by and by, and icy wind roared among the peaks and brought a skim of snow. Then Prescott shivered and pined for the lowlands and the haunts of men.

He descended at last from the peaks and entered a tiny hamlet of the backwoods, where he found among other things a two-weeks-old Richmond newspaper. Looking eagerly through its meager columns to see what had happened while he was buried in the hills, he learned that there was no new stage in the war—no other great battle. The armies were facing each other across their entrenchments at Petersburg, and the moment a head appeared above either parapet the crack of a rifle from the other told of one more death added to the hundreds of thousands. That was all of the war save that food was growing scarcer and the blockade of the Southern ports more vigilant. It was a skilful and daring blockade runner now that could creep past the watching ships.

On an inside page he found social news. Richmond was crowded with refugees, and wherever men and women gather they must have diversion though at the very mouths of the guns. The gaiety of the capital, real or feigned, continued, and his eye was caught by the name of Lucia Catherwood. There was a new beauty in Richmond, the newspaper said, one whose graces of face and figure were equaled only by the qualities of her mind. She had relatives of strong Northern tendencies, and she had been known to express such sympathies herself; but they only lent piquancy to her conversation. She had appeared at one of the President's receptions; and further on Prescott saw the name of Mr. Sefton. There was nothing by which he could tell with certainty, but he inferred that she had gone there with the Secretary. A sudden thought assailed and tormented him. What could the Secretary be to her? Well, why not? Mr. Sefton was an able and insinuating man. Moreover, he was no bitter partisan: the fact that she believed in the cause of the North would not trouble him. She had refused himself and not many minutes later had been seen talking with the Secretary in what seemed to be the most confidential manner. Why had she come back to Richmond, from which she had escaped amid such dangers? Did it not mean that she and the Secretary had become allies more than friends? The thought would not let Prescott rest.

Prescott put the newspaper in his pocket and left the little tavern with an abruptness that astonished his host, setting out upon his ride with increased haste and turning eastward, intending to reach the railroad at the nearest point where he could take a train to Richmond.

His was not a morbid mind, but the fever in it grew. He had thought that the Secretary loved Helen Harley: but once he had fancied himself in love with Helen, too, and why might not the Secretary suffering from the same delusion be changed in the same way? He took out the newspaper and read the story again. There was much about her beauty, a description of her dress, and the distinction of her manner and appearance. The President himself, it said, was charmed with her, and departing from his usual cold reserve gave her graceful compliments.

This new reading of the newspaper only added more impetus to his speed and on the afternoon of the same day he reached the railroad station. Early the next morning he entered Richmond.

His heart, despite its recurrent troubles, was light, for he was coming home once more.

The streets were but slightly changed—perhaps a little more bareness and leanness of aspect, an older and more faded look to the clothing of the people whom he passed, but the same fine courage shone in their eyes. If Richmond, after nearly four years of fighting, heard the guns of the foe once more, she merely drew tighter the belt around her lean waist and turning her face toward the enemy smiled bravely.

97

The President received the despatch bearer in his private room, looking taller, thinner and sterner than ever. Although a Kentuckian by birth, he had been bred in the far South, but had little of that far South about him save the dress he wore. He was too cold, too precise, too free from sudden emotion to be of the Gulf Coast State that sent him to the capital. Prescott often reflected upon the odd coincidence that the opposing Presidents, Lincoln and Davis, should have been produced by the same State, Kentucky, and that the President of the South should be Northern in manner and the President of the North Southern in manner.

Mr. Davis read the despatches while their bearer, at his request, waited by. Prescott knew the hopeless tenor of those letters, but he could see no change in the stern, gray face as its owner read them, letter after letter. More than a half-hour passed and there was no sound in the room save the rustling of the paper as the President turned it sheet by sheet. Then in even, dry tones he said:

"You need not wait any longer, Captain Prescott; you have done your part well and I thank you. You will remain in Richmond until further orders."

Prescott saluted and went out, glad to get into the free air again. He did not envy the responsibility of a president in war time, whether the president of a country already established or of one yet tentative. He hurried home, and it was his mother herself who responded to the sound of the knocker—his mother, quiet, smiling and undemonstrative as of old, but with an endless tenderness for him in the depths of her blue eyes.

"Here I am again, mother, and unwounded this time," he cried after the first greeting; "and I suppose that as soon as they hear of my arrival all the Yankees will be running back to the North."

She smiled her quiet, placid smile.

"Ah, my son," she said, and from her voice he could not doubt her seriousness, "I'm afraid they will not go even when they hear of your arrival."

"In your heart of hearts, mother, you have always believed that they would come into Richmond. But remember they are not here yet. They were even closer than this before the Seven Days, but they got their faces burned then for their pains."

They talked after their old custom, while Prescott ate his luncheon and his mother gave him the news of Richmond and the people whom he knew. He noticed often how closely she followed the fortunes of their friends, despite her seeming indifference, and, informed by experience, he never doubted the accuracy of her reports.

"Helen Harley is yet in the employ of Mr. Sefton," she said, "and the money that she earns is, I hear, still welcome in the house of the Harleys. Mr. Harley is a fine Southern gentleman, but he has found means of overcoming his pride; it requires something to support his state."

"But what of Helen?" asked Prescott. He always had a feeling of repulsion toward Mr. Harley, his sounding talk, his colossal vanity and his selfishness.

"Helen, I think," said his mother, "is more of a woman than she used to be. Her mind has been strengthened by occupation. You won't object, Robert, will you, if I tell you that in my opinion both the men and women of the South have suffered from lack of diversity and variety in interests and ambitions. When men have only two ambitions, war and politics, and when women care only for the social side of life, important enough, but not everything, there can be no symmetrical development. A Southern republic, even if they should win this war, is impossible, because to support a State it takes a great deal more than the ability to speak and fight well."

Prescott laughed.

"What a political economist we have grown to be, mother!" he said, and then he added thoughtfully: "I won't deny, however, that you are right—at least, in part. But what more of Helen, mother? Is Mr. Sefton as attentive as ever to his clerk?"

She looked at him covertly, as if she would measure alike his expression and the tone of his voice.

"He is still attentive to Helen—in a way," she replied, "but the Secretary is like many other men: he sees more than one beautiful flower in the garden."

"What do you mean, mother?" asked Prescott quickly.

His face flushed suddenly and then turned pale. She gave him another keen but covert look from under lowered eyelids.

"There's a new star in Richmond," she replied quietly, "and singular as it may seem, it is a star of the North. You know Miss Charlotte Grayson and her Northern sympathies: it is a relative of hers—a Miss Catherwood, Miss Lucia Catherwood, who came to visit her shortly after the battles in the Wilderness—the 'Beautiful Yankee,' they call her. Her beauty, her grace and distinction of manner are so great that all Richmond raves about her. She is modest and would remain in retirement, but for the sake of her own peace and Miss Grayson's she has been compelled to enter our social life here."

"And the Secretary?" said Prescott. He was now able to assume an air of indifference.

"He warms himself at the flame and perhaps scorches himself, too, or it may be that he wishes to make some one else jealous—Helen Harley, for instance. I merely venture the suggestion; I do not pretend to know all the secrets of the social life of Richmond."

Prescott went that very afternoon to the Grayson cottage, and he prepared himself with the greatest care for his going. He felt a sudden and strong anxiety about his clothing. His uniform was old, ragged and stained, but he had a civilian suit of good quality.

"This dates from the fall of '60," he said, looking at it, "and that's more than four years ago; but it's hard to keep the latest fashions in Richmond now."

However, it was a vast improvement, and the change to civilian garb made him feel like a man of peace once more.

He went into the street and found Richmond under the dim cold of a November sky, distant houses melting into a gray blur and people shivering as they passed. As he walked briskly along he heard behind him the roll of carriage wheels, and when he glanced over his shoulder what he beheld brought the red to his face.

Mr. Sefton was driving and Helen Harley sat beside him. On the rear seat were Colonel Harley and Lucia Catherwood. As he looked the Secretary turned back and said something in a laughing manner to Lucia, and she, laughing in like fashion, replied. Prescott was too far away to understand the words even had he wished, but Lucia's eyes were smiling and her face was rosy with the cold and the swift motion. She was muffled in a heavy black cloak, but her expression was happy.

The carriage passed so swiftly that she did not see Prescott standing on the sidewalk. He gazed after the disappearing party and others did likewise, for carriages were becoming too scarce in Richmond not to be noticed. Some one spoke lightly, coupling the names of James Sefton and Lucia Catherwood. Prescott turned fiercely upon him and bade him beware how he repeated such remarks. The man did not reply, startled by such heat, and Prescott walked on, striving to keep down the anger and grief that were rising within him.

He concluded that he need not hurry now, because if he went at once to the little house in the cross street she would not be there; and he came to an angry conclusion that while he had been upon an errand of hardship and danger she had been enjoying all the excitement of life in the capital and with a powerful friend at court. He had always felt a sense of proprietorship in her and now it was rudely shocked. He forgot that if he had saved her she had saved him. It never occurred to him in his glowing youth that she had an entire right to love and marry James Sefton if fate so decreed.

He walked back and forth so angrily and so thoroughly wrapped in his own thoughts that he noticed nobody, though many noticed him and wondered at the young man with the pale face and the hot eyes.

It was twilight before he resumed his journey to the little house. The gray November day was thickening into the chill gloom of a winter night when he knocked at the well-remembered door. The shutters were closed, but some bars of ruddy light shone through them and fell across the brown earth. He was not coming now in secrecy as of old, but he had come with a better heart then.

It was Lucia herself who opened the door—Lucia, with a softer face than in the earlier time, but with a royal dignity that he had never seen in any other woman, and he had seen women who were royal by birth. She was clad in some soft gray stuff and her hair was drawn high upon her head, a crown of burnished black, gleaming with tints of red, like flame, where the firelight behind her flickered and fell upon it.

The twilight was heavy without and she did not see at once who was standing at the door. She put up her hands to shade her eyes, but when she beheld Prescott a little cry of gladness broke from her. "Ah, it is you!" she said, holding out both her hands, and his jealousy and pain were swept away for the moment.

He clasped her hands in the warm pressure of his own, saying: "Yes, it is I; and I cannot tell you how glad I am to see you once more."

The room behind her seemed to be filled with a glow, and when they went in the fire blazed and sparkled and its red light fell across the floor. Miss Grayson, small, quiet and gray as usual, came forward to meet him. Her tiny cool hand rested in his a moment, and the look in her eyes told him as truly as the words she spoke that he was welcome.

"When did you arrive?" asked Lucia.

"But this morning," he replied. "You see, I have come at once to find you. I saw you when you did not see me."

"When?" she asked in surprise.

"In the carriage with the Secretary and the Harleys," he replied, the feeling of jealousy and pain returning. "You passed me, but you were too busy to see me."

She noticed the slight change in his tone, but she replied without any self-consciousness.

"Yes; Mr. Sefton—he has been very kind to us—asked me to go with Miss Harley, her brother and himself. How sorry I am that none of us saw you."

The feeling that he had a grievance took strong hold of Prescott, and it was inflamed at the new mention of the Secretary's name. If it were any other it might be more tolerable, but Mr. Sefton was a crafty and dangerous man, perhaps unscrupulous too. He remembered that light remark of the bystander coupling the name of the Secretary and Lucia Catherwood, and at the recollection the red flushed into his face.

"The Secretary is able and powerful," he said, "but not wholly to be trusted. He is an intriguer."

Miss Grayson looked up with her quiet smile.

"Mr. Sefton has been kind to us," she said, "and he has made our life in Richmond more tolerable. We could not be ungrateful, and I urged Lucia to go with them to-day."

99

The colour flickered in the sensitive, proud face of Lucia Catherwood.

"But, Charlotte, I should have gone of my own accord, and it was a pleasant drive."

There was a shade of defiance in her tone, and Prescott, restless and uneasy, stared into the fire. He had expected her to yield to his challenge, to be humble, to make some apology; but she did not, having no excuses to offer, and he found his own position difficult and unpleasant. The stubborn part of his nature was stirred and he spoke coldly of something else, while she replied in like fashion. He was sure now that Sefton had transferred his love to her, and if she did not return it she at least looked upon him with favouring eyes. As for himself, he had become an outsider. He remembered her refusal of him. Then the impression she gave him once that she had fled from Richmond, partly and perhaps chiefly to save him, was false. On second thought no doubt it was false. And despite her statement she might really have been a spy! How could he believe her now?

Miss Grayson, quiet and observant, noticed the change. She liked this young man, so serious and steady and so different from the passionate and reckless youths who are erroneously taken by outsiders to be the universal type of the South. Her heart rallied to the side of her cousin, Lucia Catherwood, with whom she had shared hardships and dangers and whose worth she knew; but with the keen eye of the kindly old maid she saw what troubled Prescott, and being a woman she could not blame him. Taking upon herself the burden of the conversation, she asked Prescott about his southern journey, and as he told her of the path that led him through mountains, the glory of the autumn woods and the peace of the wilderness, there was a little bitterness in his tone in referring to those lonesome but happy days. He had felt then that he was coming north to the struggles and passions of a battleground, and now he was finding the premonition true in more senses than one.

Lucia sat in the far corner of the little room where the flickering firelight fell across her face and dress. They had not lighted candle nor lamp, but the rich tints in her hair gleamed with a deeper sheen when the glow of the flames fell across it. Prescott's former sense of proprietorship was going, and she seemed more beautiful, more worth the effort of a lifetime than ever before. Here was a woman of mind and heart, one not bounded by narrow sectionalism, but seeing the good wherever it might be. He felt that he had behaved like a prig and a fool. Why should he be influenced by the idle words of some idle man in the street? He was not Lucia Catherwood's guardian; if there were any question of guardianship, she was much better fitted to be the guardian of him.

Had he obeyed this rush of feeling he would have swept away all constraint by words abrupt, disjointed perhaps, but alive with sincerity, and Miss Grayson gave him ample opportunity by slipping with excuses into the next room. The pride and stubbornness in Prescott's nature were tenacious and refused to die. Although wishing to say words that would undo the effect of those already spoken, he spoke instead of something else—topics foreign then to the heart of either—of the war, the social life of Richmond. Miss Harley was still a great favourite in the capital and the Secretary paid her much attention, so Lucia said without the slightest change in her tone. Helen's brother had made several visits to Richmond; General Wood had come once, and Mr. Talbot once. Mr. Talbot—and now she smiled—was overpowered on his last visit. Some Northern prisoners had told how the vanguard of their army was held back in the darkness at the passage of the river by a single man who was taken prisoner, but not until he had given his beaten brigade time to escape. That man was discovered to be Talbot and he had fled from Richmond to escape an excess of attention and compliments.

"And it was old Talbot who saved us from capture," said Prescott. "I've often wondered why we were not pursued more closely that night. And he never said anything about it."

"Mrs. Markham, too, is in Richmond," Lucia continued, "and she is, perhaps, the most conspicuous of its social lights. General Markham is at the front with the army"—here she stopped abruptly and the colour came into her face. But Prescott guessed the rest. Colonel Harley was constantly in Mrs. Markham's train and that was why he came so often to Richmond. The capital was not without its gossip.

The flames died down and a red-and-yellow glow came from the heart of the coals. The light now gleamed only at times on the face of Lucia Catherwood. It seemed to Prescott (or was it fancy) that by this flickering radiance he saw a pathetic look on her face—a little touch of appeal. Again he felt a great wave of tenderness and of reverence, too. She was far better than he. Words of humility and apology leaped once more to the end of his tongue, but they did not pass his lips. He could not say them. His stubborn pride still controlled and he rambled on with commonplace and idle talk.

Miss Grayson came back bearing a lamp, and by chance, as it were, she let its flame fall first upon the face of the man and then upon the face of the woman, and she felt a little thrill of disappointment when she noted the result in either case. Miss Charlotte Grayson was one of the gentlest of fine old maids, and her heart was soft within her. She remembered the long vigils of Prescott, his deep sympathy, the substantial help that he had given, and, at last, how, at the risk of his own career, he had helped Lucia Catherwood to escape from Richmond and danger. She marked the coldness and constraint still in the air and was sorry, but knew not what to do.

Prescott rose presently and said good-night, expressing the hope that it would not be long until he again saw them both. Lucia echoed his hope in a like formal fashion and Prescott went out. He did not look back to see if the light from the window still fell across the brown grass, but hurried away in the darkness.

CHAPTER XXV

THE MOUNTAIN GENERAL

It was a bleak, cold night and Prescott's feelings were of the same tenor. The distant buildings seemed to swim in a raw mist and pedestrians fled from the streets. Prescott walked along in aimless fashion until he was hailed by a dark man on a dark horse, who wished to know if he were going "to walk right over us," but the rough words were belied by joviality and welcome.

Prescott came out of his cloud and, looking up, recognized the great cavalryman, Wood. His huge beard seemed bigger than ever, but his keen eyes shone in the black tangle as if they were looking through the holes in a mask.

"What ails you, boy?" he asked Prescott. "You were goin' to walk right into me, horse an' all, an' I don't believe you'd have seen a house if it had been planted right in your path!"

"It's true I was thinking of something else," replied Prescott with a smile, "and did not see what was about me; but how are you, General?"

Wood regarded him closely for a moment or two before replying and then said:

"All right as far as that goes, but I can't say things are movin' well for our side. We're in a deadlock down there at Petersburg, and here comes winter, loaded with snow an' hail an' ice, if signs count for anythin'. Mighty little for a cavalryman to do right now, so I just got leave of absence from General Lee, an' I've run up to Richmond for a day or two."

Then the big man laughed in an embarrassed way, and Prescott, looking up at him, knew that his face was turning red could it but be seen.

"A man may employ his time well in Richmond, General," said Prescott, feeling a sudden and not unsympathetic desire to draw him out.

The General merely nodded in reply and Prescott looked at him again and more closely. The youth of General Wood and himself had been so different that he had never before recognized what there was in this illiterate man to attract a cultivated woman.

The crude mountaineer had seemed to him hitherto to be a soldier and nothing else; and soldiership alone, in Prescott's opinion, was very far from making up the full complement of a man. The General sitting there on his horse in the darkness was so strong, so masterful, so deeply touched with what appeared to be the romantic spirit, that Prescott could readily understand his attraction for a woman of a position originally different in life. His feeling of sympathy grew stronger. Here at least was a man direct and honest, not evasive and doubtful.

"General," he said with abrupt frankness, "you have come to Richmond to see Miss Harley and I want to tell you that I wish you the utmost success."

He held out his hand and the great mountaineer enclosed it in an iron grasp. Then Wood dismounted, threw his bridle over his arm and said:

"S'pose we go along together for awhile?"

They walked a minute or two in silence, the General running his fingers nervously through his thick black beard.

"See here, Prescott," he said at last, "you've spoke plain to me an' I'll do the same to you. You wished me success with Miss Harley. Why, I thought once that you stood in the way of me or any other man."

"Not so, General; you credit me with far more attractions than I have," replied Prescott deliberately. "Miss Harley and I were children together and you know that is a tie. She likes me, I am sure, but nothing more. And I—well I admire her tremendously, but——"

He hesitated and then stopped. The mountaineer gave him a sudden keen glance and laughed softly.

"There's somebody else?" he said.

Prescott was silent but the mountaineer was satisfied.

"See here, Prescott," he exclaimed with great heartiness. "Let's wish each other success."

Their hands closed again in a firm grasp.

"There's that man Sefton," resumed the mountaineer, "but I'm not so much afraid of him as I was of you. He's cunnin' and powerful, but I don't think he's the kind of man women like. He kinder gets their teeth on edge. They're afraid of him without admirin' his strength. There's two kinds of strong men: the kind that women are afraid of an' like and the kind that they're afraid of an' don't like; an' I think Sefton falls into the last class."

Prescott's liking for his companion increased, and mingled with it was a growing admiration wholly aside from his respect for him as a soldier. He was showing observation or intuition of a high order. The General's heart was full. He had all of the mountaineer's reserve and taciturnity, but now after years of repression and at the touch of real sympathy his feelings overflowed.

"See here, Prescott," he said abruptly, "I once thought it was wrong for me to love Helen Harley—the difference between us is so great—and maybe I think so yet, but I'm goin' to try to win her anyhow. I'm just that deep in love, and maybe the good God will forgive me, because I can't help it. I loved that girl the first time I ever set eyes on her; I wasn't asked about it, I just had to."

"There is no reason why you should not go ahead and win her," said the other, warmly.

"Prescott," continued the mountaineer, "you don't know all that I've been."

"It's nothing dishonest, that I'd swear."

"It's not that, but look where I started. I was born in the mountains back there, an' I tell you we weren't much above the wild animals that live in them same mountains. There was just one room to our log house—one for father, mother and all of us. I never was taught nothin'. I didn't learn to read till I was twenty years old and the big words still bother me. I went barefoot six months every year till I was a man grown. Why, my cavalry boots pinch me now."

He uttered the lamentation of the boots with such tragic pathos that Prescott smiled, but was glad to hide it in the darkness.

"An' I don't know nothin' now," resumed the mountaineer sadly. "When I go into a parlour I'm like a bear in a cage. If there's anythin' about to break, I always break it. When they begin talkin' books and pictures and such I don't know whether they are right or wrong."

"You are not alone in that."

"An' I'm out of place in a house," continued the General, not noticing the interruption. "I belong to the mountains an' the fields, an' when this war's over I guess I'll go back to 'em. They think somethin' of me now because I can ride an' fight, but war ain't all. When it's over there'll be no use for me. I can't dance an' I can't talk pretty, an' I'm always steppin' on other peoples' feet. I guess I ain't the timber they make dandies of."

"I should hope not," said Prescott with emphasis. He was really stirred by the big man's lament, seeing that he valued so much the little things that he did not have and so little the great things that he did have.

"General," he said, "you never shirked a battle and I wouldn't shirk this contest either. If I loved a woman I'd try to win her, and you won't have to go back to the mountains when this war is over. You've made too great a name for that. We won't give you up."

Wood's eyes shone with satisfaction and gratitude.

"Do you think so?" he asked earnestly.

"I haven't a doubt of it," replied Prescott with the utmost sincerity. "If fortune was unkind to you in the beginning nature was not so. You may not know it, but I think that women consider you rather good to look at."

Thus they talked, and in his effort to console another Robert forgot some of his own pain. The simple, but, on the whole, massive character of Wood appealed to him, and the thought came with peculiar force that what was lacking in Helen Harley's nature the tougher fiber of the mountaineer would supply.

It was late when they separated and much later before Prescott was able to sleep. The shadow of the Secretary was before him and it was a menacing shadow. It seemed that this man was to supplant him at every turn, to appear in every cause his successful rival. Nor was he satisfied with himself. A small but audible voice told him he had behaved badly, but stubborn pride stopped his ear. What right did he have to accuse her? In a worldly sense, at least, she might fare well if she chose the Secretary.

There was quite a crowd in the lobby of the Spotswood Hotel next morning, gathered there to talk, after the Southern habit, when there is nothing pressing to be done, and conspicuous in it were the editors, Raymond and Winthrop, whom Prescott had not seen in months and who now received him with warmth.

"How's the *Patriot*?" asked Prescott of Raymond.

"The *Patriot* is resting just now," replied Raymond quietly.

"How is that—no news?"

"Oh, there's plenty of news, but there's no paper. I did have a little, but Winthrop was short on a supply for an edition of his own sheet, and he begged so hard that I let him have mine. That's what I call true professional courtesy."

"The paper was so bad that it crumbled all to pieces a day after printing," said Winthrop.

"So much the better," replied Raymond. "In fact, a day is much too long a life for such a sheet as Winthrop prints."

The others laughed and the talk returned to the course from which it had been taken for a moment by the arrival of Prescott. Conspicuous in the crowd was the Member of Congress, Redfield, not at all improved in appearance since the spring. His face was redder, heavier and coarser than ever.

"I tell you it is so," he said oratorically and dogmatically to the others. "The Secretary is in love with her. He was in love with Helen Harley once, but now he has changed over to the other one."

Prescott shifted uneasily. Here was the name of the Secretary dogging him and in a connection that he liked least of all.

"It's the 'Beautiful Yankee,' then," said another, a young man named Garvin, who aspired eagerly to the honours of a ladykiller. "I don't blame him. You don't see such a face and figure more than once in a lifetime. I've been thinking of going in there myself and giving the Secretary something to do."

He flecked a speck of dust off his embroidered waistcoat and exuded vanity. Prescott would have gone away at once, but such an act would have had an obvious meaning—the last thing that he desired, and he stayed, hoping that the current of talk would float to a new topic. Winthrop and Raymond glanced at him, knowing the facts of the Wilderness and of the retreat that followed, but they said nothing.

"I think that the Secretary or anybody else should go slow with this Yankee girl," said Redfield. "Who is she—and what is she? Where did she come from? She drifted in with the army after the battles in the Wilderness and that's all we know."

"It's enough," said Garvin; "because it makes a delightful mystery which but adds to the 'Beautiful Yankee's' attractions. The Secretary is far gone there. I happen to know that he is to take her to the President's reception to-morrow night."

Prescott started. He was glad now that he had not humbled himself.

"At any rate," said Redfield, "Mr. Sefton can't mean to marry her—an unknown like that; it must be something else."

Prescott felt hot pincers grip him around the heart, and a passion that he could not control flamed to his brain. He strode forward and put his hand heavily on the Member's shoulder.

"Are you speaking of Miss Catherwood?" he demanded.

"I am," replied Redfield, throwing off the heavy hand. "But what business is that of yours?"

"Simply this; that she is too good and noble a woman to be spoken of slightingly by you. Such remarks as you have just made you repeat at your risk."

Redfield made an angry reply and there were all the elements of a fierce encounter; but Raymond interfered.

"Redfield," he said, "you are wrong, and moreover you owe all of us an apology for speaking in such a way of a lady in our presence. I fully indorse all that Captain Prescott says of Miss Catherwood—I happen to have seen instances of her glorious unselfishness and sacrifice, and I know that she is one of God's most nearly perfect women."

"And so do I," said Winthrop, "and I," "and I," said the others. Redfield saw that the crowd was unanimously against him and frowned.

"Oh, well, perhaps I spoke hastily and carelessly," he said. "I apologize."

Raymond changed the talk at once.

"When do you think Grant will advance again?" he asked.

"Advance?" replied Winthrop hotly. "Advance? Why, he can't advance."

"But he came through the Wilderness."

"If he did he lost a hundred thousand men, more than Lee had altogether, and now he's checkmated."

"He'll never see Richmond unless he comes to Libby," said Redfield coarsely.

"I'm not so sure," said Raymond gravely. "Whatever we say to the people and however we try to hold up their courage, we ought not to conceal the facts from ourselves. The ports of the Confederacy are sealed up by the Yankee cruisers. We have been shattered down South and here we are blockaded in Richmond and Petersburg. It takes a cartload of our money to buy a paper collar and then it's a poor collar. When I bring out the next issue of my newspaper—and I don't know when that will be—I shall say that the prospects of the Confederacy were never brighter; but I warn you right now, gentlemen, that I shall not believe a single one of my own words."

Thus they talked, but Prescott did not follow them, his mind dwelling on Lucia and the Secretary. He was affected most unpleasantly by what he had heard and sorry now that he had come to the hotel. When he could conveniently do so he excused himself and went home.

He was gloomier than ever at supper and his mother uttered a mild jest or two on his state of mind.

"You must have failed to find any friends in the city," she said.

"I found too many," he replied. "I went to the Spotswood Hotel, mother, and I listened there to some tiresome talk about whipping the Yankees out of their boots in the next five minutes."

"Aren't you going to do it?"

Prescott laughed.

"Mother," he said, "I wouldn't have your divided heart for anything. It must cause you a terrible lot of worry."

"I do very well," she said, with her quiet smile, "and I cherish no illusions."

CHAPTER XXVI

CALYPSO

It was announced that the presidential reception on the following evening would be of special dignity and splendour, and it was thought the part of duty by all who were of consequence in Richmond to attend and make a brave show before the world. Mr. Davis, at the futile peace conference in the preceding July, had sought to impress upon the Northern delegates the superior position of the South. "It was true," he said, "that Sherman was before Atlanta, but what matter if he took it? the world must have the Southern cotton crop, and with such an asset the Southern Republic must stand." He was not inclined now to withdraw in any particular from this position, and his people stood solidly behind him.

Prescott, as he prepared for the evening, had much of the same spirit, although his was now a feeling of personal defiance toward a group of persons rather than toward the North in general.

"Are you going alone?" asked his mother.

"Why, yes, mother, unless you will go with me, and I know you won't. Whom else could I ask?"

"I thought that you might take Miss Catherwood," she replied without evasion.

"No chance there," replied Prescott, with a light laugh.

"Why not?"

103

"Miss Catherwood would scorn a humble individual like myself. The 'Beautiful Yankee' looks far higher. She will be escorted to-night by the brilliant, the accomplished, the powerful and subtle gentleman, the Honourable James Sefton."

"You surprise me!" said his mother, and her look was indeed full of astonishment and inquiry, as if some plan of hers had gone astray.

"I have heard the Secretary's name mentioned once or twice in connection with hers," she said, "but I did not know that his attentions had shifted completely from Helen Harley. Men are indeed changeable creatures."

"Are you just discovering that, at your age, mother?" asked Prescott lightly.

"I believe Lucia Catherwood too noble a woman to love a man like James Sefton," she said.

"Why, what do you know of Miss Catherwood?"

His mother did not answer him, and presently Prescott went to the reception, but early as he was, Colonel Harley, the two editors and others were there before him. Colonel Harley, as Raymond termed it, was "extremely peacocky." He wore his most gorgeous raiment and in addition he was clothed about with vanity. Already he was whispering in the ear of Mrs. Markham, who had renewed her freshness, her youth and her liveliness.

"If I were General Markham," said Raymond cynically, "I'd detail a guard of my most faithful soldiers to stand about my wife."

"Do you think she needs all that protection?" asked Winthrop.

"Well, no, *she* doesn't need it, but it may save others," replied Raymond with exceeding frankness.

Winthrop merely laughed and did not dispute the comment. The next arrival of importance was that of Helen Harley and General Wood. Colonel Harley frowned, but his sister's eyes did not meet his, and the look of the mountaineer was so lofty and fearless that he was a bold man indeed who would have challenged him even with a frown. Helen was all in white, and to Prescott she seemed some summer flower, so pure, so snowy and so gentle was she. But the General, acting upon Prescott's advice, had evidently taken his courage in his hands and arrayed himself as one who hoped to conquer. His gigantic figure was enclosed for the first time since Prescott had known him in a well-fitting uniform, and his great black mane of hair and beard had been trimmed by one who knew his business. The effect was striking and picturesque. Prescott remembered to have read long ago in a child's book of natural history that the black-maned lion was the loftiest and boldest of his kind, and General Wood seemed to him now to be the finest of the black-maned lions.

There was a shade of embarrassment in the manner of Helen Harley when she greeted Prescott. She, too, had recollections; perhaps she had fancied once, like Prescott, that she loved when she did not love. But her hesitation was over in a moment and she held out her hand warmly.

"We heard of your return from the South," she said. "Why haven't you been to see us?"

Prescott made some excuse about the pressure of duty, and then, bearing his friend's interest in mind, spoke of General Wood, who was now in conversation some distance away with the President himself.

"I believe that General Wood is to-night the most magnificent figure in the South," he said. "It is well that Mr. Davis greets him warmly. He ought to. No man under the rank of General Lee has done more for the Confederacy."

His voice had all the accent of sincerity and Helen looked up at him, thanking him silently with her eyes.

"Then you like General Wood," she said.

"I am proud to have him as a friend and I should dislike very much to have him as an enemy."

Richmond in its best garb and with its bravest face was now arriving fast, and Prescott drifted with some of his friends into one of the smaller parlours. When he returned to the larger room it was crowded, and many voices mingled there. But all noise ceased suddenly and then in the hush some one said: "There she comes!" Prescott knew who was meant and his anger hardened in him.

Miss Catherwood was looking unusually well, and even those who had dubbed her "The Beautiful Yankee" added another superlative adjective. A spot of bright red burned in either cheek and she held her head very high. "How haughty she is!" Prescott heard some one say. Her height, her figure, her look lent colour to the comment.

Her glance met Prescott's and she bowed to him, as to any other man whom she knew, and then with the Secretary beside her, obviously proud of the lady with whom he had come, she received the compliments of her host.

Lucia Catherwood did not seem to be conscious that everybody was looking at her, yet she knew it well and realized that the gaze was a singular mixture of curiosity, like and dislike. It could not well be otherwise, where there was so much beauty to inspire admiration or jealousy and where there were sentiments known to be different from those of all the others present. A mystery as tantalizing as it was seductive, together with a faint touch of scandal which some had contrived to blow upon her name, though not enough really to injure her as yet, sufficed to give a spice to the conversation when she was its subject.

The President engaged her in talk for a few minutes. He himself, clad in a grayish-brown suit of foreign manufacture, was looking thin and old, the slight stoop in his shoulders showing perceptibly. But he brightened up with Southern gallantry as he talked to Miss Catherwood. He seemed to find an attraction not only in her beauty and dignity, but in her opinions as well and the ease with which she expressed them. He held her longer than any other guest, and Mr. Sefton was the third of three, facile, smiling, explaining how they wished to make a convert of Miss Catherwood and yet expected to do so. Here in

Richmond, surrounded by truth and with her eyes open to it, she must soon see the error of her ways; he, James Sefton, would vouch for it.

"I have no doubt, Mr. Sefton, that you will contribute to that end," said the President.

She was the centre of a group presently, and the group included the Secretary, Redfield, Garvin and two or three Europeans then visiting in Richmond. Prescott, afar in a corner of the room, watched her covertly. She was animated by some unusual spirit and her eyes were brilliant; her speech, too, was scintillating. The little circle sparkled with laughter and jest. They undertook to taunt her, though with good humour, on her Northern sympathies, and she replied in like vein, meeting all their arguments and predicting the fall of Richmond.

"Then, Miss Catherwood, we shall all come to you for a written protection," said Garvin.

"Oh, I shall grant it," she said. "The Union will have nothing to fear from you."

But Garvin, unabashed at the general laugh on himself, returned to the charge. Prescott wandered farther away and presently was talking to Mrs. Markham, Harley being held elsewhere by bonds of courtesy that he could not break. Thus eddies of the crowd cast these two, as it were, upon a rock where they must find solace in each other or not at all.

Mrs. Markham was a woman of wit and beauty. Prescott often had remarked it, but never with such a realizing sense. She was young, graceful, and with a face sufficiently supplied with natural roses, and above all keen with intelligence. She wore a shade of light green, a colour that harmonized wonderfully with the green tints that lurked here and there in the depths of her eyes, and once when she gazed thoughtfully at her hand Prescott noticed that it was very white and well shaped. Well, Harley was at least a man of taste.

Mrs. Markham was pliable, insinuating and complimentary. She was smitten, too, by a sudden mad desire. Always she was alive with coquetry to her finger tips, and to-night she was aflame with it. But this quiet, grave young man hitherto had seemed to her unapproachable. She used to believe him in love with Helen Harley; now she fancied him in love with some one else, and she knew his present frame of mind to be vexed irritation. Difficult conquests are those most valued, and here she saw an opportunity. He was so different from the others, too, that, wearied of easy victories, all her fighting blood was aroused.

Mrs. Markham was adroit, and did not begin by flattering too much nor by attacking any other woman. She was quietly sympathetic, spoke guardedly of Prescott's services in the war, and made a slight allusion to his difference in temperament from so many of the careless young men who fought without either forethought or present thought.

Prescott found her presence soothing; her quiet words smoothed away his irritation, and gradually, without knowing why, he began to have a better opinion of himself. He wondered at his own stupidity in not having noticed before what an admirable woman was Mrs. Markham, how much superior to others and how beautiful. He saw the unsurpassed curve of her white arm where the sleeve fell back, and there were wonderful green tints lurking in the depths of her eyes. After all, he could not blame Harley—at least, for admiration.

They passed into one of the smaller rooms and Prescott's sense of satisfaction increased. Here was one woman, and a woman of beauty and wit, too, who could appreciate him. They sat unnoticed in a corner and grew confidential. Once or twice she carelessly placed her hand upon his coat sleeve, but let it rest there only for a moment, and on each occasion he noticed that the hand and wrist were entirely worthy of the arm. It was a small hand, but the fingers were long, tapering and very white, each terminating in a rosy nail. Her face was close to his, and now and then he felt her light breath on his cheek. A thrill ran through his blood. It was very pleasant to sit in the smile of a witty and beautiful woman.

He looked up; Lucia Catherwood was passing on the arm of a Confederate general and for a moment her eyes flashed fire, but afterward became cold and unmoved. Her face was blank as a stone as she moved on, while Prescott sat red and confused. Mrs. Markham, seeming not to notice, spoke of Miss Catherwood, and she did not make the mistake of criticizing her.

"The 'Beautiful Yankee' deserves her name," she said. "I know of no other woman who could become a veritable Helen of Troy if she would."

"If she would," repeated Prescott; "but will she?"

"That I do not know."

"But I know," said Prescott recklessly; "I think she will."

Mrs. Markham did not reply. She was still the sympathetic friend, disagreeing just enough to incite triumphant and forgiving opposition.

"Even if she should, I do not know that I could wholly blame her," she said. "I fancy that it is not easy for any woman of great beauty to concentrate her whole devotion on one man. It must seem to her that she is giving too much to an individual, however good he may be."

"Do you feel that way about it yourself, Mrs. Markham?"

"I said a woman of great beauty."

"It is the same."

Her serenity was not at all disturbed and her hand rested lightly on his arm once more.

"You are a foolish boy," she said. "When you pay compliments, do not pay them in such blunt fashion."

"I could not help it; I had too good an excuse."

She smiled slightly.

"Southern men are clever at flattery," she said, "and the Northern men, they say, are not; perhaps on that account those of the North are more sincere."

"But we of the South often mean what we say, nevertheless."

Had Prescott been watching her face, he might have seen a slight change of expression, a momentary look of alarm in the green depths of the eyes—some one else was passing—but in another instant her face was as calm, as angelic as ever.

She spoke of Helen Harley and her brave struggle, the evident devotion of General Wood, and the mixed comment with which it was received.

"Will he win her?" asked Prescott.

"I do not know; but somebody should rescue her from that selfish old father of hers. He claims to be the perfect type of the true Southern gentleman—he will tell you so if you ask him—but if he is, I prefer that the rest of the world should judge the South by a false type."

"But General Wood is not without rivals," said Prescott. "I have often thought that he had one of the most formidable kind in the Secretary, Mr. Sefton."

He awaited her answer with eagerness. She was a woman of penetrating mind and what she said would be worth considering. Regarding him again with that covert glance, she saw anxiety trembling on his lips and she replied deliberately:

"The Secretary himself is another proof why a woman of beauty should not concentrate all her devotion on one man. You have seen him to-night and his assiduous attention to another woman. Captain Prescott, all men are fickle—with a few exceptions, perhaps."

She gave him her most stimulating glance, a look tipped with flame, which said even to a dull intelligence—and Prescott's was not—that he was one of the few, the rare exceptions. As her talk became more insinuating her hand touched his arm and rested there ten seconds where it had rested but five before. Again he felt her breath lightly on his cheek and he noticed how finely arched and seductive was the curve of her long yellow lashes. He had felt embarrassed and ashamed when Lucia Catherwood saw him there in an attitude of devotion to Mrs. Markham, but that sensation was giving way to stubbornness and anger. If Lucia should turn to some one else why might not he do the same?

Yielding himself to the charms of a perfect face, a low and modulated voice and a mind that never mistook flippancy and triviality for wit, he met her everywhere on common ground, and she wondered why she had not seen the attractions of this grave, quiet young man long before! Surely such a conquest—and she was not certain yet that it was achieved—was worth a half-dozen victories of the insipid and over-easy kind.

An hour later Prescott was with Lucia for a few minutes, and although no one else was within hearing, their conversation was formal and conventional to the last degree. She spoke of the pleasure of the evening, the brave show made by the Confederacy despite the pressure of the Northern armies, and her admiration for a spirit so gallant. He paid her a few empty compliments, told her she was the shining light among lesser lights, and presently he passed out. He noticed, however, that she was, indeed, as he had said so lightly, the star of the evening. The group around her never thinned, and not only were they admiring, but were anxious to match wits with her. The men of Richmond applauded, as one by one each of them was worsted in the encounter; at least, they had company in defeat, and, after all, defeat at such hands was rather more to be desired than victory. When Prescott left she was still a centre of attraction.

Prescott, full of bitterness and having no other way of escape from his entanglement, asked to be sent at once to his regiment in the trenches before Petersburg, but the request was denied him, as it was likely, so he was told, that he would be needed again in Richmond. He said nothing to his mother of his desire to go again to the front, but she saw that he was restless and uneasy, although she asked no questions.

He had ample cause to regret the refusal of the authorities to accede to his wish, when rumour and vague innuendo concerning himself and Mrs. Markham came to his ears. He wondered that so much had been made of a mere passing incident, but he forgot that his fortunes were intimately connected with those of many others. He passed Harley once in the streets and the flamboyant soldier favoured him with a stare so insolent and persistent that his wrath rose, and he did not find it easy to refrain from a quarrel; but he remembered how many names besides his own would be dragged into such an affair, and passed on.

Helen Harley, too, showed coldness toward him, and Prescott began to have the worst of all feelings—the one of lonesomeness and abandonment—as if every man's hand was against him. It begot pride, stubbornness and defiance in him, and he was in this frame of mind when Mrs. Markham, driving her Accomack pony, which somehow had survived a long period of war's dangers, nodded cheerily to him and threw him a warm and ingratiating smile. It was like a shaft of sunshine on a wintry day, and he responded so beamingly that she stopped by the sidewalk and suggested that he get into the carriage with her. It was done with such lightness and grace that he scarcely noticed it was an invitation, the request seeming to come from himself.

It was a small vehicle with a narrow seat, and they were compelled to sit so close together that he felt the softness and warmth of her body. He was compelled, too, to confess that Mrs. Markham was as attractive by daylight as by lamplight. A fur jacket and a dark dress, both close-fitting, did not conceal the curves of her trim figure. Her cheeks were glowing red with the rapid motion and the touch of a frosty morning, and the curve of long eyelashes did not wholly hide a pair of eyes that with tempting glances could draw on the suspecting and the unsuspecting alike. Mrs. Markham never looked better, never fresher, never more seductive than on that morning, and Prescott felt, with a sudden access of pride, that this delightful woman really liked him and considered him worth while. That was a genuine tribute and it did not matter why she liked him.

"May I take the reins?" he asked.

"Oh, no," she replied, giving him one more of those dazzling smiles. "You would not rob me, would you? I fancy that I look well driving and I also get the credit for spirit. I am going shopping. It may seem strange to you that there is anything left in Richmond to buy or anything to buy it with, but the article that I am in search of is a paper of pins, and I think I have enough money to pay for it."

"I don't know about that," said Prescott. "My friend Talbot gave five hundred dollars for a paper collar. That was last year, and paper collars must be dearer now. So I imagine that your paper of pins will cost at least two thousand dollars."

"I am not so foolish as to go shopping with our Confederate money. I carry gold," she replied. With her disengaged hand she tapped a little purse she carried in her pocket and it gave forth an opulent tinkle.

She was driving rapidly, chattering incessantly, but in such a gay and light fashion that Prescott's attention never wandered from herself—the red glow of her cheeks, the changing light of her eyes and the occasional gleam of white teeth as her lips parted in a laugh. Thus he did not notice that she was taking him by a long road, and that one or two whom they passed on the street looked after them in meaning fashion.

Prescott was not in love with Mrs. Markham, but he was charmed. Hers was a soft and soothing touch after a hard blow. A healing hand was outstretched to him by a beautiful woman who would be adorable to make love to—if she did not already belong to another man, such an old curmudgeon as General Markham, too! How tightly curled the tiny ringlets on her neck! He was sitting so close that he could not help seeing them and now and then they moved lightly under his breath.

He remembered that they were a long time in reaching the shop, but he did not care and said nothing. When they arrived at last she asked him to hold the lines while she went inside. She returned in a few minutes and triumphantly held up a small package.

"See," she said, "I have made my purchase, but it was the last they had, and no one can say when Richmond will be able to import another paper of pins. Maybe we shall have to ask General Grant."

"And then he won't let us," said Prescott.

She laughed and glanced up at him from under the long, curling eyelashes. The green tints showed faintly in her eyes and were singularly seductive. She made no effort to conceal her high good humour, and Prescott now and then felt her warm breath on his cheek as she turned to speak to him in intimate fashion.

She drove back by a road not the same, but as long as before, and Prescott found it all too short. His gloom fled away before her flow of spirits, her warm and intimate manner, and the town, though under gray November skies, became vivid with light and colour.

"Do you know," she said, "that the Mosaic Club meets again to-night and perhaps for the last time? Are you not coming?"

"I am not invited."

"But I invite you. I have full authority as a member and an official of the club."

"I'm all alone," said Prescott.

"And so am I," said she. "The General, you know, is at the front, and no one has been polite enough yet to ask to take me."

Her look met his with a charming innocence like that of a young girl, but the lurking green depths were in her eyes and Prescott felt a thrill despite himself.

"Why not," was his thought. "All the others have cast me aside. She chooses me. If I am to be attacked on Mrs. Markham's account—well, I'll give them reason for it."

The defiant spirit was speaking then, and he said aloud:

"If two people are alone they should go together and then they won't be alone any more. You have invited me to the club to-night, Mrs. Markham, now double your benefaction and let me take you there."

"On one condition," she said, "that we go in my pony carriage. We need no groom. The pony will stand all night in front of Mr. Peyton's house if necessary. Come at eight o'clock."

Before she reached her home she spoke of Lucia Catherwood as one comes to a subject in the course of a random conversation, and connected her name with that of the Secretary in such a manner that Prescott felt a thrill of anger rise, not against Mrs. Markham, but against Lucia and Mr. Sefton. The remark was quite innocent in appearance, but it coincided so well with his own state of mind in regard to the two that it came to him like a truth.

"The Secretary is very much in love with the 'Beautiful Yankee,'" said Mrs. Markham. "He thought once that he was in love with Helen Harley, but his imagination deceived him. Even so keen a man as the Secretary can deceive himself in regard to the gossamer affair that we call love, but his infatuation with Lucia Catherwood is genuine."

"Will he win her?" asked Prescott. Despite himself, his heart throbbed as he waited for her answer.

"I do not know," she replied; "but any woman may be won if a man only knows the way of winning."

"A Delphic utterance, if ever there was one," he said, and laughed partly in relief. She had not said that Mr. Sefton would win her.

He left Mrs. Markham at her door and went home, informing his mother by and by that he was going to a meeting of the Mosaic Club in the evening.

"I am to take a lady," he said.

"A very natural thing for a young man to do," she replied, smiling at him. "Who is it to be, Miss Catherwood or Miss Harley?"

"Neither."

"Neither?"

"No; I am in bad grace with both. The lady whom I am to have the honour, the privilege, etc., of escorting is Mrs. Markham."

Her face fell.

"I am sorry to hear it," she said frankly.

Prescott, for the first time since his childhood, felt some anger toward his mother.

"Why not, mother?" he asked. "We are all a great family here together in Richmond. Why, if you trace it back you'll probably find that every one of us is blood kin to every other one. Mrs. Markham is a woman of wit and beauty, and the honour and privilege of which I spoke so jestingly is a real honour and privilege."

"She is a married woman, my son, and not careful enough of her actions."

Prescott was silent. He felt a marked shyness in discussing such questions with his mother, but his obstinacy and pride remained even in her mild presence. A few hours later he put on his cloak and went out in the twilight, walking swiftly toward the well-kept red brick house of General Charles Markham. A coloured maid received him and took him into the parlour, but all was well-ordered and conventional. Mrs. Markham came in before the maid went out and detained her with small duties about the room.

Prescott looked around at the apartment and its comfort, even luxury. Report had not wronged General Markham when it accused him of having a quarter-master's interest in his own fortunes. It was not her fault that she became it all wonderfully well, but even as he admired her he wondered how another would look in the midst of this dusky red luxury; another with the ease and grace of Mrs. Markham herself, with the same air of perfect finish, but taller, of more sumptuous build and with a nobler face. She, too, would move with soundless steps over the dark red carpet, and were she sitting there before the fire, with the glow of the coals falling at her feet, the room would need no other presence.

"A penny for your thoughts, Mr. Wise Man," she said.

"My reward should be greater," he said, fibbing without conscience, "because I was thinking of you."

"In that event we should be starting," she said lightly. "Ben Butler and the family coach are at the door, and if you deem yourself capable of it, Sir Knight, I think that I shall let you drive this evening."

"He would be a poor captain who could not guide a vessel with such a precious cargo," said Prescott gallantly.

"You forget that you are a part of the cargo."

"But I don't count. Again it was you of whom I was thinking."

She settled herself in the phaeton beside him—very close; it could not be otherwise—and Ben Butler, the Accomack pony, obedient to the will of Prescott, rattled away through the street. He recalled how long she had been in reaching the shop by day, and how long also in returning, and now the spirit of wickedness lay hold of him; he would do likewise. He knew well where the house of Daniel Peyton stood, having been in it many times before the war, but he chose a course toward it that bent like the curve of a semicircle, and the innocent woman beside him took no notice.

The night was dark and frosty, with a wind out of the northwest that moaned among the housetops, but Prescott, with a beautiful woman by his side, was warm and cozy in the phaeton. With her dark wrap and the dark of the night around them she was almost invisible save her face, in which her eyes, with the lurking green shadows yet in them, shone when she looked up at him.

Ben Butler was a capable pony and he paid habitual deference to the wishes of his mistress—the result of long training. As he progressed at a gentle walk Prescott scarcely needed one hand for his guidance. It was this lack of occupation that caused the other to wander into dangerous proximity to the neat and well-gloved fingers of Mrs. Markham, which were not far away in the first place.

"You should not do that," she said, removing her hand, but Prescott was not sorry—he did not forget the thrill given him by the pleasant contact, and he was neither apologetic nor humble. The lady was not too angry, but there appeared to Prescott a reproachful shadow—that of another woman, taller and nobler of face and manner, and despite his manhood years he blushed in the darkness. A period of constraint followed; and he was so silent, so undemonstrative that the lady gave him a glance of surprise. Her hand strayed back to its former place of easy approach, but Prescott was busy with Ben Butler, and he yielded only when she placed her hand upon his arm, being forced by a sudden jolt of the phaeton to lean more closely against him. But, fortunately or unfortunately, they were now in front of the Peyton house, and lights were shining from every window.

Prescott stepped out of the phaeton and tied Ben Butler to the hitching-post. Then he assisted Mrs. Markham to the ground and together the two entered the portico.

"We are late," said Prescott, and he felt annoyance because of it.

"It does not matter," she said lightly, feeling no annoyance at all.

He knew that their late entrance would attract marked notice to them, and now he felt a desire to avoid such attention; but she would make of it a special event, a function. Despite Prescott's efforts, she marshaled himself and herself in such masterly fashion that every eye in the room was upon them as they entered, and none could help noticing that they came as an intimate pair—or at least the skilful lady made it seem so.

These two were the last—all the members of the club and their guests were already there, and despite the bond of fellowship and union among them many eyebrows were lifted and some asides were spoken as Mrs. Markham and Prescott arrived in this fashion.

Lucia Catherwood was present—Raymond had brought her—but she took no notice, though her bearing was high and her colour brilliant. Some one had prepared her for this evening with careful and loving hands—perhaps it was Miss Grayson. All the minute touches that count for so much were there, and in her eyes was some of the bold and reckless spirit that Prescott himself had been feeling for the last day or two.

This little company had less of partisan rancour, less of sectional feeling, than any other in Richmond, and that night they made the beautiful Yankee their willing queen. She fell in with their spirit: there was nothing that she did not share and lead. She improvised rhymes, deciphered puzzles and prepared others of her own that rivaled in ingenuity the best of Randolph or Caskie or Latham or McCarty or any of the other clever leaders of this bright company. Prescott saw the wit and beauty of Mrs. Markham pale before this brighter sun, and the Secretary seemed to be the chosen favourite of Miss Catherwood. He warmed under her favouring glance, and he, too, brought forth ample measure from the store of his wit.

Harley was there in splendid uniform, as always, but somber and brooding. Prescott clearly saw danger on the man's brow, but a threat, even one unspoken, always served to arouse him, and he returned with renewed devotion to Mrs. Markham. His growing dislike for Harley was tinctured with a strain of contempt. He accused the man's vanity and selfishness, but he forgot at the same moment that he was falling into the same pit.

The men presently withdrew for a few moments into the next room, where the host had prepared something to drink, and a good-natured, noisy crowd was gathered around the table. The noisiest of them all was Harley, whose manner was aggressive and whose face was inflamed, as if he had made himself an undisputed champion at the bowl. The Secretary was there, too, saying nothing, his thin lips wrinkled in a slight smile of satisfaction. He was often pleased with himself, rarely more so than to-night, with the memory of Lucia Catherwood's glorious brow and eyes and the obvious favour that she showed him. He was a fit mate for her, and she must see it. Wisdom and love should go together. Truly, all things were moving well with him, he repeated in his thought. Prescott was following the very course he would have chosen for him, kneeling at Mrs. Markham's feet as if she were a new Calypso. The man whom he knew to be his rival was about to embroil himself with everybody.

If he wanted more evidence of his last inference, Harley of the inflamed face and threatening brow was quick to furnish it. When Prescott came in Harley took another long draught and said to the crowd:

"I have a pretty bit of gossip for you, gentlemen."

"What is it?" asked Randolph, and all looked up, eager to hear any fresh and interesting news.

"It's the story of the spy who was here last winter," replied Harley. "The romance, rather, because that spy, as all of you know, was a woman. The story will not down. It keeps coming up, although we have a great war all about us, and I hear that the Government, so long on a blind trial, has at last struck the right one."

"Indeed," said Randolph, with increased interest. "What is it? The answer to that puzzle has always bothered me."

"They say that the spy was a woman of great beauty, and she found it impossible to escape from Richmond until an officer of ours, yielding to her claims, helped her through the lines. I'll wager that he took full pay for his trouble."

"His honour against hers," said some one.

Harley laughed coarsely.

Prescott became deathly white. He would have fought a duel then with Harley—on the instant. All the Puritan training given him by his mother and his own civilized instincts were swept away by a sudden overwhelming rush of passion.

His colour came back and none noticed its momentary loss, all eyes being on Harley. Prescott glanced at Mr. Sefton, but the Secretary remained calm, composed and smiling, listening to Harley with the same air of interested curiosity shown by the others. Prescott saw it all with a flash of intuition; the Secretary had given Harley a hint, just a vague generalization, within the confines of truth, but without any names—enough to make those concerned uneasy, but not enough to put the power in any hands save those of the Secretary. Harley himself confirmed this by continuing the subject, though somewhat uncertainly, as if he were no longer sure of his facts.

It occurred to Prescott that he might borrow this man's own weapons and fight him with the cold brain and craft that had proved so effective against himself, Robert Prescott. But when he turned to look at the Secretary he found Mr. Sefton looking at him. A glance that was a mingling of fire and steel passed between the two; it was also a look of understanding. Prescott knew and the Secretary saw that he knew. In the bosom of James Sefton respect rose high for the young man whom he had begun to hold rather cheap lately. His antagonist was entirely worthy of him.

Harley rambled on. He looked uncertainly now and then at Prescott, as if he believed him to be the traitorous officer and would provoke him into reply; but Prescott's face was a perfect mask, and his manner careless and indifferent. The suspicions of the others were not aroused, and Harley was not well enough informed to go further; but his look whenever it fell on Robert was full of hatred, and Prescott marked it well.

"What do you think of a fellow who would do such a thing?" asked Harley at last.

"I've a pretty good opinion of him," said Raymond quietly.

"You have?" exclaimed Harley.

"I have," repeated Raymond; "and I'm willing to say it before a man high in the Government, like Mr. Sefton here. Are all the powers of the Confederate Government to be gathered for the purpose of making war on one poor lone woman? Suppose we whip Grant first and bother about the woman afterward. I think I'll write an editorial on the Government's lack of chivalry—that is, I will when I get enough paper to print it on, but I don't know when that will be. However, I'll keep it in mind till that time arrives."

"I think you are wrong," said the Secretary smoothly, as one who discusses ethics and not personalities. "This man had his duty to do, and however small that duty may have been, he should have done it."

"You generalize, and since you are laying down a rule, you are right," said Raymond. "But this is a particular case and an exception. We owe some duties to the feminine gender as well as to patriotism. The greater shouldn't always be swallowed up in the lesser."

There was a laugh, and Winthrop suggested that, as they were talking of the ladies, they return to them. On the way Prescott casually joined the Secretary.

"Can I see you in the office to-morrow, Mr. Sefton?" he asked.

"Certainly," replied the Secretary. "Will three in the afternoon do? Alone, I suppose?"

"Thank you," said Prescott. "Three in the afternoon and alone will do."

Both spoke quietly, but the swift look of understanding passed once more. Then they rejoined the ladies.

Prescott had not spoken to Lucia Catherwood in the whole course of the evening, but now he sought her. Some of the charm which Mrs. Markham so lately had for him was passing; in the presence of Lucia she seemed less fair, less winning, less true. His own conduct appeared to him in another light, and he would turn aside from his vagrant fancy to the one to whom his heart was yet loyal. But he found no chance to speak to her alone. The club by spontaneous agreement had chosen to make her its heroine that night, and Prescott was permitted to be one of the circle, nothing more. As such she spoke to him occasionally as she would to others—chance remarks without colour or emphasis, apparently directed toward him because he happened to be sitting at that particular point, and not because of his personality.

Prescott chafed and sought to better his position, wishing to have an individuality of his own in her regard; but he could not change the colourless rôle which she assigned him. So he became silent, speaking only when some remark was obviously intended for him, and watched her face and expression. He had always told himself that her dominant characteristic was strength, power of will, endurance; but now as he looked he saw once or twice a sudden droop, faint but discernible, as if for a flitting moment she grew too weak for her burden. Prescott felt a great access of pity and tenderness. She was in a position into which no woman should be forced, and she was assailed on all sides by danger. Her very name was at the mercy of the Secretary, and now Harley with his foolish talk might at any time bring an avalanche down upon her. He himself had treated her badly, and would help her if he could. He turned to find Mrs. Markham at his elbow.

"We are going in to supper," she said, "and you will have to take me."

Thus they passed in before Lucia Catherwood's eyes, but she looked over them and came presently with Raymond.

That was a lean supper—the kitchens of Richmond in the last year of the war provided little; but Prescott was unhappy for another reason. He was there with Mrs. Markham, and she seemed to claim him as her own before all those, save his mother, for whom he cared most. General Wood and Helen Harley were across the table, her pure eyes looking up with manifest pleasure into the dark ones of the leader, which could shine so fiercely on the battlefield but were now so soft. Once Prescott caught the General's glance and it was full of wonder; intrigue and the cross play of feminine purposes were unknown worlds to the simple mountaineer.

Prescott passed from silence to a feverish and uncertain gaiety, talking more than any one at the table, an honour that he seldom coveted. Some of his jests and epigrams were good and more were bad; but all passed current at such a time, and Mrs. Markham, who was never at a loss for something to say, seconded him in able fashion. The Secretary, listening and looking, smiled quietly. "Gone to his head; foolish fellow," was what his manner clearly expressed. Prescott himself saw it at last and experienced a sudden check, remembering his resolve to fight this man with his own weapons, while here he was only an hour later behaving like a wild boy on his first escapade. He passed at once from garrulity to silence, and the contrast was so marked that the glances exchanged by the others increased.

Prescott was still taciturn when at a late hour he helped Mrs. Markham into the phaeton and they started to her home. He fully expected that Harley would overtake him when he turned away from her house and seek a quarrel, but the fear of physical harm scarcely entered into his mind. It was the gossip and the linking of names in the gossip that troubled him.

Mrs. Markham sat as close to him as ever—the little phaeton had grown no wider—but though he felt again her warm breath on his cheek, no pulse stirred.

"Why are you so silent, Captain Prescott?" she asked. "Are you thinking of Lucia Catherwood?"

"Yes," he replied frankly, "I was."

She glanced up at him, but his face was hidden in the darkness.

"She was looking very beautiful to-night," she said, "and she was supreme; all the men—and must I say it, all of us women, too—acknowledged her rule. But I do not wonder that she attracts the masculine mind—her beauty, her bearing, her mysterious past, constitute the threefold charm to which all of you men yield, Captain Prescott. I wish I knew her history."

"It could be to her credit only," said Prescott.

She glanced up at him again, and now the moonlight falling on his face enabled her to see it set and firm, and Mrs. Markham felt that there had been a change. He was not the same man who had come with her to the meeting of the club, but she was not a woman to relinquish easily a conquest or a half-conquest, and she called to her aid all the art of a strong and cultivated mind. She was bold and original in her methods, and did not leave the subject of Lucia Catherwood, but praised her, though now and then with slight reservations, letting fall the inference that she was her good friend and would be a better one if she could. Such use did she make of her gentle and unobtrusive sympathy that Prescott felt his heart warming once more to this handsome and accomplished woman.

"You will come to see me again?" she said at the door, letting a little hand linger a few moments in his.

"I fear that I may be sent at once to the front."

"But if you are not you will come?" she persisted.

"Yes," said Prescott, and bade her good-night.

CHAPTER XXVII

THE SECRETARY AND THE LADY

The chief visitor to the little house in the cross street two days later was James Sefton, the agile Secretary, who was in a fine humour with himself and did not take the trouble to conceal it. Much that conduced to his satisfaction had occurred, and the affairs that concerned him most were going well. The telegrams sent by him from the Wilderness to a trusty agent at an American seaport and forwarded thence by mail to London and Paris had been answered, and the replies were of a nature most encouraging. Moreover, the people here in Richmond in whose fortunes he was interested were conducting themselves in a manner that he wished. Therefore the Secretary was pleasant.

He was received by Lucia Catherwood in the little parlour where Prescott had often sat. She was grave and pale, as if she suffered, and there was no touch of warmth in the greeting that she gave the Secretary. But he did not appear to notice it, although he inquired after the health of herself and Miss Grayson, all in the manner of strict formality. She sat down and waited there, grave and quiet, watching him with calm, bright eyes.

The Secretary, too, was silent for a few moments, surveying the woman who sat opposite him, so cool and so composed. He felt once more the thrill of involuntary admiration that she always aroused in him.

"It is a delicate business on which I come to you, Miss Catherwood," he said. "I wish to speak of Miss Harley and my suit there; it is not prospering, as you know. Pardon me for speaking to you of such intimate feelings. I know that it is not customary, but I have thought that you might aid me."

"Was it for such a reason that you gave me a pass to Richmond and helped me to come here?"

"Well, in part, at least; but I can say in my own defense, Miss Catherwood, that I bore you no ill will. Perhaps, if the first phase of the affair had never existed, I should have helped you anyhow to come to Richmond had I known that you wished to do so."

"And how can I help you now?"

The Secretary shrugged his shoulders. He did not wish to say all that was in his mind. Moreover, he sought to bring her will into subjection to his. The personal sense that he was coming into contact with a mind as strong as his own did not wholly please him, yet by a curious contrariety this very feeling increased his admiration of her.

"I was willing that you should come to Richmond," he said, "for a reason that I will not mention and which perhaps has passed away. I have had in my mind—well, to put it plainly, a sort of bargain, a bargain in which I did not consult you. I thought that you might help me with Helen Harley, that—well, to speak plainly again, that your attractions might remove from my path one whom I considered a rival."

A deep flush overspread her face, and then, retreating, left it paler than ever. Her fingers were pressed tightly into the palms of her hands, but she said nothing.

111

"I am frank," continued the Secretary, "but it is best between us. Finesse would be wasted upon one with your penetrating mind, and I pay you the highest compliment I know when I discard any attempt to use it. I find that I have made a great mistake in more respects than one. The man who I thought stood in my way thought so himself at one time, but he knows better. Helen Harley is very beautiful and all that is good, but still there is something lacking. I knew it long ago, but only in the last few weeks has it had its effect upon me. This man I thought my rival has turned aside into a new path, and I—well, it seems that fate intends that he shall be my rival even in his changes—have followed him."

"What do you mean?" she asked, a sudden fire leaping to her eyes and a cold dread clutching her heart.

"I mean," he said, "that however beautiful Helen Harley may be, there are others as beautiful and one perhaps who has something that she lacks. What is that something? The power to feel passion, to love with a love that cares for nothing else, and if need be to hate with a hate that cares for nothing else. She must be a woman with fire in her veins and lightning in her heart, one who would appear to the man she loves not only a woman, but as a goddess as well."

"And have you found such a woman?"

She spoke in cold, level tones.

The Secretary looked at her sitting there, her head thrown slightly back, her eyes closed and the curve of her chin defiant to the uttermost degree. The wonder that he had not always loved this woman instead of Helen Harley returned to him. She was a girl and yet she was not; there was nothing about her immature or imperfect; she was girl and woman, too. She had spoken to him in the coldest of tones, yet he believed in the fire beneath the ice. He wished to see what kind of torch would set the flame. His feeling for her before had been intellectual, now it was sentimental and passionate.

James Sefton realized that Lucia Catherwood was not merely a woman to be admired, but one to be loved and desired. She had appealed to him as one with whom to make a great career; now she appealed to him as a woman with whom to live. He remembered the story of her carrying the wounded Prescott off the battlefield in her arms and in the dark, alone and undaunted, amid all the dead of the Wilderness. She was tall and strong, but was it so much strength and endurance as love and sacrifice? He was filled with a sudden fierce and wild jealousy of Prescott, because, when wounded and stricken down, she had sheltered him within her arms.

His look again followed the curves of her noble face and figure, the full development of strong years, and a fire of which he had not deemed himself capable burned in the eyes of the Secretary. The pale shade of Helen Harley floated away in the mist, but Lucia met his silent gaze firmly, and again she asked in cold, level tones:

"Have you found such a woman?"

"Yes, I have found her," replied the Secretary. "Perhaps I did not know it until to-day; perhaps I was not sure, but I have found her. I am a cold and what one would call a selfish man, but ice breaks up under summer heat, and I have yielded to the spell of your presence, Lucia."

"Miss Catherwood!"

"Well, Miss Catherwood—no, Lucia it shall be! I swear it shall be Lucia! I do not care for courtesy now, and you are compelled to hear me say it. It is a noble name, a beautiful one, and it gives me pleasure to say it. Lucia! Lucia! Lucia!"

"Go on, then, since I cannot stop you."

"I said that I have found such a woman and I have. Lucia, I love you, because I cannot help myself, just as you cannot help my calling you Lucia. And, Lucia, it is a love that worships, too. There is nothing bad in it. I would put myself at your feet. You shall be a queen to me and to all the rest of the world, for I have much to offer you besides my poor self. However the war may end, I shall be rich, very rich, and we shall have a great career. Let it be here if you will, or in the North, or in Europe. You have only to say."

There was then a feeling for him not all hate in the soul of Lucia Catherwood. If he loved her, that was a cloak for many sins, and she could not doubt that he did, because the man hitherto so calm and the master of himself was transformed. His words were spoken with all the fire and heat of a lover, his eyes were alight, and his figure took on a certain dignity and nobility. Lucia Catherwood, looking at him, said to herself in unspoken words: "Here is a great man and he loves me." Her heart was cold, but a ray of tenderness came from it nevertheless.

The Secretary paused and in his agitation leaned his arm upon the mantel. Again his eyes dwelt upon her noble curves, her sumptuous figure, and the soul that shone from her eyes. Never before had he felt so utter a sense of powerlessness. Hitherto to desire a thing was with him merely the preliminary to getting it. Even when Helen Harley turned away from him, he believed that by incessant pursuit he could yet win her. There he took repulses lightly, but here it was the woman alone who decreed, and whatever she might say no act or power of his could change it. He stood before her a suppliant.

"You have honoured me, Mr. Sefton, with this declaration of your love," she said, and her tones sounded to him as cold and level as ever, "but I cannot—cannot return it."

"Neither now nor ever? You may change!"

"I cannot change, Mr. Sefton." She spoke a little sadly—out of pity for him—and shook her head.

"You think that my loyalty is due to Helen Harley, but I do not love her! I cannot!"

"No, it is not that," she said. "Helen Harley may not love you; I do not think she does. But I am quite sure of myself. I know that I can never love you."

"You may not now," he said hotly, "but you can be wooed and you can be won. I could not expect you to love me at once—I am not so foolish—but devotion, a long devotion, may change a woman's heart."

"No," she repeated, "I cannot change."

She seemed to be moving away from him. She was intangible and he could not grasp her. But he raised his head proudly.

"I do not come as a beggar," he said. "I offer something besides myself."

Her eyes flashed; she, too, showed her pride.

"I stand alone, I am nothing except myself, but my choice in the most important matter that comes into a woman's life shall be as free as the air."

She, too, raised her head and met him with an unflinching gaze.

"I also understand," he said moodily. "You love Prescott."

A flush swept over her face, and then retreating left it pale again, but she was too proud to deny the charge. She would not utter an untruth nor an evasion even on so delicate a subject. There was an armed truce of silence between them for a few minutes, till the evil genius of the Secretary rose and he felt again that desire to subject her will to his own.

"If you love this young man, are you quite sure that he loves you?" he asked in quiet tones.

"I will not discuss such a subject," she replied, flushing.

"But I choose to speak of it. You saw him at the President's house two nights ago making obvious love to some one else—a married woman. Are you sure that he is worthy?"

She maintained an obstinate silence, but became paler than ever.

"If so, you have a mighty faith," he went on relentlessly. "His face was close to Mrs. Markham's. Her hair almost touched his cheek."

"I will not listen to you!" she cried.

"But you must. Richmond is ringing with talk about them. If I were a woman I should wish my lover to come to me with a clean reputation, at least."

He paused, but she would not speak. Her face was white and her teeth were set firmly together.

"I wish you would go!" she said at last, with sudden fierceness.

"But I will not. I do not like you the least when you rage like a lioness."

She sank back, coldness and quiet coming to her as suddenly as her anger had leaped up.

"You have told me that you cannot love me," he said, "and I have shown you that the man you love cannot love you. I refuse to go. Awhile since I felt that I was powerless before you, and that I must abide by your yea and nay; but I feel so no longer. Love, I take it, is a battle, and I use a military simile because there is war about us. If a good general wishes to take a position, and if he fails in the direct charge—if he is repelled with loss—he does not on that account retreat; but he resorts to artifice, to stratagem, to the mine, to the sly and adroit approach."

Her courage did not fail, but she felt a chill when he talked in this easy and sneering manner. She had liked him—a little—when he disclosed his love so openly and so boldly, but now no ray of tenderness came from her heart.

"I can give you more of the news of Richmond," said the Secretary, "and this concerns you as intimately as the other. Perhaps I should refrain from telling you, but I am jealous enough in my own cause to tell it nevertheless. Gossip in Richmond—well, I suppose I must say it—has touched your name, too. It links you with me."

"Mr. Sefton," she said in the old cold, level tones, "you spoke of my changing, but I see that you have changed. Five minutes ago I thought you a gentleman."

"If I am doing anything that seems mean to you I do it for love of you and the desire to possess you. That should be a sufficient excuse with any woman. Perhaps you do not realize that your position depends upon me. You came here because I wrote something on a piece of paper. There has been a whisper that you were once a spy in this city—think of it; the name of spy does not sound well. Rumour has touched you but lightly, yet if I say the word it can envelope and suffocate you."

"You have said that you love me; do men make threats to the women whom they love?"

"Ah, it is not that," he pleaded. "If a man have a power over a woman he loves, can you blame him if he use it to get that which he wishes?"

"Real love knows no such uses," she said, and then she rose from her chair, adding:

"I shall not listen any longer, Mr. Sefton. You remind me of my position, and it is well, perhaps, that I do not forget it. It may be, then, that I have not listened to you too long."

"And I," he replied, "if I have spoken roughly I beg your pardon. I could wish that my words were softer, but my meaning must remain the same."

He bowed courteously—it was the suave Secretary once more—and then he left her.

Lucia Catherwood sat, dry-eyed and motionless, for a long time, gazing at the opposite wall and seeing nothing there. She asked herself now why she had come back to Richmond. To be with Miss Grayson, her next of kin, and because she had no other place? That was the reason she had given to herself and others—but was it the whole reason?

113

Now she wished that she had never seen Richmond. The first visit had ended in disaster, and the second in worse. She hated the sight of Richmond. What right had she among these people who were not hers? She was a stranger, a foreigner, of another temperament, another cast of thought.

Her mind flitted over the threats, open and veiled, of the Secretary, but she had little fear for herself. There she had the power to fight, and her defiant spirit would rise to meet such a conflict. But this other! She must sit idle and let it go on. She was surprised at her sudden power of hatred, which was directed full against a woman in whose eyes—even in moments of peace—there were lurking green tints.

He had done much for her! Well, she had done as much for him and hence there was no balance between them. She resolved to cast him out wholly, to forget him, to make him part of a past that was not only dead but forgotten. But she knew even as she took this resolution that she feared the Secretary because she believed it lay within his power to ruin Prescott.

The door was opened and Miss Grayson came quietly into the room. She was a cool, soothing little person. Troubles, if they did not die, at least became more tolerable in her presence. She sat in silence sewing, but observed Lucia's face and knew that she was suffering much or it would not show in the countenance of one with so strong a will.

"Has Mr. Sefton been gone long?" she asked after awhile.

"Yes, but not long enough."

Miss Grayson said nothing and Miss Catherwood was the next to interrupt the silence.

"Charlotte," she said, "I intend to leave Richmond at once."

"Leaving Richmond is not a mere holiday trip now," said Miss Grayson. "There are formalities, many and difficult."

"But I must go!" exclaimed Miss Catherwood vehemently, all her anger and grief flashing out—it seemed to her that the gates suddenly opened. "I tell you I must leave this city! I hate everything in it, Charlotte, except you! I am sorry that I ever saw it!"

Miss Grayson went on calmly with her sewing.

"I shall not let you go," she said in her quiet, even voice. "I could have endured life without you had I never had you, but having had you I cannot. I shall not let you go. You must think of me now, Lucia, and not of yourself."

Miss Grayson looked up and smiled. The smile of an old maid, not herself beautiful, can be very beautiful at times.

"See what a burden I am," Miss Catherwood protested. "We nearly starved once."

Then she blushed—blushed most beautifully, thinking of a certain round gold piece, still unspent.

"You are no burden at all, but a support. I shall have money enough until this war ends. The Confederate Government, you know, Lucia, paid me for the confiscations—not as much as they were worth, but as much as I could expect—and we have been living on it."

The face of Lucia Catherwood altered. It expressed a singular tenderness as she looked at Miss Grayson, so soft, so small and so gray.

"Charlotte," she said, "I wish that I were as good as you. You are never excited, passionate or angry. You always know what you ought to do and you always do it."

Miss Grayson looked up again and her eyes suddenly sparkled.

"You make a mistake, a great mistake, Lucia," she said. "It is only the people who do wrong now and then who are really good. Those of us who do right all the time merely keep in that road because we cannot get out of it. I think it's a lack of temperament—there's no variety about us. And oh, Lucia, I tell you honestly, I get so tired of keeping forever in the straight and narrow path merely because it's easiest for me to walk that way. I don't mean to be sacrilegious, but I think that all the rejoicing in Heaven over the hundredth man who has sinned and repented was not because he had behaved well at last, but because he was so much more interesting than all the other ninety-nine put together. I wish I had your temper and impulses, Lucia, that I might flash into anger now and then and do something rash—something that I should be sorry for later on, but which in my secret heart I should be glad I had done. Oh, I get so tired of being just a plain, goody-goody little woman who will always do the right thing in the most uninteresting way; a woman about whom there is no delightful uncertainty; a woman on whom you can always reckon just as you would on the figure 4 or 6 or any other number in mathematics. I am like such a figure—a fixed quantity, and that is why I, Charlotte Grayson, am just a plain little old maid."

She had risen in her vehemence, but when she finished she sank back into her chair and a faint, delicate pink bloomed in her face. Miss Charlotte Grayson was blushing! Lucia was silent, regarding her. She felt a great flood of tenderness for this prim, quiet little woman who had, for a rare and fleeting moment, burst her shell. Miss Grayson had always accepted so calmly and so quietly the life which seemed to have been decreed for her that it never before occurred to Lucia to suppose any tempestuous feelings could rise in that breast; but she was a woman like herself, and the tie that bound them, already strong, suddenly grew stronger.

"Charlotte," she said, placing her hand gently upon the old maid's shoulder, "it seems to me sometimes that God has not been quite fair to women. He gives us too little defense against our own hearts."

"Best discard them entirely," said Miss Grayson briskly. "Come, Lucia, you promised to help me with my sewing."

CHAPTER XXVIII

THE WAY OUT

Prescott at three o'clock the following afternoon knocked on the door of Mr. Sefton's private office and the response "Come in!" was like his knock, crisp and decisive. Prescott entered and shut the door behind him. The Secretary had been sitting by the window, but he rose and received his guest courteously, extending his hand.

Prescott took the proffered hand. He had learned to look upon the Secretary as his enemy, but he found himself unable to hate him.

"We had an interview in this room once before," said the Secretary, "and it was not wholly unfriendly."

"That is true," replied Prescott, "and as the subject that I have to propose now is of a somewhat kindred nature I hope that we may keep the same tone."

"It rests with you, my dear Captain," said the Secretary meaningly.

Prescott was somewhat embarrassed. He scarcely knew how to begin.

"I came to ask a favour," he said at last.

"The willingness to bestow favours does not always imply the power."

"It is true," said Prescott; "but in this case the will may go with the power. I have come to speak to you of Lucia Catherwood."

"What of her?" asked the Secretary sharply. He was betrayed into a momentary interruption of his habitual calm, but settled himself into his seat and looked keenly across the table at his rival, trying to guess the young man's plan of campaign. Calculating upon the basis of what he himself would do in the same position, he could form no conclusion.

"I have come to speak on her account," continued Prescott, "and though I may be somewhat involved, I wish it to be distinctly understood that I am not to be considered. I ask no favour for myself."

"I see that you have brought your pride with you," said the Secretary dryly.

Prescott flushed a little.

"I trust that I always have it with me," he said.

"We are frank with each other."

"It is best so, and I have come for yet plainer speaking. I am well aware, Mr. Sefton, that you know all there is to be known concerning Miss Catherwood and myself."

"'All' is a large statement."

"I refer to the facts of Miss Catherwood's former presence in Richmond, what she did while here, and how she escaped from the city. You know that I helped her."

"And by doing so you put yourself in an extremely delicate position, should any one choose to relate the facts to the Government."

"Precisely. But again it is Miss Catherwood of whom I am speaking, not myself. You may speak of me, you may denounce me at any time you choose, but I ask you, Mr. Sefton, to respect the secret of Miss Catherwood. She has told me that her acts were almost involuntary; she came here because she had nowhere else to come—to her cousin, Miss Grayson. She admits that she was once tempted to act as a spy—that the impulse was strong within her. You know the depth of her Northern sympathies, the strength of her nature, and how deeply she was moved—but that is all she admits. This impulse has now passed. Would you ruin her here, as you can do, where she has so many friends, and where it is possible for her life to be happy?"

A thin smile appeared on the face of the Secretary.

"You will pardon me if I call this a somewhat extraordinary appeal, Captain Prescott," he said. "You seem to show a deep interest in Miss Catherwood, and yet if I am to judge by what I saw the other night, and before, your devotion is for another lady."

Prescott flushed an angry red; but remembering his resolve he replied quietly:

"It is not a question of my devotion to anybody, Mr. Sefton. I merely speak for Miss Catherwood, believing that she is in your power."

"And what induced you to believe that I would betray her?"

"I have not indicated such a belief. I merely seek to provide against a contingency."

The Secretary pondered, lightly tapping the table with the forefinger of his right hand. Prescott observed his thin, almost ascetic face, smooth-shaven and finely cut. Both General Wood and the Secretary were mountaineers, but the two faces were different; one represented blunt strength and courage; the other suppleness, dexterity, meditation, the power of silent combination. Had the two been blended here would have been one of the world's giant figures.

"We have begun by being frank; we should continue so," said the Secretary presently. "We seem doomed to be rivals always, Captain Prescott; at least we can give each other the credit of good taste. At first it was Helen Harley who took our fancy—a fancy it was and nothing more—but now I think a deeper passion has been stirred in us by the same object, Miss Catherwood. You see, I am still frank. I know very well that you care nothing for Mrs. Markham. It is but a momentary folly, the result of jealousy or something akin to it—and here I am, resolved to triumph over you, not because I would enjoy your

115

defeat, but because my own victories are sweet to me. If I happen to hold in my hand certain cards which chance has not dealt to you, can you blame me if I play them?"

"Will you spare Miss Catherwood?" asked Prescott.

"Should I not play my cards?" repeated the Secretary.

"I see," said Prescott. "You told me that I brought my pride with me. Well, I did not bring all of it. I left at home enough to permit me to ask this favour of you. But I was wrong; I should not have made the request."

"I have not refused it yet," said the Secretary. "I merely do not wish to pledge myself. When a man makes promises he places bonds on his own arms, and I prefer mine free; but since I seek Miss Catherwood as a wife, is it not a fair inference that her fame is as dear to me as it is to you?"

Prescott was compelled to admit the truth of this statement, but it did not cover all the ground. He felt that the Secretary, while not betraying Lucia, would in some way use his knowledge of her for his own advantage. This was the thought at the bottom of his mind, but he could not speak it aloud to the Secretary. Any man would repel such an intimation at once as an insult, and the agile mind of James Sefton would make use of it as another strong trump card in playing his game.

"Then you will make no promise?" asked Prescott.

"Promises are poor coin," replied the Secretary, "hardly better than our Confederate bills. Let me repeat that the fame of Lucia Catherwood is as dear to me as it is to you. With that you should be content."

"If that is all, good-day," said Prescott, and he went out, holding his head very high. The Secretary saw defiance in his attitude.

Mr. Sefton went the following evening to the little house in the cross street, seeking an interview with Lucia Catherwood, and she, holding many things in mind, was afraid to deny him.

"It is your friend, Captain Prescott, of whom I wish to speak," he said.

"Why my friend rather than the friend of anybody else?" she asked.

"He has been of service to you, and for that reason I wish to be of service to him. There has been talk about him. He may find himself presently in a very dangerous position."

The face of Lucia Catherwood flushed very red and then became equally pale. The Secretary noticed how her form stiffened, nor did he fail to observe the single angry flash from her eyes. "She cares very much for that man," was his mental comment. The Secretary was not less frank with himself in his love than in other matters.

"If you have come here merely to discuss Richmond gossip I shall beg you to leave at once," she said coldly.

"You misunderstand me," replied the Secretary. "I do not speak of any affair of the heart that Captain Prescott may have. It is no concern of mine where his affections may fall, even if it be in an unlicensed quarter. The difficulty to which I allude is of another kind. There is malicious gossip in Richmond; something has leaked out in some way that connects him with an affair of a spy last winter. Connect is scarcely the word, because that is too definite; this is exceedingly vague. Harley spoke of it the other night, and although he did not call Prescott by name, his manner indicated that he was the man meant. Harley seems to have received a little nebulous information from a certain quarter, not enough upon which to take action had one the malice to wish it, but enough to indicate that he might obtain more from the same source."

The Secretary paused, and his expression was one of mingled concern and sympathy. A young man whom he liked was about to fall into serious difficulties and he would save him from them if he could. Yet they understood each other perfectly. A single glance, a spark from steel like that which had passed between Prescott and the Secretary, passed now between these two. The Secretary was opening another mine in the arduous siege that he had undertaken; if he could not win by treaty he would by arms, and now he was threatening her through Prescott.

She did not flinch and therefore she won his increased admiration. Her natural colour returned and she met his glance firmly. The life of Lucia Catherwood had been hard and she was trained to repression and self-reliance.

"I do not understand why you should speak of this to me," she said.

"Merely that you might exert your influence in his favour."

She was measuring him then with a glance not less penetrating than his own. Why should she seek now to save Prescott? But she would, if she could. This was a threat that the Secretary might keep, but not at once, and she would seek time.

"Captain Prescott has done me a great service," she said, "and naturally I should be grateful to any who did as much for him."

"Perhaps some one who will do as much can be found," he said. "It may be that I shall speak to him of you later and then he will claim the reward that you promise."

It was on her lips to say that she promised nothing except gratitude, but she withheld the words. It suddenly seemed fair to a singularly honest mind to meet craft with craft. She had heard of the military phrase, "in the air"; she would leave the Secretary in the air. So she merely said:

"I am not in Captain Prescott's confidence, but I know that he will thank you."

"He should," said the Secretary dryly, and left her.

Almost at the very moment that the Secretary was going to the Grayson cottage Prescott was on his way to Winthrop's newspaper office.

There was little to be done, and a group including General Wood, who had come that afternoon from Petersburg, sat in the old fashion by the stove and talked of public affairs, especially the stage into which the war had now come. The heat of the room felt grateful, as a winter night was falling outside, and in the society of his friends Prescott found himself becoming more of an optimist than he had been for some days. Cheerfulness is riveted in such a physical base as youth and strength, and Prescott was no exception. He could even smile behind his hand when he saw General Wood draw forth the infallible bowie-knife, pull a piece of pine from a rickety box that held fuel for the stove and begin to whittle from it long, symmetrical shavings that curled beautifully. This was certain evidence that General Wood, for the evening at least, was inclined to look on the bright side of life.

Unto this placid group came two men, walking heavily up the wooden stairs and showing signs of mental wear. Their eyebrows were raised with surprise at the sight of Prescott, but they made no comment. They were Harley and Redfield.

Harley approached Winthrop with a jovial air.

"I've found you a new contributor to your paper and he's ready to bring you a most interesting piece of news."

Winthrop flipped the ash off his cigar and regarded Harley coolly.

"Colonel!" he said, "I'm always grateful for good news, but I don't take it as a favour. If it comes to the pinch I can write my newspaper all by myself."

Harley changed countenance and his tone changed too.

"It's in the interest of justice," he said, "and it will be sure to attract attention at the same time."

"I imagine that it must be in the interest of justice when you and Mr. Redfield take so much trouble to secure its publication," said Winthrop; "and I imagine that I'm not risking much when I also say that you are the brilliant author who has written the little piece."

"It's this," said Harley. "It's about a man who has been paying too ardent attentions to a married woman—no names given, of course; he is a captain, a young man who is here on leave, and she is the wife of a general who is at the front and can't look after his own honour. Gossip says, too, that the captain has been concerned in something else that will bring him up with a jerk if the Government hears of it. It's all written out here. Oh, it will make a fine stir!"

Prescott half rose from his seat, but sank back and remained quiet. Again he imitated the Secretary's example of self-repression and waited to see what Winthrop would do. General Wood trimmed off a shaving so long that it coiled all the way around his wrist. Then he took it off carefully, dropped it on the floor with the others, and at once went to work whittling a new one.

"Let's see the article," said Winthrop.

Harley handed it to him and he read it carefully.

"A fine piece of work," he said; "who wrote it—you or Redfield?"

"Oh, we did it together," replied Harley with a smile of appreciation.

Redfield uttered a denial, but it was too late.

"A fine piece of work," repeated Winthrop, "admirably adapted to the kindling of fires. Unfortunately my fire is already kindled, but it can help on the good cause."

With that he cast the paper into the stove.

Harley uttered an oath.

"What do you mean?" he cried.

"I mean that you can't use my paper to gratify your private revenge. If you want to do that sort of thing you must get a newspaper of your own."

"I think you are infernally impertinent."

"And I think, Vincent Harley, that you are a damned fool. You want a duel with the man about whom you've written this card, but for excellent reasons he will decline to meet you. Still I hate to see a man who is looking for a fight go disappointed, and just to oblige you I'll fight you myself."

"But I've no quarrel with you," said Harley sullenly.

"Oh, I can give you ample cause," said Winthrop briskly. "I can throw this water in your face, or if you prefer it I can give you a blow on the cheek, a hard one, too. Take your choice."

Prescott arose.

"I'm much obliged to you, Winthrop," he said, "for taking up my quarrel and trying to shield me. All of you know that I am meant in that card which he calls such 'a piece of good news.' I admire Colonel Harley's methods, and since he is so persistent I will fight him on the condition that the meeting and its causes be kept absolutely secret. If either of us is wounded or killed let it be said that it was in a skirmish with the enemy."

"Why these conditions?" asked Redfield.

"For the sake of others. Colonel Harley imagines that he has a grievance against me. He has none, and if he had the one that he imagines he is certainly in no position to call me to account. Since he will have it no other way, I will fight him."

117

"I object," said Winthrop with temper. "I have a prior claim. Colonel Harley has tried to use me, an unoffending third party, as the instrument of his private revenge, and that is a deadly offense. I have the reputation of being a hot-blooded man and I intend to live up to my reputation."

A glass of water was standing by the cooler. He lifted it and hurled the contents into Harley's face. The man started back, strangling and coughing, then wiped the water from his face with a handkerchief.

"Do you dispute the priority of my claim over Captain Prescott?" asked Winthrop.

"I do not," said Harley. "Mr. Redfield will call on you again in my behalf within an hour."

Prescott was irresolute.

"Winthrop," he said, "I can't permit this."

"Oh, yes, you can," said Winthrop, "because you can't help yourself."

Then General Wood upreared his gigantic form and ran the fingers of his left hand solemnly through his black whiskers. He put his bowie-knife in its sheath, brushed the last shaving off his trousers and said:

"But there's somebody who can help it, an' I'm the man. What's more, I mean to do it. Colonel Harley, General Lee transferred your regiment to my command yesterday and I need you at the front. I order you to report for duty at once, and I won't have any delay about it either. You report to me in Petersburg to-morrow or I'll know the reason why; I go myself at daylight, but I'll leave a request with the Government that Captain Prescott also be despatched to me. I've got work for him to do."

The man spoke with the utmost dignity and his big black eyes shot fire.

"The king commands," said Raymond softly.

Wood put his hand on Harley's arm.

"Colonel," he said, "you are one of my lieutenants, and we're thinkin' about a movement that I've got to talk over with you. You'll come with me now to the Spotswood Hotel, because there's no time to waste. I don't reckon you or I will get much sleep to-night, but if we don't sleep to-night we'll doze in the saddle to-morrow."

"The king not only commands, but knows what to command," said Raymond softly.

It was the general of the battlefield, the man of lightning force who spoke, and there was none who dared to disobey. Harley, himself a brilliant soldier though nothing else, yielded when he felt the hand of steel on his arm, and acknowledged the presence of a superior force.

"Very well, General," he said respectfully; "I am at your service."

"Good-night, gentlemen," said Wood to the others, and he added laughingly to the editors: "Don't you boys print anythin' until you know what you're printin'," and to Prescott: "I reckon you'd better say good-by to-morrow to your friends in Richmond. I don't allow that you'll have more'n a couple of days longer here," and then to Harley: "Come along, Colonel; an' I s'pose you're goin' out with us, too, Mr. Redfield."

He swept up the two with his glance and the three left together, their footsteps sounding on the rickety steps until they passed into the street.

"There goes a man, a real man," said Raymond with emphasis. "Winthrop, it takes such as he to reduce fellows like you and Harley to their proper places."

"It is unkind of him to kidnap Harley in that summary fashion," said Winthrop ruefully. "I really wanted to put a bullet through him. Not in a vital place—say through the shoulder or the fleshy part of the arm, where it would let blood flow freely. That's what he needs."

But Prescott was devoutly thankful to Wood, and especially for his promise that he, too, should speedily be sent to the front. What he wished most of all now was to escape from Richmond.

The promise was kept, the order to report to General Wood himself in Petersburg came the next day and he was to start on the following morning.

He took courage to call upon Lucia and found her at home, sitting silently in the little parlour, the glow from the fire falling across her hair and tinting it with deep gleams of reddish gold. Whether she was surprised to see him he could not judge, her face remaining calm and no movement that would betray emotion escaping her.

"Miss Catherwood," he said, "I have come to bid you farewell. I rejoin the army to-morrow and I am glad to go."

"I, too, am glad that you are going," she said, shading her eyes with her hands as if to protect them from the glow of the fire.

"There is one thing that I would ask of you," he said, "and it is that you remember me as I was last winter, and not as I have appeared to you since I returned from the South. That was real; this is false."

His voice trembled, and she did not speak, fearing that her own would do the same.

"I have made mistakes," he said. "I have yielded to rash impulses, and have put myself in a false position before the world; but I have not been criminal in anything, either in deed or intent. Even now what I remember best, the memory that I value most, is when you and I fled together from Richmond in the cold and the snow, when you trusted me and I trusted you."

She wished to speak to him then, remembering the man, stained with his own blood, whom she had carried in her strong young arms off the battlefield. With a true woman's heart she liked him better when she was acting for him than when he was acting for her; but something held her back—the shadow of a fair woman with lurking green depths in her blue eyes.

"Lucia!" exclaimed Prescott passionately, "have you nothing to say to me? Can't you forget my follies and remember at least the few good things that I have done?"

"I wish you well. I cannot forget the great service that you did me, and I hope that you will return safely from a war soon to end."

"You might wish anybody that, even those whom you have never seen," he said.

Then with a few formal words he went away, and long after he was gone she still sat there staring into the fire, the gleams of reddish gold in her hair becoming fainter and fainter.

Prescott left Richmond the next morning.

CHAPTER XXIX

THE FALL OF RICHMOND

Two long lines of earthworks faced each other across a sodden field; overhead a chilly sky let fall a chilly rain; behind the low ridges of earth two armies faced each other, and whether in rain or in sunshine, no head rose above either wall without becoming an instant mark for a rifle that never missed. Here the remorseless sharpshooters lay. Human life had become a little thing, and after a difficult shot they exchanged remarks as hunters do when they kill a bird on the wing.

If ever there was a "No Man's Land," it was the space between the two armies which had aptly been called the "Plain of Death." Any one who ventured upon it thought very little of this life, and it was well that he should, as he had little of it left to think about. The armies had lain there for weeks and weeks, facing each other in a deadlock, and a fierce winter, making the country an alternation of slush and snow, had settled down on both. The North could not go forward; the South could not thrust the North back; but the North could wait and the South could not. Lee's army, crouching behind the earthen walls, grew thinner and hungrier and colder as the weeks passed. Uniforms fell away in rags, supplies from the South became smaller and smaller, but the lean and ragged army still lay there, grim and defiant, while Grant, with the memory of Cold Harbour before him, dared not attack. He bided his time, having shown all the qualities that were hoped of him and more. Tenacious, fertile in ideas, he had been from the beginning the one to attack and his foe the one to defend. The whole character of the war had changed since he came upon the field. He and Sherman were now the two arms of a vise that held the Confederacy in its grip and would never let go.

Prescott crouched behind the low wall, reading a letter from his mother, while his comrades looked enviously at him. A letter from home had long since become an event. Mrs. Prescott said she was well, and, so far as concerned her physical comfort, was not feeling any excessive stress of war. They were hearing many reports in Richmond from the armies. Grant, it was said, would make a great flanking movement as soon as the warmer weather came, and the newspapers in the capital gave accounts of vast reinforcements in men and supplies he was receiving from the North.

"If we know our Grant, and we think we do, he will certainly move," said Prescott grimly to himself, looking across the "Plain of Death" toward the long Northern line.

Then his mother continued with personal news of his friends and acquaintances.

"The popularity of Lucia Catherwood lasts," she wrote. "She would avoid publicity, but she can scarcely do it without offending the good people who like her. She seems gay and is often brilliant, but I do not think she is happy. She receives great attention from Mr. Sefton, whose power in the Government, disguised as it is in a subordinate position, seems to increase. Whether or not she likes him I do not know. Sometimes I think she does, and sometimes I think she has the greatest aversion to him. But it is a courtship that interests all Richmond. People mostly say that the Secretary will win, but as an old woman—a mere looker-on—I have my doubts. Helen Harley still holds her place in the Secretary's office, but Mr. Sefton no longer takes great interest in her. Her selfish old father does not like it at all, and I hear that he speaks slightingly of the Secretary's low origin; but he continues to spend the money that his daughter earns.

"It is common gossip that the Secretary knows all about Lucia's life before she came to Richmond; that he has penetrated the mystery and in some way has a hold over her which he is using. I do not know how this report originated, but I think it began in some foolish talk of Vincent Harley's. As for myself, I do not believe there is any mystery at all. She is simply a girl who in these troublous times came, as was natural, to her nearest relative, Miss Grayson."

"No bad news, Bob, I hope," said Talbot, looking at his gloomy face.

"None at all," said Prescott cheerily, and with pardonable evasion.

"There go the skirmishers again."

A rapid crackle arose from a point far to their left, but the men around Talbot and Prescott paid no attention to it, merely huddling closer in the effort to keep warm. They had ceased long since to be interested in such trivialities.

"Grant's going to move right away; I feel it in my bones," repeated Talbot.

Talbot was right. That night the cold suddenly fled, the chilly clouds left the heavens and the great Northern General issued a command. A year before another command of his produced that terrific campaign through the Wilderness, where a hundred thousand men fell, and he meant this second one to be as significant.

Now the fighting, mostly the work of sharpshooters through the winter, began in regular form, and extended in a long line over the torn and trampled fields of Virginia, where all the soil was watered with blood. The numerous horsemen of Sheridan, fresh from triumphs in the Valley of Virginia, were the wings of the Northern force, and they hung on the flanks of the Southern army, incessantly harrying it, cutting off companies and regiments, giving the worn and wounded men no respite.

Along a vast, curving line that steadily bent in toward Richmond—the Southern army inside, the Northern army outside—the sound of the cannon scarcely ever ceased, night or day. Lee fought with undiminished skill, always massing his thin ranks at the point of contact and handling them with the old fire and vigour; but his opponent never ceased the terrible hammering that he had begun more than a year ago. Grant intended to break through the shell of the Southern Confederacy, and it was now cracking and threatening to shatter before his ceaseless strokes.

The defenders of a lost cause, if cause it was, scarcely ever knew what it was to draw a free breath. When they were not fighting, they were marching, often on bare feet, and of the two they did not know which they preferred. They were always hungry; they went into battles on empty stomachs, came out with the same if they came out at all, and they had no time to think of the future. They had become mere battered machines, animated, it is true, by a spirit, but by a spirit that could take no thought of softness. They had respected Grant from the first; now, despite their loss by his grim tactics, they looked in wonder and admiration at them, and sought to measure the strength of mind that could pay a heavy present price in flesh and blood in order to avoid a greater price hereafter.

Prescott and Talbot were with the last legion. The bullets, after wounding them so often, seemed now to give them the right of way. They came from every battle and skirmish unhurt, only to go into a new one the next day.

"If I get out of all this alive," said Talbot, with grim humour, "I intend to eat for a month and then sleep for a year; maybe then I'll feel rested."

Wood, too, was always there with his cavalry, now a thin band, seeking to hold back the horsemen of the North, and Vincent Harley, ever a good soldier, was his able second.

In these desperate days Prescott began to feel respect for Harley; he admired the soldier, if not the man. There was no danger too great for Harley, no service too arduous. He slept in the saddle, if he slept at all, and his spirit never flinched. There was no time for, him to renew his quarrel with Prescott, and Prescott was resolved that it should never be renewed if there were any decent way of avoiding it.

The close of a day of incessant battle and skirmish was at hand, and clouds of smoke darkened the twilight. From the east and from the west came the low mutter and thunder of the guns. The red sun was going down in a sea of ominous fire. There were strange reports of the deeds of Sheridan, but the soldiers themselves knew nothing definite. They had lost touch with other bodies of their comrades, and they could only hope to meet them again. Meanwhile they gave scarcely a glance at the lone and trampled land, but threw themselves down under the trees and fell asleep.

A messenger came for Prescott. "The General-in-Chief wishes you," he said.

Prescott walked to a small fire where Lee sat alone for the present and within the shelter of the tent. He was grave and thoughtful, but that was habitual with him. Prescott could not see that the victor of Fredericksburg and Chancellorsville had changed in bearing or manner. He was as neat as ever; the gray uniform was spotless; the splendid sword, a gift from admirers, hung by his side. His face expressed nothing to the keen gaze of Prescott, who was now no novice in the art of reading the faces of men.

Prescott saluted and stood silent.

Lee looked at him thoughtfully.

"Captain Prescott," he said, "I have heard good reports of you, and I have had the pleasure also to see you bear yourself well."

Prescott's heart beat fast at this praise from the first man of the South.

"Do you know the way to Richmond?" asked the General.

"I could find it in a night as black as my hat."

"That is good. Here is a letter that I wish you to take there and deliver as soon as you can to Mr. Davis. It is important, and be sure you do not fall into the hands of any of the Northern raiders."

He held out a small sealed envelope, and Prescott took it.

"Take care of yourself," he said, "because you will have a dangerous ride."

Prescott saluted and turned away. He looked back once, and the General was still sitting alone by the fire, his face grave and thoughtful.

Prescott had a good horse, and when he rode away was full of faith that he would reach Richmond. He was glad to go because of the confidence Lee showed in him, and because he might see in the capital those for whom he cared most.

As he rode on the lights behind him died and the darkness came up and covered Lee's camp. But he had truly told the General that he could find his way to Richmond in black darkness, and to-night he had need of both knowledge and instinct. There was a shadowed moon, flurries of rain, and a wind moaning through the pine woods. From far away, like the swell of the sea on the rocks, came the low mutter of the guns. Scarcely ever did it cease, and its note rose above the wailing of the wind like a kind of solemn chorus that got upon Prescott's nerves.

"Is it a funeral song?" he asked.

On he went and the way opened before him in the darkness; no Northern horsemen crossed his path; the cry of "Halt!" never came. It seemed to Prescott that fate was making his way easy. For what purpose? He did not like it. He wished to be interrupted—to feel that he must struggle to achieve his journey. This, too, got upon his nerves. He grew lonely and afraid—not afraid of physical danger, but of the omens and presages that the night seemed to bear. He wondered again about the message that he bore. Why had not General Lee given some hint of its contents? Then he blamed himself for questioning.

He rode slowly and thus many hours passed. Mile after mile fell behind him and the night went with them. The sun sprang up, the golden day enfolded the earth, and at last from the top of a hill he saw afar the spires of Richmond. It was a city that he loved—his home, the scene of the greatest events in his life, including his manhood's love; and as he looked down upon it now his eyes grew misty. What would be its fate?

He rode on, giving the countersign as he passed the defenses. With the pure day, the omens and presages of the night seemed to have passed. Richmond breathed a Sabbath calm; the Northern armies might have been a thousand miles away for all the sign it gave. There was no fear, no apprehension on the faces he saw. Richmond still had absolute faith in Lee; whatever his lack of resources, he would meet the need.

From lofty church spires bells began to ring. The air was pervaded with a holy calm, and Prescott, with the same feeling upon him, rode on. He longed to turn aside to see his mother and to call at the Grayson cottage, but "as soon as possible," the General had said, and he must deliver his message. He knocked at the door of the White House of the Confederacy. "Gone to church," the servant said when he asked for Mr. Davis.

Prescott took his way to Doctor Hoge's church, well knowing where the President of the Confederacy habitually sat, and stiff with his night's riding, walked and led his mount. At the church door he gave the horse to a little negro boy to hold and went quietly inside.

The President and his family were in their pew and the minister was speaking. Prescott paused a few moments at the entrance to the aisle. No one paid any attention to him; soldiers were too common a sight to be noticed. He felt in the inside pocket of his waistcoat and drew forth the sealed envelope. Then he slipped softly down the aisle, leaned over the President's pew and handed him the note with the whispered words, "A message from General Lee."

Prescott, receiving no orders, quietly withdrew to a neighbouring vacant pew and watched Mr. Davis as he opened the envelope and read the letter. He saw a sudden gray pallor sweep over his face, a quick twitching of the lips and then a return of the wonted calm.

The President of the Confederacy refolded the note and put it in his pocket. Presently he rose and left the church and Prescott followed him. An hour later Richmond was stricken into a momentary dumbness, soon followed by the chattering of many voices. The city, the capital, was to be given up. General Lee had written that the Southern army could no longer defend it, and advised the immediate departure of the Government, which was now packing up, ready to take flight by the Danville railroad.

Richmond, so long the inviolate, was to be abandoned. No one questioned the wisdom of Lee, but they were struck down by the necessity. Panic ran like fire in dry grass. The Yankees were coming at once, and they would burn and slay! Their cavalry had already been seen on the outskirts of the city. There was no time to lose if they were to escape to the farther South.

The streets were filled with the confused crowd. The rumours grew; they said everything, but of one thing the people were sure. The Government was packing its papers and treasures in all haste, and the train was waiting to take it southward. That they beheld with their own eyes. Great numbers of the inhabitants, too, made ready for flight as best they could, but they yet preserved most of their courage. They said they would come back. General Lee, when he gathered new forces, would return to the rescue of the city and they would come with him. The women and the children often wept, but the men, though with gloomy faces, bade them be of good cheer.

Prescott, still with no orders and knowing that none would come, walked slowly through the crowd, his heart full of grief and pity. This was his world about him that was falling to pieces. He knew why the night had been so full of omens; why the distant cannon had escorted him like funeral guns.

His first thought was now of his mother, and his second was of Lucia Catherwood, knowing well that in such a moment the passions of all the wild and lawless would rise. He hurried to his home, and on his way he met the Secretary, calm, composed, a quiet, cynical smile on his face.

"Well, Mr. Sefton," said Prescott, "it has come."

"Yes," replied the Secretary, "and not sooner than I have expected."

"You are leaving?" said Prescott.

"Yes," replied Mr. Sefton, "I go with the Government. I am part of it, you know, but I travel light. I have little baggage. I tell you, too, since you wish to know it, that I asked Miss Catherwood to go with us as my wife—we could be married in an hour—or, if not that, as a refugee under the escort of Miss Grayson."

"Well?" said Prescott. His heart beat violently.

"She declined both propositions," replied the Secretary quietly. "She will stay here and await the coming of the conquerors. After all, why shouldn't she? She is a Northern sympathizer herself, and a great change in her position and ours has occurred suddenly."

Their eyes met and Prescott saw his fall a little and for the first time. The sudden change in positions was, indeed, great and in many respects.

The Secretary held out his hand.

"Good-by, Captain Prescott," he said. "We have been rivals, but not altogether enemies. I have always wished you well where your success was not at the cost of mine. Let us part in friendship, as we may not meet again."

Prescott took the extended hand.

"I am sorry that chance or fate ever made us rivals," the Secretary went on. "Maybe we shall not be so any longer, and since I retire from the scene I tell you I have known all the while that Miss Catherwood was not a spy. She was there in the President's office that day, and she might have been one had she yielded to her impulse, but she put the temptation aside. She has told you this and she told you the full truth. The one who really took the papers was discovered and punished by me long ago."

"Then why——" began Prescott.

The Secretary made a gesture.

"You ask why I kept this secret?" he said. "It was because it gave me power over both you and her; over her through you. I knew your part in it, too. Then I helped Miss Grayson and her when she came back to Richmond; she could not turn me away. I played upon your foolish jealousy—I fancy I did that cleverly. I brought her back here to draw you away from Helen Harley and she drew me, too. She did not intend it, nor did she wish it; but perhaps she felt her power ever since that meeting in the Wilderness and knew that she was safe from any disclosures of mine. But she loved you from the first, Captain Prescott, and never anybody else. You see, I am frank with myself as I have tried always to be in all respects. I have lost the field and I retire in favour of the winner, yourself!"

The Secretary, bowing, walked away. Prescott watched him a minute or two, but he could see no signs of haste or excitement in the compact, erect figure. Then he hastened to his mother.

He found her in her parlour, prepared as if for the coming of some one. There was fervent feeling in her look, but her manner was calm as she embraced her son. Prescott knew her thoughts, and as he had never yet found fault with them he could not now at such a time.

"I know everything, Robert," she said. "The Government is about to flee from Richmond."

"Yes, mother," he replied, "and I brought the order for it to go. Is it not singular that such a message should have been delivered by your son? Your side wins, mother."

"I never doubted that it would, not even after that terrible day at Bull Run and the greater defeats that came later. A cause is lost from the beginning when it is against the progress of the human race."

There was mingled joy and sadness in her manner—joy that the cause which she thought right had won; sadness that her friends, none the less dear because for so many months they had taken another view, should suffer misfortune.

"Mother," Prescott said presently, "I do not wish to leave you, but I must go to the cottage of Miss Grayson and Miss Catherwood. There are likely to be wild scenes in Richmond before the day is over, and they should not be left alone."

The look that she bent upon her son then was singularly soft and tender—smiling, too, as if something pleased her.

"They will be here, Robert," she said. "I expect them any minute."

"Here! in this house!" he exclaimed, starting.

"Yes, here in this house," she said triumphantly "It will not be the first time that Lucia Catherwood has been sheltered behind these walls. Do you not remember when they wished to arrest her, and Lieutenant Talbot searched the cottage for her? She was at that very moment here, in this house, hidden in your own room, though she did not know that it was yours. I saved her then. Oh, I have known her longer than you think."

Stirred by a sudden emotion Prescott stooped down and kissed his mother.

"I have always known that you were a wonderful woman," he said, "but I gave you credit for less courage and daring than you really have."

Some one knocked.

"There they are now," exclaimed Mrs. Prescott, and hurrying forward she opened the door. Lucia Catherwood and Charlotte Grayson entered. At first they did not see Prescott, who stood near the window, but when his tall form met their eyes Miss Grayson uttered a little cry and the colour rose high in Lucia's face.

"We are surprised to see you, Captain Prescott," she said.

"But glad, too, I hope," he replied.

"Yes, glad, too," she said frankly.

She seemed to have changed. Some of her reserve was gone. This was a great event in her life and she was coming into a new world without losing the old.

"Miss Catherwood," Prescott said, "I am glad that my mother's house is to be the shelter of Miss Grayson and yourself at such a time. We have one or two faithful and strong-armed servants who will see that you suffer no harm."

The two women hesitated and were embarrassed. Prescott saw it.

"You will not be bothered much by me," he said. "I have no instructions, but it is obvious that I should go forth and help maintain order." Then he added: "I saw Mr. Sefton departing. He bade me good-by as if he did not expect ever to be in Richmond again."

Again Lucia Catherwood flushed.

"He said a like farewell to me," she said.

Prescott's gaze met hers, and she flushed deeper than ever as her eyes dropped for a moment.

"I hope that he has gone forever," said Prescott. "He is an able man and I admire him in many ways. But I think him a dangerous man, too."

"Amen," said Miss Charlotte Grayson with emphasis. Lucia was silent, but she did not seem to be offended.

He went presently into the street, where, indeed, his duty called him. When a capital, after years of war, is about to fall, the forces of evil are always unchained, and now it was so with Richmond. Out from all the slums came the men and women of the lower world, and down by the navy storehouses the wharf-rats were swarming. They were drunk already, and with foul words on their lips they gathered before the stores, looking for plunder. Then they broke in the barrels of whisky at the wharf and became drunker and madder than ever. The liquor ran about them in great streams. Standing ankle deep in the gutters, they waded in it and splashed it over each other. Hilarious shouts and cries arose and they began to fight among themselves. Everywhere the thieves came from their holes and were already plundering the houses.

Steadily the skies darkened over Richmond and a terrified multitude kept pressing toward the railroad station, seeking to flee into the farther South. Behind them the mad crowd still drank and fought in the gutters and the thieves passed from house to house. Again and again the cry was raised that the Yankees were here, but still they did not come. Many fancied that they heard far away the thunder of the guns, and even Prescott was not sure. He went once to the Harley house and found Helen there, unafraid, quieting the apprehensions of her father, who should have been quieting hers. She, too, would stay. Mrs. Markham, she told him, was already on the train and would follow the Government. Prescott was very glad that she had gone. He felt a mighty relief to know that this woman was passing southward and, he hoped, out of his life.

Twilight came on and then the night, settling down black and heavy over the lost capital. The President and his Cabinet were ready and would soon start; the small garrison was withdrawing; an officer at the head of men with torches went about the city, setting fire to all the property of the Government—armouries, machine shops, storehouses, wharves. The flames shot up at many points and hung like lurid clouds, shedding a ghastly light over Richmond.

The gunboats in the river, abandoned by their crews, were set on fire, and by and by they blew up with tremendous explosions. The reports added to the terror of the fleeing crowd and cries of fright arose from the women and children. The rumours which had flown so fast in the day thickened and grew blacker in the night. "All the city was to be burned! The Yankees were going to massacre everybody!" It was in vain for the soldiers, who knew better, to protest. The Government property, burning so vividly, gave colour to their fears.

It seemed as if all Richmond were on fire. The city lay lurid and ghastly under the light of these giant torches. Wandering winds picked up the ashes and sifted them down like a fine gray snow. Wagons loaded with children and household goods passed out on every road. When the President and his Cabinet were gone, and the whistling of the train was heard for the last time, the soldiers disappeared up the river, but the streets and roads were still crowded with the refugees, and the fires, burning more fiercely than ever, spread now to private houses. Richmond was a vast core of light.

Prescott will never forget that night, the sad story of a fallen city, the passing of the old South, the weepings, the farewells, the people going from their homes out upon the bare country roads in the darkness, the drunken mob that still danced and fought behind them, and the burning city making its own funeral pyre.

Midnight passed, but there was still no sign of the Yankees. Prescott wished that they would come, for he had no fear of them: they would save the city from the destruction that was threatening it and restore order. Richmond was without rulers. The old had gone, but the new had not come.

The wheels of some belated guns rattled dully in the street, passing up the river to join in the retreat. The horsemen supporting it filed by like phantoms, and many of them, weatherbeaten men, shed tears in the darkness. From the river came a dazzling flash followed by a tremendous roar as another boat blew up, and then General Breckinridge, the Secretary of War, and his staff rode over the last bridge, already set on fire, its burning timbers giving them a final salute as they passed. It was now half way between midnight and morning, and blazing Richmond passively awaited its fate.

CHAPTER XXX

THE TELEGRAPH STATION

It had been a night of labour and anxiety for Prescott. In the turmoil of the flight he had been forgotten by the President and all others who had the power to give him orders, and he scarcely knew what to do. It was always his intention, an intention shared by his comrades, to resist to the last, and at times he felt like joining the soldiers in their retreat up the river, whence by a circuitous journey he would rejoin General Lee; but Richmond held him. He was not willing to go while his mother and Lucia, who might need him at any moment, were there, and the pathos of the scenes around him troubled his heart. Many a woman and child did he assist in flight, and he resolved that he would stay until he saw the Northern troops coming. Then he would slip quietly away and find Lee.

He paid occasional visits to his home and always the three women were at the windows wide awake—it was not a night when one could sleep. The same awe was on their faces as they gazed at the burning buildings, the towers of fire twisted and coiled by the wind. Overhead was a sullen sky, a roof of smoke shutting out the stars, and clouds of fine ashes shifting with the wind.

"Will all the city burn, Robert?" asked his mother far toward morning.

"I do not know, mother," he replied, "but there is danger of it. I am a loyal Southerner, but I pray that the Yankees will come quickly. It seems a singular thing to say, but Richmond now needs their aid."

Lucia said little. Once, as Prescott stood outside, he saw her face framed in the window like a face in a picture, a face as pure and as earnest as that of Ruth amid the corn. He wondered why he had ever thought it possible that she could love or marry James Sefton. Alike in will and strength of mind, they were so unlike in everything else. He came nearer. The other two were at another window, intent on the fire.

"Lucia," he whispered, "if I stay here it is partly for love of you. Tell me, if you still hold anything against me, that you forgive me. I have been weak and foolish, but if so it was because I had lost something that I valued most in all the world. Again I say I was weak and foolish, but that was all; I have done nothing wrong. Oh, I was mad, but it was a momentary madness, and I love you and you alone."

She put down her hand from the window and shyly touched his hair. He seized the hand and kissed it. She hastily withdrew it, and the red arose in her cheeks, but her eyes were not unkind.

His world, the world of the old South, was still falling about him. Piece by piece it fell. The hour was far toward morning. The rumble of wagons in the streets died. All the refugees who could go were gone, but the thieves and the drunkards were still abroad. In some places men had begun to make efforts to check the fire and to save the city from total ruin, and Prescott helped them, working amid the smoke and the ashes.

The long night of terror come to an end and the broad sun flushed the heavens. Then rose again the cry: "The Yankees!" and now report and rumour were true. Northern troops were approaching, gazing curiously at this burning city which for four years had defied efforts, costing nearly a million lives, and the Mayor went forth ready to receive them and make the surrender.

Prescott and the three women followed to see. He was stained and blackened now, and he could watch in safety, slipping out afterward to join his own army. The fires still roared, and overhead the clouds of smoke still drifted. Afar sounded the low, steady beat of a drum. The vanguard of the North was entering the Southern capital, and even those fighting the fires deserted their work for awhile to look on.

Slowly the conquerors came down the street, gazing at the burning city and those of its people who remained. They themselves bore all the marks of war, their uniforms torn and muddy, their faces thin and brown, their ranks uneven. They marched mostly in silence, the people looking on and saying little. Presently they entered the Capitol grounds. A boy among the cavalry sprang from his horse and ran into the building, holding a small tightly wrapped package in his hand.

Prescott, looking up, saw the Stars and Bars come down from the dome of the Capitol; then a moment later something shot up in its place, and unfolding, spread its full length in the wind until all the stripes and stars were shining. The flag of the Union once more waved over Richmond. A cheer, not loud, broke from the Northern troops and its echo again came from the crowd.

Prescott felt something stir within him and a single tear ran down his cheek. He was not a sentimental man, but he had fought four years for the flag that was now gone forever. And yet the sight of the new flag that was the old one, too, was not wholly painful. He was aware of the feeling that it was like an old and loved friend come back again.

Then the march went on, solemn and somber. The victors showed no elation; there were no shouts, no cheers. The lean, brown men in the faded blue uniforms rarely spoke, and the watchful, anxious eyes of the officers searched everywhere. The crowd around them sank into silence, but above them and around them the flames of the burning city roared and crackled as they bit deep into the wood. Now and then there was a rumble and then a crash as a house, its supports eaten away, fell in; and at rare intervals a tremendous explosion as some magazine blew up, to be followed by a minute of intense, vivid silence, for which the roaring flames seemed only a background.

The drunken mob of the under-world shrank away at the sight of the troops, and presently relapsed, too, into a sullen silence of fear or awe. The immense cloud of smoke which had been gathering for so many hours over Richmond thickened and darkened and was cut through here and there by the towers of flame which were leaping higher and higher. Then a strong breeze sprang up, blowing off the river, and the fire reached the warehouses filled with cotton, which burned almost like gunpowder, and the conflagration gathered more volume and vigour. The wind whirled it about in vast surges and eddies. Ashes and sparks flew in showers. The light of the sun was obscured by the wide roof of smoke, but beneath there was the lurid light of the fire. The men saw the faces of each other in a crimson glow, and in such a light the mind, too, magnified and distorted the objects that the eye beheld. The victorious soldiers themselves looked with awe upon the burning city. They had felt, in no event, any desire to plunder or destroy; and now it was alike their instinct and wish to save. Regiment after regiment stacked arms on Shockoe Hill, divided into companies under the command of officers, and disappeared down the smoking street—not now fighters of battles, but fighters of fire. The Yankees had, indeed, come in time, for to them the saving of the city from entire ruin was due. All day they worked with the people who were left, among the torrents of flame and smoke, suppressing the fire in places, and in others, where they could not, taking out the household goods and heaping them in the squares. They worked, too, to an uncommon chorus. Cartridges and shells were exploding in the burning magazines, the cartridges with a steady crackle and the shells with a hiss and a scream and then a stream of light. All the time the smoke grew thicker and stung the eyes of those who toiled in its eddies.

Man gradually conquered, and night came upon a city containing acres and acres of smoking ruins, but with the fires out and a part left fit for human habitation. Then Prescott turned to go. The Harley house was swept away, and the Grayson cottage had suffered the same fate; but the inmates of both were gathered at his mother's home and he knew they were safe. The stern, military discipline of the conquerors would soon cover every corner of the city, and there would be no more drinking, no more rioting, no more fires.

His mother embraced him and wept for the first time.

"I would have you stay now," she said, "but if you will go I say nothing against it."

Lucia Catherwood gave him her hand and a look which said, "I, too, await your return."

Prescott's horse was gone, he knew not where; so he went into the country on foot in search of Lee's army, looking back now and then at the lost city under the black pall of smoke. While there, he had retained a hope that Lee would come and retake it, but he had none now. When the Stars and Bars went down on the dome of the Capitol it seemed to him that the sun of the Confederacy set with it. But still he had a vague idea of rejoining Lee and fighting to the last; just why he did not understand; but the blind instinct was in him.

He did not know where Lee had gone and he learned that the task of finding him was far easier in theory than in practice. The Northern armies seemed to be on all sides of Richmond as well as in it, to encircle it with a ring of steel; and Prescott passed night after night in the woods, hiding from the horsemen in blue who rode everywhere. He found now and then food at some lone farmhouse, and heard many reports, particularly of Sheridan, who, they said, never slept, but passed his days and nights clipping down the Southern army. Lee, they would say, was just ahead; but when Prescott reached "just ahead" the General was not there. Lee always seemed to be fleeing away before him.

Spring rushed on with soft, warm winds and an April day broke up in rain. The night was black, and Prescott, lost in the woods, seeking somewhere a shelter, heard a sound which he knew to be the rumble of a train. Hope sprang up; where there was a train there was a railroad, and a railroad meant life. He pushed on in the direction whence the sound came, cowering before the wind and the rain, and at last saw a light. It might be Yankees or it might not be Yankees, but Prescott now did not care which, intent as he was upon food and shelter.

The light led him at last to an unpainted, one-room shanty in the woods by the railroad track, a telegraph station. Prescott stared in at the window and at the lone operator, a lank youth of twenty, who started back when he saw the unshorn and ghastly face at the window. But he recovered his coolness in a moment and said:

"Come in, stranger; I guess you're a hungry Reb."

Prescott entered, and the lank youth, without a word, took down some crackers and hard cheese from a shelf.

"Eat it all," he said; "you're welcome."

Prescott ate voraciously and dried his clothing before the fire in a little stove.

The telegraph instrument on a table in a corner kept up a monotonous ticking, to which the operator paid no attention. But it was a soothing sound to Prescott, and with the food and the heat and the restful atmosphere he began to feel sleepy. The lank youth said nothing, but watched his guest languidly and apparently without curiosity.

Presently the clicking of the telegraph instrument increased in rapidity and emphasis and the operator went to the table. The rapid tick aroused Prescott from the sleep into which he was falling.

"Tick-tack, tick-tack, tick-tack," went the instrument. A look of interest appeared on the face of the lank youth.

"That instrument seems to be talking to you," said Prescott.

"Yes, it's saying a few words," replied the operator.

"Tick-tack, tick-tack, tick-tack!" went the instrument.

"It's a friend of mine farther up the line," said the boy. "Would you like to hear what he's saying?"

"If you don't mind," replied Prescott.

It was very warm in the room and he was still drowsy. The boy began in a mechanical voice as of one who reads:

"General Lee surrendered to General Grant to-day——"

"What's that?" exclaimed Prescott, springing to his feet. But the boy went on:

"General Lee surrendered to General Grant to-day at Appomattox Court House. The Army of Northern Virginia has laid down its arms and the war is over."

Prescott stood for a moment like one dazed, then staggered and fell back in his chair.

"I guess you're one of that army, mister," said the boy, hastily bringing a cup of water.

"I was," replied Prescott as he recovered himself.

He stayed all night in the hut—there was nothing now to hurry for—and the next morning the lank youth, with the same taciturn generosity, shared with him his breakfast.

Prescott turned back toward Richmond, his heart swelling with the desire for home. The sun came out bright and strong, the rain dried up, and the world was again young and beautiful; but the country remained lone and desolate, and not till nearly noon did he come in contact with human life. Then he saw a half-dozen horsemen approaching—whether Northern or Southern he did not care—it did not matter now, and he went on straight toward them.

But the foremost rider leaped down with a cry of joy and wrung his hand.

"Bob, Bob, old boy!" he said. "We did not know what had become of you and we had given you up for dead!"

It was Talbot, and Prescott returned his grasp with interest.

"Is it true—true that Lee has surrendered?" he asked, though knowing well that it was true.

Talbot's eyes became misty.

"Yes, it is all so," he replied. "I was there and I saw it. We went down to Appomattox and the Yankees came right after us—I don't know how many strong, but too strong for us. Grant would never let us alone. He was there at our heels all the time, and Sheridan kept galloping around us, lopping off every straggling regiment and making our lives miserable. When we got to Appomattox we found the Yankees were so thick that we stayed there. We couldn't move. There weren't more than fifteen thousand of us left, and we were starved and barefoot. The firing around us never stopped. Grant kept pressing and pressing. Bob, I felt then that something was going to happen."

Talbot stopped and choked, but in a moment he went on:

"Our generals had a big talk—I don't know what they said, but I know what they did. A messenger went over to Grant's army, and by and by General Grant and a lot of officers came and met General Lee and his staff, and they went into a house and talked a long time. When they came out it was all over. The Army of Northern Virginia, the victor of so many great battles, was no more. We couldn't believe it for awhile, though we knew that it must come. We hung around Marse Bob, and asked him if it was true, and he said it was. He said when a war was over it was over. He said we were beaten and we must now stop fighting. He told us all to go home and go to work. It was an undivided Union; the war had settled that and we must stick to it. General Grant had promised him that we shouldn't be harmed, and he told us to think no more of war now, but to rebuild our homes and our country. We loved Marse Bob in victory, but we love him just as much now in defeat. We crowded around him and we shook his hand and we would hardly let him go."

Talbot choked again, and it was a long time until he continued:

"General Grant did everything that he promised General Lee. He's the right sort all through—so is the Yankee army. I've got nothing against it. They never insulted us with a single word. We had our own camp and they sent us over part of their rations. We needed them badly enough; and then General Grant said that every man among us who had a horse was to take it—and we did. Here I am on mine, and I reckon you might call it a gift from the Yankee General."

The little group was silent. They had fought four years, and all had ended in defeat. Tears were wiped from more than one brown face.

"We're going to Richmond, Bob," said Talbot at last, "and I guess you are bound that way, too. You haven't any horse. Here, get up behind me."

Prescott accepted the offer, and the silent little group rode on toward Richmond. On the way there Talbot said:

"Vincent Harley is dead. He was killed at Sailor's Creek. He led a last charge and was shot through the heart. He must have died instantly, but he did not even fall from the saddle. When the charge spent its force, the reins had dropped from his hands, but he was sitting erect—stone dead. It's a coincidence, but General Markham was killed on the same day."

Prescott said nothing, but Thomas Talbot, who never remained long in the depths, soon began to show signs of returning cheerfulness. They stopped for a noon rest in a clearing, and after they ate their scanty dinner Talbot leaped upon a stump.

"Oyez! Oyez!" he cried. "Attention all! I, Thomas Talbot, do offer for sale one job lot of articles. Never before was there such an opportunity to obtain the rare and valuable at such low prices."

"What are you selling, Tom?" asked Prescott.

"Listen and learn," replied Talbot, in sonorous and solemn tones. "Gentlemen, I offer to the highest bidder and without reserve one Confederacy, somewhat soiled, battered and damaged, but surrounded by glorious associations. The former owners having no further use for it, this valuable piece of property is put upon the market. Who'll buy? Who'll buy? Come, gentlemen, bid up. You'll never have another such chance. What do I hear? What do I hear?"

"Thirty cents!" called some one.

"Thirty cents! I am bid thirty cents!" cried Talbot.

"Confederate money," added the bidder.

A laugh arose.

"Do you want me to give you this property?" asked Talbot.

But he could get no higher bid, and he descended from the stump amid laughter that bordered closely on something else. Then they resumed their journey.

CHAPTER XXXI

THE COIN OF GOLD

Prescott had been at home some months. Johnston's army, too, had surrendered. Everywhere the soldiers of the South, seeing that further resistance would be criminal, laid down their arms. A mighty war, waged for four years with unparalleled tenacity and strewn all the way with tremendous battles, ceased with astonishing quickness.

The people of Richmond were already planning the rebuilding of the city; the youthful were looking forward with hope to the future, and not the least sanguine among them were a little group gathered as of old in the newspaper office of Winthrop. They had been discussing their own purposes.

"I shall stay in Richmond and continue the publication of my newspaper," said Winthrop.

"And I shall bring my wandering journal here, give it a permanent home and be your deadly rival," said Raymond.

"Good!" said Winthrop, and they shook hands on the bargain.

General Wood said nothing about his own happiness, which he considered assured, because he was to be married to Helen Harley the following month. But some one spoke presently of the Secretary.

"Gone to England!" said Raymond briefly.

Raymond mentioned a little later a piece of gossip that was being circulated quietly in Richmond. A million dollars in gold left in the Confederate treasury had disappeared mysteriously; whether it had been moved before the flight of the Government or at that time nobody knew. As there was no Confederate Government now, it consequently had no owner, and nobody took the trouble to look for it.

Prescott was in London a few years later, where he found it necessary to do some business with the great banking firm of Sefton & Calder, known throughout two continents as a model of business ability and integrity. The senior partner greeted him with warmth and insisted on taking him home to dinner, where he met Mrs. Sefton, a blond woman of wit and beauty about whom a man had once sought to force a quarrel upon him. She was very cordial to him, asking him many questions concerning people in Richmond and showing great familiarity with the old town. Prescott thought that on the whole both Mr. Sefton and his wife had married well.

But all this, on that day in Winthrop's office, was in the future, and after an hour's talk he walked alone up the street. The world was fair, life seemed all before him, and he turned his course to the new home of Helen Harley. She had grieved for her brother awhile, but now she was happy in her coming marriage. Lucia and Miss Grayson were with her, helping to prepare for the day, and making a home there, too, until they could have one of their own.

Prescott had noticed his mother's increasing love for Lucia, but between Lucia and himself there was still some constraint; why, he did not know, but it troubled him.

He knocked at the Harley home and Helen herself answered the door.

"Can I see Miss Catherwood?" he asked.

"She is in the next room," she replied. "She does not know that you are here, but I think you can go in unannounced."

She opened the second door for him at once and he entered. Lucia was standing by the window and there was a faint smile on her face, but the smile was sad. She was looking at something in her hand and Prescott's eyes caught a yellow gleam.

His step had been so light that Lucia did not hear him. He came nearer and she looked up. Then her hands closed quickly over the yellow gleam.

"What have you there?" asked Prescott, suddenly growing brave.

"Something that belongs to you."

"Let me see it."

She opened her hand and a gold double eagle lay in the palm.

"It is the last that you left on Miss Grayson's doorstep," she said, "and I am going to give it back to you."

"I will take it," he said, "on one condition."

"What is that?"

"That you come with it."

She flushed a rosy red.

"Won't you come, Lucia?" he said. "Life is not life without you."

"Yes," she said softly, "I will come."

127

THE END.

Made in the USA
Las Vegas, NV
16 July 2022

51677595R00072